Only You

A Mephisto Covenant Book

He's living on the edge – she's completely broken.

Orphaned at six and sent to live with abusive relatives in Bucharest, Mariah learned early in life to box up violent, agonizing memories and put them in permanent mental storage. Now almost nineteen, she has a paying job, a tiny apartment, and a plan to attend university. She loves her independence and is steadily overcoming her past, but when an enigmatic stranger walks into the pub where she works and the trajectory of her life changes yet again, she begins to wonder if she'll run out of mental shelf space.

The only females unafraid of the Mephisto brothers are the extremely rare Anabo, born without Original Sin. Over one hundred years ago, Phoenix was first to find one, but he made a fatal mistake and she was murdered by his oldest brother and enemy, Eryx. Phoenix soldiered through the next century wrapped up in grief and guilt, his only outlet planning takedowns of those who pledged their souls to Eryx. When one of his brothers brings Mariah to Mephisto Mountain, he's torn between his instinctive, powerful need to pursue her, and his certainty that he can never have her.

Drawn into the world of the Mephisto, Mariah sees the pain and misery Eryx unleashes on humanity, and the boxes in her mind begin to fly open, one by one. All that keeps her from slipping off the edge is her unlikely, sexually charged friendship with Phoenix. He's incredibly screwed up; she's completely broken. It would take a miracle for them to find happiness. Then Eryx brings the war for Hell to a whole new level, forcing Mariah and Phoenix to make a choice that will bind them together for all eternity, or rip them apart forever.

ONLY YOU

A MEPHISTO COVENANT BOOK

STEPHANIE FEAGAN

ONLY YOU
A Mephisto Covenant Book

Stephanie FeaganCopyright © 2013 Stephanie Feagan
All Rights Reserved

Pink Publishing, LLC

ISBN: 1940431042
E-Book 978-1-940431-06-2
Print   978-1-940431-04-8

BISAC Code: FIC027120FICTION / Romance / Paranormal
Key words: New Adult, angels, Hell, alpha male, sexy, Mephisto Mark, paranormal romance

Please Note

Cover Design by The Killion Group
Interior Format by The Killion Group
and Author E.M.S.
Photograph © Paula Kubiak

DEDICATION

For Mike – They're all for you

LEXICON

Aurora – First child of Adam and Eve, born before the fall of mankind, who was lost from Eden and began a line of descendants born without Original Sin who came to be known as Anabo.

Mephistopheles – The dark angel of death who ferries souls bound for Hell. He is Lucifer's second in command, and has many thousands of minions to aid him in his work.

Elektra – An Anabo Mephistopheles fell in love with over a thousand years ago. She bore him seven sons, in secret, without God or Lucifer's knowledge. Before her eldest was compelled to jump to his death and be resurrected to immortality, he murdered Elektra to release her spirit and alert God and Lucifer to the existence of his younger brothers, to save them from his fate of losing all light in his soul. The remaining brothers were blessed by God at death, ensuring they retained the light of Elektra when they came back as immortals.

Mephisto – Six immortal brothers, sons of the dark angel, Mephistopheles, and the Anabo, Elektra. Their sole purpose is to capture those who've pledged their souls to their oldest brother, Eryx, and imprison them in Hell on Earth. By virtue of the blood of Mephistopheles, they are bound for Hell when the world ends, or when Eryx is finally defeated, unless they fulfill the Mephisto Covenant.

Anabo – Pronounced *uh-nah-bo*. A human born without Original Sin. Extremely rare. An Anabo may be recruited to be a Lumina, or she can become Mephisto via a change in DNA when she's kissed by a Mephisto. If she's immortal, the change to Mephisto is permanent. If she's not immortal, she can ask Lucifer to be returned to how she was before the kiss. If an Anabo wishes to become like other humans, she can request to lose Anabo and Lucifer will make it happen.

Eryx – Eldest brother of the Mephisto, oldest son of Mephistopheles, Eryx lost all light in his soul when he became immortal. An anomaly, his soul belonging to neither God nor Lucifer, to fill the hopelessness within, he wants to take the reins of Hell from Lucifer and thereby control all of mankind and eradicate free will, dooming all humans who are not Anabo to Hell.

Lucifer – Ruler of Hell, the down to God's up, dark to the light, he is mankind's conscience, the reason for free will. Mankind is fallen and have the choice to rise above it, or not.

Lumina – Exceptional humans with extraordinary light in their souls, recruited by the Mephisto to become immortal and live and work with them on Mephisto Mountain. A recruit dies and is resurrected by God to be a living angel. Luminas may marry other Luminas, but are discouraged from interacting with humans.

Purgatory – A spirit meant for Heaven, but unable to ascend because of their anger at God, usually because of something occurring just before or during death. They are sent to work for the Mephisto to learn humility, acceptance and forgiveness from the Luminas.

Hell on Earth – A labyrinth of caverns deep within the Earth, carved out by Lucifer to imprison those who pledge their souls to Eryx.

Lost soul – One who pledges his or her soul to Eryx. Upon death, their soul is absorbed by Eryx, making him stronger. When he believes he is strong enough, he will declare war on Lucifer and attempt to take over Hell. The Mephisto and Luminas know the lost souls by the shadow across their eyes. If captured, they die in Hell on Earth, their spirit unable to escape and add to Eryx's strength.

Skia – In Greek, *skia* means shade, or shadow. Skia agree to become immortal followers of Eryx, and hand their soul to him upon resurrection. They are drones, incapable of free will, enslaved to Eryx's commands. The Skia are Eryx's recruiters, and search constantly for humans who are vulnerable, who are likely to pledge their soul. The shadow across Skia eyes are much darker than the lost souls because their spirits already belong to Eryx. Unlike the lost souls who die when they're sent to Hell on Earth, the Skia are immortal, and live in eternal misery and horror if they're captured. They have strength equal to the Mephisto and are specifically chosen by Eryx for their exceptional intelligence, which makes them cunning and more difficult to capture.

The Mephisto Covenant – God's promise to the Mephisto of redemption and a chance of Heaven if they win the love of a woman and selflessly love her in return. They are limited to extremely rare Anabo females because all other human girls are afraid of them.

Kyanos – A small island in the North Atlantic, surrounded by a mist created by Mephistopheles over a thousand years ago to hide Elektra and his sons from God and Lucifer. When the youngest Mephisto became immortal, they left Kyanos, but still return for councils, or for punishment.

Council – A meeting of the Mephisto on Kyanos, a trial of sorts to determine guilt and punishment of a Mephisto who's broken a hard rule. Punishment is usually a period of solitary time on Kyanos, which is primitive and cold.

Mephisto Mark – An internal mark made by a Mephisto to an Anabo during sex, allowing the Mephisto to mentally search for and find her, as they do with each other. If the Anabo is immortal, the mark is permanent. If she's still human, it is not and can be replaced by another mark, or erased entirely by Lucifer.

Scent – A particular scent attached to an Anabo, Lucifer's way of indicating which Mephisto she is meant for. If an Anabo is found and any of the brothers could go for her, it would be a free-for-all, a fight to the death – and they can't die. To keep order, Lucifer attaches a scent to an Anabo, and the Mephisto who don't catch it are instinctively not attracted to her.

Mephisto Mountain – Several thousand acres of land high in the southern Colorado Rockies above Telluride, populated by Lumina cottages, the Mephisto mansion, and outbuildings. The boundary is circled by the Kyanos mists, making everything Mephisto on the mountain invisible to humans and inaccessible to anyone but the Mephisto, Anabo, and Luminas.

Meet the Mephisto: http://www.stephaniefeagan.com/meet-the-mephisto/

"I am part of the part that once was everything,
Part of the darkness which gave birth to light…"
Mephistopheles, from Goethe's *Faust*

CHAPTER 1

~~ MARIAH ~~

Within a minute of his arrival, I knew the guy in black was going to be a problem. Unlike the other men in the pub who'd arrived several hours earlier to watch hockey on Gustav's ancient television and were now very drunk, this one walked in at half past midnight, stone cold sober. Alone. He took a seat at a table next to the wall, not far from the loud group in the middle, and swept his gaze across the dim, smoky room. His inspection stopped at me.

I was used to guys sizing me up to decide if I was worth hitting on. I worked in a bar, after all. But this one's black-eyed stare was different. Inquisitive and intense. As if he knew me.

I had zero sexual vibes from him, and as much as anything, that made me nervous. If an interested guy didn't want sex, he was a wild card. Could he be with the police? My heart raced and I talked myself back to calm. He certainly wasn't dressed like a policeman. Probably no older than twenty-one, he was tall and broad with a handsome face, and wore his long, black hair in a ponytail that reached just above the spot between his shoulder blades. Who was he? And what did he want?

Only one way to find out. I went to his table and asked what he'd like to drink. He ordered whiskey, neat, and thanked me when I delivered it, but didn't attempt to make conversation. I washed glasses behind the bar, cleaned a table in the corner, helped Gustav tally up the evening gross, and all the while, I could feel the new guy's stare.

Nimbly avoiding grasping hands and crude come-ons, I deposited a round of vodka and beer to the hockey fans, then carried my tray over to his table. Despite all of my instincts screaming that something was horribly awry, I smiled as if my life had been lacking until he appeared; genuine and warm without suggesting anything. Friendly and hospitable. I earned very good tips with my smile. "Can I bring you another whiskey?"

"Where do you go after you're done here? Where do you live?" His voice was deep, his Romanian perfect. Too perfect for a Romanian. I decided he was either British or American.

Determined to ignore his unnerving stare, I never lost my smile. "In an apartment, with a cat and the mice she's too lazy to kill. So, how about another drink?"

"Yeah, I'll have another one."

When I returned with his second whiskey, he handed me a U.S. one hundred dollar bill. A pay-off of some kind? I gave one millisecond's thought to refusing it before I folded it into my pocket. If I had a prayer of attending university, I needed all the money I could get my hands on. Ignoring my uneasiness, I grinned at him. "I had a feeling you're American."

He pointed to the chair across the table. "Give me two minutes."

"I can't sit down or Gustav will be angry. I'm sorry." I wasn't sorry at all. What was it about this guy that set my teeth on edge?

"I know who you are."

So he *did* know me, but how? Never abandoning my barmaid guise, I laughed and pointed to the name badge I wore above my left breast: MARIAH. "It's not a secret."

"I know a lot more about you than your name. You were born in a tiny village fifty miles from here to an older couple who thought they couldn't have children. Not quite two years later, they had another daughter. When she was four, they were killed in a car wreck and you and your sister came to live with your mother's cousin here in Bucharest."

Mention of my sister was all it took to send me into extreme panic, but this guy went so much further. He knew things I'd never shared with anyone. Not even Gustav or his mother, Marta, the only two people in the world I'd ever considered remotely close to me. No longer able to keep up my bogus smile, I eyed him apprehensively. "Who are you?"

"My name is Kyros."

"What do you want?"

"I want to know how your sister wound up at an orphanage. Did your mother's cousin take her there?"

This needed to stop. Now. "My sister died. You've got the wrong story, or the wrong person." I mentally placed Kyros in a box, shoved it into a space next to all the others, then turned and walked away.

He stayed where he was and drank his whiskey and continued watching me, but I would not be afraid of him. He'd been boxed; him and his black staring eyes and nosy questions and unfathomable knowledge of my most closely held secret. Once something went in a box, it was no longer a threat.

As it grew closer to two in the morning, the regular patrons began to trickle out of Gustav's like the last foamy dribble of a finished beer keg. When the only guy left was Kyros, I went to his table and picked up his empty glass. "We're closing now. You should go, because if you don't, Gustav will make you."

"I know she didn't die, Mariah. She was adopted by a man who became the American president."

Blood rushed and roared in my ears, making me lightheaded. He *knew*. He didn't just know of my sister's existence. He knew who she was *now*, in real time. I could no longer hide my panic and my voice shook ever so slightly. "Please tell me who you are."

"I'm a friend of your sister." He pulled a stuffed patchwork rabbit out of his trench coat pocket and handed it to me.

My mouth went dry. "Oh, my God." A thousand memories floated around me as I ran my fingers across his stitches and his button eyes. Tears clogged my throat when I saw the tiny embroidered initials inside the bunny's right ear. *V.A.* Viorica Ardelean. My baby sister.

Kyros's box came flying out at me, the lid flung too far away for me to shove it back on and make this stop killing me.

His voice was low and earnest. "I came to Bucharest to find

who made him, to have it repaired. It took all day yesterday and most of today, but I finally found a little shop in a village fifty miles from here, and the woman who made this was still there. She remembered your family. All I want to know is why your sister wound up at an orphanage."

Desperate to make him stop, make him go away, and equally determined not to show my desperation, I said calmly, "If you're her friend, you'll leave right now and never, ever tell her what you've learned."

"She and I are a lot more than friends, and I can't keep something like this from her. I'd like to keep it from everyone else in the world, but not from her. She's going to want answers, and there's no doubt she'll want to see you, but for now, I just want to know why she was in an orphanage."

Dressed in black leather, with a scruff beard and a hard edge to him that could only come from an unforgiving life, he looked like a criminal. Why would my sister, the adopted daughter of a wealthy family who now lived in the White House, have anything to do with this guy? She wouldn't. He had to be lying. I took a step closer to him. "How did you get the rabbit? Did you steal it when you stole her? Did you have something to do with her kidnapping?"

That surprised him, and he blinked. "I rescued her."

"You're a liar. She was left in Hyde Park by her captors."

"That's what the world believes, but that's not what happened. You tell me about the orphanage, and I'll tell you the real story of her abduction."

If only he didn't have the rabbit. Viorica's rabbit. It was her treasure, her heart, and the only thing I'd allowed her to take when we ran away all those years ago. This guy couldn't possibly have it unless he was very close to my sister. I didn't know what he might do with what he'd learned, but I had to know more. Had to protect Viorica. After all I'd done to make sure she was safe, I wouldn't allow anyone to threaten her happiness and peace of mind.

I shot another glance at Gustav, who was busy cleaning the bar, then whispered to Kyros, "I took her there."

He looked incredulous. "Why? *How?* You were six."

Gustav's voice rumbled across the pub. "That floor's not

going to mop itself, Mariah."

Facing the inevitability of talking to Kyros about Viorica, I handed the rabbit back to him. "I'll be done here in an hour. Meet me outside, down at the corner."

Kyros immediately got to his feet and walked out.

An hour later, my mind having run in circles while I mopped and cleaned, I said goodbye to Gustav before stepping outside into the cold night. In the faint light from the streetlamp at the corner, I saw Kyros waiting just beyond the door. I looked up at him and said, "Let's walk."

He fell in with me as I went down the street, and I sensed his impatience. At the corner, while we waited for cars to pass, I looked up at him again. "Is there any way I can convince you not to tell my sister about me?"

He shook his head. "Not a chance. Why don't you want her to know? Wouldn't you like to see her?"

More than I wanted anything, I wanted to see my sister. But not yet. Not now. I kept my attention on the top button of his coat. "It's just that I want her to be happy, and nothing about any of this is good. I thought that someday, when we're older, when she's settled and not living in the White House under a microscope, I'd see her and explain. She'd want to know. But she's still so young, barely seventeen."

"Barely? She'll be eighteen in three weeks."

I met his eyes. "She was born on Christmas Day. She just turned seventeen. I turned eighteen last February."

"Did the orphanage not know how old she was?"

I shook my head. "They didn't know anything about her. Either they made up a birthday for her, or her adopted parents did."

"Please tell me what happened."

His voice had softened. Noticing the concern in his expression and the light in his eyes, I realized what hadn't been evident before. "You're in love with her, aren't you?"

"Does it matter?"

It mattered a lot, but I didn't say so. I wondered if Viorica felt the same about him? "How are you here? And why? No guy I know would come so far to get a girl's stuffed animal repaired. There must be a million places you could have gone to in the States."

He barely blinked, but I knew he lied when he said, "I'm here for a family funeral. Jordan's rabbit was torn up because of me, an accident, and she's so attached to it, I thought it'd make her happy if I found where it was made and took a picture. I didn't expect to find out so much, but now that I know, I'd like to have the whole story."

Why did he lie? I supposed he didn't trust me any more than I trusted him. But he was in love with my sister, and since he had the bunny, she must feel something for him. He was determined to tell her about me. My only hope of convincing him to keep quiet was to tell him the whole bloody truth. When he knew, when he understood, he'd change his mind, I was certain.

I focused on the button again and took a deep breath.

Speaking of it meant remembering. I hated him for coming to Romania, for walking into Gustav's, for digging and asking and making me do this. I carefully drew a very old box from the deepest recesses of my mind and hesitantly lifted the lid. "My mother's cousin, Nadia, was married to a horrible man named Emilian. We'd only been living there a week when he broke my arm. He'd get angry and lock me in a closet and wouldn't give me any food for days at a time."

He clenched his hands into fists and I could feel anger roll off of him.

I ignored it. "It's said that very young children who are abused don't know it's not normal, because that's all they know. So maybe if our parents hadn't been so loving, I wouldn't have understood how wrong it was. But I knew he was evil, and as much as I hated what he did to me, I couldn't bear watching him torment Viorica. She was so happy, so sweet, and I didn't want what happened to me to happen to her. So I took her and ran away."

"Where did you go? Where did you *plan* to go?"

"As you said, I was six. I had no plan. I just knew I had to get her out of there. Emilian was already pinching her hard enough to leave bruises. I sometimes wonder if God led me, because I took refuge inside a church that happened to have an orphanage. I hid there for two days, trying to decide if I should ask the priest for help, but I was afraid he'd call Emilian and we'd be sent back. I'd been watching what went on at the building across the street, the children in the play yard, and the nuns who looked after them. I realized those children lived there, that they had no parents, no family. So I took Viorica late in the night and left her on the doorstep, rang the bell, then hid to watch, to make sure the nuns took her in."

The cars had long since passed, and I stepped off the curb, restless and anxious to get home. I wanted him to go away. I wanted to shove all of this night into a box and go to sleep and when I woke up tomorrow, it'd be life as usual.

"Why did you leave her?" Kyros asked. "Why didn't you stay, as well?"

If only that had been an option. "I knew if I didn't go back and make up a story about Viorica, Nadia would search for us, and she might look where orphans live." I stared down at the sidewalk as we traveled from one rundown part of Bucharest to another. The air was frigid, and I buried my hands deeper in the pockets of my old coat, wishing I had fur-lined gloves like Gustav's. "So I went back and told her I had gotten lost when Viorica and I followed a dog down the street. We couldn't find our way home, and when we were in a crowd of people, a lady picked up my sister and took her away. Maybe because Viorica was such a beautiful child, Nadia believed my story. She made a halfhearted attempt to find her, but I know they were glad to be rid of her."

"Didn't they call the police?"

He didn't get it. Not yet. I glanced up at him. "Emilian wouldn't let Nadia call."

"What about neighbors? Didn't anyone ask what happened to your sister?"

"If anyone noticed one of us was missing, they must have assumed she'd been visiting or something. We'd only been there two months when I ran away. And even if they were curious, no way they would have knocked on the door and asked. Emilian and Nadia never spoke to their neighbors and had no friends. You really can't imagine what horrible people they were."

"You'd be surprised. I'm kind of an expert on evil people."

It hit me then what it was about Kyros that was so odd, what set him apart from other guys. There was an air of darkness about him, a faint but distinct feeling of doom. I checked him out as we walked. "You seem . . . different. How do you know my sister?"

"It's a long story." As we turned a corner, he asked, "Didn't Emilian and Nadia recognize Jordan when her adoptive father became president, and she became a public figure?"

There it was, the question I'd known he'd ask, that I'd tried to prepare for. Didn't matter. This box I had hidden deep and well, but I could never completely lose it. That it existed at all was my certain damnation. It was why I never attended mass. Hadn't since . . . "Nadia died from cancer before he was elected president, but yes, Emilian knew it was Viorica, and he had big plans to demand money in exchange for not taking her back. He also wanted to extort money for his silence. How would it look if the American president had adopted a child with legitimate guardians? That President Ellis didn't know wouldn't have made any difference, because there would be people who'd insist he *did* know. Emilian would have threatened to go public, and play up how Viorica was stolen from him. I was so afraid for her. She didn't know any of this, and having that slime crawl out of the gutter and come after her family . . . I couldn't let it happen. By then, I was almost fourteen, and after all that time, after what I did to save her from Emilian, I wasn't going to let him screw up her life."

"How did you stop him?"

I killed him. "It turned out I didn't have to do anything. He died when his house burned down. He was a drunk, and a smoker. He passed out with a cigarette, and that was that."

"When did Nadia die?"

"When I was twelve. After she was gone, Emilian started . . ." I paused, horrified by what I'd almost said. Had I been that close to saying it? Kyros's peculiarity was getting to me. "Everything got worse," I finished lamely.

He fell quiet and I wondered if he guessed. He was young, but an old soul. I had a feeling Kyros knew about men like Emilian.

He asked in a low, hoarse voice, "After he died, what did

you do?"

"I lived with the woman across the road, who wasn't unkind, but she expected me to work for my keep. I cooked and cleaned, and when I was old enough, I went to work for her son."

"Gustav?"

I nodded. "He's gruff and hard, but generous, and he makes sure none of the customers get out of hand. About six months ago, his mother passed on and he sold her house. That's when I got my own apartment."

"Are you . . . with someone?"

"No. I'm never going to be with someone. I don't even date." I shot him another glance. "I don't like men."

"You mean, you're—"

"No, I just don't like guys. You saw, in the bar. You know. And after Emilian . . ." I couldn't possibly be close to anyone, ever. I was dirty. Damaged. And the thought of . . . no. I was absolutely content to be alone. I determinedly slid the lid back on that box and shoved it where it belonged, in the darkest part of my mind. "So, are you going to tell me how you met my sister, and about her kidnapping, and who you really are? Because I'm pretty sure you're not a regular guy."

"What makes you think so?"

"There's something about you, a little bit spooky. No offense."

"None taken. As soon as we get to your apartment and you get your cat, I'll tell you everything."

Panic returned. "What do you mean, get my cat? Do you think I'm going somewhere with you?"

"I'll explain when we get there, and you can decide if you want to go, or not."

He could explain whatever, but no chance I was going anywhere with him. Especially if it involved seeing my sister. I had to convince him to keep my existence a secret from her. "Just so you know, if you didn't have her bunny, I wouldn't be taking you to where I live, and I wouldn't have told you anything. I don't ever talk about her with anyone."

"How do you know it's the same bunny?"

Because I still saw it in my dreams, my little sister's arms around him while she watched me back away from the orphanage steps, her lip trembling. She cried and tried to follow. I told her I'd be back to get her in the morning, that she just needed to keep the nuns company for a little while, but she knew I lied. She was so smart, even as a tiny child. With tears on her round cheeks, she held her bunny and watched me disappear into the shadows.

But I didn't say any of that to Kyros. I simply said, "Viorica's initials are embroidered inside his ear."

We reached my building, and he followed me inside and up seven flights of unsteady stairs without comment. It was past three in the morning, but some of my neighbors were up, loud music coming from behind several of the doors along my hallway, the guy in 742 shouting at his girlfriend, and somewhere, glass broke.

As soon as I opened the door and stepped inside my very tiny apartment, Olga wound between my legs, meowing her greeting. I picked her up and turned, about to introduce her to Kyros when he reached for my arm. Before I could pull away or tell him to back off, everything went dark and the floor disappeared.

I sucked in a harsh breath, too stunned to scream.

Seconds later, my feet were once again on solid ground and light returned. Except I was no longer in my apartment.

Where was I? *How had he brought me here?* Confused and angry, I clutched Olga against my chest and stepped back from Kyros. "Holy God, *what* just happened?" I dashed a look around what appeared to be a circular grand hall. *Very* grand. My brain registered rosewood and gilt, life-size portraits, and a vast expanse of white marble decorated with an ornate inlaid onyx *M,* where I now stood. To my left was a grand staircase, to the right, a gigantic door. A domed ceiling soared three floors above me, painted with angels and clouds.

Kyros was about to say something, but a deep voice from above distracted him. I knew very little English, but I understood two words I'd read in a badly translated Dickens novel: *Yorkshire* and *heather.*

Then a girl spoke and I understood nothing of what she said.

A couple appeared at the top of the stairs. They caught sight of me and instantly stopped moving, staring at me with shocked expressions. She was blond and beautiful, tall and graceful, and there was something different about her that I noticed immediately. All around her, the atmosphere seemed a tiny bit brighter. It was astonishing and I wondered what would make her body do that. Where was this place? Fairyland? Maybe I'd been hit on the head and was dreaming this. Or maybe I was struck by a car and was now dead on the street, and my spirit was on the other side. But, no, that couldn't be. No way a girl like that would be in Hell.

By contrast, the guy next to her looked exactly as I imagined a guy from Hell. His eyes were black as midnight and he had a ferocious scowl. He was tall and broad with dark features very similar to Kyros's. His brother. This had to be his brother. Was Miss Glowlight his sister? Or was she attached to the brother?

Did I care? Not really. I wanted to be taken home. I had to work two shifts tomorrow and I needed sleep. And food. I also needed to wash out my pants so I could wear them again. I only had the one pair, and a pair of jeans, but Gustav didn't like me to wear jeans at work. I had a lot to do, and being brought to this freaky place in the middle of the night was not on the list.

The girl asked Kyros a question in English, her voice communicating a note of wonder. I caught "Jordan's sister," but didn't understand anything else. She continued talking and asking questions as she hurried down the stairs toward me.

Her companion, Sir Frownsalot, stayed on the top step, completely still.

She said something to me, and all I caught was the name, Sasha. Then she turned to Kyros with a brilliant smile and exclaimed in an excited voice. I imagined she said something like, "We need an exhausted barmaid with a cat! How clever of you to bring her!"

Looking skeptical, Kyros jerked his gaze to me and said in Romanian, "I don't think so, Sasha. She's exceptional, but not Anabo."

Of course I wasn't Anabo. I was Romanian. And furious. Olga meowed in protest when I squeezed her too tightly.

Smiling at me, the blond rattled off more meaningless

words.

Equally bewildered and irritated, I said, "I don't speak English."

She nodded and said in Romanian, "I'm Sasha. Poor thing, you look scared to death. Please don't be. You're safe here."

My definition of safe and hers were miles apart. I said to Kyros, "Please take me home."

"I know this is confusing," he said, "but no one's going to hurt you, I swear it."

Getting hurt wasn't the issue. I didn't feel threatened. But I'd been brought here against my will. I was in a weird place with strangers – and no one asked. I didn't get the chance to say no. Old anger surged and I clasped Olga tighter, forcing it back in the box. Anger never helped. It brought more pain. Always.

Kyros asked the guy at the top of the stairs, "Can you see it, Phoenix?"

See what?

His expression had changed from anger to disbelief. He was staring hard at me, as if he was powerless to look away. "No, but I can feel . . . I can . . . ." His voice was low and rough.

Spellbound by his black eyes, I forgot to be upset about Kyros bringing me here against my will. I lost the thread of wondering how he'd done it. The beautiful girl faded, along with the exquisite grand hall and every conscious thought but one: the guy named Phoenix despised me. His loathing slid down the wide staircase to wrap around me, making my breath catch, and no matter how hard I tried, I couldn't not stare back. I couldn't stop the shiver in my belly. And I couldn't fathom why someone I'd never seen before would hate me this much.

CHAPTER 2

September 6, 1888
Yorkshire, England

Standing with my brothers, circling the Mephisto M in the center of the great hall's flagstone floor before we leave for London and what promises to be an excruciatingly difficult and exhausting takedown, I'm surrounded by the scent of heather. Mathilda had the Purgatories who serve as housemaids go out to the moors and gather up great bunches of the tiny purple flowers, which are now stuffed into vases and crockeries all about the house. I know I will never smell heather and not think of Yorkshire. It is wild and beautiful, sometimes savage, though more accommodating than Russia and infinitely more jolly than Greece, but perhaps I only think so because these are modern times. Greece was almost nine hundred years ago, after all, and we haven't lived in Russia since just after Catherine the Great died.

Key looks at me and each of my brothers in turn, silently communicating his expectations and his authority. He does this before every takedown and I'm always reminded of a wolf pack, of the alpha asserting his superiority. It's needless with Kyros. We accept that he's leader of the Mephisto, but he's compelled to give us this look, and waits for a nod before moving on to the next brother.

We will take out the lost souls tonight, and tomorrow we'll begin planning the next takedown. It never stops, never ends.

I feel energized by the scent of the heather, anxious to be gone.

Jax says into our silence, "On three." He begins to count.

Moments later, I'm standing at the entrance to the Duchess of Rothschild's ballroom, cloaked so no one can see me. The last time I was here was to attend a masquerade ball held by the sixth Duke of Rothschild, and we were not invisible – only disguised. My brothers and I wore masks and pretended to be Russian aristocrats. We danced and drank champagne and every single one of us found a bed partner for the evening; even Zee, who generally finds it difficult to speak to females without offending them.

Tonight's ball is held by the eighth Duke of Rothschild, a celebration to commemorate his second wife's thirtieth birthday. This night, we aren't here to dance, or look for willing girls. We're here to take out seventy-nine people who were faithless and gullible enough to hand their souls to Eryx.

I scan the sea of color swirling around the dance floor, searching for our oldest brother. Key had said Eryx might be on to our plan, that he might show up and attempt to stop us. In all the smiling, flushed faces, I don't see Eryx's. I'm relieved, but to be absolutely sure, I concentrate carefully, mentally searching for him. His location comes to me in little waves of awareness. He's nowhere close to London. I stay focused and eventually I know he's in the mountains of Romania, walking the halls of Erinýes. He won't be interfering with tonight's takedown. He doesn't know. I feel glad, and smug. This one is huge – he will lose a large group of his followers after we're done.

At the far end of the room, just behind the musicians' dais, Jax holds up a finger, then two, then three, and as one, he and I throw a freeze across the entire Mayfair house. The music and the dancers instantly stop and all conversation ceases. The only movement in the large room is by us and three Skia, Eryx's immortal minions who convinced the other seventy-six souls to turn their backs on God and follow their master. Our inability to freeze Skia and their ability to see past our cloaks never fails to hamper takedowns, and tonight is no exception.

Giles St. John sees me scarce seconds after the freeze and grabs his frozen dance partner around the neck. "I'll snap her like a twig," he threatens.

"Go ahead," Key says, winding his way through the stiff,

still crowd toward St. John. "Just know that no matter what
you do in the next two minutes, it won't change your fate."
  St. John lets go of the woman and makes a mad dash toward
the terrace doors, but Key pops there before him and easily
overtakes him, disappearing immediately.
  In the southeast corner of the room, a similar scene plays
out between the queen's favorite chancellor and Denys. The
man manages to land a punch to Denys's face, but seconds
later, they, too, disappear.
  The third Skia is wilier, but Ty finds his hiding place
beneath the musicians' dais and drags him out, ignoring the
man's shouts and curses, never flinching when the Skia buries
a dagger in his arm. As soon as they are gone, Jax, Zee and I
begin carrying the lost souls to the gates. I grasp the arm of a
beautiful young woman with blond hair, wide blue eyes and
porcelain skin. She is Lady Georgiana Rutledge, daughter of
the Earl of Longbourne, a debutante just finishing her first
season in London. Rumor has it she will marry the Duke of
Rothschild's eldest son, a brilliant match that will join two of
England's oldest families.
  I feel nothing but a pang of regret that one so young and
lovely has traded her soul to Eryx. I wonder what she asked
for, what she considered worth her soul. But I don't give it
much more than a flash of thought before I take the arm of her
intended in my other hand and transport from the glittering
ballroom to the barren desert of the Arabian Empty Quarter.
The couple is still frozen and make no move or sound when I
drop them to the sand that hides the gates to Hell on Earth.
Key chants, waiting for Lucifer to open the gates and allow the
Skia and lost souls to fall in.
  I pop back to London to ferry two more lost souls, then two
more and so on, until my brothers and I have emptied the
ballroom of them. The freeze will soon fade. We hurry to
transport the rest of the ball guests to the back of the
townhouse, standing their statue-like bodies in and around the
cook's vegetable garden and in the mews, where they would be
if they ran from a burning house. When they wake from their
frozen state, they'll be disoriented and won't remember
running from the house, but will assume they did when they see

flames and smoke.

Key, Denys and Ty are almost done placing the lost souls' doppelgangers in the ballroom. Jax is readying to set a catastrophic fire. I run to the last room with people, an anteroom where there are low settees and comfortable chaises filled with dowagers and matrons who spend time at balls sipping madeira while they gossip and reminisce. As I expected, it is filled with old ladies, all frozen, but I'm surprised to find one who isn't old. Or frozen.

Sitting on a chair next to the fire is a mirror image of Lady Georgiana, but this girl is surrounded by soft light, almost a glow. I blink. I move toward her, forgetting about the old ladies, about the takedown, about everything in the universe but this girl. Staring at me, her hand moves to her throat. Why isn't she frozen, like all the others? She's ethereal, lit from within. My confusion lifts as I realize she must be Anabo, something I've never seen in all my nine hundred years of immortality.

I'm awed.

She doesn't get up or make any attempt to run from me, despite her obvious fear. Her blue eyes widen as I come closer.

I catch the scent of heather and my heart races. Long ago, when we first learned about the Mephisto Covenant, our father said when an Anabo is meant for us, we will know by her scent. After centuries of waiting and hoping, I've found my Anabo. It seems fitting that she smells of heather.

"Hello," I say. "What's your name?"

"Jane," she whispers. "I'm Lady Jane Rutledge."

Georgiana's twin. I face the fact that even beyond being a son of Hell, I have another huge obstacle to winning this woman.

Less than fifteen minutes ago, I killed her sister.

~~ PHOENIX ~~

I was so dizzy, I didn't move a muscle, afraid I'd hurtle down the stairs as if it were a landslide. It would be the ultimate indignity to fall in a heap at her feet.

Oh, God rhythmically repeated in my head, over and over

like a squeaking wheel. I wasn't sure who I was angrier with –
Key, or God. That my brother would bring this girl to Mephisto
Mountain without asking, without warning, was infuriating.
But why would God make her smell like heather? Like Jane?
Was this a divine joke?

We'd moved from Yorkshire to Colorado to get away from
the memories, and the heather, and here it was, right in the
house, making me euphoric, suicidal, and enraged all at once.

The scent filled my head and I was gripped with an extreme
need to draw closer, to snatch her right off of the onyx *M*, to
carry her away somewhere and take every stitch of her clothes
off and just feel her skin. Soft. It would be so soft. It had been
over one hundred years since I'd felt a woman's skin, since I'd
touched a woman's hair, since I'd felt anything but the burn of
guilt and the yawning hollow of loneliness. I didn't even know
her name. I couldn't see her glow, but I knew she was Anabo,
and I knew, against all the odds, against everything that
followed the laws of karma and fate, that she was intended for
me. The worst of all my brothers, the one who let my Anabo
die, I had been gifted with another, while three of my brothers
had none.

I hated God for making her smell of heather. I hated her for
existing. I hated Kyros for his arrogance. But mostly, I hated
myself for wanting her, for betraying Jane.

Jane, who was kind, beautiful and gently bred. A lady,
always.

This girl was dressed in skintight black pants, cheap, worn
boots with low heels, and a shabby coat. Her dark hair was
pulled into a ponytail at the back of her head. Her eyes were
the color of the evening sky, not quite gray and not exactly
blue, lined with thick, dark lashes. Anabo always have blue
eyes. Jane's had been the color of cornflowers, wide, innocent
and filled with compassion.

She was sublimely fine.

This girl was rough.

And clearly something was wrong with her. She had no
glow and her eyes were almost dark. Maybe she wasn't entirely
Anabo.

No, that made no sense. There was no such thing as shades

of Anabo. Like being pregnant – you either were, or you weren't. Because of her scent, and Sasha's unquestioning declaration, I knew she was Anabo. But something was way off about her. This was a good thing. I couldn't possibly want a defective Anabo. I'd steer clear of her until I could convince Key to take her back; put her out of my mind and forget her. I wouldn't think about her skin, or the fullness of her bottom lip, or the uncertainty in her eyes as she stared back at me.

Oh, fuck.

I was an idiot. A fool in deep denial. I couldn't bullshit myself that I didn't want her. She was the most beautiful thing I'd seen since Jane, and it took every ounce of willpower to stay where I was. I knew if I moved at all, my body would go to hers of its own volition. I wanted her with crushing desperation.

And I could never have her.

"Phoenix?" Key had the strangest look on his face, almost as if he wanted to cry. But that couldn't be. Kyros hadn't cried since the night Eryx murdered our mother, over a thousand years ago. "This is Mariah. I brought her here because I think she should become a Lumina."

Mariah. A beautiful name. Why couldn't she be called Bertha or Helga? Why couldn't she have a face like a horse, a third eye, some kind of horrifying growth? Why couldn't she smell like sheep shit?

It wouldn't matter. I'd want this woman no matter her name, appearance, or scent. Instinct and a thousand years of loneliness demanded it, because what she could do for me was light-years from the superficiality of those things. Unlike every other human female on planet Earth, this one had the ability to love me.

The thought was horrifying. Jane died because she loved me.

Sasha slid an arm around Mariah's shoulders and Mariah carefully and politely stepped away. Sasha's touch bothered her and I wondered why. The orange tabby meowed again, then made her escape, leaping from Mariah's arms to dash across the hall and disappear beneath the middle console, the one with a portrait of Jane next to it.

My gaze was drawn to her beautiful, innocent blue eyes. Jane. Who loved me.

With one last look at Mariah, I popped away from the Mephisto house and landed in Yorkshire at the foot of Jane's grave. I stared at her headstone and cursed Kyros. And God. And Mariah.

CHAPTER 3

~~ MARIAH ~~

One second he was standing up there glaring at me; the next, he disappeared into thin air. I was ravenously hungry and completely exhausted. Maybe I imagined it?

But no, Phoenix Who Despised Me really did disappear, and Kyros really did bring me here via magic, which meant there must be the devil about. Mama used to tell stories about fantastical things, and all of them taught a moral lesson to small children – magic and such is the work of the devil. I later learned that the devil is at work everywhere, and there's nothing at all magical about it. I'd met the devil, and his name was Emilian. After that, nothing particularly frightened me. People popping in and out was incredible and weird, but not scary.

Still, this was an eerie place with bizarre people and I was torn between serious concern for Viorica and the absolute necessity of leaving immediately.

Self-preservation won the day. I walked toward the console where Olga hid and coaxed her out, swung her up into my arms and turned back to Kyros. "Take me home now."

He and Sasha exchanged a look before he said evenly, "I'm asking you to stay, Mariah. Jordan will want to see you and it's much safer for the two of you to visit here than at your apartment, or in the White House."

I walked to where he stood and made one last plea. "It will upset her to find out about me, and it's cruel because there's no way we can maintain any kind of relationship while she's the president's daughter. Later, maybe when she's at university,

I'll see her."

Again, they looked at each other before Kyros said, "She won't be going to college. She isn't . . ." He stopped talking.

I was more than alarmed. I was afraid. "Why won't she go to college? Is something wrong with her?" Holy God, I'd never survive if she died. Viorica was everything to me. She was why I got up every day. The thought of her living a happy life with parents who loved her was what got me through the worst of things. "Is she ill?" He didn't reply and Sasha shifted her weight, clearly uncomfortable. *"Tell me!"*

"No, she's not sick. Far from it. Jordan will live a long life. Longer than you'd imagine."

"What does that mean?"

He slid his hands into the pockets of his leather trench coat. "There's a lot to tell you about us, and I'm certain Jordan will want to be the one who does. For now, have something to eat, get some rest, and plan to stay a few days with us. She has school and other commitments, but she can be here every night and the two of you can get reacquainted. I'd also like you to get to know my brothers, and Sasha."

If his other brothers were as awful as Phoenix, I'd take a pass on getting to know them. "I have to work tomorrow." I needed the money. I saved most of what I earned, stashing it away for when I enrolled at university. Missing work wasn't an option.

"Tell Gustav you need some time off."

He said it as an order, and my back went up. "I'll do no such thing."

"Doesn't he have other help?"

"Yes, but I need the shifts."

Sasha laid a hand on his arm and said something in English, which I found insulting. "Have the courtesy to speak so I can understand."

She apologized and said in Romanian, "I said that you probably need the money and he should respect that."

Kyros said, "I'll pay you to stay. Whatever you want."

Before I could tell him what I thought of his offer, Sasha scolded him. "Key, you can't offer her money. It's offensive."

He looked genuinely surprised. "Why? We've got more

money than anyone on the planet. I'm happy to give her as much as she wants, but at a minimum, she could at least take what she'll miss earning over the next week. I want her to stay. We *need* her to stay."

I was bemused. "Are your parents aware of your willingness to hand money over to strangers?"

"My mother is long dead and my father isn't . . . we live here, just me and my brothers and Sasha and the household staff."

I was about to ask more questions because the whole setup was dodgy, but he held up a hand and shook his head. "I know you're tired, Mariah. Please, just eat and rest, and I promise Jordan will explain everything later."

Looking from him to Sasha, then glancing around the grand hall, I considered my options. There weren't many. I was confident he'd take me home if I insisted, but there was evidently no talking him out of telling Viorica about me, and once that happened, I wanted to see her. This place, strange as it seemed and wherever it was, would be a safe venue. I gave Kyros a quick nod.

"Good." He smiled and it transformed his face. "Very good." He flicked his wrist and a tall dark-skinned man appeared from the shadows beneath the staircase. Dressed in balloon pants and a turban, he looked like a character out of *Arabian Nights*. "This is Deacon, our butler and self-appointed morality police. Deacon, this is Jordan's sister, Mariah. See that her cat is fed and watered, then taken to the bedroom next to Jordan's."

The man wouldn't look me in the eye, but asked my shoulder, "Her name?"

"Olga." I handed her over. "She will vomit if you give her fish."

"Then I shall not give her fish." He gently stroked Olga's head while he looked at Kyros. "Dinner is waiting. Am I to ask Mathilda to serve?"

"No. Give Olga to Dani with instructions, then we'll have dinner."

Deacon disappeared and I scarcely blinked. "Odd clothing choice for a butler."

"He's a Moor. It's how he was dressed when he died," Kyros said.

I hoped he hadn't just said that Deacon was dead. "I don't understand."

"You will."

I turned my gaze to Sasha. "So he's a zombie." I was joking, sort of, and expected her to smile.

Instead, she said soberly, "He's a ghost – a spirit who deserves Heaven but can't make it because he's mad at God. His family was slaughtered during the Crusades and he's still holding a grudge against God for letting it happen. Most spirits like that are sent to Purgatory to wait it out, but some are sent here to serve the Mephisto in hopes servitude and interaction with the Luminas will help them get over it so they can ascend. All of the household staff are Purgatories."

I remembered Key had told Phoenix he thought I should become a Lumina. It couldn't be any weirder than a Purgatory. Could it? "What's a Lumina?"

Sasha said, "They're extraordinary people who become immortal and live here on Mephisto Mountain and help the Mephisto."

"Who are the Mephisto?"

"Key and his brothers." She smiled then. "And me. And soon—"

"Let's eat," Kyros said, "and let Jordan tell her the rest."

Kyros thought I should become immortal and stick around to help out? Help with what? Counting his money? I began to wonder if I'd finally slipped off the edge. I always worried I'd lose it one day, but imagined it'd be a dramatic moment where I'd stand on a rooftop and shout and throw rocks at God and they'd take me off to jail where I'd rot. Instead, I was in a house in some alternate universe with people who wanted me to live forever.

That would be the worst thing possible. Living forever meant never losing the past, and while I wasn't quite ready to die just yet, I didn't exactly dread it either, even though I knew death meant Hell. I was certain of that because of . . .

I wouldn't look in that box again. I would take all of this at face value, and see my sister and she'd explain what went on here, and then I'd go back to my own life.

Suddenly aware of a delicious smell, my stomach growled.

"Come along and meet my brothers."

I walked between him and Sasha toward the rear of the grand hall where there was a double door entry into a cavernous dining room to the right and a wide hallway with a lot of doors to the left. It occurred to me that the house was lit entirely by candlelight. Looking up, I saw electric fixtures, but none of them were on. Of all the weird things about this night, this struck me as one of the oddest.

Just as we cleared the entrance to the dining room, four guys with the same coloring, similar features, and who were as tall and broad as Kyros and Phoenix stood from their chairs and stared at me with looks ranging from incredulous to suspicious. Tonight just got more fun. I longed for my apartment and my bed, to be curled up with Olga, drifting off to sleep.

Instead, I was facing the Inquisition.

Kyros walked ahead of me and stopped at the end of the very long table. "This is Mariah, Jordan's sister. She's going to stay a few days." He looked at me before he began to point. "The tallest one there is Titus. We call him Ty. He's an animal lover. Ty, you'll have to meet Mariah's cat, Olga."

Ty managed a small smile, but I could tell he wasn't happy about my presence.

Kyros pointed to the one with a buzz cut, a diamond stud in one ear and a tat of a question mark on his neck. "That's Xenos, who we call Zee. He's our musician."

Zee was conflicted, unsure if I was interesting or annoying. "Where did you come from?" he asked.

"Bucharest," I replied. "Your Romanian is perfect."

"All our languages are perfect."

"All?"

"We know every language spoken on Earth."

"Why? How?"

"It's a job requirement, and we were born this way." He looked to Kyros. "Why is she here?"

"We'll talk about it later," Kyros said firmly. He pointed to the guy across the table from Ty and Zee. "That's Ajax. When we're not mad at him, we call him Jax."

This one walked toward us and slipped an arm around Sasha while he smiled at me. Now I knew who Sasha was: attached to Ajax.

"Hello, Mariah. I'm glad to meet you." He looked at Kyros. "I hope you know what you're doing, brother."

Sasha said, "Isn't it amazing how much she resembles Jordan? She has that same . . . skin tone, doesn't she? Practically glows."

Jax's smile faded by degrees while he stared at me like I was a germ under a microscope. He murmured, "It must run in their family."

"Phoenix met Mariah just after Key brought her here, but unfortunately he won't make it to dinner. He had to go see Jane."

Who was Jane? I felt bad for her having to suffer a visit from Phoenix.

I'd swear Sasha and Jax carried on an entire conversation without saying a word, then Jax shot a questioning look at Kyros, who nodded. Jax smiled at me again, wider this time. "I'm glad you're staying for a while, Mariah."

"Thank you." I turned my attention to the last guy, arguably the best looking of all of them, and that was saying a lot.

"Denys is the youngest," Kyros said. "He drinks too much and chases women."

"Kyros!" Sasha was clearly shocked. She gave me an apologetic smile. "Denys likes to laugh and have a good time. That's all."

I met Denys's gaze and saw right past his grin. There was agony in his eyes and I wanted to tell Kyros he was an oblivious ass, but I didn't because Denys's demons weren't my business. He made some light quip about girls being more fun to chase than guys and I smiled like I thought it was funny, but he kind of made me want to cry.

"Well, then," Kyros said, "now you know the Mephisto. Enjoy your dinner, and Sasha will see to it that you're comfortable in a guest room."

"Aren't you eating?"

"I have some things to do. I'll be back later, with Jordan." And just like Phoenix and Deacon, he disappeared.

So this was really going to happen. After so many years and so much dreaming of this moment, I was going to see Viorica. I wasn't ready and was convinced she would be more upset than glad, but if it was inevitable, I would accept it and focus on my joy. My heart beat a little faster and I was both anxious and delighted.

When I turned back to the table, the other brothers were still and quiet, staring at me with that same focused attention I'd received from Phoenix, but without the hostility. Something about me was fascinating, which was an entirely new experience. I just wished I knew what it was.

Jax went to the chair at the opposite end of the table and pulled it out. "Sit in Key's chair, Mariah. That'll make it easier for us to stare at you."

I was fairly certain he was joking, a tease to clue his brothers in that they were being rude. Didn't work. They still stared.

Sasha moved close and whispered, "We don't have visitors here, especially girls."

Ah, so their attention was because I was female. I debated telling her I wasn't remotely interested in guys, but then I noticed the sparkle in her eyes, her obvious pleasure at having some female companionship, and I didn't have the heart to be negative. I certainly had no issues with women. Not that I had many friends, but I considered Gustav's fiancé my friend. She'd just become a teacher, having graduated from university the previous summer. It was Sophia who'd urged me to begin saving for school so I could become something other than a barmaid. Looking at Sasha's hopeful gaze, I smiled before I went around the table to accept Jax's invitation to Kyros's chair.

As soon as I'd removed my coat and Jax hung it on the back of the chair, I sat down. Jax took his seat, Sasha sat beside him, and Deacon reappeared, bending low to serve from a huge silver tray he balanced in one hand. He set what looked like some kind of beef dish on the thin, elegant china plate in front of me, and it was all I could do to wait for everyone else to be served before I picked up my fork and began to eat. It was, without a doubt, the best thing I'd ever tasted. I'd scarcely taken three bites before Deacon was back to serve tiny carrots with some kind of glaze, a soufflé of butternut squash, and thin, steamed green beans. As soon as he'd finished that round, he came back with yeasty rolls. I was so focused on my food, so hungry and so happy to be eating something this delicious, it was a moment before I realized Zee had asked a question. I looked at him as I took a drink of ice water from a crystal goblet. "I'm sorry, what did you say?"

"I asked what you normally eat. Do you live alone? Do you cook? When was the last time you ate?"

"Are you just curious, or was I being overzealous?"

"Both."

Zee was a guy who said exactly what was on his mind. I liked that. "I work at a pub six days a week, from eleven in the morning until three in the morning, so I eat most of my meals there. Gustav's menu is limited, mostly cabbage soup and sausages. Yes, I live alone, no I don't cook because I don't have a kitchen, and the last meal I had was yesterday at four, Romanian time. I had a brown roll and fish stew. Gustav made it because it was Sunday. Hockey day. We have a lot of patrons on hockey and football days."

"Must be hard to work in a pub," Denys said.

I nodded and continued eating. They all exchanged glances, silently communicating something, but I didn't much care. If the food was always this incredible during my stay, I intended to take full advantage of it. And if they thought I was curious because I was so involved with my plate, I was fine with it. I wondered what would be for dessert?

Deacon came back with a fruit and cheese board and I thought I might laugh with happiness. It was simply marvelous. I'd just taken a bite from a slice of a crisp pear when Phoenix walked through the doorway, which I was directly facing, being situated in Kyros's chair.

That was terribly unfortunate. Just when I was having such a lovely time, Mister Thundercloud had to show up. Maybe Jane told him to scram.

The atmosphere around the table changed immediately, and I sensed an enormous amount of anxiety.

Jax again took the lead. He said a little too loudly with an edge of forced joviality, "Glad you could make it, Phoenix. Hans has outdone himself tonight."

Phoenix came to stand at the other end of the table and ignored Jax, all of his focus on me. "Where did he find you?"

I swallowed the bite of pear. "At Gustav's Pub in Bucharest."

"So you're a drinker." His voice indicated he wasn't at all surprised. Why did he have such a low opinion of me? He didn't know the first thing about me.

"I work there, and no, I don't drink. I can't afford it."

"You're poor."

"Very. Is this why you're so offended by me? Because I'd much rather be poor than shallow."

"I'm many things, but I assure you I'm not shallow."

"But you *are* offended by me. Don't deny it."

"I want you to go away."

"We don't always get what we want."

I was aware of the others moving their heads back and forth in unison as we sparred, and I had the urge to laugh.

"You think this is funny?"

"I think it's ridiculous. You don't know me at all, but you've decided to dislike me based on my appearance."

"That shirt is too low-cut, and your pants are too tight."

"I told you, I work in a pub. Provocative clothing earns me better tips."

He looked ready to explode, he was so very angry. "You're a whore."

Sasha gasped. Jax stood and said, "That's enough."

"Is that it, Mariah? Do you dress like this so the men in the pub will pay you extra in hopes you'll go home with them?"

"That's it exactly."

"And do you?"

"Do I what?"

"Do you go home with them?" His hands were clenched into fists and his handsome face was flushed with fury.

There was a time when I'd have been frightened, but those days were long over. I would never be afraid of an angry man again. Whatever he said, whatever he did, I would separate myself from it and nothing would bother me. So let him be mad for no reason other than his prejudice and egotistical need to hold himself above me. His opinion meant nothing. "Whether I do or don't isn't up for discussion. Back off."

"Answer me! *Now!*" He positively bellowed.

I opened my mouth to answer so he'd shut up and leave me alone, but never got the chance. With such speed, he moved in a blur, Zee was out of his chair and knocking Phoenix to the floor.

The fight that followed was bloody and vicious. The other brothers surged to their feet and rushed to that end of the dining room to break it up. Sasha looked at me and said, "I'm so sorry, Mariah. He's . . . Phoenix has some problems."

I didn't bother telling her it was all right. Why lie? The table shook, and china and crystal crashed to the floor.

While I listened to the sound of fists hitting flesh, of grunts and curses and shouts of fury, certain boxes tried to slip free in my mind. I ate more of the pear, some of the cheese, and concentrated on holding the boxes in place, but they kept sliding out and I couldn't stop them. Determined to stay calm and above what was happening right in front of me, my mind took me where I always went as a last resort – home. Not my tiny, dilapidated apartment. The home where I lived until my parents died.

Small and cozy, set back from the road in a copse of trees, it was just a few miles from the nearest village. There was a stone fireplace and a braided rug and a little dog named Beet, because he liked beets. And Mama in her chair by the fire, darning socks, replacing buttons, telling Viorica and me Romanian folktales. Nothing bad could ever happen to me when I was there, stretched across the rug petting Beet, or sitting cross-legged with Viorica while we sang for Papa, or drinking warm cider after playing in the snow. The sum of all contentment was that braided rug by the fire.

So I finished eating the pears and cheese and stayed there on the rug and hardly noticed when Sasha reached for my arm and said it was time to go upstairs and rest. Olga would be there. She'd snuggle up against me and we would sleep and when we woke up, everything would be better. Mornings were my favorite. Emilian never got up in the mornings. I always had them to myself, to read, or walk in the park, or sit on the roof and dream.

I smiled at Sasha while I slowly withdrew my arm from her grasp and stepped away. She took my coat from the chair and led me from the dining room. Other than blood on the rug, there was no evidence of the fight. The chairs had all been righted, the broken dishes swept up. I said, "Crushed eggshells will get that out."

Sasha gave me a peculiar look.

"It's true. I cleaned for Marta, so I know lots of housekeeping tricks."

We were halfway up the stairs. "Who is Marta?"

"She was Gustav's mother. She was one of those hard women with a rough voice. She was strict, but kind. I went to live with her after . . . when I found myself alone at fourteen."

"Will you tell me how you came to be separated from Jordan?"

"No." I followed her up another flight of stairs and down a wide hallway with beautiful paintings and more candles. "I don't talk about my sister to anyone."

"I understand."

"No, you don't. Let's not talk any more. I have a headache." I needed Olga. I wanted to lie in the dark and be very still, and then no one would find me. I'd be invisible.

"Mariah," Sasha said when we were inside a pretty bedroom with pale pink walls, a crackling fire and a beautiful candelabra on a beautiful desk. "You're not making any sense. Look at me."

I turned from searching for Olga and looked directly into her eyes. "What doesn't make sense?"

"You said you will be invisible."

"Did I?" Oh, God, I was losing myself. Viorica would be here soon. She couldn't see me like this. I sucked in a deep breath and tried to smile while I lied. "It's just that these headaches make me slightly disoriented. If I lie down in the dark for a while, I'll be fine."

"I'll have Mathilda bring some medicine."

I didn't need medicine. I needed to be alone. "Yes, that'd be lovely, thank you." Who was Mathilda? How many strangers did I have to meet today? I wanted to go home to my apartment, where I'd be blessedly alone. And safe.

She went to a small plastic box on the wall by the door, pressed a button and said, "Mathilda, would you bring some Tylenol to Mariah's bedroom?"

I'd barely had time to sit on the chair by the fire before a plump woman appeared in the center of the room. She wore a long brown dress with a crisp white apron and her brown hair was in a tidy bun at the nape of her neck. Something, her smell of gingerbread, I think, reminded me of my mother, and I instantly liked her. She came toward me and reached for my hand and patted it while she smiled down at me with soft, warm brown eyes. "There now, puir lamb, Deacon told me how you came to be here. 'Tis a disgrace the way those boys act sometimes, pilfering sweet girls right out of their homes, brawling in the dining room, talking disrespectful to a gentle soul. But ye've naught to worry about. Mathilda is here now, and our Sasha. We'll have you right as rain in no time."

I blinked up at her, completely confused. "You spoke English and I understood."

"'Tis because I'm of the spirit world, child. I can't really talk, but your spirit hears mine and there's no language."

I wasn't sure what entranced me more – my ability to understand her thickly accented English, or how much I enjoyed her holding and patting my hand. I typically couldn't abide anyone touching me.

She looked at Sasha. "What's Tynedol?"

"Tylenol. It's medicine for headaches. You'll have to ask a Lumina to get some at a drug store."

"If there's no Tylenol," I said, wishing I hadn't lied about the headache because this was becoming way too complicated, "I can take anything. Plain old aspirin will be fine."

Sasha said, "There's no medicine of any kind in the house. Nobody here ever needs it. We're immortal, so we don't get sick, and if we're injured, we heal very quickly."

Jax's voice came through the plastic box. "War room meeting. Now."

I was wondering what a war room was when Mathilda said, "Go on, Sasha. I'll look after Mariah. I'll call Brody and have him go get the Tynedol."

"Tylenol." Sasha looked at me. "I'm sorry I have to go. I swear I'll be back as soon as possible. Are you going to be okay?"

"I'll be fine." I hated that she'd seen me crack around the edges. "I'm tired and it's been a very strange night."

"I'm sorry to say it's going to get stranger still. I've been here just over a year. I know how you feel right now."

"Thank you," I said, mildly curious to know how she came to be with the brothers. How had she met Jax? How did she become immortal?

She disappeared and I looked up at Mathilda. "Have you seen my cat?"

"Yer kitty is still in the kitchen, enjoying a second dish of cream. Dani will bring her up directly."

"I can't go to sleep without her." She was my warning system. Olga meowed whenever someone came close to her. If I was asleep and she meowed, I knew what was about to happen. I could be ready. I could go home in my head and be ready.

"She'll be here, never you worry." Mathilda let go of my hand and bent to pick up my foot. "For now, let's get you comfortable so you can have yer lie-down." My right boot came off, followed by the left, and before I knew it, I was dressed in only my bra and panties. My very old bra and panties. She looked me over and tsked. "We'll be finding you some new unmentionables. For now," she went to a door and opened it, revealing a closet, and unhooked a fluffy white robe from within, "slip this on and get into bed."

The robe was heavenly. The sheets were even better. And the bed was amazing. Soft and warm and comfortable. I felt a thousand times better. I listened to her tell someone on the other end of the plastic box to go to town and buy some Tynedol. A male voice replied, "Tylenol?"

"That's it," she said. "We've a guest and she's needing a headache powder. Sasha says Tynedol is the thing."

I could hear a smile in the guy's voice. "I'll get your Tynedol right away and bring it right up."

"Thank ye, Brody, there's a good lad."

"Mathilda?" I asked.

She turned from the plastic box. "Yes, child?"

"Why are you here? What happened to make you mad at God?"

Moving to the chair by the fire, she sat and arranged her skirts before she said quietly, "In eighteen-fifty-two, I was housekeeper to an aristocrat at a manor house in Surrey. I had a daughter, a bright, happy girl I named Prudence – Pru for short – and she lived with my sister, but I always brought her to be with me for the week of Christmas. When Pru was twelve, she came to visit and all was fine and good, except she'd learned to read and I couldn't keep her out of his lordship's library. One night, I woke up and she wasn't in bed with me, so I went to find her."

Mathilda paused, and I stiffened. I knew what was coming. I wanted to stop her, but I didn't. I couldn't. I'd asked, and if she was brave enough to tell me, I had to be brave enough to listen. I hadn't seen it going this way, but I was in it now.

"I found her in the library with his lordship. She were on the floor and he . . . even after more than a century, I remember just the way she sounded, breathless and scared. She kept whispering, 'Mum,' and he said if she screamed, he'd sack me and I'd never work again. He never knew I was there, he was so busy violating my girl. I grabbed the fireplace poker and whacked him on the head. Killed him. Pru didn't last the night before she passed on. She bled and didn't stop. The constable came and I was arrested. They said at the trial that I hit him fourteen times. I don't reckon I remember, but I suppose they were right, and the day after they found me guilty, I was executed for killing a titled gentleman, but he weren't no gentleman, Miss Mariah. He was an animal and if I had it to do over, I'd kill him just the same."

I swallowed again and again and barely managed to whisper, "Why do you blame God? You should be angry at the devil."

"For taking my baby. He could have let her live. She would have healed."

I stared up at the ceiling and mentally stood on *that* box. I would *not* let the lid come off. "Her body would have healed, but not her mind. I think God was merciful, taking her to Heaven so she didn't have to finish growing up with . . ."

Mathilda came to the side of the bed, bent and smoothed the hair from my brow. "Ye're a gentle soul and my heart hurts for you, same as it did for my sweet Pru."

"You don't think I mean—"

"Shhh, I know, love. I know. Close yer eyes now and sleep and I'll be right here when you wake up. Nobody will pester ye."

For the first time since I'd rescued her from the street when I was thirteen, I fell asleep without Olga.

~~ PHOENIX ~~

I knew Jax would call a war room meeting. I considered leaving before he did, so I'd have an excuse for not attending, but I was never one to hide from my screw-ups. In my bathroom, changing out of bloody clothes, I heard Jax's voice on the intercom and faced what was sure to happen. He would call a council. We'd convene on Kyanos; my brothers and Sasha would debate whether I was deserving of punishment – and there was no doubt I deserved it – then mete it out. I'd probably pull a month of solitary on Kyanos. Maybe that'd be for the best. By the time I returned to Colorado, Mariah would be gone.

I didn't think it was possible to loathe myself more than I had when Mariah first appeared, but not so. I'd lost my grip and the darkest side of me took over. I thought that battle won years ago, thought I had perfect control over the Mephisto in me. Far from having won, I was worse than before Jane. I imagined Mariah lying naked with another guy, and over one hundred years of hard won self-control flew right out the window. I became a caricature of myself; a ravening beast. I shouted at her and called her a whore.

Nothing had ever made me more glad than when Zee knocked me down and made me stop. Since Jane, I'd tried to be more of what she wanted me to be – a gentleman. I tried to be considerate of women. It was part of the reason I never accompanied my brothers when they went looking for sex. Jane had shown me what lies within a woman's soul and no matter how much I craved the feel of a woman's body, I could never step over that line again. Not when I knew it was nothing but sex. And it could only ever be about sex. Because of their fear, no human woman could stay with one of us. Only an Anabo. I had self-righteous disdain for my brothers' never-ending hunt for meaningless one-night stands, but I was infinitely worse. I'd verbally attacked an Anabo.

I'd be lucky if I pulled less than six months on Kyanos.

Taking a deep breath, I popped down to the basement, to the war room in the center of a maze of offices and computer banks where the Luminas worked, ready to face the music. Everyone but Key was there, Jax standing next to Sasha at one end of the large oval table that dominated the flagstone floor, Ty in his chair with the thirty-third version of Gretchen, his favorite mastiff, right beside him, Zee leaning against the wall with the world map and white board, and Denys in front of the huge flat screen on the opposite wall.

"Where is Kyros?" I asked. It was highly unusual to have a war room meeting without our leader. I hated his guts at the moment, but that was beside the point.

They all looked solemnly at me while Jax said, "He's in Bucharest, doing some investigative work to learn more about Mariah. Later, he's going to Washington to tell Jordan she has a sister." He looked conflicted. "She'll be in the gym at ten for a training session. I don't like knowing this when she doesn't, but Key said to go along, business as usual and let him tell her. There's something . . ." Jax stopped and sighed. "He looked like he might cry. Whatever he already learned about Mariah, it's bad."

I hadn't imagined that Key was close to tears. *Jesus.* What was so bad that it would make Kyros cry? Maybe Mariah *did* take guys home with her. For money. Was she so destitute, she'd turned to whoring herself?

That overwhelming feeling of helpless rage washed over me and I focused on the world map hoping to make it subside. My eyes were drawn to Romania. Where Mariah was from; where Eryx lived. It was a strange coincidence, and not a happy one.

He was extremely active at the moment. He'd convinced a

lot of big dogs in Washington to trade their souls to him, and unless my takedown plan was a success, control of the United States was within his reach. Except he was tripping himself up like he always did, a victim of his own dark soul. He still had some human tendencies, just as we did, but he was missing a key ingredient all humanity needed to achieve success in anything – hope. What made people, including us, keep going, even in the face of defeat, was a deep-seated need to maintain self-respect. We were all sons of Hell, but all of us except Eryx kept the part of our mother that was hope and dignity.

Eryx lost that when he died and crossed into immortality, extinguishing all light in his soul. It was why I didn't believe he would ever succeed in his grand plan to take out Lucifer and rule Hell.

It was why, after his scheme to convert the president through coercion by kidnapping Jordan backfired on him, he hadn't stayed the course and gone after other powerful people in Washington. Instead, once he realized she was Anabo and had become immortal, he became less interested in controlling the U.S. and more obsessed with Jordan. Unlike Jane, who he'd murdered so she could never become immortal or Mephisto, who he'd never once considered keeping, he wanted Jordan to live with him, do what he did, and bear his sons.

But, then, Jordan was the complete opposite of Jane. Self-assured, assertive, and outspoken, she was the product of her background. Growing up as the only child of the man who became president of the U.S. gave her an edge on leadership abilities. And the wherewithal to stand up to Kyros.

Jane had grown up extremely sheltered, in a different era, where women were much less forthright. But all that aside, if they switched places, Jane would always be quiet and reserved and Jordan couldn't not be a natural leader. It was the strength in her that attracted Eryx. He knew she was now immortal and becoming Mephisto, but he was fanatical and wouldn't give up trying to figure out a way to get her away from Kyros.

He wouldn't want Mariah to stay with him. She wasn't like Jordan. She wasn't like Jane, either, but she wouldn't appeal to him as Jordan did. He would see her as leverage to get at Jordan, then . . .

My mind went straight down the rabbit hole, despite all my attempts to stop it. Thoughts of Eryx and Jane and Jordan and Mariah led to one final, horrible conclusion: he'd kill her. He'd wait until I arrived to rescue her, then slit her throat. It would be exactly as it had been with Jane.

Mariah's only hope was if I stayed away from her. If she wasn't marked, Eryx couldn't sense her existence, couldn't find her, would never know she was Anabo. She'd live the rest of her life until she was very old and die like all humans and go to Heaven because she was Anabo. And I'd lose all hope of ever waking up with someone beside me in my bed, of having someone to talk to, a woman whose body and soul could bring me any measure of peace, because this was the way it had to be. This was what I deserved. This was my penance for Jane.

Sweet, gentle Jane. Her death was a vulgar horror. And it was my fault. Like a movie on repeat, I relived her death in my head yet again, remembered the look of desperation in her perfect blue eyes as she begged me to bring her back – and her heartbreak when she understood I couldn't.

Eryx had laughed.

He watched me try, watched Jane bleed out in my arms while I forced every ounce of energy in my body into hers, and when it was clear she was gone forever, he laughed.

Sometimes I woke to the sound of his laughter, ringing through the years.

I hated him with every immortal cell in my body.

I kept my eyes on Romania and barely heard Jax when he said, "Key will tell us more as soon as he can. I called this meeting in the meantime because we need to all be on the same page about Mariah." From my peripheral vision, I saw him sweep his gaze around the room. "You all got that she's Anabo, right?"

Everyone nodded. Zee said, "She has no glow."

"Yes, she does," Sasha said. "It's just very dim."

"What's wrong with her?" Ty asked.

"I don't know," Jax said, "but she's definitely Anabo, and Jordan's sister. We owe her every courtesy and all due respect." He looked at me then. "Phoenix, we get it, but we can't stand aside and allow you to abuse her. For one thing, it's cruel, but there's also the future to consider. If she's miserable, there's no way she'll ever agree to stay, as a Lumina or as Mephisto. She'll leave because of your behavior, and that's not fair to her, or to us. If you can't control yourself around her, I think it's best if you leave and stay away until she's had time to learn and understand who we are and what we do, and decide, on its own merit, if she wants to join us."

I looked away from Romania and met the gaze of my closest brother. Jax and I had always understood one another, so I was well aware of the subtext in his speech: *Get the fuck over it.* Whatever understanding he'd had of how it was for me had dissolved the instant he met Mariah and knew she was Anabo. I wanted to leap across the distance between us and pound him until he begged for mercy. "Is this a rhetorical question, brother?"

Ajax drew himself up. "I'm dead-ass serious. You went off the rails tonight. Either you've got the ability to not do that again, or you don't. Decide. Now."

I took a quick assessment of their expectant faces before I refocused on Jax. "Fuck you."

"Not rising to the bait. Answer the goddamn question."

I looked at Zee, who shook his head. "Already beat the shit out of you. Not gonna happen again."

Ty shrugged. "I'd enjoy getting into it with you, Phoenix, but it won't help. You need to figure out how to deal, or leave."

Sasha simply cocked one delicate brow.

Denys glared at me and said in a low voice, "It's not fair, and I'm man enough to say what everyone's thinking. Because you're all fucked up, you think you don't deserve her, but at the same time, because she's not pure and perfect like Jane, you'd rather throw her away like yesterday's leftovers than even *try.* I'd take her in a heartbeat if I could. I wouldn't give a damn if she had sex for money, or if she'd fucked every guy in Romania for free. She'd be *mine.* What, you think you're some kind of special case because of Jane? No, Phoenix, all you are is a sanctimonious, self-righteous asswipe on a perpetual guilt trip. Fuck *you.*"

Never in our lives had I heard Denys say something like that. I was so stunned, I had no reply.

I was still taking it in when he added, "Next time . . . there'd better not be a next time. We'll send your ass to Kyanos for the next century. We spent the last century tiptoeing around any mention of Jane, always trying to protect you. I'll be damned if we'll spend the rest of eternity handling you with kid gloves because you can't handle that you *have another Anabo!*" He slammed his fist on the table and it cracked, right down the middle. A thousand years old, made from a Kyanos hickory, and my baby brother, the joker, the perennial party guy, the one who was rarely serious about anything at all, broke it in a passionate rage.

With fury in his black eyes, he looked up from the crack and spat at me before he disappeared from the war room.

"Damn," Zee murmured, "shit just got real."

I took a heavy breath and said to all of them, "It's best if I leave, at least for now. I'll figure things out, and she can be here and get to know Jordan again without any more drama." I said to Sasha, "I'm sorry," because she knew what this meant. She understood like they didn't. Mariah was my responsibility, and I was abandoning her. Until Jordan came to be with us permanently, it would be up to Sasha to walk Mariah through the minefield that was our lives.

At her nod, I left.

CHAPTER 4

~~ MARIAH ~~

Olga meowed.

I jerked awake, then lay utterly still, eyes squeezed shut while my mind took me away from what was about to happen. I waited on the braided rug by the fire and listened to the wind at the windows and said little girl prayers and, in the part of my mind that could never entirely leave, I prayed he'd be too drunk.

I came awake more fully and remembered he was dead and wanted to weep with relief. But Olga had meowed. Someone was here.

Opening one eye a tiny bit, I remembered where I was. I lifted my head and saw Mathilda sitting by the fire, reading a book. A bottle of Tylenol sat on the desk, alongside a glass of water. And leaning against the wall next to the door was Phoenix – the reason for Olga's meow. He was dressed as Kyros had been, in black leather pants with heavy black boots and a long, black leather trench coat. I wondered what it was that they did. I would ask Viorica.

Thinking of seeing her, my anticipation returned and I wished I had something nicer to wear. For all that I was insulted by what Phoenix said, he was spot on with his critique. My clothes were fine for pub work, but inappropriate for anywhere else. If I could go to my apartment, I would change into a sweater and my jeans.

He pushed off the wall to stand straight. "I'm here to apologize, Mariah."

I wondered if Sasha and his brothers made him do this,

although he did actually sound sincere, so maybe not. I closed my eyes and stroked Olga's soft fur. "Apology accepted."

He didn't leave. I could still feel him watching me.

After a while, he said, "How long will you stay?"

"A week."

"I'll be gone, so I won't see you again."

"Okay."

He still didn't leave. I opened my eyes and looked across the room at him. He stared at me with a contradictory expression of anger and need. "Was there something else?"

"No, I . . . no."

"Well, goodbye then."

"I really am sorry, Mariah. Whatever my problems are, it's grossly unfair to make you suffer for them."

I wondered what his problems were, then decided I didn't care. I would never see him again. "Everyone has problems, and sometimes they bleed over onto others. It's okay, Phoenix. Let's just forget it."

Still, he didn't leave. I rolled to my back and sat up, disturbing Olga, who jumped to the floor and went straight to Phoenix. She purred loudly, butting her head against his boot. When he reached down to pick her up, I knew he wasn't going to leave right away. I was cursing this fact when he looked at me again, only this time, there was no anger, no hatred. Instead, all I saw was yearning. Not sexual, exactly, although there was that, but more a plea, a want of some kind. Mesmerized, puzzled, and improbably sad, I couldn't look away.

Mathilda continued reading, and maybe she was listening, maybe she wasn't, but I had a feeling she knew every tiny detail of what went on in this house, so there was no point worrying about her presence. I asked Phoenix, "What is it about me? Do I remind you of someone?"

"Yes."

"Was she friend or enemy?"

"Friend." He continued petting Olga, who continued to purr.

The room was darker than before, only two of the six candles in the candelabra lit, lending an air of intimacy that was helped by the light of the fire. Something far beyond my comprehension tugged at me, demanding my attention, but I was lost and didn't know what to do. Our eyes met again and I had the sudden certainty that I'd remember this moment all the rest of my life. "Did you love her?"

I saw it in his eyes, *no*, but he said out loud, "It doesn't matter now. She's gone, long ago."

"Did she leave you?"

"She died."

"Do I look like her?"

"No. But you're like her in another way." He walked toward the bed and stopped just at the edge to set Olga down. Tail straight with indignation, she went to curl up at the end. He loomed over me and I bent my neck to look up at him.

"Let me touch your hair," he whispered. "Just this once."

It was a strange request, something I'd never allow any guy to do for any reason, but the way he asked, the look in his eyes . . . I couldn't refuse. Reaching behind my head, I pulled the ponytail loose and my hair fell across my back and shoulders. He lifted one hand and gently stroked down before slipping his fingers into the middle to cradle my head. I could feel his warm palm against my nape as he bent lower and whispered, "Don't stay, Mariah. They'll try to talk you into it, but don't. Go home, marry a nice boy, have some babies and live to be very old."

His face was scarce inches from mine. He was closer than I ever let anyone come, and I began to feel anxious. I caught the tangy sweet scent of oranges, which seemed very odd. "I intend to go home."

"Good." I thought he might kiss me, but he didn't, and I was glad and sad all at the same time. I'd never been kissed. I'd never wanted it. Never expected to want it. How strange that my first stirring of curiosity was for a guy who'd insulted me. He did seem genuinely sorry, and now his gaze moved across my face as if he was memorizing it, as if it mattered.

His expression was sad when he released me and stood straight. "Goodbye, Mariah. I wish . . ."

"What do you wish?"

He huffed out a breath and said, "A happy life for you."

Then he was gone and I stared at the imprint of his boots on the rug where he'd been. I couldn't shake the feeling that something momentous just occurred, but it hadn't. He petted my hair, told me to go home and have a happy life, and he left. Other than him disappearing into thin air, nothing at all out of the ordinary about it.

So why did I feel as if someone just walked over my grave?

I'd gotten out of the shower, which Mathilda insisted I take, and slipped back into the white robe when Sasha knocked and came in. I was struck all over again by her beauty. Small wonder Jax was in love with her.

She saw me in the doorway to the bathroom and said with a wide smile, "Key just called. He'll be here with Jordan in about twenty minutes."

"I'll get dressed."

"Yer clothes are clean and waiting for you in the closet," Mathilda said.

"Thank you." It was a very big closet. I went inside, closed the door and quickly dressed, wishing all over again that I had something else to wear. Back in the bathroom, I blow dried my hair, pulled it into a ponytail, then returned to the bedroom.

Mathilda was gone, so Sasha and I sat and made small talk until there was a knock at the door. She swung it open, and there was Kyros, holding my sister's hand.

Sasha said, "Mariah and I were just talking about cats."

As Viorica stepped into the room, Olga wound around her ankles, meowing loudly, but she didn't pay her much attention; all of her focus was on me. I got up from where I'd been sitting at the end of the bed. She was petite and beautiful, more so in real life than in press photos or on television, and she had that same ethereal light that Sasha had. Her hair was glossy and dark and her eyes were the color of bluebells, just as they'd been when we were small, just as they were in my dreams.

"Mariah," she whispered.

"Viorica," I replied.

We rushed toward one another and I wrapped my arms around her and she threw hers around me and we both cried.

Overwhelmed, I didn't notice when Kyros and Sasha left.

~~ PHOENIX ~~

In Yorkshire, in the countryside close to the moors where we used to live, it was snowing. Despite where I stood at the foot of her grave, staring at her name, I couldn't focus on Jane. All I could think about was watching Mariah wake up. When I had stepped inside the room, the cat meowed, and I saw her body stiffen beneath the covers. I could feel her tense awareness, and knew she was afraid. Terrified. But not of me. She didn't know I was there until moments later when she opened her eyes and saw me. Her expression was unhappy; not scared. She didn't like me, but at least she wasn't afraid of me.

Like it mattered.

But there was no denying what I'd witnessed. Mariah was horribly afraid of something and I wanted to know, what?

In the middle of my thoughts, Key materialized, carrying two rapiers. Was he fucking kidding? He looked through the falling snow at me, and I glared at him. "No. Just . . . *no.*"

Ignoring me, sliding out of his coat, he tossed it aside and moved toward me, gripping the hilt of one sword in position to begin a match. He tossed the other into the air, and for a nanosecond, I thought about letting it split my head in two, but it wouldn't kill me; it would merely hurt for a while. I might relish a different kind of pain, but the prospect of skewering Key held a lot more appeal. I caught it in the nick of time. "You arrogant, overbearing piece of *shit,* you had no right. *None.* There was no discussion, no request."

"She's all that's good. And she's Jordan's sister."

"I don't give a damn if she's *our* sister. Nobody brings a Lumina recruit to the mountain without asking."

"Let's skip the bullshit, Phoenix. Do you want to fight, or do you want to stand there and yell at me?"

"I'd like to cut your heart out and feed it to the buzzards."

Key whipped his rapier through the air. "Bring it."

I lunged, and Key parried, the loud ping of steel against steel ringing through the cold morning air. Next to Jax, Key'd always been the best of us when it came to swords, but not today. I had cold, steady rage running through me. At that moment, I hated Key as much as I hated Eryx.

I fought with single-minded purpose, grunting my satisfaction when I thrust my blade into his only weak spot and pierced his side. He redoubled his effort, but I forced him into retreat, and we moved around the perimeter of Jane's grave. Key missed dinner and it must have been a long time since he'd eaten anything. He was weakening. "Take her back."

"You can't be serious. Her life is crap, Phoenix."

He made another thrust, but I easily deflected and countered with my own, slicing into his upper arm.

"She's not just some girl, not just Jordan's sister. She's Anabo, and we need her."

"*I* don't need her." I let finesse slip and became more savage in my attack, my rapier moving with lightning speed.

Grimacing in pain after I sliced across his chest, Key came back and slipped beneath my guard, landing a hard jab into my shoulder. "She's another soldier in our dirty war."

I went after him and made another slice across his chest, shredding what was left of his shirt so that it hung in tatters from his shoulders. The snow on the ground was stained with blood, mostly Key's. I was like a rabid dog, practically snarling. "*Always* about the job, isn't it, brother? God forbid you do *anything* that isn't about Mephisto."

He lost his momentum after that and I wondered if what I'd said actually filtered through to his brain. It wasn't much longer before he gave up. When I went for his heart, he didn't raise his sword to protect himself, and I stopped with the tip of my rapier an inch from his chest. "You're going to let me take you out?"

"I'm not *letting* you do anything. I'm fucking exhausted. Just do it." When I hesitated, he said, *"Do it!"*

He wasn't the only one who'd lost the heart for this. I moved the sword slowly away from him. "No." He took my rapier when I held the hilt toward him, and I turned and walked back to Jane's grave. He needed to know the truth. Maybe that was part of the reason he came here, where he knew he was unwelcome. He had to know what to do about Mariah. Had to know if I would cave in to instinct and loneliness and share what I was with her. He thought it was so simple. Thought I could eventually set aside my guilt and grief over Jane and move on. But he didn't know the truth. No one did. Except me, and I had to live with it for the rest of eternity. I would never drag Mariah into the Hell that was my life. I wouldn't ruin whatever hope she had of happiness. And I wouldn't put her at risk from Eryx. "You need to think real hard about talking her into staying, Kyros, because she won't be Mephisto, and if that's all she means to you, it's cruel to keep her on the mountain."

"That's not all she means to me. She's Jordan's sister. She's been through a lot, and she needs us to help her find her way back to her own humanity."

Didn't he know I had enough guilt for a thousand lifetimes? Surely he wasn't standing there trying to add more guilt to my plate. "If you think I'll feel sorry for her, you've—"

"She wouldn't want anyone to feel sorry for her. She's all about Jordan, and if all she can ever be is a Lumina, I think that's just fine. There's no rule that says a Mephisto has to accept an Anabo, just like they don't have to accept us."

A Lumina. Yeah, that'd just be so awesome. She'd be there on the mountain, day after day, year after year, century after century, working with all the other Luminas, and one of them was bound to fall for her and I'd spend forever watching her with another guy. I'd never survive. I'd eventually be unable to stand it and would walk into a church, onto holy ground, where I'd burst into flames and die and be sent straight to Hell, to be with Lucifer and my father and all the wretched souls who lost their way. It was fitting, I supposed. I'd certainly lost my way. "So there's no way you'll take her back?"

"If you knew . . . if you could see where she lives, and what she's got in this world, and if you could understand how she feels about Jordan, you wouldn't want her to go back. Besides, it's not as if her being away from the mountain will make any difference. She'll still be Anabo, and you're still Mephisto, and you know she exists. It's not going to make her any less tempting."

Jerking my gaze to Key's, I scowled. And lied. "I'm *not* tempted. I'm not interested at all. And that's not going to change, *ever*."

Key's gaze moved to the headstone. "Of course Jane would

want you to stay true to her, and you're nothing if not loyal, Phoenix."

Pure hyperbole. Did the arrogant son of a bitch really think I'd fall for it? I opted to take it at face value and nodded as I said, "She's got nothing to worry about."

Time marched on, as it always does, and I know he expected me to say something.

I didn't.

Then, while I waited for him to go away, he blew my mind. "I'm sorry, Phoenix."

I turned my head to look at him, shocked by the grief in his black eyes. Jordan had done this to him. As much as his chemistry gave her the DNA to become Mephisto and have the ability to kill the lost souls despite the Anabo in her, she gave Key enough of herself to affect a subtle but undeniable shift in the way he looked at the world. But I was too angry to be glad about it. Too frustrated and bitter. "Did the mighty leader of the Mephisto just *apologize*? Is this the apocalypse?"

He immediately bent to get his coat and I was positive it was to keep me from seeing his tears. I was astounded all over again. Kyros was cold, distant, and hard. Always. He was all about his job and his duty as the head of our family, as leader of the Mephisto.

When he straightened up again, his coat folded across one bloody arm, he had himself back under control. "I wish I'd known she's Anabo so I could have warned you. I'd never have done that to you, but I just didn't know."

I believed him. He was sincerely sorry. It had been a misstep, and Key never made mistakes. He hadn't known Mariah was Anabo – but he knew she was exceptional because he could feel what was within her, what set her apart from all other humans. A well of goodness, of kindness and compassion that didn't judge, that wasn't selective. Born without Original Sin, Anabo were unique, and very rare. Mariah was different, though. Something was wrong with her. The blue of her eyes was dark, and she'd lost her light. "Why can't we see it?"

"Because of her life. She's been . . . things have happened that caused her to . . . ." He stopped talking and sighed.

I watched snowflakes land on my brother's dark hair and

waited.

Finally, he said, "She's broken."

That hit me hard and I flinched before I quickly refocused on Jane's grave. "Go home and eat, Key. You're still bleeding, and you're pale as a ghost."

I suppose he understood that I couldn't talk anymore. While I stared at Jane's gray, dreary headstone and wondered what had happened to break Mariah, Key disappeared.

~~ MARIAH ~~

My reunion with my sister was bittersweet: extremely joyous and heartbreakingly sad, all at once.

We sat on the chairs in front of the fire and before I'd talk about me or our shared history, short as it was, I insisted Viorica tell me about her life, about her adoptive parents and being the First Daughter. When she told me about her mother dying of breast cancer four years ago, she cried, but there was something more, something beneath her tears that was infinitely more tragic than Mrs. Ellis's too early death. I watched her carefully as she spoke, noticing the feminine way her hands moved, the light in her eyes, the confidence in her voice. What bothered me was her Romanian. She spoke it perfectly, just like all the others who called themselves Mephisto. Zee had said they knew every language on Earth. I was certain Viorica knew far more than the average teenager, and she undoubtedly studied French, Spanish, maybe even German, or Chinese, but would she know Romanian? Perhaps she remembered bits and pieces from her early childhood, but what were the odds she'd speak it so fluently now?

With dread in my gut, before she was done telling me her life since I'd seen her last, I interrupted and asked, "Why are you here? Who are these strange people to you?"

She turned her bluebell eyes toward the fire and fell quiet.

I waited.

Finally, she said, "I'm as strange as they are, Mariah. I was killed when I was kidnapped, and Key brought me back to life. We were going to let the world believe that my abductors dropped me into the ocean, but on a training mission in

London, I was recognized, and had to make up a story to explain where I'd been. I came back to the States, to my dad at the White House, but I'm going to fake die at my birthday party in a couple of weeks and after that, I'll be here permanently." She turned to look at me. "I'll never die. I've agreed to stay here with the Mephisto and do what they do."

Concentrating carefully, I kept my face devoid of any emotion. I swallowed the overpowering need to cry and scream and rail at God, opened a new box, put this inside, firmly affixed the lid, and slid it on the shelf next to the others. Instead of screaming, I asked, "What is it that they do?"

"Have you ever heard of Mephistopheles?"

The night Emilian died, I'd made it a certainty that I'd meet Mephistopheles. "He's the dark angel of death who carries souls to Hell."

"He's also Key's father. He and his brothers and Sasha call him M."

That explained a lot. Didn't make it better; in fact, I wished I was still asleep and was dreaming this. "Who is their mother?"

"She was an Anabo who M found in a market in Greece over a thousand years ago. He broke a million rules of Heaven and Hell and fell in love with her."

This was the second time I'd heard the word Anabo. I now knew about Purgatories and Luminas. The Mephisto brothers were the sons of the dark angel of death. Really, how much weirder could this be? "What is an Anabo?"

Viorica smiled. "People born without Original Sin. Before Eve ate the apple, she had a daughter, but the girl wandered away from Eden and was lost. She began a line of descendants who are all without Original Sin. They became less and less over time, and now, there are almost none."

"There's no such thing," I told her, certain of this. "Everyone sins. It's the pull of darkness none of us can escape."

"Believe what you like, Mariah, but they do exist. Sasha is Anabo." She smiled. "And so am I."

Before I could stop it, my mind tripped back in time and I could see her at the table, too short to reach, trying to eat her soup, spilling a little when the bowl tipped. Emilian exploded out of his chair and backhanded her so that she flew from her chair and hit the wall. She crumpled into a little ball and he shouted at her to get up. She saw me coming to get between her and him, to distract him, and quickly scrambled to her feet, looked up at Emilian and said she was sorry, please could she finish. He picked up the bowl and poured the rest of her soup on her head. Her beautiful eyes weren't angry. They were filled with confusion and sorrow. She felt sorry for him. He was a brutal fiend and she felt bad for him.

That was the night I knew I had to get her away from him.

I looked at her now and knew she was no different. She would never want revenge, no matter the provocation. She'd always stand up for herself, but a part of her would feel sorrow.

"Anabo are the only people who can become Mephisto," she continued, "and the more there are, the better."

"Why? What do the Mephisto do?"

She lost her smile and gave me a sober look. "They take out people who've pledged their souls to the oldest brother, Eryx."

I glanced around the pretty pink room with the cheerful fire and candles in sconces and candelabras and the softest bed and a sumptuous rug and a bathroom almost as big as my one room apartment. "Where are we, Viorica?"

"Colorado. In the mountains. This house exists only to us, and the Luminas and Purgatories. Ordinary people can't see it, and Eryx can't find it."

"Tell me about Eryx."

I drifted a bit while she told me, either because I'd heard too much already, or I was infinitesimally losing reality as the night wore on. Maybe I was simply exhausted. It was two in the morning in the United States, eleven in Romania. I'd had maybe four hours of sleep. And I'd spent almost every moment since Kyros walked into Gustav's trying to hold back all the boxes. I'd added to the towering stacks, and they all threatened to come crashing down. *Too much*, my mind screamed while my heart continued to break over Viorica's death and resurrection. I grieved for her, for the eternal life she'd chosen, and for the inevitability of never seeing her again.

Somewhere in her explanation, she said humans weren't

allowed here unless they were Luminas. I didn't want to be a Lumina. I wanted to go home, and the real world and this one weren't compatible. Viorica would live here and join the others when they captured those who'd traded their souls to the oldest brother, a megalomaniac who couldn't stop looking for some way to replace the lost light of his soul and thought taking over Hell and abolishing free will would solve everything.

"God and Lucifer didn't know about M's sons. He'd hidden his Anabo behind a mist of secrecy on a tiny island in the north Atlantic he called Kyanos. When they turned eighteen, they became immortal, and Eryx, as the oldest, was first. When he died, he lost all the light he had from his mother, so when he came back, he had a soul darker even than Lucifer's. Before he died, he knew what would happen to him, and to save his younger brothers from the same thing, he killed their mother. That was the only way he knew to make God aware of their existence. Every brother after Eryx was blessed by God before he became immortal, so they kept their mother's light."

I struggled to remain focused. Her words flowed over me, settling into my mind like falling snow, delicately clinging to conscious thought. She continued explaining how Eryx sacrificed his mother and himself for his brothers, then became the only soul in existence that wasn't wanted by anyone – neither God, nor Lucifer. He spent his days convincing gullible, desperate people to pledge their faith in him, and once they said yes, there was no going back. The Mephisto captured them and put them in a place where they could never escape, killing them in the process, but ensuring Eryx would never have their soul, which he needed to increase his power. When he had enough of humanity to tip the scales, he'd declare war on Lucifer and the real fight for Hell would begin.

The Mephisto worked constantly to keep him from acquiring enough, and very soon, my sister would join their ranks. "How will you feel about killing someone, Viorica?"

"They're lost. It's for the good of humanity."

"Yeah, that's what Hitler said."

"It's not the same at all."

Maybe not. My head was about to explode and I wasn't up for arguing. It wouldn't do any good anyway. Viorica would stay here, no matter what I said.

It was fantastical, all of it, and I began to wonder if this was actually happening, or if I'd taken a walk off the edge of sanity and was only imagining it. I'd read about people who lost sight of reality and lived in their own world, talking to people who weren't there, thinking they went somewhere when really, they were sitting on a chair all the time. I was something of an expert on traveling somewhere in my mind, but I did it on purpose. Maybe my mind had decided to take a trip all on its own.

Looking at Viorica, I knew this was real. She was real. She'd grown into an amazing young woman. I didn't know if what had happened to her was good or bad, but I was absolutely certain she'd be the best at whatever she did, and everyone in this house would benefit from her being here. I loved her so much. If I never saw her again after this week, I'd make it be okay by reminding myself that she was happy. And she was. Her lovely eyes lit up when she talked of Kyros. She didn't know it yet, but she was mad about him. And I already knew he was in love with her.

Viorica finished telling me about the Mephisto, and Eryx and the lost souls and Sasha and Jax and her relationship with Kyros, then said, "Okay, you know everything about me. It's your turn."

I'd seen the way she and Kyros looked at each other before she came in the room. They were very close. I had no doubt he'd told her everything I'd said to him, which meant she knew why I took her to the orphanage, and what happened after. I saw no reason at all to talk about it anymore, and especially with Viorica. I'd saved her from Emilian – why give her the details of what I'd made certain she would miss? Better to skip over it and move on. "I'm happy to talk about our parents, what I can remember of them, or my life now, but everything in between is best left unsaid, Viorica. I hope you understand."

She didn't. But after considering me for a while, she must have decided not to push. I was relieved.

"What did our parents look like?"

"I have some photographs I can show you if Kyros will take me home to get them."

Clearly impatient and unwilling to wait for him to return, she asked, "If I take us to the orphanage, can you direct me from there?"

I nodded, and two minutes later, we stood on the steps of the old church. We held hands and looked across the street for a while at the orphanage, which was now a youth center, before I said, "I live close enough to walk, if you like."

Viorica nodded and I led her away from the church and down the street. It was snowing and she pulled up the hood of her jacket. As we walked, I couldn't stop remembering the two of us walking this way fourteen years ago, except in the opposite direction. Her hand tightened around mine, and I knew she had the same thoughts.

When we arrived at my apartment, I offered her tea, but I could tell she didn't want to stay. She was nervous and jumpy. "If I'm caught here, there'll be no way to explain it, like there was in London. Is it all right if we go back to Colorado?"

I was disappointed, but didn't show it. I nodded agreement, then turned to the shelf where I kept a few dishes and Marta's old toaster. Next to Mrs. Ellis's book about life in the White House, which I'd saved up to buy when I was sixteen, and between my Bible and Kafka's *The Metamorphosis*, was our mother's thin photo book, which I'd found among Nadia's things when she died. She'd had it all that time and I never knew. Typical of her to withhold anything that might bring me comfort. "The pictures are here, in this album," I said to Viorica. I turned with it in my hand. "I promised I'd stay for a few days, and I've already called Gustav to tell him I'm taking off of work, but I don't have any clothes in Colorado. Maybe I should get some while I'm here."

Viorica nodded. "Good idea."

I laid the photo book on the bed and went to the curtain I'd hung across the narrow niche where I kept my clothes. I took out my jeans, a couple of cotton blouses, and the gray sweater Marta had given me for Christmas two years ago. I added two pairs of panties and a T-shirt to sleep in, then rolled it all up and strapped a belt around it. Turning, I smiled at Viorica. "I'm ready."

She was moving closer to reach for my hand and take us

back to Colorado when the door flew open, startling me, and a guy in blue coveralls came in. I was shaken and unsure what to do or how to protect my sister, but it wasn't Viorica he was after. He scarcely glanced at her before he turned to me.

I felt his hands at my shoulders, pushing me back until I fell on the bed. He came down on top of me, shoving my shirt up past my bra. I went completely still. To fight was to make him angry, and it would hurt so much worse. He'd do other things and I'd die of the pain, except I never died. I just kept living, and then he'd come back. He always came back. I tried to go home in my head, but couldn't, so I stared up at the ceiling of my tiny, shabby apartment, the first place I could ever call my own, where I'd felt safe, but now realized it was all an illusion, and waited for him to be through. And stayed as still as a corpse so he wouldn't hurt me worse.

Suddenly, he collapsed, and the weight of him pressed all the air from my lungs. I heard Viorica mumble something in English, then she asked in Romanian as she shoved the man off of me, "Do you know this guy?"

"No, I've never seen him before." She had smashed his head with Marta's toaster, so hard there was a dent. And the stranger's head was bleeding. Remembering she'd said Mephisto have superhuman strength, I smiled up at her. "You're really strong, aren't you?"

She returned my smile, but her eyes were filled with anguish. "Yes. Very . . . strong," she whispered. "Let's go home now."

I didn't remind her that I was home already. I sat up, tugged my shirt down, reached for the photo book and my bundle of clothes, and accepted Viorica's hand. "Maybe we should drag him out into the hall."

"I'll get Key and come back for him, Mariah. He's a lost soul."

I almost looked at him to see if he was different from someone whose soul still belonged to God, but I didn't. I couldn't. I shoved the stranger into a box, slipped him onto a shelf, and mentally turned away. I would dream about this, but while I was conscious, he didn't exist.

CHAPTER 5

October 6, 1888
London

It's past ten o'clock before we're done with tonight's takedown, especially difficult because there were more than the usual number of Skia; all trained swordsmen. Two managed to escape, infuriating Jax, who's still in Afghanistan with Zee, searching.

I return home, quickly eat to renew my energy, bathe and change into clean clothes, then transport to London, to the musicale held at Mrs. Mangrum's, cousin to the Earl of Longbourne. Her familial status is the only reason Jane and her family are in attendance. Otherwise, they are still in mourning for Georgiana and don't attend social events.

From where I materialize at the back of the drawing room, I look around and don't see Jane. Backing out, I walk around the townhouse, cloaked, searching for her. I find her in the solarium, in her trolley chair, reading a penny dreadful by the light of the gas lamp next to a bank of orchids, her eyes wide as she reads. It must be a scary part.

She looks up and smiles. "I'm a horrible person, aren't I? But honestly, Phoenix, listening to Miss Davenport mangle Mozart becomes tiresome." She folds the paper and neatly tucks it up under her hat, then wheels her chair closer to me. "How did your takedown turn out?"

"Fine." I don't tell her what happened. She doesn't like hearing details of what we do because it reminds her of Georgiana, and it's still too raw and painful. I glance at her chair and revive our only disagreement. "Jane, please let me

fix you."

Ever patient, denying me the argument I'm spoiling for, she shakes her head. "This is why Georgiana sold her soul, so I'd be able to walk, and she never knew until it was too late that her sacrifice wouldn't make a difference. Your brother tricked her into believing I would walk, and now she's gone to a horrible place with no chance of Heaven. I know you don't understand. You've said so. But I can't walk, knowing what she gave up for me."

I'm frustrated past the breaking point, tired of dancing around the truth to spare her more pain. She needs to know. I walk behind her chair and begin to push her through the solarium, talking to the heather pinned to the top of her hat as we go. "The day after the fire, I talked to my father about Georgiana. I needed to know why she handed her soul to Eryx."

"He said it was for me to walk. Why are you telling me this again?"

"Because I didn't tell you all of it. Georgiana didn't sacrifice herself because she cared about you. It was vanity and nothing else. She imagined that the two of you would debut together and hold London in the palm of your hand. She hated that you can't walk, was embarrassed by your infirmity. You want so much to believe she was as noble as you, but she wasn't. Georgiana was spoiled, selfish, and angry at you because of what you are."

Jane says nothing. We're on our second go-round of the solarium before she finally speaks. "You wouldn't lie to me to get your way, would you?"

"I did lie to spare you from hurt, so it's not as though I can claim any high moral ground, but I'm not lying now. Your sister looked like you, but any resemblance ended there. So your refusal to let me fix you because of some sense of equitable justice is misguided and wrong."

She is quiet until we're on the third lap. "I thought she had changed," Jane whispers. "I hated what she did, but held on to believing she did it for a selfless reason." She pauses. "For me."

I wait for her to agree to allow me to heal her spine, but minutes pass and she says nothing. I'm about to ask her thoughts when she says over the squeak of one trolley wheel, "That day we went riding, after my horse threw me, she confessed she'd sabotaged my saddle so I wouldn't be able to ride with her and Robert. He liked me, and she couldn't stand it. We were thirteen and far too young to be socializing, but old enough to be intrigued by the opposite sex. He was the son of a tenant on the estate, a boy neither of us could be seriously interested in, but it didn't matter to Georgiana. She craved attention and admiration, and resented any I received, unless it was for the both of us, as a set, like a pair of perfectly matched Staffordshire dogs up on a mantel. She hadn't known the mare would throw me, and she cried and begged me to forgive her. And to not tell our parents."

I grip the back of her chair to keep from cursing. "This is whose memory you're trying so desperately to honor. Why, Jane? Don't you see, walking again is where you'll find equitable justice. Agreeing to join us and do what we do is how you even things out."

"My parents just lost a child, Phoenix. I can't do this to them."

"I can wait. In the interim, I want you to walk and gain your strength back."

"If I walk again, there will be expectations."

"They'll want to marry you off."

"It's certain that they will. How will you feel to see me betrothed?"

"Unhappy." I stop pushing the chair and go around to kneel in front of her, taking her hands in mine. "But if I know you'll eventually be with me, I can stand anything."

She smiles, but her cornflower blue eyes are forlorn. "Will you love me, Phoenix?"

"I want to."

"I've never had that. My parents favored Georgiana, and I see the way they look at me, as if they wish it had been me who died in the fire instead of my sister."

I don't argue. She's not wrong, but I don't know what to say to reassure her.

She leans forward in her chair and kisses me for the second

time. The first was a week ago, after I brought her a new
supply of penny dreadfuls. I drop her hands and grasp her
shoulders and return the kiss, wishing she wasn't wearing the
hat, wondering how soft her hair might be. I remember what M
said about kissing, that to begin her metamorphosis into
Mephisto, there has to be an exchange of saliva. I tentatively
touch her lips with my tongue and she pulls back quickly, eyes
wide with surprise. I say, "It's what a man and a woman do,
Jane."

Leaning forward again, she allows me to kiss her more
deeply, but it's awkward and we stop rather quickly. She sits
back and smiles at me. "Come to my room at one. We'll be
home by then and Rose will have put me to bed. What do I need
to do to prepare?"

"Nothing," I say, getting to my feet. "It will be a while
before you can walk because your legs have lost so much
muscle, but once your spine is healed, if you'll exercise every
day, the strength will come back."

"You'll help me, won't you?"

"Of course."

A voice drifts into the solarium from the central hall. Jane's
mother, talking to Mrs. Mangrum. "Yes, Louisa, I'm aware we
tend to indulge her, but can you blame us? Crippled as she is,
with no prospects, it's not as though she misses opportunities
when she steals away like this."

"Such a pity. She's so lovely."

"A dreadful waste, yes. If only Georgiana . . ." She doesn't
finish. She doesn't need to. Her meaning is clear.

Jane looks up at me with sad eyes. "I'll see you at one."

I squeeze her hand in farewell before I disappear.

~~ PHOENIX ~~

I spent more time in Yorkshire, standing in the place where
our house had been before Lucifer built the one in Colorado
and made this one disappear, walking the streets of the nearby
village, sitting on the garden wall of the Longbourne estate to
stare at the clipped, leafless rose bushes. Jane loved roses.

Staying made no difference. As hard as I tried to keep Jane

front and center in my thoughts, Mariah intruded over and over. What had happened to her? Why had Jordan been adopted, but not Mariah? How had she wound up working in a pub?

I went home to change out of my bloody clothes – it was beginning to be a habit today – then, without a plan or even a reason, I popped myself to Bucharest, to the oldest district, which was recently enjoying a revival, a lot of the buildings being renovated, shops and restaurants and living spaces cropping up on every street. I cloaked myself and swiped a cup of coffee from a cart because I didn't have any Romanian money, then sat on a park bench and Googled Gustav's.

I finished the coffee while I watched women with strollers and men in suits walk past. Children played in the snow, squealing when they slipped and fell. A teenaged couple made out beneath a tree. It was lunchtime. Despite the snow, some people sat on other park benches and ate. Gustav's would be crowded. A good time to go, I decided.

After I tossed the coffee cup in the trash, I disappeared, and seconds later, landed on the street where Gustav's was located, instantly struck by oppressive gloom. This was one of the poorest districts in Bucharest, some of the streets unpaved, most of the buildings from the Soviet era; giant gray boxes of depressing unimaginative sameness.

This street was paved, with a sidewalk, and I decloaked to walk north. The sign was fairly new, which meant Gustav hadn't been in business all that long. Inside was less crowded than I'd expected, but there were a respectable number of patrons eating cabbage soup and sausages, drinking a pint before they'd head back to wherever they worked. Every one of them was male. A waitress hurried between the tables, looking frazzled. Pushing forty, with bleached blond hair and too much make-up, she wore something similar to Mariah's clothes, but they hung from her rail thin body like a tired dishrag. The customers never looked at her.

The bar was dingy and smoky, and the tables and chairs were ancient, mismatched and chipped. I supposed Gustav bought the place as-is, renamed it, and carried on. An eighties pop song played from a boombox at the back. Zee would have heart failure.

Imagining Mariah coming here day after day, I became more depressed. No wonder Key didn't want to bring her back.

I took a seat at the bar and ordered a beer from a burly thirtyish guy with a gap between his two front teeth. When I handed him a credit card, he said, "Cash only."

"All I have is American money."

"That'll work." He took my twenty and didn't give me any change.

He didn't appear to recognize me as someone who looked like Key, which meant Key must have erased his memory of him the night before.

While he worked the bar, I asked, "Where's Mariah today?"

He jerked his head up and narrowed his eyes at me. "Who wants to know?"

"I'm an old friend of hers and thought I'd see her while I'm in Bucharest. Somebody told me she works here."

Back to washing beer mugs, he shook his head. "Bad luck, then. Had something come up and she took off the week." While he rinsed, he added, "How'd you say you know her?"

"I didn't."

He looked up again, even more suspicious than before. "You're not with the police, are you?"

The police? Why the hell would he ask if I was with the police? "No. Is Mariah in some kind of trouble?"

"Not that I know of, but if a policeman walks in, she usually takes a break." He looked me over. "Are you somebody who knew Emilian?"

With no clue who he was talking about, I lied. "Yes."

He added more mugs to the soapy water. "Were you friendly with him?"

Picking up on his tone, I shook my head. "Not really."

"Makes sense. You look to be twenty, twenty-one, so you were what, sixteen or seventeen when he died?"

"Sixteen," I said with a nod. So Emilian had been dead four or five years. Who was he? I took another drink of the beer. "I did some work for him."

"And that's when you met Mariah, eh?"

"That's right." Was Emilian her father?

"After the fire, she came to live with me and my mother, but I don't remember ever seeing you around."

"We moved away before the fire. I didn't know about it."

"Bad business. I never got on with Emilian. Nobody did. The guy was a drunk, a mean bastard who got what was coming to him. We lived across the road, and after Nadia died, my mother wanted Mariah to live with us, but he wouldn't agree. Said we weren't family. But he wasn't either. Nadia was Mariah's blood, and once she was gone, he had no reason to make her stay with him except she was free help."

"How did the fire start?"

"Passed out with a cigarette and caught the bed on fire. Mariah was asleep, and by the time she woke up, it was too late to save Emilian or the house. She was lucky to get out alive. She felt bad about it, and I told her and my mama told her, she couldn't have saved him." He stepped toward me and lowered his voice. "The way I see it, the world's better without him in it. Sure better for Mariah. I know he beat up on her, and a man who does that deserves to roast like a sausage in his own bed."

I wished Emilian was still alive. I'd love to beat him until he was dead, and I wouldn't care that Lucifer would be pissed and I'd be severely punished. I'd break the you-can't-kill-people rule and gladly spend eternity in Hell to pay for the privilege of killing him.

Shaken to my bones and seriously disturbed, my mind took my thoughts from Point A to Point B to Mariah not liking to be touched to Mariah waking up in abject terror. Had Emilian done more than hit her? My gut seized up, and I drank more of the beer, this time not for appearances.

Now I got why Key had been on the verge of crying.

Gustav plunged his hands back into the water and washed more mugs. "Kind of turned into a hobby of mine, looking after her. I'd sure hate to find out you don't treat her right, if you happen to run into her again."

Remembering how I'd acted at dinner last night, I wanted to kick my own ass. "Do I look like a guy who wouldn't treat her right?"

"Sure do."

"Fair enough, but I'm not a guy who beats up girls."

Without my asking for it, he took my mug and topped it off. I liked Gustav. I was glad he and his mother had been there for Mariah.

I took the risk of saying the wrong thing in hopes of getting more information from him. "Mariah used to talk about going to school. Is she taking classes while she works here?"

"Not yet, but my fiancé, Sophia, is helping her get her application together for university." He grinned at me. "I told her how to dress and how to act to get tips from these guys who drink my beer. Mostly nobody tips in Romania. But she's doing all right, and I expect she'll have saved up enough to start school next year. How about you? Are you in school?"

I was always in school. We had Luminas whose only job was to teach us what we didn't know, and in the last hundred years, there was more and more we didn't know. But I shook my head at Gustav. "I'm doing some charity work at the moment."

"Huh. Didn't figure you for a do-gooder. What kind of charity?"

"I guess you could say I do clean-up work for God." And Lucifer.

"I see. A religious man."

Some other time, that would have been funny.

He'd finished washing the mugs and was now concentrating on clearing dishes from the bar. "Might not want to talk too much about God to Mariah."

"Has she lost her religion?"

"Not for me to say, but she never goes to mass. Sophia asks her all the time, but she says she's too busy."

An Anabo who never went to a place of worship? They were drawn to churches and synagogues and mosques. After his redemption, Jax had gone all over the world with Sasha to all sorts of spiritual havens, including a shaman's hut in the Amazon. To an Anabo, the doctrine made no difference. If it was a place for God by any name, they were compelled to be there on a regular basis to refill the well.

But Mariah avoided mass.

And she was afraid of the police.

Had she started the fire? Had she killed Emilian? Was he a

lost soul? His behavior indicated he was, but humans who weren't lost souls were just as capable of evil. If he wasn't lost, and Mariah killed him . . . *impossible.* No matter how far removed she was from the Anabo inside of her, she couldn't kill someone who still belonged to God.

But what if she did?

It'd cause more pain than she could endure. She'd either go mad or lose Anabo. She had already lost most of her light, and her eyes were somewhere between blue and gray.

Did Kyros know all of this?

Forcing my mind to leave it alone for now, I asked, "Does Sophia work here?"

"God, no. She's a teacher. Smart girl, my Sophie." His smile was wry. "But maybe not that smart, since she said she'd marry me, eh?"

"I think she'll do okay." I drained the beer and set the mug down. "Thanks, Gustav."

"My pleasure. If you're around next week, come back and Mariah will be here."

"Yeah, I'll do that." I slid from the stool and walked toward the door, erasing his memory of me as soon as I was outside.

~~ MARIAH ~~

Viorica was extremely upset and trying hard to hide it when she took me back to Colorado. We'd barely gotten to the pink bedroom when she gave me a transparently fake smile and said way too brightly, "Well, here we are! I'll just call Mathilda to come up and . . ." Her finger was already on the button. "Mathilda, could you come to Mariah's room, please?" She stepped back from the plastic box and kept her gaze away from mine.

"Viorica, are you crying?"

She turned to me, blinking rapidly, and smiled harder. "Of course not." She folded her arms across her chest as if to stop herself from fidgeting. "I'm going to find Key so we can go back and get that guy, then I have to go home and dress for school. I'll be back tonight and we'll look at the pictures."

Mathilda appeared next to the fireplace, her expression

creased with worry. "What's happened?"

Viorica swallowed so hard I heard it, then said in that same too-bright voice, "We went to Mariah's apartment to get a photo album, and while we were there, a lost soul busted in. He went after Mariah and I knocked him out, so Key and I have to take care of him."

Take care of him. They were going to kill him. I backed up and sat on the end of the bed. "Do you have to? Can't we just let him leave on his own? He'll come around eventually, and go get medical help." They both looked at me as if I'd just suggested we lob a nuclear bomb on a nursery school. "What's the point in killing the man? I'm fine. He didn't hurt me."

"Mariah, didn't you understand what I told you earlier? This is all the Mephisto do, all they've done for centuries. If we let the lost die and release their souls to Eryx, he gets that much stronger. Nobody knows when he'll decide he's ready, but the day he declares open war on Lucifer, the world will be thrown into mass chaos. He's still tied to Earth. His war has to be fought here, and it won't be like any war we've ever seen. It'll be everywhere and catastrophic. Millions will suffer."

"Who's to say he'd win? Maybe it's time to let him go, let him declare war and be defeated. He can't beat Lucifer and God."

"God wouldn't be involved. This is all about who controls Hell."

"Of course God would be involved. He wouldn't let so many suffer."

"They suffer now, Mariah."

I felt a little like I'd been slapped and looked down at the thin photo book and my tiny bundle of clothes, most of what I owned. "Yes," I agreed, "they do."

"It's all about Original Sin and free will. There's a dark side to humanity, but they can choose to live above it. If Eryx were in control, he wouldn't care how a person lived their life – they'd be doomed to Hell from birth. No one would try, and the world would self-destruct."

She was so passionate and righteous and completely sure of what she was saying, I admired her enormously, even though I didn't agree. I raised my head. "Maybe everyone has a dark side, but I don't think they rise above it to escape Hell. Some people are compassionate and selfless because they love others, and it has nothing to do with some spiritual race for Heaven." Her frustration with me was clear, but I needed to say this. "Even if they know Hell is waiting, they'll love others just the same, and when they get to Hell, they'll *still* love others. Maybe they'll make Hell obsolete. Maybe that would be the silver lining if Eryx were to win his war."

She gave up trying not to cry. With fat tears spilling over, she said in a surprisingly strong voice, "Who are you talking about, Mariah? Who are these selfless people? Because everyone I know, even the kindest, warmest, most generous people, have their moments of rage and vengeance and jealousy." Turning away, she said to the silk draperies covering the window, "You believe what you believe because you see the world through the filter of who you are. You think others are like you, but they're not."

"I'm human. I have a dark side. And there's a chance I'll be heading south on the day I die, but that doesn't make me want to give up on humanity."

Viorica swiped at her tears and said softly, "I love you, Mariah. I will never be angry with you, never doubt you, never let anything bad happen to you. Do you believe me?"

I stood and went to her and pulled her close. "I'm the big sister, remember?"

She squeezed me tight around the waist and mumbled into my shoulder, "Let me be that for you, just for a while."

I petted her hair and said, "Only if you stop crying. You're getting snot all over my best work blouse."

She leaned back and smiled at me. "I'll see you tonight." Then she stepped away and disappeared.

Mathilda reached for my bundle I'd left on the bed and undid the belt holding it together. "I hope ye brought more unmentionables, Miss Mariah. Ah, I see ye did. Gracious, child, these have holes."

I almost made a joke about Holy Panties, but decided not to when I realized Mathilda was also crying.

There was some subtext here that I couldn't read and didn't understand. I was just going to have to pay closer attention.

~~ PHOENIX ~~

I needed to think. My mind worked better when my hands were occupied, but going home to the shop to work on a bike wasn't an option. I popped to Harrods in London, bought clothes and a leather bag, mostly for appearances, then checked into a Mayfair suite at Claridge's. After an enormous room service meal of everything English that I liked and missed, I showered, then sat in long boxers at the desk by the window and started a list of the things Mariah needed to fix her life.

Money was at the top. She'd no doubt argue and say she couldn't take our money, but she would. Eventually. Second on the list was a decent place to live. I wrote Bucharest with a question mark. Maybe she'd like to live somewhere else for school. Maybe London. I'd buy her a townhouse and hire household help to cook and clean and drive her to school. Next on the list was *learn English*.

Then, *clothes*. Sasha could take her shopping and buy what she needed for school. Maybe some party clothes. I wondered if she ever went to parties. Unlikely. She probably didn't know people who had parties, and had no time for them even if she did. She'd meet people at school who would invite her to social things. Maybe she'd meet a nice guy at university. An engineer. A lawyer, or a doctor. A guy who would provide for her. Maybe somebody in international business who'd take her on trips. I wondered if she'd ever traveled. Did she want to travel?

I imagined her touring the Hermitage in St. Petersburg with another guy, thought about what would be going through his mind while he watched her exclaim over a Fabergé egg, where he'd take her afterward, what he'd do to her . . . Madness. I had to stop thinking about her with any kind of possessiveness. Mariah wasn't mine – could never be mine.

I looked again at my list. What was she interested in? Did she read? What kind of books would she like? I read constantly, anything and everything. I wrote down my favorite titles to give to her, just in case she was a reader.

I added several more items to the list, then wrote *doctor*. I'd take her to wherever was considered the best medical facility in the world and she'd have everything checked out. Humans needed shots, I knew, so she'd have those. And a lady parts doctor would examine her and make sure nothing was wrong so if she wanted to have children, she could. I didn't linger too long thinking about that. I remembered every second of how it had been with Jane. Blood and tears, shame and recriminations – and we'd done it all on purpose. I couldn't fathom what Mariah must have suffered – if my instincts were right about Emilian. How old had she been? Twelve? Thirteen?

The nice Claridge's pencil broke between my fingers.

I looked through the sheers down to Brook Street. It was now midafternoon in London, still morning in the States. I wondered how Mariah's reunion with Jordan had gone. Jordan would be in school now, with Key, who stayed with her because of the difficulty in being Mephisto and going about in the real world for an extended amount of time. What was Mariah doing? Maybe sleeping.

I drew the drapes to block the light and got into bed, but didn't fall asleep for a long while. When I finally did, I dreamed about Jane and the night we had sex for the first time. The only time. Except in my dream, she didn't stop bleeding, and my healing powers wouldn't work. I panicked and went for help, but when I got back with the doctor, she'd morphed into Mariah, who lay there still as stone. I ran to the side of the bed and she looked up at me with no fear in her eyes, as if nothing was out of the ordinary, as if she wasn't bleeding to death. She said my name, "Phoenix." Then she said it again, and I said, "Mariah," and she said my name again, and I said hers, and this went on and on, and I couldn't stop, and I wanted her to say something besides my name, wanted her to let me help her, let the doctor save her, but she just kept saying my name, and I said hers, and all the while she was bleeding and dying.

I jerked awake, instantly aware of Jax at the end of the bed, repeating my name while he shook my foot. I sat up and blinked. "What's wrong? What's happened?"

He ran his hands through his hair before he said in a tired, dull voice, "Eryx knows she's Anabo."

Holy hell. I came more awake. "How?"

"Jordan took her to her apartment in Bucharest to get some pictures of their parents, and while they were there, a lost soul came in and assaulted Mariah. Shoved her shirt up to see her birthmark. Jordan thought he intended to rape Mariah, so she smashed his head with a toaster."

"Is Mariah hurt?"

"I just saw her and she seemed fine."

"What about the lost soul? Did Jordan kill him?"

"No, just knocked him out. When she and Key went back for him, he'd made his way down to another floor and was texting Eryx."

"How did the guy even know to look?"

"Eryx hacked into the GPS system on Jordan's phone. It's Secret Service high tech that works anywhere on the planet. Eryx is tracking her every move, and when he realized she was in Bucharest, he texted one of his locals and told him to follow her and see what she did. The guy texted back with a photo of Mariah and Jordan and, since they look so much alike, Eryx told him to see if the other one had an Anabo birthmark, which he did before Jordan beaned him. When he came to, he went through Mariah's things, and before he left the apartment, he sent Eryx her name."

This was bad. Really bad. Cataclysm bad. I got out of bed and went to take a piss, thoughts racing around my head while I tried to think of some way, *any* way I could fix this. Back in the bedroom, I opened the drapes, realized it was nighttime in London, and closed them again. Jax followed me into the sitting room and we sat by the fireplace. I said, "She'll have to move and change her name. If he doesn't know where she goes, or who she is, he can't touch her. She can live a normal life and he'll never find her."

Jax slowly shook his head. "The instant Jordan goes to see her, and she will, no matter how risky it is or how much Key insists she can't, Eryx will know." He saw me open my mouth to speak, and held up a hand. "Jordan will be marked within a month, Phoenix. I'm not sure she and Key will even make it that long. And once she's marked, Eryx won't need GPS to find her."

"Yeah, no shit." Had he really said that to me, of all people? As if I hadn't spoken, Jax continued. "He's so obsessed with her, it'll be forever before he'll leave her alone. A hundred years from now, she and Key will have an entire family and there will be Eryx whenever Jordan leaves the mountain, still trying to talk her into staying with him."

"Since when are you a fan of hyperbole?"

Jax shot me a look. "My point is, I don't think Eryx will give up on Jordan for a very long time."

I shook my head. "Jordan's immortal, so Key's mark will be permanent, and she can never give Eryx what he wants."

"She can never give him children, but he's gone over the edge with this obsession. I think he wants her to be with him, regardless."

Assigning normal human emotions to Eryx was dangerous, but I wondered if there was still something in him that needed a tie to another soul. Chasing Jordan, even though he had to know she was ultimately unattainable, was a sign of desperation, and it had nothing to do with keeping her from Key. It certainly wasn't to keep her from becoming Mephisto. He was way too late for that. No, his obsession was all about his need for her to be with him.

Which meant Jax was dead on the money. Eryx wouldn't give up, even after Jordan was marked. Mariah would be at risk for a very long time.

I sat back and looked at the cut roses on the mantel. "So Mariah has two choices – leave the mountain and be murdered by Eryx, or stay and become a Lumina."

"That's the way I see it. And for the short-term, until Jordan has Key's mark, Eryx could use Mariah as leverage to coerce Jordan, so it's not only Mariah who's at risk. There's no way Key's letting her leave."

My list could now be made into a paper airplane and flown into oblivion. "Did Jordan tell her she's Anabo?"

"No. She and Key want to keep it from her at least until the end of the week so she can get to know everyone and let it all soak in at a distance. If she doesn't know, she has no investment, no decision to make."

"So she'll spend the week thinking she's going home on

Sunday, and when the time comes for her to leave, Jordan and Key will say, oh, by the way, this is Hotel California. You can never leave. And she's supposed to be okay with this. She's not going to be upset or angry that she was lied to all along. It won't bother her that everyone knew and she didn't. Is that how it'll be, Jax?"

My brother slumped back in his chair and glowered at me. "You got a better idea?"

I didn't. Yet.

"It'd be different if she was . . . if there wasn't something wrong with her."

"There's nothing *wrong* with her. She's had some bad shit in her life, but that doesn't make her *wrong*. It makes her wounded. And I think bullshitting her, in some stupid misguided attempt to protect her, is the worst possible idea. Jesus, that's cruel. Protecting her means helping her understand what she is and what her options are, not lying to her."

"Are *you* going to tell her?"

"Of course not. Jordan should tell her."

"Well, she won't and Key won't, and no one else is going to tell her and risk getting his ass kicked, including me. I'd have been furious if anyone had interfered with Sasha and me." He rubbed the stubble on his chin. "Since you're not taking the lead, it's got to fall to someone. Key brought her, so he's ultimately responsible for her."

"He's completely biased on Jordan's behalf. I think this calls for a war room meeting and everyone should have a say in how to go forward."

Jax's gaze slid away from mine and I already knew what he was going to say. "We just had a meeting, and everyone agreed it's best to wait to tell her."

Before I could tell him I was pissed that they'd met without me, Key appeared just inside the foyer of the suite and focused on Jax. "I need to talk to him alone."

Jax got to his feet and said to me before he left, "Don't do anything stupid."

I assumed he meant, *Don't tell Mariah she's Anabo*, which only served to prove that his definition of stupid and mine were not the same.

After Jax was gone, Key wandered around the sitting room, peeked through the drapes, reached out to touch one of the roses, picked up a porcelain figurine and bounced it in his hand.

"You're nervous. And you're bugging the hell out of me. Say what you came to say."

He set the figurine down and came to stand behind the chair Jax had just vacated. "I didn't tell the others, but I think you should know something about Mariah."

"Emilian?"

His shock was obvious. "How do you know?"

Suddenly feeling way too exposed, I stood and went to the window, opened the drapes and willed off the lights in the sitting room. Watching the cars and pedestrians on Brook Street down below, I told Key about the way Mariah woke up and what I'd learned at Gustav's.

When I was done, he said, "I had my suspicions, but Jordan verified it."

"Did Mariah tell her?"

"No, she wouldn't talk about anything of her life after their parents died, but when that guy busted into her apartment and assaulted her, Jordan says she made no move to fight. She just . . . laid there."

The drapery wand my hand was wrapped around snapped in two.

"After she left Mariah with Mathilda, she came to get me so we could go collect the lost soul. Cried so hard, it took me a while to understand her. She thinks Mariah has insulated herself so completely, she won't let anything affect her, good or bad. She says it's not unusual for survivors of sexual abuse to remove themselves from what's happening to them. They can also be self destructive – cutting, drug abuse, sleeping around. And depression is almost universal."

"What does sexual abuse do to an Anabo?"

Key didn't answer for a long time. I counted twenty cars before he said, "Evidently they wrap themselves in cotton and avoid any kind of emotion."

"Avoiding it doesn't make it go away. It's all inside, waiting like a sleeping volcano, isn't it?"

"I . . . she . . . yes. To keep it asleep, her mind takes her somewhere else when she perceives a threat or something upsets her. Sasha said she checked out last night after you and Zee got into it. For over twenty minutes, she sat there eating a pear as if nothing at all was happening. Didn't seem aware of the end of the fight or Deacon cleaning up. When Sasha took her upstairs, she said she needed to become invisible. Sasha asked what she meant and that's when she came back. Looked embarrassed and said she was just tired."

She'd tried to be invisible when she was with Emilian. I wanted to know exactly what he did to her. I wanted to fix it. "Do you think she killed him?"

"I think she knew when the bed caught fire and did nothing to stop it, or save him. What he did to her is eating away at her, but this is what's destroying her. I asked M, and he said Emilian wasn't a lost soul. Just an evil fucker who enjoyed beating up on little girls. When M took him to Hell, he didn't cry and beg for another chance like most of them do. He shouted all the way. The thing is, Mariah didn't do it because she hated him, or to get rid of him so he'd stop hurting her. It was to protect Jordan. He was planning to extort money from President Ellis in exchange for keeping quiet and not taking her back."

"How did Jordan wind up in an orphanage in the first place?"

"Mariah took her there. They'd been living with Nadia and Emilian a week when he broke Mariah's arm. He locked her in a closet for almost a week." Key continued telling her story and I wanted to pick up the furniture and hurl it through the window. Mariah had been six years old, still practically a baby, and she was wandering the streets of Bucharest with her four-year-old sister. Once Jordan was safe, Mariah went back to Emilian to make sure she stayed safe.

I came dangerously close to losing my shit. "Mariah told you this when you found her?"

"Yes. And she never said out loud that Emilian raped her, but I knew as much from what she didn't say as what she did. I don't think she'd have told me jack if she hadn't been so desperate that I not tell Jordan about her."

I tapped the broken drapery hardware against my palm. "So why *did* you tell Jordan? Doesn't Mariah matter? Why did you take it on yourself to bring her to the mountain? Now, she's stuck, and she'll hate it, and not only because I'm an ass or because we're all sons of Hell or because we spend our days killing people. Don't you see? She's had no say in pretty much anything that's happened in her life. She's finally making her own calls, then there you are, screwing it up for her. And this is a permanent screw-up, Kyros. You've completely altered the trajectory of her life, and she's sitting in Colorado trying to make the best of being talked into staying a *week*."

"I'm aware it's an epic clusterfuck, and all my fault, but continuing to apologize and wring my hands isn't going to fix things. All we can do is move forward." He came to stand beside me and looked down at the street. "There *is* a solution to the problem."

I broke the wand again. Now I had two pieces of it. "It can't happen, Key."

"It won't be easy. It was impossible for Jax, and I screw it up with Jordan daily. I have no idea how things will turn out between us. For you, it's . . . she's so broken, and you're so fucked up, but she can't leave, and you need her. Can't you try?"

My anger settled and I huffed out a breath. "It's not that I don't *want* to try, it's that I *can't*. So leave it alone. It's never going to happen."

I expected him to pick at it, but instead, he said quietly, "Then the only other solution is for her to lose Anabo. We could tell her what she is and give her that option. If she went for it, she could go back to Bucharest after Jordan is with us permanently, and Jordan could visit her without worrying about Eryx. If she's no longer Anabo, she can't become Mephisto, so he'll lose the motive to kill her, and Jordan will be out of reach, so he won't want her for leverage."

My insides twisted. She'd be lost to me forever, extinguishing all hope. In spite of everything, even knowing I could never have her, there was still the promise of hope, and I wanted to hold on to it like a fugitive clings to dreams of mercy. But what I wanted didn't make a damn bit of difference. "She deserves to know, Key."

"Then tell her. We all think it should wait, but it's your call, your decision." He looked up from the street and grasped my shoulder. "I'd do anything to change it, Phoenix. All of it – Jane, Eryx, Mariah."

"I know."

He disappeared, and I was alone again.

CHAPTER 6

~~ Mariah ~~

After Viorica was gone, Mathilda insisted I sleep some more, but I felt like I'd barely drifted off when she woke me and said it was time for breakfast. It was worth having to wake up. So many things to eat, all of them delicious, and I made a glutton of myself once again. Zee watched me take a second helping of Eggs Benedict and laughed. Ty joked that his chickens were going to demand overtime pay for all the eggs they'd need to lay to feed my appetite. I went along with their teasing and didn't alter my plan to eat as much as I wanted. I even tried kippers, but decided I'd skip those next time.

When breakfast was done, Sasha took me on a tour of the house, and we started in the library on the ground floor. To a booklover, it was paradise. Two stories tall, with a catwalk that went around the middle and several library ladders, it was elegant and comfortable with deep wingback leather chairs, low cushioned sofas and two desks. Wide, tall windows looked out on snow covered mountains and a glorious blue sky. A portrait of a woman in a Regency era gown hung above the mantel of a huge fireplace. "That's a Lumina named Mirabelle," Sasha said. "She's in Washington right now, pretending to be Key's aunt."

"Why?"

"He's going to school with Jordan until it's time for her to be here, so to make it all look legit, he rented a townhouse and Mirabelle is there as his aunt, and Brody as his brother."

Across the grand hall from the library was a living room large enough to host a huge party. I was wondering who would

come to a party since humans weren't allowed, when Sasha
said, "The Luminas come sometimes, after a particularly
difficult takedown or one that required them to do a lot of extra
work. We also have weddings here."

That struck me funny. Holy matrimony in a house of Hell.
"Who officiates weddings?"

"A guy named Samuel. He was a Quaker."

"What is he now?"

She looked as if the question surprised her. "A Lumina."

"How many Luminas are there?"

"One hundred twenty two. In a couple of months, it'll be
one hundred twenty three. Cora and Miguel are expecting."

"Luminas have babies?"

"It's rare because they have to get a specific dispensation,
but yes, for sure."

I wondered who gave them dispensation – God, or the
Mephisto? What a strange place this was.

Over the next several hours, I saw the rest of the house. It
was enormous, with winding corridors, a turret, and multiple
staircases; beautiful, with priceless artwork and lovely
antiques; a little spooky, with twenty unoccupied bedrooms on
the third floor. I didn't ask, but I assumed they were for
children, when and if the brothers had any. Did they have to get
dispensation?

We bypassed the second floor, where there were six suites.
For six brothers. The fourth floor was a finished attic, most of
which held lots of shelves with storage boxes neatly lined
along them, random pieces of furniture, and old trunks from
back in the day. A smaller area was enclosed as Sasha's studio.
Two skylights and three windows bathed the room in light.

"I've always loved art," she told me, "and planned to study
restoration. There's a Lumina named Andres who's a very
accomplished artist. We passed several of his pieces in the
hallways, and he painted the portrait of Mirabelle in the library.
He's been teaching me different techniques for my own work,
and he lets me help clean the artwork in the house."

I didn't comment on what she said, that she'd had to give up
her plans in order to be here. I felt bad for her, but she seemed
okay with it, so who was I to judge? I had plans, and maybe

they were too big and unreachable, but I was determined to try. I looked around the studio and saw hundreds of pencil sketches and a dozen half-finished oils – all of them with the same subject. "Are you getting Jax just right before you move on to something else?"

She laughed. "Andres says I have art ADD, so he's making me finish Jax before I can start anything new."

"I took an art class in school once. My teacher told me to stick to literature."

"It's very relaxing. Maybe I could teach you? We could come up tomorrow morning."

"That'd be nice, thank you." I would be lousy at it, but it was a way to pass the time until Viorica came to visit.

Lunch was yet another smorgasbord of deliciousness. When we were almost done, the cook, Hans, came out of the kitchen to meet me. He was short and stocky with blond hair, blue eyes and spoke German. He wore an army uniform I was certain was from World War I, and I wondered what his story was, but didn't ask. He seemed pleased by my praise of his cooking, and said, "If you'd like to have something Romanian, you have only to ask."

Intrigued all over again by my ability to understand a language I didn't know, I thanked him and said, "I'm sure you'd do Romanian food a favor, but it's enjoyable for me to try new things."

He smiled and sketched a short bow before he went back to the kitchen.

Sasha had picked up on my love of the library, and suggested we spend the afternoon reading, but there weren't any titles in Romanian. "No worries," she said. "Tell me what you'd like to read."

I'd seen a translated version of a Stephen King novel in a bookstore a few weeks earlier. I mentioned the title and she said, "I'll be right back," then disappeared.

I wandered around and looked at the books, some of them very old, some leather-bound, some barely published, they were so new. I wished I could read English. I could stay here forever and still not read all of them. Reading was my favorite thing to do. I loved to dive headfirst into a book and live someone else's life for a little while, and it made no difference if their life was fiction, or real. Novels, history, biographies – I read anything and everything. The Bucharest public library, with its quiet stacks and tucked away chairs, was where I usually spent my days off. I couldn't imagine living here, with this library right in my own home. It would be glorious.

Barely ten minutes after she'd left, Sasha returned, looking very pleased, the King novel in her hand. "I'm terrible at transporting," she said. "On takedowns, I usually wind up in the wrong place and Phoenix has to come get me to take me to the right place. But just now, I went exactly where I wanted to go."

"It's a strange thing to do."

"Very strange." She grinned at me. "But awesome."

After she handed the book to me, she took a seat on one of the wingback chairs by the fireplace, which now had a crackling fire, courtesy of Deacon. Her book, I noticed, was a paperback with a picture of a woman in a Victorian dress, which was coming off of her shoulder, and a guy standing behind her in a pirate shirt. "What is that book?"

"A romance novel. Don't tell the guys. They'll give me grief and strike copy-cat poses and tell me all the reasons this is an entirely inaccurate portrayal of how it was in the olden days."

"Is it?"

"Don't know, don't care." She slipped off her boots, curled her legs beneath her in the chair, and settled back to read. "It's marvelous and racy, and I'm dying to find out if the earl killed his first wife."

"Is he the guy in the pirate shirt?"

"No, the earl is the heroine's husband, and he's one spooky dude. The guy in the pirate shirt was accused of killing the wife, so he went on the run and masquerades as a thief, but really he's the rightful earl, and he's trying to out the bad guy as a murderer so he can clear his name and reclaim his title."

"How do you know so much about aristocratic titles?"

"From romance novels." She looked over the top of the book at me. "You want me to read it to you? I can translate as I go."

I wanted it more than I wanted to know what was for dinner. Which is how I 'read' my first romance novel.

⮞⮜⮞⮜

Hours later, Sasha was almost to the very end. Other than a quick bathroom break and Mathilda delivering tea at mid-afternoon, we'd remained in our chairs while Sasha read and I stared up at Mirabelle and listened, completely enraptured.

The bad earl had been executed for murdering his first wife. The rightful earl was back in society's good graces, and he proposed to the heroine. I wanted her to say, *maybe later*, and retire to the country to grow her favorite roses and ride her beloved horse and have the vicar over for tea. She had a lovely house where she could do all of that. But she didn't. She said yes, and the earl carried her off to bed.

Sasha didn't seem the slightest bit embarrassed when she read that part. I'm certain I was as red as a beet. On the other hand, it was absolutely fascinating, and I was so intrigued, I decided I'd find romance novels in Romanian as soon as I was back in Bucharest. The idea of sex as something wonderful was completely foreign to me and I wondered if the author of that book made it up like she'd used inaccurate history. Sex was scary and horrible and painful. I couldn't in my wildest imagination consider it something a woman would ever want. I'd had friends in school who I'm certain had sex – I knew because they got pregnant – but I assumed they'd been forced into it. I assumed all women were forced or coerced, or they suffered through it to make babies, or ensure they received something in return, like food, or a roof over their head, or a husband, or money, or even just a steady boyfriend.

But what if I was wrong?

I wished I knew Sasha better. She seemed okay with reading about it. Was she okay with having it with Jax? But I didn't know her well at all, and even if I did, I didn't think I could ask. I'd have a hard time talking about it without disturbing certain boxes, and that was to be avoided. Always.

No, better not to ask or even wonder. But I was going to the library to search for romance novels as soon as I was back home.

Dinner was roasted chicken with herbs, tiny potatoes,

asparagus, acorn squash, salad, and chocolate layer cake. After I ate the last crumb, Zee jokingly offered me his cake, and they all laughed when I took it. Deacon brought him another slice and delivered a glass of ice cold milk to me. Heaven.

Afterward, I went to my room to wait for Viorica's visit, and since I didn't expect her for at least two hours, I started the Stephen King. With Olga snoozing in my lap, I'd just read page five when there was a knock at my door. Surprised that Viorica was early, I called out, "Come in," and the door swung inward.

My smile of welcome hit the road.

Not Viorica.

Phoenix.

His expression was inscrutable, and I was instantly beset with anxiety. Why was he here? What did he want? Mathilda wasn't with me. I was all alone on the third floor of this monstrous mansion. Twenty empty bedrooms. Earlier, I'd thought it was creepy. Now, I realized it was dangerous.

I was wondering how long I could barricade myself in the closet before he knocked the door down when I remembered he could pop himself anywhere he liked. There was nowhere I could go that he couldn't get to me. Anxiety swiftly turned to panic.

The lights went off at the same time every candlewick in the room burst into flame, and my panic slid right into hysteria.

"Don't be afraid of me, Mariah."

How did he know? I'd perfected the art of never showing any emotion whatsoever. "I'm not afraid," I lied. "I'm just wondering why you're here. You said you'd be gone this week."

"I had a change of plans."

He closed the door and I eyed the distance between my chair and the closet. I could hit the number three button on the plastic box and call Mathilda, but he was standing in front of it.

"Did you have an enjoyable day?"

The last thing I wanted to do was chat about my day. I wondered what he'd think if I told him Sasha read a romance novel to me, sexy bits and all. It might give him ideas, or make him think I was interested. *Good God.* I pasted on my Gustav's smile and said, "It was a wonderful day. Sasha is an excellent docent. She says tomorrow she'll teach me to paint."

He walked farther into the room and it was all I could do to stay where I was and not bolt from the chair, dash around him and run out the door. I'd race down the stairs to the front hall. Deacon would be there, adjusting the portraits or fiddling with the cut flowers on the middle console. I could ask him to get Mathilda. Or Sasha.

"Mariah, relax. I'm not going to do anything but talk to you."

I didn't relax. Last night, I hadn't noticed how very large he was, and he became much larger the closer he came. Huge, really. His legs were long, his thighs thick with muscle beneath faded jeans. His scuffed brown boots were gigantic. He wore a starched white button-down shirt with PDK embroidered in black on the pocket, size ginormous to comfortably cover his torso and arms. Not only was he much bigger than me, he was Mephisto. Superhuman strength. If he decided to . . . I didn't have a prayer.

Olga meowed.

He was next to my chair now. He bent to reach down, and I froze.

Olga's green eyes slid to half closed, and she purred when he scratched behind her ears.

I watched his big hand against her ginger fur. Closely clipped nails, long fingers, no hair on the back, a visible vein. It was a strong, masculine, beautiful hand. Looking up, I met his black-eyed gaze, and he said softly, "What's her name?"

"Olga. She likes you."

"I suspect she likes everybody." His hand began to stroke, slowly, gently, and I barely was able to not shiver when his fingers grazed my belly.

"We had a bad start," he said. "I'd like to begin again and be friends."

"Okay." I'd agree to be whatever he wanted if he'd just step back. Or show any kind of emotion and give me a clue of his real intention.

His eyes were on mine. "You're very good at this, but I've been alive a thousand years. I have more practice."

I whispered, "What do you want?"

"To be your friend."

I searched for sincerity and found nothing at all. "It's a nice thought, but I won't be here that long."

He came a little closer. "That depends."

"On what?"

His gaze searched my face before he settled on my eyes again. "Amazing. You're scared to death and all I see is this sweet little smile."

"I'm not—"

"Let's strike a bargain, Mariah. You don't lie to me and I won't lie to you. I'll tell you everything right out, good or bad."

"Maybe if we'd known each other for years and years, we'd have that kind of trust."

"Maybe you could give me a chance."

"A chance for what?"

"To help you. Because you're going to need help."

"I'm doing all right, but thank you."

He petted Olga once more, then stood straight. "I want to tell you something, but first I need you to stop being afraid of me. What can I do to set your mind at ease?"

"Call Mathilda to be here with us."

He shook his head. "This needs to be between you and I and no one else."

That sounded alarming. If he was genuine in his desire for me to relax, he really had no clue how to make it happen. "Back up and sit down. You're so . . . big. And turn the lights on."

The lights came back as he took his seat on the chair opposite mine. He smiled and, just like Kyros, it transformed his face. He was intensely handsome. "Better?"

I nodded and set aside the book I still held in my hand. "Viorica will be here at ten."

"I'll be gone by then." He laid his arms on the wingback's rests and looked completely relaxed, his long legs stretched before him, right boot crossed over the left. "My brothers and Sasha and Jordan want to wait until the end of the week to tell you, but I think you should know now. You can let them know about this conversation, or not. Entirely up to you."

"Why wouldn't I tell them?"

"Because they'll ramp up the pressure for you to stay, and you might like a week of no expectations. If they think you're unaware of their true motivation, they'll court you instead of selling you on why you should stay."

Now thoroughly confused, I said, "You're speaking in riddles."

"Are you still afraid?"

"Less afraid," I admitted, "and becoming aggravated."

He smiled again. "You have a temper."

An instant, unwanted memory of smoke and flames skittered across my mind. "You have no idea."

His smile faded, his fingers ever-so-slightly gripped the ends of the armrests, and his eyes became solemn, almost sad.

I caught a hint of oranges and wondered where it came from. He appeared serene and calm, but his tightened fingers gave him away. Whatever he had to say must be terrible. Was it about Viorica? My heart beat faster as I impatiently waited for him to begin.

~~ PHOENIX ~~

She was more beautiful to me tonight than she'd been the night before. No doubt she'd be more so tomorrow, and the day after. Despite knowing the color of her eyes was due to all the trauma in her life, I was bemused by their smoky blue. Her dark, silky hair was down today and she wore a pair of jeans with a hole in the knee and a threadbare sweater. She'd taken off her boots to curl up in the chair, but had sat up straight as soon as I came in, no doubt readying herself to run. I looked down at her small, pretty feet, at her clean, rounded nails. No polish. Sasha always had polished toes, courtesy of Dani, who loved playing beauty shop, and Sasha gladly played along. Would Mariah like getting her toes done?

I noticed her book was a Stephen King, one of his later ones – one of my favorites.

I took false courage from that, like it was a sign, and began talking. She listened carefully, and once in a while she asked a question, but mostly she sat there with Olga racked out in her lap and stared at the fire and never, even once, allowed any emotion to cross her face. I told her everything, including how an Anabo becomes marked when she has sex with a Mephisto. I expected some reaction to that. Disgust, or fear. *Something.* But, no. I told her that love, the real deal, not lust or infatuation, was the only chance my brothers and I had of Heaven when the end of the world came, and the only females who could stick around long enough to fall in love were Anabo. I explained it was our covenant with God, given to us when we became immortal and took up the fight against Eryx. It was what gave us hope. And finally, I circled around and told her she was intended for me.

Nothing. *Nada.* No reaction except to ask, "The girl you told me about last night, the one who died, was she Anabo? Was she meant for you?"

I knew there would be questions about Jane. I just wasn't sure I was up for answering. "She was, but Eryx murdered her before she became immortal."

"He found her because she was marked."

"Right."

She looked at me. "Why did you mark her before bringing her here, where she'd be safe?"

Of course she'd zero in on that. "I didn't know. None of us did. She was the first Anabo we'd ever found."

"If you and the others could sense it, what made you think Eryx couldn't? He can sense each of you, so it logically follows he'd sense a new Mephisto, just as you did."

Guilt, my old companion, pushed at me, but I managed to shove it back. "There's more to the story, and it doesn't matter. I'm only telling you because you deserve to know all the facts now, instead of when the others decide you should know."

She turned her attention to Olga. "Are you sure I'm Anabo?"

"I'm sure. Kyros didn't know because he couldn't see your glow. Sasha did. If you still don't believe, think about your birthmark. There's a tiny, cursive *A* with a sunburst around it just beneath your right breast. It's the sign of the Anabo. Sasha has it and so does Jordan." So did Jane. Until that night, when she . . . I turned my thoughts away from remembering and watched Mariah, hoping for any sign of her feelings about all of this.

She didn't refute me because she couldn't deny the physical proof of what she was, but she did say, "It makes no sense at all. I understand about Sasha and Viorica. I can feel what they are, can see it in them." Her hands slowly rubbed Olga's fur. "But I'm not without sin. Not even close."

I wished she'd tell me, if not all of it, at least about Emilian. But I couldn't push. It had to come from her need to talk about it, and that might not happen for a very long time. After Key left my room at Claridge's, I'd read two books and countless websites about adult survivors of abuse and sexual assault. Maybe I was going at this all wrong, but I had to do something to help her. Had to work around my own completely fucked up life and try to salvage hers. She was meant for me, and abandoning her to the other Mephisto wasn't just wrong. It was a replay of Jane.

No matter how this ended, whether she stayed or didn't, I wanted no regrets. She was already at high risk because of Key bringing her here, and Jordan taking her back to Bucharest. Her best hope was knowing everything, so that whatever they suggested in the future, she could make an informed decision.

Without being obvious, she'd watched me carefully from the instant I walked in, gauging my body language and facial expression for any sign of imminent threat. She was in a constant state of war, suspicious and guarded around all males, except maybe Gustav. It had to be exhausting. How did she work in that pub with all those guys? I knew what guys were capable of, especially when they'd been drinking. I was a guy, and a son of Hell, which made me an expert on men behaving badly. Mariah had lived through the lowest, worst thing any male could do to a female, yet she worked with men, day in and day out, in a job that lent itself to disrespect and assumptions about her sexuality. I'd thought the exact same thing and accused her of it.

Zee should have stabbed me in the heart instead of merely punching my face.

Mariah wasn't quite as petite as Jordan, and had more

curves for sure, but she was on the small side, edging close to too thin, probably because she didn't get enough to eat. Zee had told me how enthusiastic she was at meals. She was physically small and emotionally wounded, but ferociously protective of her sister, wasn't a pushover, and she worked fourteen hour shifts in the midst of what frightened her most.

I could kick anybody's ass, and Mariah would lose in one go-round with a strong wind, but she had infinitely more courage than I did.

I finally addressed what she'd said. "Being born without Original Sin doesn't mean you're incapable of doing something out of line. It's the intent that's crucial. No matter what you've done that you consider a sin, you didn't do it for selfish reasons."

She moved, making Olga jump from her lap, and got to her feet to reach for the poker. I started to get up and do it for her, but realized she needed to be doing something while she talked. Muddling around in the coals, she shoved them this way and that before she set aside the poker and lifted a split log from the holder next to the fireplace. As she bent to set the log on the coals, I caught myself staring at her perfect ass and quickly looked away. I patted my leg in invitation to Olga, and she jumped up to settle on my thighs.

Mariah was still jacking with the fire, still bent over. I willed the lights to dim, thinking it'd make her stand and look at me. But, no, she stayed there with the poker, trying to get the new log to catch.

She didn't turn when she spoke, and her voice was so soft and quiet, I almost didn't hear her. "Did Kyros tell you about me?"

"Yes."

"So you know about Emilian."

"He died in a fire he caused by passing out with a cigarette when he was drunk."

Gripping the poker like a weapon, she wheeled around, her eyes darker, but still devoid of what she was feeling. "I could have saved him," she said in a low, even voice, "but I didn't. I stood there and watched him die before I ran from the house. I stood in the road and watched that house of horrors burn to the ground and never blinked. Never felt the tiniest bit of remorse. I still don't." She turned and picked up the Stephen King book, set it on her chair, then picked up a smaller book that had been beneath. Turning back, she tossed it in my lap, eliciting a grouchy meow from Olga. I looked down and saw it was a photo album.

"You're holding the only things I saved. I had time to go back to my room and retrieve the photos and my cat. I didn't call for help, didn't scream, didn't do anything until I was certain he had to be dead. Then I ran downstairs and out the door."

Abruptly turning back to the fire, she was much more aggressive with the log. I hoped it'd catch fire soon. She was going to hurt herself if she beat on it much longer.

I opened the photo book, looked at the first page and quickly closed it, along with my eyes, but the image of her as a small child, smiling as she held Jordan's hand, was burned into my brain. How long was it after this picture was taken that Emilian broke her little arm? I struggled for control. I couldn't lose it in front of her. Me flying into a furious rage was the last thing she needed.

I opened my eyes and caught her staring at me.

She waved the poker around. "I killed him the same as if I'd poured petrol on him and lit a match."

"You were motivated by survival instinct and the need to protect Jordan."

The poker lowered. "That's how I've justified it to myself all these years, but there's a part of me that rejoiced when he was gone. I hated him. I prayed every day that he'd die."

"God didn't take him out because you asked him to. He didn't take him out at all. Emilian did it to himself."

"I didn't save him, and I could have."

"You sure take a lot on yourself, Mariah. How do you know he hadn't had a heart attack? He could have been dead before the fire started. He might have aspirated on his own vomit. Alcoholics do that."

"You just said that intent is everything. I intended to let him die, so whether or not he was still breathing isn't relevant."

"Okay, let's assume you played a part in his death. It's not murder. If it was, there'd be intent to kill, and because you're Anabo, you're incapable of the intent. If by some odd twist in the cosmos you were able to intentionally kill him, you'd lose Anabo immediately. Your birthmark would disappear. Your glow would go away."

"So because I have an unusual birthmark and Sasha thinks I have good skin tone, I get a pass? God forgives me for letting a man die? That's awesome. Maybe I should parlay this amazing gift into financial gain. I could rob a bank and still go to the front of the line at the pearly gates."

"You think you're damned to Hell."

"Of course I am." She dropped the poker back in the fireplace tool stand and walked around the room. "You have to swear never to tell Viorica about Emilian, about what I did."

"Whatever we talk about is between us and no one else, Mariah."

She sat at the end of the bed, stared at the floor for a moment, then stood and walked around some more. She stopped at the desk, picked up a bottle of Tylenol, shook it, turned it within her palms, tossed it from hand to hand. She wanted to say something, was searching for the right words.

"You can trust me, Mariah."

Wrong thing to say. She set the bottle down and frowned at me. "You're a son of Hell, a guy who made a snap judgment call and insulted me, and as soon as you figured out I'm not who you thought, that I can be your ticket to Heaven, here you are playing Mr. Understanding. Am I supposed to fall at your feet and trust you and love you? Suppose I was stupid enough to do that. How long before I'd wind up like the other girl?"

I took a deep breath. "Her name was Jane."

"My name is Mariah, and I'm alive right now because I learned early in life not to trust anybody."

"What about your sister? Do you trust her? Because she's the reason you're blown. Taking you to Bucharest was worse than foolish. It was a disaster."

"She's a victim. I don't blame her for what happened."

I noticed she didn't argue that she *did* trust Jordan.

She went to her chair, moved the King book, and sat down. "Thank you for telling me everything."

"Will you think about staying?"

For the first time since I'd arrived in her room, I saw something besides a false smile. She was bitter. "What's to think about? If I lose Anabo, if you ask Lucifer to take away whatever's left of the light in my soul, I'm for sure going to Hell. If I keep my birthmark, there's a chance this isn't all a grand joke and maybe I can redeem myself by staying here on Hell Mountain and killing more people. I can also be with my sister, something I'd assumed was impossible."

"You understand if you stay, you can't remain human. You have to become a Lumina. And incidentally, they never kill people. They help us find the lost souls, and take care of records and false identities when we need them, and provide other kinds of assistance, but they almost never go with us on takedowns. It's traumatizing and takes weeks for them to recover. And they don't take the lost to the gates of Hell on Earth. Only the Mephisto do that."

"I've worked since I was six. So I'll be a Lumina and work here. Same difference."

So bitter, so angry, and so alone. I reminded myself of what I'd just spent all day reading. Somewhere in all that mistrust and anger was a little girl who smiled joyfully when her parents took her picture, who loved unconditionally and trusted God and humanity, who was lost in a spiral of cruelty. She was still in there, and maybe it'd take the next century to coax her out, but I wouldn't give up. I wouldn't allow her to hide behind sarcasm. "What did you plan to do with your life, Mariah?"

"I was going to become a pop star and live in Hollywood."

Her life had just done a one-eighty. She wasn't a crier, or one to bemoan cruel fate. Mariah wouldn't do anything that might reveal what she was really feeling. Paradoxically, the rage she'd never been allowed to feel was the reason she couldn't admit out loud how badly this hurt. All she could do was be flippant and sarcastic. "What were you really going to do?"

Her gaze dropped to Olga. "Be a pediatrician. When I was younger, there was a doctor. She tried to help me."

"You wanted to help other kids."

She looked up and lost her sad eyes. "No, I wanted to make

a lot of money."

More sarcasm. "It's like you're spoiling for a fight."

"Maybe I am."

I stood, and Olga ran under the bed. "I'm game. Give me your best shot."

She sprang to her feet and stood two feet away, all pretense gone. She was furious. "I saw that look on your face. You tried to hide it before I saw, but you were too late."

I knew, but said anyway, "What look?"

"Pity! You feel *sorry* for me! I *hate* that, and I hate you for feeling it. I'm poor and an orphan and the man who was supposed to take care of me was pure evil, but I'm not some pathetic loser who deserves your pity, you arrogant, self-satisfied goat. Hand it to somebody who feeds and thrives on being a victim. Don't *ever* come in here again and look at me like I'm a sad case."

"Am I supposed to ignore your past? Because you sure as shit didn't ignore mine."

"Oh, sad puppy because I pointed out that it was your fault the other girl died. I see what's up with you, Phoenix. You're carrying a suitcase full of guilt around your neck so everyone can see it, so they'll all know how sorry you are that she died and it was all your fault, and oh, woe to you because you have to live with losing your Anabo."

"You've gotta be joking. If I have a suitcase full of guilt, you're hauling around a metric ton of it. You're so guilty, you're sure Lucifer is getting your room ready. What difference does it make if he is or he isn't? You're either sorry you didn't save the evil son of a bitch, or you're not. Own it, Mariah."

Somehow, there was now less than a foot of distance between us. The scent of heather was incredible. And I could see her glow. Slightly. Or maybe she was just so pissed off, her body was generating heat.

"I already said I'm not sorry."

"I already heard you, but maybe I don't believe you."

"Why do I smell oranges? Oh, my God, it's driving me crazy."

"The same reason I smell heather."

She glared up at me. "It is *never* happening."

"I never asked."

"You don't have to. I can see it in your eyes."

We were closer, and *she* was the one moving. Two more inches and we'd be touching, and she didn't like being touched. If she touched me, it would be huge. An hour ago, she'd been afraid of me. That she was this close now was extreme progress. "Well, what do you expect? I'm eternally an eighteen year old guy and I haven't touched a girl in over a hundred years. You land on my doorstep with your dark hair and pretty face and sexy body. If I didn't want you, I'd be dead. But wanting something and having it are two very different things."

"You love that you're a paragon of self-control, don't you? I bet Denys and the others go out all the time and you stay here and congratulate yourself for your superior morality." Contact. She moved so close, her breasts were against my chest. I wondered if she was even aware. "But there's a side to you that's far removed from all the guilt and martyrdom."

"There's no such side. What you see is what there is." She was blowing my mind. I wanted to tell her to stop talking. I'd die if she stopped talking.

"Oh, there's a side, and it's wild and scary and if you let it loose, you don't really know if you can control it."

"And you would know this, how?"

"I saw it at dinner last night. That's who you are. I get it now, why you were so upset when I arrived, why you were so mad about how I earn a living, what you imagined and how it made you feel. You went with it, which isn't something you do, ever."

I hadn't felt this alive in a century. Maybe ever. I wanted to slip my fingers into her long hair and kiss her until she couldn't breathe. Her lips parted and she looked anxious and anticipatory. "I won't," I whispered.

"I haven't ever," she replied, now staring at my mouth. "I never wanted to."

"Until now?"

"Until now." She frowned and shook her head. "No, not now. I'm not interested at all."

"If I ever kiss you—"

"I'll begin turning to Mephisto. You said that already."

"Then maybe it'd be better if you didn't stand this close. I might get the wrong idea."

She didn't budge.

"Are you testing me, Mariah?"

"No, I just happen to like standing here next to you. Must be the oranges."

"Are we done fighting?"

"For now."

"Who won?"

Her smoky blue eyes met mine. "Draw."

I swallowed and didn't trust myself to move an inch. I breathed in the scent of her shampoo, all mixed up with the heather. She was so small and wounded, and I was overwhelmed with hardcore, down-and-dirty brute protectiveness. I wanted to hold her near and keep anything from hurting her ever again. I wanted to buy her beautiful things and take her all over the world and feed her delicious food and ask her a million questions. I wanted to kiss her on her mouth, and all over her soft body. I wanted to make love to her and show her it wasn't painful and horrible and wrong.

All these things I wanted, and could never have because I could never love her. More than anything in the universe, Mariah needed love. She deserved a guy who was capable of giving her that. And that guy wasn't me.

She stepped back before she blinked up at me. "You're very sad now. Why?"

Her intuition was more precise than a laser. I reached out to stroke her hair. "I just wish . . ."

"What do you wish?"

"For you to have a happy life."

She pushed my hand away from her head. "Oh, please. You wish *you* had a happy life. You wish things hadn't gone so wrong with the other girl. Maybe you even wish, if it had to happen, that it hadn't been your fault. And right now you wish I were something different. Something better."

"Careful, Mariah. That chip on your shoulder is showing."

"Don't deny it."

"I'm not even going to give it enough credence to deny it.

Haven't you been listening? You're it, my one and only, and for me, it's got nothing to with a ticket to Heaven. It's about a thousand years of fucking loneliness. Jane was in my life less than three months and yeah, I'm guilty and angry at myself, but that is nothing to do with you or how I feel about you."

"If I'm all you've got, why aren't you trying? Obviously, it's because you'd rather have no one than me."

Damn. Hadn't seen that coming. God, why were girls like this? Why did they have to needle into things that were simple and turn them into a complicated minefield? "Let's not forget what I am. All my instincts want me to take you right off this rug, carry you away somewhere, and keep you all to myself until they make me come back. I'm selfish enough to do that, and egotistical enough to think you'd be okay with it. But as much as I have those instincts, I'm smart enough to know it'd never last. You'd resent me. You've spent your whole life answering to someone else, and I want you to be in control of what happens to you."

"Ah, I see. So you're making this great sacrifice for my sake. I think I'll talk to Kyros about giving you a medal."

"I have no idea why we're talking about it. You don't want me."

"True, but it's not you in particular. I don't want anybody."

"Someday, you might. It just can't be me."

"Yes, we covered that. You'd rather be alone than with me."

Frustrated and angry, I held her face in my hands and said, "I'd rather be alone than fuck up your life."

She blinked. "Too late."

Her hair was silky soft on my fingertips and her skin was warm and inviting. I stared down into her wide eyes and almost kissed her. I wanted it *so* much. "I can't love you. Even if a miracle happened and you loved me, I couldn't love you back. You deserve love, Mariah. Hold out for it and never settle."

"You're ridiculous."

"You're harsh."

"You're such a guy. In a whole houseful of guys. So you had this horrible terrible thing happen over a hundred years ago, and in all that time you've never talked to anyone about it."

She didn't understand, and I wanted her to. "Jane was perfect. Beautiful, graceful, compassionate, smart, and she loved me. But I—"

"Didn't love her, so now you think that if you couldn't love Miss Perfect, you must be too damaged, too screwed up to be capable of love. Is that it?"

When I made no reply, because I was trying to process that she'd just summed up over a century of misery in one sentence, she said, "She was perfect for someone else. That's why you feel guilty. She loved you and you didn't love her. God sent her to you and you accepted it, but way deep down in a place you never acknowledge, you wondered, why her?"

I knew I should let go of her, stop stroking the smooth curve of her cheeks, drowning in the scent of heather, wishing I could kiss her. "I did love her, in my way."

"Now who's lying? You said we had a bargain."

"Not lying." I travelled back in time and remembered the look in her eyes, her complete heartbreak. No one knew, no one saw. Just me. "I did love her. I *did*."

"I'm sure you felt affection, and that other thing guys feel, but it obviously wasn't enough, because here you are, unredeemed. Now you have another Anabo, and this time, God sent me." She gave me a sad smile. "Poor Phoenix. You just can't catch a break."

"Don't do that."

"I'm not being self-deprecating, if that's what you think. It's just that I can see who you are and what you'd need to be mad about someone, and I don't have it."

I slid my hands further back, into her hair to hold her head. "You don't know me at all, so how could you have a clue what I need? It doesn't matter anyway. This isn't about me. It's about you, and what's ahead, and I'm going to help you through all of this so you can be happy."

"I'm not a weekend project, Phoenix. You can't fix me and lay out a golden path of perfect happiness for me and redeem yourself for whatever you did wrong with her. It doesn't work like that."

"How does it work?"

She grasped my shirt in her hands while she looked up into

my eyes. "Don't try so hard. Don't push. Let's just agree that we're going to be friends."

"I don't have any friends except my brothers, and Sasha and Jordan. If I did, I suspect I wouldn't want to kiss them the way I want to kiss you."

Her gaze went to my mouth again. "I've never done it, and you're so out of practice, it's certain we'd both be bad at it and disappointed."

"Guess it's a good thing we can't."

"Yeah," she murmured, "I guess."

I dropped my hands and turned toward the door but stopped when there was a knock. Quickly turning back, I saw something in her eyes before she could hide it. I wasn't absolutely sure, but I thought it might have been desire.

This was going to kill me.

CHAPTER 7

~~ Mariah ~~

Viorica loved the photos. She teared up several times, her
small fingers tracing the outline of one picture in particular.
We'd fallen asleep on the braided rug, her clutching her bunny,
me clutching her. I suppose our mother thought it was cute, and
so she snapped a picture.

I told her all I could remember about them, and I know she
wanted to feel some connection, but she'd been barely four
when they died. They were strangers to her.

Just before she left, she hugged me close and whispered, "I
love you, Mariah. I wish we'd . . . thank you for what you did."

"There's no call for gratitude, Viorica. I did what I did and
now we're together again. Let's look forward." I knew I wasn't
leaving and so did she, but she didn't know that I was aware. I
wished she'd tell me the truth.

She smoothed my hair, probably because Phoenix had
mussed it – he had a thing for my hair, it seemed. "You've
known me all your life as Viorica, but it sounds strange to me.
Would it bother you an awful lot to call me Jordan?"

If I didn't know I was staying, this would have been a clue.
Why did it matter what I called her if I was gone in a week,
never to see her again? I nodded and smiled at her. "Of course
I'll call you whatever you like. Jordan, it is."

She left then, on her way to the second floor to see Key. I
wondered what they did when they were alone. Was she
marked? I had an instant reaction to the thought. I wanted to go
downstairs and punch Kyros in the nose.

I was alone again, but everything was changed. I tried to

read more of the King book, but my mind wandered away from the words on the page. Uneasy and restless, I wasn't ready to turn in. I needed to let go. I hadn't done it in a very long time. There hadn't been the need.

Sliding into my coat, I took a candle from the candelabra, left my room and went to the stairs, climbing to the fourth floor. Inside the attic, I flipped the light switch and blew out the candle, then walked behind the rows of shelves with boxes to a door I'd noticed earlier. It opened onto a tiny terrace, covered in snow. It took me a while to shove all the snow through the stone posts beneath the railing, and dragging an antique French chair through the shelves and the door wasn't easy, but I finally had a place where I wouldn't be disturbed.

I sat for a long time and stared out at the moonlit, snow-covered mountains without really seeing them, my breath visible in the frigid night air. Hands clenched into fists inside my coat pockets, I whispered, "Not fair, not fair, *not fair*." All my hopes and dreams – gone. Everything I'd thought to be – gone. My hard won independence – gone. Bending forward, I buried my face against my thigh and screamed until my throat was raw, and repeated in my head, over and over, *Not fair.*

Viorica who wasn't Viorica; my baby sister who I didn't really know at all, a girl named Jordan who was strong, sure of herself, and capable, and she'd chosen to be here with these ghosts of humanity. I didn't choose this, yet here I was. I never chose to take Nadia's place in Emilian's twisted world of pain and cruelty, but for two years of my life, that's exactly what I was. I didn't choose to cook and clean for Marta and Gustav, but the alternative was to be on the streets, to starve and sell myself.

Not fair!

I screamed harder and my hands bled from my nails digging into my palms.

Why did my parents have to die? Why did Emilian have to be an evil bastard? Why couldn't Nadia have been kind? She was my *family*, and she treated me like dirt, like I was less than dirt, and never once tried to stop Emilian.

Then she died and left me alone with him.

I stopped screaming and sat up quickly, sucking in deep

breaths, forcing my mind to stop. I had to stop. I couldn't think about it. I squeezed my eyes shut and imagined the shelves and the boxes, all of them neatly stacked, all of them holding those memories I couldn't remember without losing myself completely.

The past six months had been hard, so hard, but they'd been *mine*. I'd had my own space, my own money, my own plans. University would never happen. I'd not be a doctor. I'd be a drudge and work for the Mephisto. And Phoenix would feel sorry for me, and I'd hate it every day of my life. Which would now last forever.

I slumped over and stared at the flagstones of the terrace, at the snow caught in all the cracks. I was enraged at God, at Lucifer, at Mephistopheles, at Kyros and every soul who lived on this mountain. How could I ever find peace of mind or a solid direction when nothing I did ever made any difference?

Maybe this was penance for what I did to Emilian. Maybe this was God's way of telling me I had to repent, had to forgive Emilian.

I shifted in the chair. No way. I hated him as much in that moment as I had the night he died. I remembered watching him burn. My joy was enormous. Joy. Over a man's death.

God would never forgive me and I'd never forgive Emilian. I still had a date with Mephistopheles. It'd just be much further in the future, when the end of the world came.

I realized suddenly that I'd slid that box right off the shelf, removed the lid and examined the contents, all without panicking. For the first time since the night Emilian died, I could remember it and not be afraid. I'd never admitted my part in his death to anyone, until tonight. Until Phoenix. I still wasn't entirely sure why I'd done it. He'd just told me life as I knew it was over, that I was stuck on this mountain for the foreseeable future, and even when I'd be able to leave, it'd be for short periods. I'd live here for the remainder of eternity. Then he told me I was incapable of sin and I knew he was so wrong. I wanted him to know, wanted him to understand that whether I was Anabo or not, I killed somebody and that was a sin against God and humanity. It didn't matter who Emilian was or what he did. So long as he was alive, he had the opportunity to ask forgiveness, to redeem himself. I had no right to interfere by helping his life end.

I knew all these things, but I couldn't be sorry.

Maybe I'd wanted Phoenix to fully realize why I'd never be with him, why I'd never be with anyone. I was nothing of the light he spoke of – I was dark, dirty, damaged. If he couldn't love Miss Perfect, he'd never, ever love me.

Not that I wanted him to. It was better this way. Less complicated. But I did feel a little bad for him because he had no choice at all – just me. And I was a thousand times less worthy than the other girl.

I supposed whatever subconscious reason I'd felt compelled to tell him didn't matter. My confession had given me the ability to remember without being petrified. He'd said we'd be friends, and I was okay with that. I wasn't afraid of him. I actually liked him quite a lot. It wasn't his fault everything had changed – he was simply the messenger.

A slip of paper appeared from below and twirled in the wind, round and round until it landed at my feet on the terrace. It was a fortune from a Chinese fortune cookie. In English, of course. I slipped it into my coat pocket, thinking I'd translate it later, wondering who had take-out Chinese. I was hungry. I thought about the chocolate cake we'd had at dinner. Maybe there was some left.

Nothing was different than it had been an hour ago, but I did feel somewhat better. Letting it go, screaming into myself while I sat on the roof of Emilian's house had been my only way of dealing. After Nadia died and he found a new way to torture me, I was angry and scared and I fought, and it was a long time before I learned that to be completely still didn't excite him as much as my anger. He got off on my fear and fury, and once I realized it, I never again got angry in front of him. I climbed on the roof and screamed into my legs.

I got to my feet, washed my bloody hands in the snow, then dragged the chair back inside and made my way downstairs, tricky because there was very little light on the upper staircase, just what filtered up from below.

In the grand hall, Deacon was nowhere to be seen, and I took the opportunity of solitude to look at all the portraits.

Sasha had said they were Luminas. Each gigantic gilt frame had a small, brass plate at the bottom with names and dates. I wondered if the date was the year of their birth, the year they became immortal, or the year the portrait was painted. The clothing ranged from Elizabethan, with ruffs and funny men's pantaloons, to early twentieth century, with white linen suits and big hats. The most beautiful of all the women was a blonde who sat next to a dainty secretary, a spaniel at her feet. I moved closer to see what she held in her hand. A gold chain dangled from her slender fingers, and at the end, against the skirts of her blue silk Victorian dress, was a bejeweled golden bird. A phoenix.

I looked at the name plate. *Lady Jane Rutledge 1888.*

She was an aristocrat. She must have come from a wealthy family. She wore big, beautiful pearl drop earrings, a sapphire and diamond pendant, and her spectacular dress matched her tranquil, lovely eyes, the color of spring crocuses.

I stared up at her for a very long time, wondering why Phoenix hadn't loved her. I grew sad for her. It had to be terrible to love someone when they didn't love you back.

Turning away to head for the kitchen, in hopes I could nab a piece of cake, I was glad of my certainty that I'd always be alone. I would never be in Jane's position because I would never be romantically in love. And I'd never be unwise enough to fall for a guy like Phoenix. He had heartbreaker written all over his handsome face.

As I crossed through the dining room to the kitchen, I remembered with perfect clarity just how much I'd wanted him to kiss me. I was curious, and he was the first guy in my entire life I'd ever wanted to kiss. But that was nothing like love. It was lust, which came out of nowhere and surprised me, but I couldn't deny it. Maybe Sasha's romance novel had opened a tiny door somewhere in my soul.

Didn't matter. I wasn't going to kiss him, ever. I didn't want to be Mephisto. I could never capture a human being and send him to his death. The fight alone would bother me, but knowing I was about to kill someone . . . never happen. Emilian's death had altered my entire life, and not all to the good. I was done with death.

Hans was in the kitchen. It was a quarter to midnight. I said hello and he beamed as if very pleased to see me. "Why are you still here?" I asked. "Don't you ever sleep?"

"No, we Purgatories have no need of sleep, or food."

"How do you cook such delicious things without eating any of it, without tasting?"

He pulled a jug of milk from one of three gigantic refrigerators and set it on the island in the middle of the huge kitchen. "I have many volunteers among the Luminas who taste for me, but mostly, I cook from memory. When I was alive, I was a chef in Cologne. Then there was the war, and I died and was sent here, to cook for the Mephisto." His blue eyes sparkled. "Because of the need to feed their strength, they eat a lot and often, and always appreciate what I prepare. Except Jax, who refuses to eat sauerkraut."

"I love sauerkraut."

"I think maybe you enjoy all food. This is why I love to cook, to sustain the soul as well as the body." He turned away and when he turned back, he had the cake in his hands. He set it down and said, "You're here for a slice, aren't you?"

"How did you know?"

He became serious and nodded as if it all made perfect sense. "For a while, you'll eat too much, especially the sweets. You come to my kitchen at midnight, there can only be one thing you want." He cut a slice and was just handing it to me when Zee walked in, barefoot, wearing a pair of ratty sweatpants and a faded Aerosmith T-shirt.

He saw me take the cake and laughed.

"It's a good thing I don't have an eating disorder. Every time I turn around, you're laughing at me about food."

Sobering instantly, he said, "Have I been a jackass? I do that a lot."

I smiled at him. "It's all good, Zee. I was teasing you."

"Ah, okay. Well, then, let's both have some cake and laugh at each other."

Hans cut him a slice, handed each of us a glass of milk, then shooed us out of the kitchen.

In the dining room, I was about to sit at the table, but Zee nodded toward the hall. "Let's go watch some TV while we eat."

I followed him across and down the wide hallway to a door that led into a candlelit room with a huge flat screen TV, several black leather couches and deep club chairs with ottomans, a white rug, and a treat bar at the back of the room with fountain sodas, baskets of boxed candies, and a popcorn machine.

He took a seat on one of the couches and set his glass and plate down before he chose a remote from a basket of them on the coffee table. He looked at me, still standing slack-jawed in the doorway. "Have a seat, Mariah. What would you like to watch with your cake?"

I wasn't altogether comfortable being alone with him, but he seemed completely focused on cake and TV. Perceiving no threat, I took a seat at the other end of the couch, set down my plate and glass, and slipped out of my coat. "I mostly watch sporting programs and news because that's what Gustav always has on at the pub. I don't have a TV at home."

"Do you go to see movies?"

"Not often." Mostly never.

He took a bite of his cake and as he swallowed, he eyed me speculatively. "You're probably not a girl who likes blow up movies, but I can't really see you getting into chick flicks, either." He turned the TV on and pulled up a list, all in English.

Moments later, he said, "We'll start this one and if you hate it, say so and we'll watch something else. It's in English, but I've set it for Romanian subtitles."

I was surprised when it turned out to be an animated movie. *UP.* I polished off my cake before the first scene was done, which was a good thing because the second scene had me crying my eyes out. Zee smiled. "Sasha has seen this three times, and she *still* cries."

It was sweet and so sad, then heartwarming and funny. I was delighted and loved every second of it. When it was done, we watched the credits, which were as enchanting as the movie. I decided I'd watch it again, later, by myself. "Thank you," I said from where I was snuggled into the couch, covered by a cashmere throw.

He scooted closer and pointed to different buttons on the

remote, explaining how to load a movie, how to make it have subtitles. He had it connected to a computer program that would translate any movie. I wished I could understand English so I wouldn't need subtitles. Here was one upside to becoming a Lumina – I'd be able to speak all languages. I could watch any movie I liked and understand what they were saying.

"I'll get you a TV for your room and you can watch in there. You can also stream movies off of the Internet, in case there's one we don't already have. Not likely, but just in case."

"I don't have a computer."

He turned his attention from the remote and gave me a shocked look. "Why? Are you a technophobe?"

"I don't know what that is, but I don't think so. I'm just very short on funds, and computers are expensive. I used one at school to write papers, and I've used one at the library for different reasons, but I don't know much about them, and I've only been on the Internet a few times." I smiled up at him. "You look like I just told you I wear a fur pelt and club small animals for dinner."

"It's just weird these days. I'll get you a laptop, and teach you how to use it."

Another clue. Why would he buy me such an expensive item if I weren't going to stay? I nodded and said thank you, then sat up and refolded the throw. "I'm going to bed, where hopefully I'll sleep. My days and nights are all mixed up."

"It'll get better in a week or so."

For stealth guys who spent their lives sneaking up on the lost souls to capture them, they weren't trying very hard to keep me in the dark about the truth to things.

He walked me all the way upstairs to my door and patted my shoulder as I told him goodnight. He seemed suddenly shy and awkward. "If there's anything you need, I mean anything at all, or if you just want to talk, or hang out and watch a movie or listen to music, I'm here for you."

"I'll remember. Thank you."

"Do you play any instruments?"

I shook my head and resisted smiling because he was so serious, but what a joke. Like Emilian would have paid for me to have music lessons. In return for cooking and cleaning,

Marta had paid for my clothes and food. It wasn't as if she owed me anything extra.

"Would you like to learn? I could teach you anything you like."

"Why?"

"Because music makes everything better. Just listening to it changes your world, but being able to make it . . ." He was so solemn. "That's magic. The music room is at the end of the hall where the TV room is, so come there tomorrow and you can decide if you want to learn. If you don't, that's okay. I'll play things for you and you'll tell me I'm brilliant and I'll be happy."

"What if I don't think you're brilliant?"

He shrugged. "Lie."

"Deal. But maybe day after tomorrow, because I'm scheduled for a painting lesson with Sasha in the morning."

"No hurry. We've got all the time in the world." Unaware he'd just dropped yet another clue, he gave me another awkward pat on my shoulder and disappeared.

CHAPTER 8

November 6, 1888
Yorkshire

Tonight Jane will meet my family. Waiting for Deacon to finish knotting my tie, I'm nervous and fidgety. He looks at me from solemn dark eyes. "I've reminded your brothers of their manners. They will be best behaved."
"What if their best behaved isn't good enough?"
"Your lady will not think so. Because you have love and respect for them, so will she."
I hope he's right. Taking a quick look in the mirror, I feel ridiculous dressed this formally in the middle of the night, but this is the only time Jane can sneak away for a visit. I nod to Deacon and pop out of my bedroom and into Jane's.
In the dark, in a chair next to her window, she waits for me. I can see her, but she peers into the darkness without seeing me. She still doesn't have enough Mephisto to see in the dark. I wonder how long it will take.
"Phoenix?" she whispers.
"I'm here," I say, moving toward her.
She stands, already dressed in her shift. I'm disappointed and slightly ashamed of wishing I'd seen her take off her night-rail. Nothing is so beautiful as a naked woman, and this one is mine. I'm impatient to move forward, but very aware I have to move slowly. She's still firmly on the fence about me, and Mephisto. She's been in London the past week for fittings of gowns she's to wear for her season next year. She'll officially be on the marriage mart, and with her beauty, her family, and her charm, she's sure to have an abundance of proposals.

It's imperative I convince her to stay with me, with my brothers, before she's offered up to all the eligible bachelors in England. I can't withstand that kind of competition. Maybe she'd be more inclined if she wasn't still so put off by what we do. It's the Anabo in her, and the only thing that will change how she feels is increasing the Mephisto within her soul.

It takes almost twenty minutes for me to help her dress, and I miss the simplicity of earlier times. Women are so buttoned up these days, it's absurd. I wish she could just throw on trousers and a shirt and be done with it. I suggest it, and as I expected, she's horrified. "I can't meet your brothers in men's clothing. It'd be indecent."

I wish she'd be indecent. Just once. I wish she'd become Mephisto more quickly. We kiss every night before I leave her room after my visit, but it's never what I want it to be. Always awkward, consistently short-lived. I've begun to wonder if taking her to bed will speed things up. The idea has merit, but the execution will be challenging, to say the least. Jane is so proper, so ingrained with society's notions of respectability. The freedom of women to enjoy their own desire without guilt waxes and wanes through the years. It's my misfortune that the time I find my Anabo is during a pendulum swing to the furthest side of strict morality. Women do not have fun in 1888. Jane lives her life inside, reading, or embroidering, or arranging flowers someone else cuts and brings to her. The one acceptable outdoor activity, besides sedate strolls and croquet, is riding, and Jane has a healthy fear of horses. Not that I blame her, but all of my urging for her to try again falls on deaf ears. She refuses. I've even offered to let her ride Bailey, the wee, sweet Shetland pony Ty brought home two years ago. No, she says. Riding is for other people.

I love riding. Love horses. Love letting mine have his head to race across the moors. I love to be outside. Staying inside all the time is painful. I don't understand her lack of curiosity. There are so many things to see in the world, adventures and beautiful places and unusual food and different people. Jane is content to stay at home and read. I like reading, but how much more fun it is to live my life than read about someone else's.

"Have you thought more about the balloon launch?" I ask

hopefully.

"I don't understand your fascination with those death traps," she says with a catch in her breath as I tighten the laces on her corset.

I explain. Again. "Imagine being up in the air. You can see forever in every direction. Haven't you ever wished you could fly?"

"I'm scared being as high as a horse's back. Being close to the clouds sounds petrifying." She smiles as her gown settles over her head and I turn her to begin the long row of buttons. "I'll go and watch you, if you like."

"No, it's not the same."

"Don't be cross with me, Phoenix."

I imagine the rest of eternity with her. Will we lead separate lives? "I'm not cross. Just disappointed."

Finally, she's encased in her blue silk armor. I reach for her hand. "Ready?"

She nods and I transport us to the front hall of the Mephisto house. I expect her to look around, to ask questions, but her cornflower eyes are firmly affixed to the staircase. "How lovely to walk up those stairs," she murmurs. "Thank you for healing me, Phoenix."

"Of course." I offer her my arm and we begin climbing. At the landing, I look down at her before we proceed to the doors into the drawing room. "Thank you for coming tonight."

"It's my pleasure." She smiles at me. So sweet, so pretty. So perfect. "Shall we?"

My stomach is in knots as Deacon opens the doors and we step inside the room. They are all there, dressed as I am. Zee is playing the piano. Beethoven. Ty sits in a chair before the fire, his mastiff, Gretchen at his side. Key stands next to the fireplace, hands folded behind his back, his long hair bound in a silk tie. Jax sits at the card table, endlessly shuffling a deck. I wonder where Denys is.

They all come forward, and I've introduced each of them to Jane, thinking it's going well, about to invite her to sit down to wait for tea, when Denys appears. He's dressed in work clothes; black leather and heavy boots. Holding a glass of whiskey in one hand and a red corset in the other, he's grinning. And loud. "'ello, Janie, m'dear! I've brought you a present." He weaves toward us and she draws a bit closer to my side.

I watch what happens next the same way I'd witness a train wreck – morbidly fascinated and completely unable to stop it.

When he's only a few feet away, he stops, his eyes grow wide and he stares at her. "You're the most beautiful thing I've ever seen in my whole goddamned wasted life. If my brother wouldn't hate me forever, I'd take you away with me and never bring you back." His jolly mood is history. Fat tears well in his eyes and he looks at me. "Lucky. Shit, you're so fucking . . . lucky." He looks down at the corset in his hand before he hurls it into the fire. "Not funny. Aw, Christ, 's not funny." He turns back to Jane and sniffs long and loud, obviously trying to not cry. "I'm s'sorry, Lady Jane. I mean no disrespect. And I promise if you decide to stay with us, I won't ever off. . . ins . . ." He swallows. "Treat you like anything but the lady you are." He sways slightly and blinks at her.

"Jane," I say, "this is my youngest brother, Denys."

She moves forward and kisses him on the cheek. "You're very kind," she says in her soft voice.

He tries desperately to stand straight, but he's too drunk and she's unbalanced him. Before I can stop him, he's falling into her and they both go down in a tangle of blue silk and black leather. I'm reaching for Jane when I see Denys kiss her. Not a brotherly peck. He holds her head and kisses her full on the mouth. I'm reeling with the need to smack him around for his betrayal and impertinence – drunk, be damned – when it registers somewhere in my brain that Jane is kissing him back.

I'm certain no one notices. Not even Denys. As soon as I've retrieved Jane and she's standing next to me, her breath coming in short little gasps which I refuse to believe is anything but the tightness of her corset, I say to Denys, "You need to leave."

He rolls to his side and curls into his misery. If I wasn't so angry, I'd feel sorry for him. As it is, I want to haul him up by his collar and shake him until his balls rattle.

Key steps up and lifts Denys to his feet before they both disappear.

The visit is over. My other brothers are so uncomfortable, it hangs in the air like a noxious odor. Jane is blushing, staring at the floor where Denys had been, smoothing her hair from its muss.

Without letting her say goodbye, I grasp her arm and take her back to her room at the Longbourne estate. As soon as we arrive, I draw her close and kiss her. I want it to be amazing. I want her to want it. But she doesn't. I don't. A terrible, traitorous thought has planted itself in my head and no matter how many times I whack it down, it grows again.

Maybe God got it wrong.

~~ PHOENIX ~~

My dreams were weird again that night. Not scary. Nobody was dying. Mariah and I argued about strange topics, like whether or not Harley-Davidson manufactured the best motorcycle engines. In the dream, she knew as much as I did about bikes, and I'd been building them since they were first invented. The dream meandered along and we were standing on top of the Eiffel Tower arguing about gender politics, religion, and finally, about whether caviar was wretched excess, or the most delicious food on Earth and therefore worth the money. Then we were eating caviar on a bed in Morocco and she was naked and the rest of the dream took awesome to new heights.

I woke up in my cold, empty bed with a raging hard-on and said into the dark of my room, *"Damn."* It had seemed so real.

I'd never had an argument with Jane. I'd tried, and failed. She gave in, or changed the subject. She never got angry, never called me on my bullshit, never told me to step off. I stopped trying because it seemed cruel. I argued with Jax instead. And the Luminas, and Deacon, who gave as good as he got. After Jane died, I would let it build, then argue with other guys in pubs. It typically never ended well. I had cost the family a lot of money rebuilding pubs. And spent a lot of time on Kyanos arguing with myself because I pulled months and months of solitary after beating the everloving shit out of men who turned a perfectly good argument into something personal. I never threw the first punch, but once one was out there, I gladly took the bait. I was usually drunk and forgot I was infinitely stronger than my opponent. It never ended with me losing. Except I'd be sent to Kyanos, which was a huge loss. I hated it there. I hated being so alone. There was nothing to do, no plans to make, no one to argue with.

If Mariah stayed, if we could be friends, she'd dish it out and always understand it was as much for the adrenaline rush as to make her point. Just thinking of getting into it with Mariah had me smiling.

And thinking of getting into bed with her had me groaning. It would never happen. It couldn't. I needed to read something like algebraic theory before bed tonight. Maybe I'd dream simultaneous equations instead of simultaneous . . . other things.

Damn, that was a hot dream. If I knew for sure it'd be the same, I'd go back to sleep and dream it all over again.

I'd never had a sex dream about Jane. She would have been glad to know, but I felt guilty. Jesus, my whole fucking life was a guilt trip and it seemed I could never get off the train.

I needed to lay off thinking about it. I had things to do today. Rolling over, I saw it was six in the morning, already two in the afternoon in Bucharest. I showered and dressed, and by two-thirty local time, I was back in the park with a cup of stolen coffee and my phone, Google-mapping Mariah's apartment building. I'd gotten the address from Key, who'd asked me to clean it up. Whether Mariah returned to Bucharest or stayed on the mountain, there needed to be no blood from the lost soul in her apartment.

I suspected Kyros also wanted me to see where she lived, and I was certain of it when I finally found it and went inside and began climbing seven flights of rickety stairs. He wanted me to know what her life was like in Bucharest. He knew how it would make me feel. So maybe I knew he was manipulating me, but it didn't alter that he was right.

Gustav's was depressing, but her apartment made me angry. The building was falling apart and stunk of meth, there were cockroaches everywhere, and I know I saw a rat beneath the stairs on the fifth floor.

Inside her apartment didn't make me feel any better. It was one small room with a narrow bed that was more like a cot. A tiny table and one chair sat next to a thin window that looked out at a concrete wall. One corner of the room was partitioned off by a half wall, barely hiding a toilet and a sink. I assumed she had to go down the hall to take a shower. No telling what kind of people shared the communal bathroom, but from the sound of some guy shouting and another one cussing at the top of his lungs, and a sound I could only assume was a body hitting the floor, my money was on scary as shit. The showers were yet another place where Mariah must feel exposed and afraid.

I felt all the weight of her life in my chest, bumping against my heart.

When I ripped the bloody blanket from the bed, the scent of heather drifted up from her sheets. The blood had seeped through, so I took the sheets, as well, and rolled all of it into a ball that I left by the door for the time being. I looked closer at the shelves attached to the wall next to the door and noticed she had exactly three books: The Bible, Kafka's *The Metamorphosis,* and *Life in the White House*, a photograph book Jordan's mom had done for charity before she passed. Other items on the three shelves included chipped dishes, a bag of cat food and two small kitty bowls, a box of the Romanian version of Pop-Tarts, some toiletries, a tin box full of odds and ends like rubber bands, old, short pencils and safety pins, and a coffee can stuffed full of Romanian money. There was a slip of paper inside with a tally. She'd drawn a pot of gold at the bottom; encouragement, I supposed.

The dented toaster was on the floor next to the bed and when I picked it up, the plug came loose and fell out. I bent to retrieve it and noticed a box beneath her bed. Curious, I shoved aside hesitation of invading her privacy and pulled it out to lift the lid.

There were hundreds of photocopies of articles and pages from books, all of them about survivors of abuse and sexual assault. I sat on the bed and went through that box and saw notes she'd made in the margins, words and phrases she'd circled. I noticed a lot of the pages were wrinkled, as if they'd been wet. She'd cried over these words.

I read for hours, until it was dark outside in Bucharest and I willed on the light, which was an exposed bulb in the ceiling. When I was done reading, I laid on her narrow bed and stared up at the peeling paint and wondered what she thought about while she laid here before she went to sleep. This apartment was so horrible, it would have to get an update to be considered sketchy. I could hear the scurry of tiny rodent feet in the walls. But I had a feeling Mariah loved it here. This was her very own, a place that was just hers, where she didn't have to answer to anybody.

If she stayed with us and became a Lumina, she'd have her own cottage. She could decorate it however she liked. She would live there and come to the mansion every day to work, and hang out with the other Luminas. They went skiing and hiking. Sometimes they took pack trips deeper into the mountains even than where we lived. They were forever having get-togethers, dinners, barbecues, game nights, and in the warmer months, sports. Lots of sports. Jax had an entire basketball league. They played baseball, rode horses, rode the bikes I built for them, and had picnics in the meadow. Life on our mountain was a certain kind of Hell for my brothers and I, but for the Luminas, it was never-ending bucolic tranquility. They were dead and resurrected to immortality. Living angels. No matter what, they were always at peace, and they played as hard as they worked.

Mariah would like it. And as time passed, she'd heal. I'd help her. I'd coax her into opening up, and she'd eventually get it all out and muck it around and look at it and talk about it and be mad about it and finally, eventually, make peace with it.

I roused off the bed and gathered up the sheets and blanket and the old toaster, turned off the light, then popped back to Colorado. I went first to Mathilda's housekeeping room, where she had a desk and shelves filled with all sorts of cleaning supplies, and several sewing tables where some of the Purgatories made and repaired our work clothes. Bolts of black leather stood in one corner. Through a wide doorway was the laundry with several washing machines and dryers, ironing boards and deep sinks.

Mathilda looked up from the list she was making and smiled at me. "Master Phoenix. What can I do for ye?"

I dropped the toaster in the trash, then set the soiled sheets on the laundry table and explained what they were. "I think you should throw them away and get Mercy to buy new. Even if Mariah stays with us, I want her apartment neat and clean." M would provide a doppelganger and someone, probably Gustav, would find it and think it was Mariah. She'd want to know he didn't find her on a bed without sheets. I have no idea how I knew this – I just did.

"I also want Mercy to buy her some clothes. Tell her to buy some of everything. Whatever girls wear. And other girly stuff. Whatever Mariah doesn't like, Mercy can return."

Mathilda nodded as I spoke, then said, "The first thing she needs is a warm coat. She'll catch her death in that rag she's wearing today."

"What are you talking about? Is she outside for some reason?"

"Oh, aye. She took a painting lesson this morning from Miss Sasha, then they had an early lunch and went out with Jax, Ty and Denys to ski."

Surely Sasha and my brothers weren't at the Telluride lifts. Surely they'd taken Mariah cross-country skiing, right here on our mountain. Or maybe they were snowshoeing and Mathilda was confused. They wouldn't take Mariah away from here, where she was safe from Eryx. Trying not to panic, I closed my eyes and concentrated carefully until I found Jax.

Then I panicked. And my fury nearly choked me. Opening my eyes, I said, "I gotta go."

"I heard them talking about it before lunch," Mathilda said. "Eryx is at Miss Jordan's school, too wrapped up in her to be following any of you. They made a plan to stay with Mariah at all times, so they could pop her back here if need be."

Mathilda hated it when we fought, and we did it a lot. She was trying to pacify me so I wouldn't kick Jax's ass. To be kind, I nodded and said, "I'm sure it's fine." Then I popped myself to the base of the lifts at Revelation Bowl and found my brother, fully intending to tell him he had exactly as long as it would take me to return Mariah to the mountain to prepare for war.

He'd shoved his Oakleys to the top of his head, so I could see his eyes when he turned to face me. Before I could say anything, he pointed his ski pole toward the run right in front of us. "I've never seen anyone learn this fast, and she's been laughing since we got here. Sasha is holding Eryx's location in her head, because she's awesome at that, and he's in D.C. panting after Jordan. Calm the fuck down and let her have some fun."

I heard her laughter from halfway up the mountain, saw her racing toward us, Sasha right behind her, Denys and Ty on either side of her. She was dressed in navy, a snug cap over her head and goggles covering her eyes. Her nose was sunburned.

"We went first to the shop at Mountain Village and rigged her out. She made a couple of runs on the bunny slopes, then insisted we take her on some blue runs, and this is her first run on a black diamond. Look at her. She's fearless. A natural. And she loves it."

My anger dialed back to a low boil, probably because the sound of her laughter made my insides flip around. I wished I was skiing with her. I'd only skied a few times. But then, I rarely did anything outside. I wore my horsehair shirt of guilt and wouldn't allow myself to do things I'd once considered fun. I hadn't been on a horse since the invention of automobiles. I built bikes for everyone on the mountain, but didn't have one of my own. Denying myself anything that could be considered fun and enjoyable, including sex – *especially* sex – had seemed a small price to pay for what I did to Jane.

Watching Mariah shout her triumphant joy as she came closer to me at breakneck speed, my want, my *need* to join her was a physical thing that coiled around me and squeezed so hard, I was breathless.

Her stop was flawless. She was breathing hard, laughing up at me as she moved her goggles to her cap. Her eyes were bluer, I could see her glow, and her scent was beautiful. My brothers and Sasha skied up just behind her and looked at me with obvious anxiety. They knew I was pissed.

Mariah didn't. I bit back what I wanted to say to them and

instead said to Mariah, "I wish you weren't a liar. That whole *I'm poor* thing really had me going. Clearly you've lived in Switzerland your entire life and trained with the Olympic team."

"This is the most fun I've ever had. It's such a rush! And the mountains are beautiful, and all the snow." Still breathing hard with exertion, making her breasts rise and fall, she looked down at my boots. "Where are your skis?"

Peeling my gaze away from her chest, I focused on her eyes. "I don't have skis."

"What? Why? Go get some and ski with me."

"I'd love to, but I have to work on—"

"Are you scared? I mean, it's dangerous, I guess, but it's not like you're ever permanently hurt. If I get hurt, Sasha says she can fix me."

The only thing in the world I was scared of was what I could do to her if I wasn't constantly on guard. She was so wounded. I had to keep that front and center in my mind at all times. Had to be careful and not step over a line. Not only my words, but actions and even thoughts.

I fought to keep from looking at her breasts again. Jesus, that dream had me undone. I wished I could see her as I saw Sasha – like a sister. I'd never, even once, had a sexual thought about Sasha. Strange, because honestly, I had sexual thoughts about most women. Except for the Luminas. I was a son of Hell, but even I couldn't have impure thoughts about angels.

Would this low hum of sexual awareness disappear once Mariah became a Lumina? Could I then see her as a beautiful girl and not a hot woman I'd sell my soul to see naked, to touch, just once? I cleared my throat and said, "I assure you I'm not scared of skiing."

"Then work later and ski with us now."

I leaned down and whispered, "You're away from the mountain, at risk."

With her face scarcely two inches from mine, she whispered back, "They think I don't know, but Sasha is keeping Eryx front and center in her mind. He's in Washington and I'm nowhere on his radar. Come on, Phoenix, don't worry so much. Go get some skis and do this with me, just for a little while."

"I'd rather take you home."

"Three more hours until dark, then I'll go back and stay there until it's safe for me to leave again."

I knew I should say no. It was a needless risk. But the look on her face, the sound of her laughter – I wanted to hear it again and again. I sighed. "All right, fine, but the second you ski too far away from any one of us, we're going back. *Capice?*"

She grinned at me and my heart thudded hard against my ribs. "Let's race."

I groaned, then we all popped down to Mountain Village so I could get some skis. And food. I hadn't eaten and was starving.

We went in the Blue Dog Grill and ordered crab claws, chicken kabobs, and burgers. Mariah ate almost as much as Sasha, who ate far more than an ordinary human girl because of Mephisto. I wondered if Mariah was too poor to buy food? She obviously relished what she ate, seeming to enjoy every single bite.

When we were back up on the slopes, she beat me twice, I beat her twice, and Jax said we had to have a tie-breaker, which is how we wound up at the top of the most difficult run at Revelation Bowl. I looked down at the almost vertical drop, at the tiny figures that were Jax and the others waiting for us at the bottom, and asked her, "Are you sure about this?"

"You're chicken, aren't you?"

"They say chicken in Romania?"

"It's a worldwide euphemism for cowards."

"I doubt that."

"Look it up." She schussed left ski, then right ski, gripping her poles, focused on the slope. "Are you in, or not?"

This was going to be epic. "I'm in."

"Prepare to lose, my friend."

"I'm out of practice." I was never actually *in* practice. Until today, I'd skied four times my whole life, and those were related to a takedown back in the fifties. I learned, practiced, then we did the takedown, and my skiing career was over.

"Excuses already? You must think you're going to lose."

My competitive nature roared to life. "Not hardly."

"Okay, on three."

We counted together and as soon as we both said three, I pushed off. Just as I'd thought, it was incredible. Exhilarating. I risked a glance at her and saw she was laughing. We were neck and neck, moving faster and faster. I could see Jax and the others clapping and yelling. I'm pretty sure they were all rooting for Mariah, which only made me want to win that much more.

Unfortunately for my manhood, she smoked me, probably because I tried to be tricky and jumped a mogul instead of skiing around it. My landing almost sent me crashing, and by the time I'd regained my balance, she was ten yards ahead, and I never caught up.

When we were with the others, she pulled off her goggles and hat and high-fived Sasha. And she laughed. For the first time in a thousand years, I didn't mind losing. I'd do it over and over, just to hear her laugh.

~~ MARIAH ~~

I'd never had a real holiday until that first week on Mephisto Mountain. As much as I wished Viorica would tell me the truth, a part of me was glad to keep up the ruse that I would be leaving on Sunday. I had no commitments, no pressure, no job to do. It was glorious.

On Wednesday morning, I had my first piano lesson from Zee. It went infinitely better than my painting lesson. I would never be an artist, but I loved music, loved the chance to learn an instrument. Especially the piano. I stayed in Zee's music room for several hours, his enthusiasm infectious. He played for me, all sorts of instruments, and when he picked up a mandolin, he talked me into singing with him. I'm certain he knew every song ever sung, and when he started playing some of the old folksongs my mother used to sing, that she'd taught to me and Viorica, I joined in. He stopped singing while I gained momentum and when I was done, he said solemnly, "You sound like Nora Jones."

I'd never heard of Nora Jones, so he played some of her music on an iPod he had hooked up to a complicated system of speakers that enveloped me in sound. I couldn't understand what she sang, but her voice was low and smoky. Sexy. I guffawed. "No way do I sound like that."

He insisted that I did and said, "There are some Luminas who like to play. We get together once a week or so and jam a little. You'll have to join us."

I wasn't sure if he was sincere or just being nice.

"I take all of this way too seriously, but it's what I live for. I wouldn't ask you if I didn't want you. Music deserves respect and your voice can't do anything but make it magical."

"What about the piano?"

"You need to practice every day, at least an hour of scales. Be here next Wednesday morning for another lesson."

"I'm leaving on Sunday."

He turned from the sound system and shook his head. "We both know you're not leaving. I'm going along with the others, but let's not bullshit each other."

"How do you know?"

He rubbed one big hand across his extremely short hair. "I just . . . do. I can't explain. Sometimes, I just know shit." He walked toward the door. "I'll buy your computer and TV this afternoon and set it up in your room tomorrow." Without saying goodbye, he left.

Zee was a weird one, but I liked him.

I sat at the piano and practiced my scales and wondered where Phoenix was. He'd been at breakfast, but left as soon as he was done. He'd been quiet and hadn't said anything to me beyond, "Good morning." I assumed he wasn't friendly because of the ruse, but it still bugged me. Moody people bugged me. I'd sworn once I was away from Emilian, I'd never be around anyone who brooded, who was prone to fits of anger. He wasn't at lunch and I wanted to ask Jax where he was, but didn't want to look interested.

After lunch everyone except Phoenix and Zee went snowshoeing and they showed me all around the mountain. I saw the Lumina cottages made of stone and logs, some big, some small, all charming. We circled three stone buildings that were the stables and barn. Ty said he'd bring me on Friday for a look-see of all the animals inside. We went inside another stone building that used to be the dairy, but had been converted to a gym with a shiny wooden floor and basketball hoops at either end. The room that was once the creamery was now a workout room with all kinds of equipment.

"We workout five times a week," Jax said. "And we train here."

"What do you do to train?"

Sasha cleared her throat. "Oh, just learn and practice some moves we use to capture the lost souls."

I had a feeling there was a lot more to it, but didn't press. I didn't really want to know.

When we returned to the house, we ended up in the back, where there was a formal garden, currently frozen in ice and snow. Farther back was an enormous heap of glass, metal and wood, and next to it were the remnants of a very large fire. "What happened?"

Denys said quietly, "That was Key's greenhouse. He spent the past century building it, and destroyed it in about three hours a couple of weeks ago."

"Why would he do that?"

"Your sister told him it would never happen between them."

"I don't understand. She's clearly mad for him."

They all exchanged a look before Jax said, "Key is a little different than the rest of us. When we were boys on Kyanos, he and Eryx were very close and did everything together, usually without us tagging along. After Eryx died and came back, Key had a duty to hate him, to defeat him, and he's stuck by that all this time, but he loved Eryx so much, it's extremely hard for him. He's always kept to himself, spending time with his plants and bees, taking care of the money, doing his leader thing. When Jordan came into his life, he thought it would be different. He thought he'd have a chance to let go of the past and be at peace. But Jordan hates Eryx more than any of us do, except Phoenix, so when she realized how Key feels about him, it was too much for her. She told him she could never love him." He nodded toward the mangled mess at the back of the garden. "This is how he dealt with it."

"Why does she hate Eryx so much?"

"He was behind her kidnapping, and when she was taken,

the lost souls shot her boyfriend, Matthew. He was paralyzed. She died at Eryx's hand, and if Key hadn't brought her back, if he hadn't been there to rescue her, Eryx would have brought her back and marked her so she'd be bound to him forever. Now Eryx is at her school. He's taken five of her friends' souls and she worries there'll be more. She worries he'll offer to heal Matthew in exchange for his soul. And all the while, he's trying to convince her to go with him to Romania, to live with him and give him sons he thinks will be some superpower version of himself, with a strain of Anabo that will lure more people to him. Her entire life changed because of Eryx."

My eyes were drawn to movement in an upstairs window and when I looked up, I saw Phoenix staring down at me. "They'll work it out," I said, never moving my gaze from Phoenix's face. "Jordan has been sheltered most of her life so she's still idealistic and passionate about her convictions. She hasn't learned yet that life is all about compromise."

Denys was closer to me, also looking up at Phoenix. "What concession has he offered to you, Mariah?"

"What do you mean?"

"He insulted you, but you've forgiven him and I wonder what he did to earn it."

Feeling more than hearing the underlying anger in his words, I turned my head to look at him. "He apologized."

He scowled. "That's it?"

"Is there something else?"

He looked up again, as did I, but Phoenix was no longer at the window.

"Be careful, Mariah."

My cheeks burned with the flush of anger that swept through me. "Of what? Phoenix? Do you think I'm some meek little flower cowering in a corner, hoping the big, bad Mephisto won't step on me? Do I look like someone who lets people run over me? *Do I?*" I realized my voice had risen and they were all staring at me.

"What you look like is somebody as fucked up as he is." Denys's beautiful face could be carved from granite, his jaw was set so tight, and his eyes were as hard as obsidian. "You have no clue what you're getting into here."

I did have a clue, but he didn't know that. I stepped back, aware I'd woken a sleeping bear and stirred up some unresolved hostility between him and Phoenix.

Jax moved toward the middle of three doors in this side of the mansion. "Too heavy, Denys. Mariah is supposed to be enjoying her visit, so leave it alone and let's go watch a movie. It's about to become a blizzard."

Like he'd flipped a switch, Denys lost his angry expression and laughed. "I do suck at the serious."

Once again, I saw past the laugh and knew his torment.

The rest of the day was without drama, and after dinner, Viorica came to visit. She seemed anxious and I asked if everything was all right. I expected her to open up, at least a little, but she gave me her too-bright smile, the one I knew was fake, and told me everything was just great. I wondered if our relationship would always be this superficial. I hoped not. I hoped she was so closed up because she was continuing the illusion that I was an ordinary human who would go back to my ordinary life come Sunday.

I slept without dreaming again, which was odd, but wonderful, and Olga and I woke up to a winter white world. I'd never seen so much snow. My bedroom window faced the front of the mansion and when I opened the drapes, I saw drifts that nearly covered the tall gas lamps that ran down the drive. At breakfast, everyone said they had things to do until after lunch, so I spent the morning in the library, reading a romance novel in Romanian. It, along with four others, had appeared in my room the day before with a note from Sasha that said simply, *Enjoy!*

I did enjoy it. I was just to a good part, wherein the hero in the story, a prince of some make-believe country, got told off by the heroine, an artist who'd been commissioned to do his portrait, when Phoenix came into the library. He was dressed in faded jeans and a long sleeved black T-shirt with a motorcycle logo. He hadn't shaved, and his scruff beard made him look more dangerous. And more attractive, if that was possible.

He walked to me and looked down at the book in my hand. "*Savage Hearts*? You're kidding. You've got to be kidding."

His disdain made me want to laugh. "So you've read this book and you're not a fan?"

"No, I have definitely *not* read that book."

"Then you shouldn't be a prejudicial snobby ass about something you know nothing about." I curled tighter in the wingback and went back to reading.

Annoying me, he took the opposite seat. "What's the attraction? I don't get it."

I looked at him over the top edge of the book. "What's the attraction of any book? It's a story about somebody with a problem and I want to see how he overcomes it."

"What's his problem?"

"He's a prince, and people are trying to kill him so the villain can take over the throne of his country after his father dies."

"Who's the chick with half her clothes falling off?"

I turned the book and looked at the heroine. "It's not a faithful rendering. In the book, she wears plain gray frocks with an apron because she's a painter."

"Maybe later she wears that red dress and it falls off and the prince stands behind her on a seaside cliff and looks pensive. Without his shirt."

"It's marketing. They sell more books with pretty people on the cover. The heroine is actually plain and the prince is . . . well, he's like this picture. What difference does it make? It's a good story, and I was just to a good part, so hush with your judgmental self." I went back to reading. I'd reread the line, *"Your impertinence is intolerable,"* for the third time when Phoenix said, "Read it to me."

"What? No! Get your own book." I'd already skipped around to find the sexy bits, and they were entirely too descriptive for me to read aloud. Especially to him. I felt myself blush just thinking about it.

"You're embarrassed because it's a romance novel and you're ashamed of reading it."

I sat up and glared at him. "I'm embarrassed because it has certain scenes in it that would be awkward to read out loud."

"You mean it's *pornographic?*" He held out a hand. "Let me see."

Holding the book close to my chest, I shook my head. "It's not pornographic. Just a bit racy."

He grinned at me then, like a badly behaved little boy, his eyes lit with mischievousness. "If you don't read it to me, I'm going to steal it from you and read the racy parts at dinner, out loud, to everyone."

"Then I'll stay in my room and have Mathilda bring my dinner."

"Then I'll come to your room and read them to you while you eat."

"I hate you."

"Aw, come on, Mariah. I'm seriously curious. You can skip over those parts if you want. Just read it to me until lunch."

Glancing at the tall grandfather clock in the corner, I said, "That's over four hours from now. Don't you have work to do?"

"I'm stuck at the moment. Sometimes I read when I'm hung up, and I'd just as soon have you read to me."

"Fine, but you have to promise not to mock it and make fun."

"I swear." He settled back in his chair and folded his hands across his belly. "Okay, go."

I turned to the beginning and started over. Right after I passed page fifty, he interrupted and asked, "Did you just skip a kissing scene?"

"Maybe."

"Read it."

"You said we'd be friends. Friends don't make friends do things that'll make them uncomfortable."

"It's just a kiss. If you and I can't, we can at least read about people who can."

With my face flaming, I went back and read the scene. When it was done, after Danielle told Prince Rupert he was a dishonorable cad and vowed to paint him with a hook-nose, Phoenix said, "This is bullshit. Real people don't kiss like that. You shouldn't be reading this because you'll have unrealistic expectations."

"I read murder mysteries, but I don't expect to solve homicide cases based on what I read. Give me some credit,

Phoenix. It's called fiction for a reason." I looked at him and saw he was frowning. He was actually concerned about this. I sighed and said, "Okay, I'll bite. How is this so different from a real kiss?"

"It's too perfect. Neither of them are awkward. Real kisses, if everybody's on board and eager to do it, are messy and too rushed, or too slow, or frustrating, but they're always exciting. It's the promise of things to come that makes a kiss awesome. It's shared intimacy, like a secret, and if it's forbidden, it's that much hotter. Prince Rupert and the painter just had a movie kiss, everything staged perfectly, nothing out of place. Their teeth didn't bump. Neither of them were worried about bad breath. Her father is in the next room and there are people who could come in and catch them, but they're not hurrying, or worried. It was all beautiful and perfect until she remembered he's a putz and broke it off and stepped back to give him what for."

"He's not a putz, whatever that is. He's just conflicted."

"He's all hot for her but can't have her because she's a peasant and the court schemers will use it against him if he marries a commoner. If he'd use his brain, he'd see a way to have Danielle *and* the throne. As it is, he's stealing perfect kisses from a woman he thinks he can't have and planning to marry the lady next door because her father is Sir Somebody at court. Rupert's the prince, for God's sake, the future king. He can marry whomever he bloody well wants, but no, he's going to bend to what the schemers want instead. Like I said, he's a putz. Danielle should pack up her paints and hit the road. There's probably some nice blacksmith back in her village who'd make her a fine husband, who'd give her sloppy, passionate kisses."

"I'm so happy you don't write romance novels."

He looked genuinely surprised. "Why? Because I'd have her marry the smithy instead of the prince?"

"Let's continue, shall we? Maybe Prince Rupert will develop a brain you approve of later in the story."

He slumped further down in his chair and his long legs stretched before him. "Okay."

I read on, and didn't skip the next few kissing scenes. The

plot became more complicated when one of the schemers began romancing Danielle, swearing he was on the prince's side, working undercover to spy on the conspirators. She devised a clever way of leaving information for the prince through her paintings. Everything was coming to a head. The king had died. The villain was turning the people against the prince, who was now king. The mole was revealed as the real villain when Rupert tricked him, using the clues in Danielle's paintings to trip him up.

And in between all the subterfuge and court conspiracies, Rupert and Danielle kissed a lot. And other things. Every time I skipped those scenes, Phoenix insisted I go back and read them. Then, close to the end, the kisses and the other things led to the two of them on a sofa in the turret room where the prince sat for his portrait. Sex was clearly up next. I stopped reading, flipping ahead to get past it.

"If you don't read it," Phoenix said in a low, throaty voice, "you're chicken. Look, I'm going to close my eyes and you can pretend I'm not here."

"Impossible. You're huge."

"Please."

I cleared my throat and began to read. He'd lied because he didn't close his eyes. He stared at me the whole time, and I fumbled and stuttered and it was just awful.

He reached over, plucked the book from my hands, then sat back and read it aloud to me. I closed my eyes and listened to the deep timbre of his voice and felt too warm.

When the scene was over, he stopped reading. I heard the tick of the grandfather clock, the crackle of the fire, the ping of cutlery from the dining room as Deacon set the table for lunch. I kept my eyes closed, childishly hoping he'd think I'd fallen asleep.

"I get it now."

I made no reply. I honestly couldn't speak, too nervous and embarrassed to even open my eyes. I wished more than anything that I'd refused to read the book to him. Why had I believed he'd let me skip over the sexy bits? He was a guy, and they were all obsessed with sex. I decided I hated him. I would open my eyes, get up, snatch my book away from him and leave the library. I'd go to my room, with Olga, and ask Mathilda to bring my lunch. I'd stay there until—

"He kind of had to be a putz in the beginning so he could grow as a character and deserve the painter. And she had to back off from feeling like somebody less-than because she came from peasant stock. The story is good, but it's really all about the characters, isn't it? Are all romance novels like this?"

"I don't know. This is only my second."

"Do you want me to read the rest, or do you want to?"

"Go ahead," I said, opening my eyes to stare at the fire.

He did, and just like the bad earl-good earl story, everyone was happy in the end.

"It's the ultimate escapism," he said as he closed the book. "They figuratively ride off into the sunset and live happily ever after. They never fight over money, or whose turn it is to change diapers, or which minivan to buy."

"Prince Rupert is rich, so they'll have a nanny, and it's in the olden days before they invented cars."

"There are other things to argue about, but these two will see eye to eye until they die. I guess that's appealing to people who like romance novels."

"That's not what appeals to me."

"What is it, then? Do you like that she's not a beauty and Prince Handsome falls in love with her anyway?"

"Well, that *is* nice, but no, that's not why I enjoyed the book."

"It's that they triumphed over the bad guy."

"You have to admit it's very satisfying."

"True, but most commercial fiction is some derivative of good winning over evil. What is it about romance novels in particular that you like?"

Did he seriously think I would answer?

Silence fell again and my eyes were drawn upward, to Mirabelle in her beautiful dress. I wondered what her story was. How had the Mephisto found her? What did they say to convince her to become a Lumina? Was she with someone? Had she been with someone when they found her? Andres had painted a twinkle in her eyes and a soft, playful smile on her mouth.

"I'm just as clueless as you are, Mariah."

I didn't pretend to not know what he was talking about. Still staring at Mirabelle, I said, "You've been alive a thousand years, and I know how you've spent the past hundred years, but I'm also certain of how you spent the nine hundred before those."

"It's true I've had a lot of meaningless hook-ups with girls I barely knew and never saw again. What I mean is that I don't know what it'd be like with someone I know well and care about."

Finally, I looked at him. "What about the other girl?"

"Why won't you say her name?"

"I say her name."

"No, you always call her 'the other girl.' Why?"

"I don't want to talk about her. I don't like comparing, or being held up to her standard. She was sweetness and light, someone fine and beautiful. I'd prefer to ignore her. As for how you felt about her, I know you didn't love her, but you felt something for her. So you're *I'm clueless* line is a lie, and you said we wouldn't lie to each other."

"Yes, I felt something for her, but it was . . ." Now he was the one staring up at Mirabelle. "We had sex once, and it was a mistake. It was too soon, too rushed. We both knew it, but I didn't realize just how big of a mistake it was until . . . anyway, what I've experienced is nothing like what's in this book."

"Maybe the author got that wrong like she got kissing wrong."

"Maybe." He dropped his head and looked at me. "I guess I'll never know."

"And I will?"

"Perhaps. If you stay, you'll be here for a very long time. There could be someone, sometime – another Lumina."

"How do you know there won't be another Anabo for you?"

"It wouldn't matter if there were a hundred more. I'm never going to be with anybody."

"Was it so bad that you have to punish yourself for the rest of eternity?"

He stood, came close, and handed me the book. "Yes." Turning, he walked out of the library.

Seconds later, Deacon's solemn voice came across the intercom speaker above the open library doors "Lunch is served. Allah is good."

CHAPTER 9

Phoenix missed lunch again, but today I wasn't surprised. He'd been upset when he left the library, so I suspected he'd chosen to eat in his room. Or maybe he went somewhere else. I was halfway glad, because I still felt insanely awkward after the book reading and subsequent conversation.

He wasn't sitting at the table with his usual quiet scowl, but there was a pall over everyone, an odd undercurrent flowing through the dining room that I couldn't pin down. Even Jax and Sasha were quiet and more focused on their plates than each other.

As soon as everyone finished, they left without goodbye. After Sasha was gone, it was just me, finishing my apple dumpling. Deacon said as he picked up my dessert plate, "There has been an omen."

"What does that mean?"

"Mathilda found the omen in your coat pocket."

"An omen from a Chinese fortune cookie?"

He stepped back from the table and stared out the windows at the world of white. "You did not know what this fortune foretold?"

"It was in English. And it wasn't my fortune cookie." I remembered it flying through the air and landing at my feet on the small terrace outside the attic. "The slip of paper was on . . . it was on the ground and I picked it up."

"The omen came to you, the only human on the mountain. You are the messenger."

I dabbed my mouth with my napkin and laid it on the table. I was not a superstitious person, or given to believing in omens, but asked anyway, "What does it say?"

He looked me right in the eye, which was so unusual, I stiffened. "The Mephisto will suffer a great loss by straying from the path."

"What does it mean? What kind of loss? In a takedown?"

He looked away and said to the windows, "The loss of a Mephisto."

"But they can't die."

"They can be lost. They can go to the dark side and join Eryx. They can die. To stand on holy ground is to die by fire."

I remembered then that Phoenix had told me none of them could go in a church or any other spiritual haven without burning to death. Except Jax, because he'd been redeemed by his love for Sasha. As for joining Eryx, I thought about what Jax told me yesterday. Kyros still felt something for his brother besides hate. Would he abandon his younger brothers and a thousand years on this side of the war to join Eryx? Impossible. He was crazy for Viorica, and leaving the Mephisto meant leaving her.

No, the omen must mean one of them would die. No wonder they were so solemn and quiet. "Who sent it?"

"Lucifer."

The hair at the base of my scalp raised, and I pushed back from the table, taking my time before I stood to get my reaction under control. When I faced Deacon, I was outwardly calm. "Do they blame me for the omen?"

"They do not. Their concern is for Kyros and his Mephisto, who are exposed. Until they are here within the security of the Mephisto Mountain, they are in extreme danger." He gave a slight bow of his head, then disappeared.

His Mephisto. Viorica was one of them now. She could be the one foretold to die.

But no, Phoenix had said that as much as she was now Mephisto, she was still Anabo, still able to stand on holy ground. She could never die. Neither could Sasha. The omen must be about Kyros.

Leaving the dining room, I made my way upstairs with a heavy heart.

In my room, Mathilda was there with a young, pretty dark-haired Lumina named Mercy who had a French accent and a multitude of bags from different stores, bulging with clothes and shoes. "So this is why you took my coat," I said to Mathilda.

"'Tisn't warm enough for this mountain. Come along and try these clothes and see what ye like."

I spent the next hour in and out of the closet, trying on everything from bras to jeans to sweaters to dresses. There were boots and shoes and socks and mittens, cosmetics and perfume and hair clips and jewelry. It was all beautiful, made of the finest materials, bought from stores I'd never been in, would never have dreamed of visiting. It was everything I'd never had. I asked Mercy, "How can all of this fit so well?"

She grinned at me. "We are the same size, even height, so I tried on, and if it fit, I bought it."

At half past two, Mathilda left and came back with tea, and Sasha arrived just in time to share. She seemed less gloomy than she'd been at lunch and when I asked about the omen, she waved it away. "Lucifer does this every once in a while, and it's not so much an omen of what will happen as a warning of what can happen if we don't walk the straight and narrow. The Mephisto are fairly autonomous, but there are rules we can't break, and suggestions we're expected to listen to."

"Is Kyros doing something Lucifer would consider straying from the path?"

"I don't think so, but things in Washington are weird. Eryx is acting extremely out of character and it has everyone spooked. Probably none more than Lucifer."

"What's he doing that's so out of character?"

"Just being in the real world is strange. He's very reclusive and usually stays at his home in Romania. He goes out only rarely, and then to find Skia recruits. He moves them around to strategic locations and they're the ones who find people willing to pledge their souls. But ever since Jordan was discovered in London and had to go back to Washington, Eryx has been there, pretending to be a regular guy, a new student at her school."

"Brody says Eryx is going out with Jordan's best friend," Mercy said. "They eat lunch at the same table, are in a lot of the same classes, and he's constantly staring at Jordan. Brody says it's creepy."

"What does he hope to gain?" I asked. "Jordan will never give him what he wants."

Sasha slumped back in the chair by the fire. "That's why everyone's freaked out. We're sure he's planning something." She widened her eyes. "I hope you're keeping that dress. It's marvelous and you look beautiful in black."

I looked in the long mirror Mathilda had pulled from the closet. "I never wear dresses. It feels weird."

"Put those black boots on," Sasha said.

After I did, Mercy clapped. "*Oui!* Perfect!"

Mathilda nodded. "Very fetching, Miss Mariah."

They were all three caught up in dressing me and we didn't talk of the omen or Eryx again, but as soon as they left my room, Mercy and Mathilda carting off what didn't work and what needed to be washed before wearing, I dressed in a new pair of jeans and a pale blue sweater and the boots and went downstairs to find Phoenix. I had no idea which of the six suites on the second floor was his, so I knocked on the first door I came to, which I knew already was Zee's because the floor was vibrating and I could hear the low thump of a bass guitar.

I was amazed he'd heard my knock, but within a few seconds, the door swung wide and he jerked a thumb, indicating I should come inside. He was dressed only in black leather pants, and I was taken aback by the expanse of his chest, of his hard body and muscled arms. He had a beautiful tat of the Mephisto *M* on his right bicep. "Have a seat and I'll be out as soon as I'm dressed." He took off through a doorway that led to a bathroom, and I saw him pass through another doorway into a large closet.

I looked around and decided his room was exactly as I'd have imagined. It was huge, furnished with warm and worn antiques, a beautiful rug, and pale green silk on the colossal bed. On the wall with the bathroom door was a black marble fireplace with a portrait of the brothers hanging above it. They stood in front of a beautiful house with onion domes and intricate woodwork, each of them dressed in seventeenth century clothing, Ty with a mastiff, Kyros with long hair, and

Phoenix holding the reins of a horse. Zee, Ajax, and Denys sat at a small table on the lawn. Below the painting, on the right side of the mantel, was a small bronze of a nude woman sitting on a delicate chair, playing a violin, her metal hair flowing to her waist. When Zee found an Anabo, I hoped she liked music.

Butter yellow silk draperies were open and afforded a sweeping view of the mountains. Just in front of the windows was a shiny black grand piano. On the wall opposite the fireplace was a sound system that took up the entire wall, stacked within beautiful mahogany shelves. A rock song I vaguely recognized was playing at the moment, so loud I could feel my bones vibrating. I liked it. The room was Louis XVI does Led Zeppelin.

Zee came out of the bathroom fully dressed in a black T, heavy black boots and a black leather trench coat that reached his ankles. Walking to the opposite wall, he turned off the music and faced me. "What's up?"

"I'm looking for Phoenix."

"He's gone. Didn't say where."

My disappointment must have shown.

"You want to tell me about it?"

I eyed his clothes. "You're about to leave. I don't want to keep you."

He shrugged. "You can go with me. Probably do you good to get out of here for a while, and besides, if you're going to be one of us, you need to see how we do things."

"I'm not going to be—"

"I'm not going to argue about it. Just go with me, you can tell me what's up, and after I'm done, I'll take you for coffee." He smiled. "And cake."

"I'm not supposed to leave the mountain. Kyros worries Eryx will take me and use me for leverage to get Jordan to do what he wants."

"He probably would if he knew where you were, but he won't. He's not thinking about you at all right now. The crazy bastard is crazy obsessed with your sister."

"That's what I wanted to talk to Phoenix about."

He came toward me. "Hold my hand and don't let go."

I took his hand. "Do I need a coat?"

Instantly, we were in my room, and he said, "Get one."

As soon as I'd shrugged into the wool pea coat Mercy had brought, he took my hand again. "Where are we going?"

"Moscow."

Seconds later, we stood on a snow-covered sidewalk several meters away from a corner streetlamp. Zee pulled me beneath the overhang of a building, into the shadows. It was just after one in the morning in Moscow, and patrons were leaving the nightclub across the narrow road from where we stood. Every time the door opened, I could hear the loud beat of techno music and see flashing colored lights. "Are we going in?"

"No, it's unnecessary, which is good because there are things in there you'd rather not see. We're waiting for a guy and his posse to leave, and we're going to follow to see where they go. He'll have some hopefuls with him, and I want to know where he takes them because it might lead us to more lost souls. He's a Skia who's flown under the radar for over twenty years."

"How do you know someone is Skia or a lost soul?"

"They have a shadow across their eyes. *Skia* means shadow in Greek. Skia shadows are so dark, it's hard to see their eyes. The lost souls also have a shadow, but it's way less intense. You won't be able to see shadows until you're Mephisto."

I didn't want to argue the point, so I asked if Luminas could see the shadows.

He nodded. "There are some Luminas whose only job is popping all over the world to look for lost souls and Skia. When they find them, it's my job to do reconnaissance. I give what I discover to Phoenix, who plans a takedown, and when we do it, Jax commands."

I felt a chill and when I looked at Zee, he was ghostly, almost transparent. "What just happened?"

"I put us under a cloak so no one can see us, with the exception of the Skia, whose name is Viktor. We're going to walk far enough behind him to not be obvious, but close enough that we don't lose him. If he turns around for any reason, I'll pretend to kiss you so he won't see my face. Got it?"

"As long as you don't actually kiss me."

"I'd *never* kiss you, Mariah. It'd be like kissing my sister. Like kissing Sasha." He made a face. "She's like a brother. Except she's a girl." He huffed out a breath. "Trust me, I'd never kiss you like that."

I was supposed to be pretending I didn't know I was Anabo or that I was intended for Phoenix, but Zee appeared to know I was aware, so I said, "This must go with the scent thing."

"If an Anabo was available to any of us, we'd kill each other fighting for her. Except we can't die, so we'd take each other out, over and over, and never catch any Skia or lost souls. And I'm sure the Anabo would be so disgusted with the lot of us, she'd take off and never come back. The smell thing is weird, I guess, but God had to make an end-run around what we are. Lucifer made it so we're not remotely attracted to an Anabo whose scent we don't know."

"What if you found an Anabo intended for you and you didn't get along with her?"

"Is this a general question, or are we getting into Phoenix and his fucked up head?"

"Just generally. Like, what if you found an Anabo who wasn't into music at all?"

He shook his head. "Never happen. Everybody else in the world can go around and look for somebody to hang out with. Sometimes they pick wrong. They can move on and find someone else. For me and my brothers, because Anabo are so rare, we get one shot, maybe two. God wouldn't send us an Anabo we aren't compatible with."

"What if you don't ever love her?"

He looked away from the nightclub door to focus on me. "The salient question is if *she* will love *me*." He rubbed a hand across his short hair. "Can we stop talking about this? It bugs the shit out of me."

"Why?"

"I hate sappy crap. The idea of love is ridiculous anyway. It's a construct dreamed up by humans to put a nice face on sex. Getting naked with somebody is sanctioned if there's some deep emotional attachment, but really, it's two people making babies. Instinct and nature are not love."

I wondered what it was when a grown man raped a twelve-year-old?

Quickly shutting down that line of thinking, I asked, "How'd you get to be such a cynic?"

"My father's the dark angel of death, best buds with the devil. How do you think?" He took a deep breath and stared across at the door to the nightclub, watching each person who came out. "I told you I *don't* want to talk about it."

Wow. Testy much? "Okay, so I won't talk about it." I followed his gaze to the nightclub door. "If he's never seen you before, how could Viktor know who you are?"

"Eryx schools his Skia about us, makes them memorize our photos, tells them how we operate and how we dress. They know. They always know. And they typically run, but sometimes, they stand and fight. If he runs, we'll chase, but if he turns on me, we're out of here. Just stay close."

I nodded and silence fell. It began to snow and I was somewhat mesmerized by the beauty of the flakes in the color of the lights when the nightclub door opened. I failed to notice when Zee slid an arm around me, but jerked out of my reverie when he turned me and began walking. I saw a group of six guys ahead of us, some short, some tall, but otherwise homogenous in dark coats and fur hats. Despite nighttime, I could see them very well in the lights of the city reflected from the low cloud cover. If I hadn't already known they weren't like an ordinary group of guys, I'd have questioned why they were so quiet. They'd just left a nightclub at half past one in the morning, but instead of laughing, or arguing, or singing, or talking too loud – all the things drunk people do – they were silent.

We followed several meters behind until they came to a well-lit boulevard and turned right. At the corner of the building, Zee slowed to a stop and peeked around. "They're about to go inside an apartment building. Hang on."

I waited, then went along when he grabbed my hand and turned the corner. The group was at the entrance to a building down the block, talking beneath a streetlight. The tallest had his back to us, gesticulating, clearly trying to convince the others to go inside. "Is that Viktor?"

"Right. His pigeons are having second thoughts."

There were very few other pedestrians, and traffic was light; mostly taxis and a lumbering bus that left smelly diesel fumes in its wake.

Zee stopped beneath a tree in the sidewalk and reached inside his coat to withdraw a pack of cigarettes. "I've never been much of a smoker," he said as he lit one, "but it gives me an excuse to loiter while I'm spying." He held the pack out to me. "Want one?"

Remembering the stench of old smoke on Emilian, I swallowed the bile in my throat and shook my head. I moved to stand upwind of him.

It was freezing cold and I wished I'd remembered to pick up the mittens Mercy had bought for me. I shoved my hands deeper in my coat pockets and darted looks at the group. Zee continued to smoke. "Will you follow and try to talk them out of pledging?"

"Definitely not. We're never about that, Mariah. People do what they do and we're forbidden to interfere with free will. If those guys decide to follow Eryx, my only interest in them will be taking them out so they can't sucker more people, then die and help Eryx grow stronger."

"If you're not going to interfere, why are we standing here? That's obviously where Viktor lives, so now you know."

"I don't know for sure. It might be one of the others' building. The shortest guy is a lost soul; Viktor's bait. He's telling those guys how awesome his life is since he pledged."

"How do you know?"

"I can hear him." He looked down at me. "We can see in the dark and hear things even dogs can't hear. Just be patient. They're all about to say yes and go inside, then I'm going to get closer and check it out to see if there are other lost souls who live there."

"Are we going inside?" I didn't want to. Real bad, I didn't. This was beginning to creep me out.

"No, we won't go inside."

"Then how will you know if there are more?"

"I just know. It's kind of like a sixth sense. I can put my hands on the building and know how many of Eryx's are inside."

"That's . . ." I was going to say weird, but didn't. "Interesting."

"It's fucking weird." He tossed the cigarette to the snowy ground, pulled me toward him, and embraced me.

"Is he looking?"

"He turned and is now facing us."

"Does he see us?"

"Yes, but we look like lovers under a tree." He bent his head and nuzzled my neck, murmuring into my hair, "Just put your arms around me and stay like this for a minute."

Not liking his nearness but understanding the reason, I complied, and at the same time, peeked around him to see what the group was doing.

That's when I saw Viktor's face.

Time stood still.

My heart stopped.

The boxes in my head exploded.

Viktor was my worst nightmare come to life. Every memory I'd so carefully avoided for so many years drowned me in a tidal wave of horror and agony. I sucked in a breath and nearly climbed inside Zee's coat, clutching his shirt, gasping for air.

"What the . . . Mariah, what's wrong? Jesus! *What?*"

"We have to go *now!* Please, please, *get me out of here!*" I couldn't breathe. I was dizzy with fear and disbelief.

"*Tell me.*"

"Emilian," I breathed. "It's Emilian." I didn't understand how, couldn't manage even one coherent thought. All I knew was that the devil stood less than fifty meters away. "Oh, God, it's *Emilian!*"

"Who the fuck is Emilian?"

I held bunches of his T-shirt in my hands and went over the edge. "Zee, please, you've got to take me back! *Now!*"

"I will, as soon as you tell me—"

Pushing away from him, I turned and took off running, mentally screaming, my hands curled into fists of rage and terror, cutting my palms. *How could it be?* I saw him die. How could he be here, in Moscow, alive and well? Had he seen me?

I heard heavy footsteps pounding behind me. He was coming closer. He would catch up to me, grab me, hit me, and drag me into the dark and hurt me *that* way. *Oh, God, oh, God, please, please help me!*

His hands were on me and I sobbed aloud before I closed my eyes and went limp. I couldn't be angry, couldn't show fear. It would be so much worse. He'd get out his knife. He'd strip off my clothes and scream ugly horrible things while he cut me.

Desperately trying to go away in my head, I heard his annoyed voice. "Don't ever run like that again. You have no idea what could happen to you."

He was already in a rage. Because I ran. Because I didn't make it easy for him. My body moved when he picked me up, but I barely noticed. I was at home, on the braided rug with Beet. On the chair next to the fire, Mama darned socks and sang. I wished she could hear me. I wished she could save me from what was about to happen. I called out to her, but she didn't hear, didn't stop singing.

Turning my head, I saw Phoenix sitting on Papa's chair, reading a book. "Help me," I whispered, and he looked up from the book and smiled, soft and gentle. "Come sit with me and I'll read to you." I got to my feet and went to him and he cradled me in his lap and read words I didn't understand, but I didn't care. I rested my head on his shoulder and inhaled the sweet scent of oranges while I waited for Emilian to be done. I prayed that this time, I would die.

CHAPTER 10

~~ PHOENIX ~~

I was sitting in the Green Room at the White House, frustrated with planning this über-complicated takedown, when Zee appeared. Breathing hard, he looked as freaked as I'd ever seen him. "Come home. Now."

Standing, I transported to the front hall and as soon as Zee was there, he nodded toward the stairs. "Mariah. Something's very wrong with her."

I didn't ask any questions before I popped upstairs to her room. She was in a chair by the fireplace, arms around her knees, curled into a ball of fear and misery, her very dark eyes blankly staring at nothing. My heart plummeted to my boots.

Olga sat beside the chair, and when I moved closer, she meowed. Mariah instantly drew herself into a tighter ball, and whispered, "Please, God, let it be over." Olga, I realized, was her warning system. She meowed when someone came near, waking Mariah so she knew what was about to happen to her. Except Mariah wasn't asleep right now. She was somewhere else, but she wasn't unconscious. What the hell had sent her off like this?

Her slender body shivered, and my breath caught. I scooped her up, turned and sat, settling her in my lap, wrapping my arms around her. Her arms twined around my neck and she nestled her head in the crook. She was still in another place, but I could feel the tension ease out of her. Her scent was so slight, I almost couldn't catch it.

Zee stood a few feet away, looking shell-shocked.

"Tell me what happened." I didn't think Mariah was aware

of her surroundings, but just in case, I spoke in English.

With his eyes on Mariah, he told me how they spent the past hour. I was so freaked, I couldn't muster much anger for Zee. That would come later. For now, my only concern was Mariah. "Do you have a photo of Viktor?"

He handed me his phone. Viktor was a gaunt, gray-faced man in his forties with hard, dark eyes. I punched the contacts button and hit the one for my father. As soon as he answered, I said, "I need your help."

"Can it wait?"

"No."

Seconds later, he was there, dressed in his usual black suit and red tie, holding a small gray dog under one arm and his phone in the other hand. He looked from my face to Mariah's and back again, and maybe I imagined it, but he looked pleased. "What can I do for you?"

I held up Zee's phone. "Emilian?"

He peered at the photo before shaking his head. "Dead ringer, but no. Emilian had green eyes and a scar on his cheek. Who is this guy?"

"Viktor Petrov."

M slipped his phone into his pocket and handed the dog to Zee. "Give him to Titus. I just took his master out and accidentally took him with me. He can't go back now." The dog yipped and M petted its head while he was thinking, searching the bank of knowledge he had available to him to know details of every soul on Earth. Then he looked at me. "He's a relative of Emilian's. An uncle on his mother's side." He gave me a quick biography of Emilian's immediate family and ended by looking at the photo again. "The resemblance is striking." He glanced at Mariah, who was still in another world. "She saw him?"

"Yes. In Moscow, with Zee, who was tailing him."

Zee was still pale as a ghost. "Who *is* Emilian?"

M said in his dry, just-the-facts voice, "Her guardian. He abused her from the moment she went to live with him when she was six, and raped her repeatedly from when she was twelve until he died when she was fourteen. He stroked out right after he lit a cigarette, fell on his bed, and it caught fire."

He looked at Zee's wide, horrified eyes. "This goes no further. She's had a bad enough time without everyone in this house talking about it." He turned to me again. "I suggest you don't take her off the mountain again until she's come to terms with what he did to her."

I glared at Zee. "Everyone was on orders to make sure she doesn't leave."

"Because of Eryx," Zee said defensively, "and he's so wrapped up in mooning over Jordan, he's not paying any attention to Mariah."

M said, "Eryx is the least of her worries. What's in her head is far more dangerous and frightening than Eryx."

"Are you serious?" Zee was incredulous. "Eryx will *kill* her."

"Look at her, son. Do you think she's afraid of death?"

M came close and bent to gently stroke her hair. I watched in stunned disbelief. Not since our mother died had I seen my father express anything close to affection.

Her soul must have recognized who he was because she looked up at him with relief and whispered, "I'm ready to go."

"It's not your time," he murmured.

She leaned her head into his hand and closed her eyes. "He came back."

"No, he's never coming back."

"Promise?"

"I promise." He moved his hand across her face and she instantly went to sleep, her head falling against my shoulder. He focused on me, his expression stern. "Whether you claim her or not, she's your responsibility."

"I'm aware."

"What do you plan to do to help her?"

"I've been reading books about survivors and how they make peace with their pasts."

"And?"

"It involves a lot of talking. Getting it out and allowing herself to feel all the rage."

M glanced at Mariah. "I'm sure talking it out will be helpful, but she's a born warrior. Teach her to fight. Let her work the rage out of her system. Show her how to protect herself."

"She'll never need to protect herself again. I'll make sure of it."

Jerking his gaze back to me, he was angry. "Like in Moscow?"

He'd mined her memory to see what had happened. I wasn't sure what he'd seen that made him this angry, but I knew Zee and I were walking a narrow line. "Zee was with her all the time. She was never in any danger, except in her own head."

"Exactly. She ran and Xenos chased. She thought he was Emilian, and if she knew how to fight, she would have turned to stand her ground. She would have realized he wasn't the threat she thought. Instead, when he caught her, she was so terrified, her mind slipped right off the edge." He bent again and ran the back of his fingers across her cheek. "You and your brothers suffer. I know this. But nothing you've lived through in a thousand years of life could help you understand what she has endured, because you've never been overpowered or helpless. Let her use all that rage to her advantage. Teach her to fight."

"She'll be a Lumina," I said, hiding my astonishment at his gentle compassion for Mariah. "They never fight."

He unbent and said, "She's not cut out to be a Lumina. Make her Mephisto."

That pissed me off. "Since when do you make that call?"

In a blink, he was hovering over me, holding my face in his hands. "Since you seem incapable of doing what's in the best interests of everyone on this mountain, including Mariah. Let it go, Phoenix." He shook my head, angry and frustrated with me. "*Enough.*"

"You know why I can't," I whispered.

"I only know why you won't, but somewhere along the way, you lost yourself and all the reasons it mattered. Of what use is a one-armed man who cuts off his other arm to make amends? His sacrifice doesn't make him a martyr. It makes him a liability." Blowing me away completely, he kissed my forehead before he disappeared.

Holding the little dog, Zee collapsed in the chair opposite mine. "I'm sorry," he said, staring at her. "You no doubt want to kick my ass into next week."

"Forget it," I said. "Just keep an eye on her when I'm not around and make sure nobody else takes her off the mountain."

His eyes were filled with sorrow. "This is rough, brother."

I stood and carried her to the bed, laying her down on her pillow. I pulled off her boots and moved her around to remove her coat. After I spread the throw at the end of the bed over her, Olga jumped up and curled into the curve of her belly. Her arm went around the cat and I'd swear she seemed more at ease. I knew she'd be out of it for several hours. M had put her under as he'd done with us at different times in our lives, sending us to a level of unconsciousness that allowed rest without dreams, without memory.

Still bemused by his affection for Mariah and the kiss he gave me before he left, I started a fire in the grate, then sat down again. The dog was falling asleep in Zee's lap.

"I bought her a TV," he said. "Planned to install it when we got back from Moscow. A couple of nights ago, we watched *UP* and she cried."

"Sasha cries every time she watches it. Must be a girl thing."

"I guess." He looked toward the fire. "You wanna talk about it?"

"Not really."

"Okay, but can I just say one thing?"

"Go ahead."

Still staring at the fire, he said, "I agree with M."

"There are things you don't know, Zee. It's best this way. Leave it alone."

"Best for who? Not her."

"Yes, for her. I can't give her what she needs."

"She could be Mephisto and not yours."

"If she's Mephisto and not mine, she has no one and no possibilities. She can't be with a human, or a Lumina, or any of our brothers. Look at who she is. Imagine her turning into some warrior princess, fighting Skia, taking out the lost souls, then coming back here to a room of her own with nobody to share her life with. She'd suffer as we have and hate the loneliness, except worse because more than anything, she needs somebody to love her."

"I'd love her if I could."

Knowing how he felt about love and romance, I recognized his statement for what it was – guilt and grief. He didn't know it yet, but neither guilt nor grief made for anything that lasted. Not for the first time, I wondered what sort of girl would arrive in his life. "It's all moot anyway. She doesn't want to be Mephisto. She thinks she let Emilian die in the fire, so she has a complete aversion to violence of any kind. No way she'd learn to use a blade."

"Will you tell her what M said about Emilian?"

"When she's ready to hear it." I looked toward the bed. "I have no idea how she'll be when she wakes up." Would she be back to that perfect picture of calm acceptance that hid her true feelings? Would I be starting all over again with her?

It was promising that, in the grip of fear so great her mind had taken her somewhere else, she put her arms around my neck and settled into my lap with complete ease.

"Does Key know about her?"

"He's known since before he brought her here."

"I'll tell him what happened. M's bound to bring it up, and Key will be pissed we didn't clue him in."

"He gave strict orders not to take her off the mountain. He may call a council on you."

Zee shrugged. "I probably deserve it. Either way, I think he should know, and I should be the one to tell him."

Before I could respond, Deacon's solemn voice came through the intercom. "Dinner is served. Allah is good."

"Go on," I said. "I'll have Mathilda bring us something to eat later, after Mariah wakes up."

"What should I tell the others?"

"Say Mariah isn't feeling well, and I'm still at the White House."

Holding the sleepy dog, Zee stood and went to the side of her bed. Olga meowed, but Mariah didn't wake.

Zee said, "She's known all week that she's Anabo, but hasn't let on except to me, because I called her on it."

I didn't ask how he knew. He knew the same way he knew other things. We'd never known why, or how it worked, but

Zee had a gift that went far beyond intuition. He simply knew certain things, but rarely divulged details. I wondered sometimes if what landed in his mind was the reason he was odd. I suspected he knew things all of us would rather not know. Disturbing things. He drowned out the thoughts with music, and when that wasn't available, he worked within a narrow box that was his own sanity. He'd always been a strange one, talking to himself, drawing bizarre pictures, and he wrote constantly. He had locked trunks in the attic, and I was certain they were filled with his journals.

Denys liked to joke that if Zee wasn't Mephisto, he'd be a serial killer. Zee laughed it off, but I knew it hurt him. Behind his metal music and odd behavior and contempt for romantic love, he was probably the most sensitive of us all; even Ajax, who tried and failed to hide his sentimental nature. I told Denys to back off with the serial killer jokes, and he did, but it didn't change that Zee was weird.

Maybe that's why I wasn't mad at him for what he'd done with Mariah. He stood there watching her sleep, and I could feel his pain and regret.

When he turned and walked toward me, he said, "The cat's not an ordinary kitty. Somebody sent her to watch over Mariah and be a solace to her."

"I wonder who?"

"Someone divine. Maybe an angel. Maybe God. All I know for sure is that she's devoted to Mariah and will be until she dies. The cat, I mean. Until the cat dies." He looked down at the dog he held before he disappeared without a goodbye.

Minutes ticked by and turned into an hour, then two. I stoked the fire and watched her sleep, my mind searching for a way to fix her that didn't involve turning her to Mephisto. Because as much as I resented what M had said, the rational side of me had to admit it made sense. I thought about how she skied – fearless. If she had Mephisto and all the instincts that went with it, she'd be incredible. Unstoppable. After Jax taught her to use a knife, to fight to win, she'd be empowered. She wouldn't be afraid when Olga woke her up. She'd fly out of bed with a blade in hand and take out the threat before the cat was done with her meow.

But I couldn't do it to her. As much as it would help, it would hurt. Mathilda was right. Mariah was a gentle soul, more so than Sasha or Jordan. Even more than Jane. Mephisto would change that. *And,* a small voice I couldn't silence said, *she'd be infinitely more tempting.*

Eliminating all of her other options so that I was the only guy she could choose meant she had no choice. Knowing that, knowing myself, it would be impossible to stay away from her. Maybe I could do it for a few years. Maybe I'd even make it a hundred years. But at some point, I'd crack. I'd go after her in earnest, and she'd be lonely enough to accept. She'd regret it. She'd be too close, and she'd know what I'd hidden from my brothers all these years.

I poked at the fire, fighting to stifle my never-ending frustration and anger. Why was I like this? What sick twist of fate gave me this much of my father? Why couldn't I have been born with more of my mother, like Jax? Even Zee in all his weirdness was more like Mana than I was.

Thinking of her, I slammed the poker against a flaming log and watched it explode into fiery pieces. She'd died because our father wouldn't confess his secrets to Lucifer. Eryx sacrificed himself for the rest of us, murdering his own mother so Lucifer and God would know we existed – something M should have taken care of before Eryx was grown. It was Eryx's last act of compassion, and the worst thing that could have happened to him before he was compelled to jump to his death from the Kyanos cliffs. He came back with a soul black as midnight, a threat to all of humanity. So much pain and horror, all because M wouldn't step up and do the right thing.

I was just like him. I wouldn't tell the truth, and Jane died; murdered by the same brother who murdered our mother.

I couldn't be with Mariah. Ever. I had something dark and horrible in me, just as M did, and maybe I'd be kind to her, seduce her, and give her sons, just as M did for my mother, but I would hurt her in the end. She was so wounded, it seemed the greatest tragedy that God sent her to me. Of all of us, why me? Why not Ty, who lived to heal what was injured and make it whole again?

Hearing a noise, I jerked my head around. Mariah stirred

and rolled to her back, throwing one arm above her head. I noticed something in her hand and got up to go look. Olga meowed as soon as I came close, and Mariah's body went stiff and still.

That made my chest hurt. How long would it be before she lost her fear? Would she ever? "It's me," I said quietly. "You're home now and safe." I saw her palm when she uncurled her hand from the fist she'd made. It was splotched with dried blood, and I wondered what she'd done to hurt it. Zee hadn't said that she fell.

She opened her eyes and looked up at me with no expression at all.

Damn. I'd been so hopeful she wouldn't go back to how she was in the beginning. I debated what to do. I wanted to pick her up and hold her for a while and assure her everything would be all right, but what if she freaked out? I was in way over my head. All I could do was go on instinct. I kept my distance and asked, "How are you feeling?"

"What time is it?"

"Half past eight. You've been asleep a couple of hours."

"Did I imagine that Mephistopheles was here?"

"No."

"He told me Emilian didn't come back. He promised he'd never come back. Did he know why that man looked exactly like Emilian?"

"He's a relative."

I expected her to ask more questions, but she didn't. She laid there and stared at me a while longer, then said, "It was nice by the fire. Thank you."

"I didn't think you knew."

"Of course I knew. I go home in my head and . . ." She paused and I heard her swallow. "You'll think I'm crazy."

"No. Tell me."

"I imagine I'm home on the rug by the fire and my mother is there and I'm safe. This time, you were there, too, and I sat on your lap and you read to me. It was lovely."

"You sat on my real lap for a while. Do you remember?"

She shook her head. Then she moved to make room, and said, "Sit down, Phoenix. You're so tall and I can't see your face because it's too dark in here. Why do you never turn on the lights? Why candles? Because the twenty-first century called and they'd like you to live there."

She was making a joke. She asked me to sit. Maybe we hadn't returned to square one after all. "I'll be right back." I went in the bathroom and ran warm water on a washcloth. Taking it to the bed, I sat and reached for her hand, but she held it away from me. "Let me clean it, Mariah." She nodded and stared up at the ceiling while I washed away the dried blood, revealing four perfect half-moon cuts. While I cleaned her other hand, I said, "Since we can see in the dark, we don't need that much light. It can even bother us at times. And I suppose we lived so long with candlelight, we like it." I set the washcloth on her nightstand, then held her hands, thinking to heal them, but she made a soft sound of protest and pulled them away from me.

"Promise me," she whispered.

"I promise." I smoothed her hair away from her brow. "What did I promise?"

"Don't tell the others. Tell Zee not to say anything. And especially don't tell Viorica."

"We think we have to tell Key."

"He'll tell her."

"No, he won't. She's having a rough time right now, so the last thing he wants is for her to worry about you."

"I went downstairs to find you to talk about her, and the omen, but you were gone and Zee said I should go with him to learn what you all do, even though I told him I'm not going to be Mephisto. He's a funny one, but I like him. I'm sure after what happened he thinks I'm a head case, and I guess maybe he'd be right. Do you think Viorica is going to be okay? Is Kyros going to be lost? Does Lucifer send omens very often? Why did he send it to me?"

She was progressively getting more wound up. I continued stroking her hair and said calmly, evenly, "Zee is a head case, and believes people in glass houses shouldn't throw stones. He feels bad for putting you in that situation, but he didn't know about Emilian. He does now, but don't worry about that. He's not one to carry tales. Your past is yours to talk about if you want, and otherwise, no one will know who doesn't already. As for Jordan, she's incredibly strong, and will be just fine. It'll be hard for her to let her father go, because they're so close and she's all he has now, but she will, and Kyros will not be lost, and all will be well. Lucifer sends his messages through a human, although it's always in the real world because there are no humans here. We get omens and messages on restaurant receipts, newspapers, even the sides of busses. Don't be frightened by the omen, or that he sent it to you."

"He said the Mephisto shouldn't stray from the path. What does it mean?"

"I don't know. It'll make sense later, and we'll remember what he said and act accordingly. Don't fret, Mariah. Jordan's fine."

"You said she's having a hard time right now. She won't tell me anything at all. What's happening?"

"She feels guilty about Matthew. Her time's running out and she wants to make things right with him before she leaves the real world. Her father is under a lot of pressure because so many things are going wrong in the United States right now." I smiled at her. "And she's working things out with Key, which would make anybody stressed. He's not easy."

"Do you think she loves him?"

"Yes, but she doesn't fully realize it yet." Finding Mariah was the turning point, I was certain. Not because she was Jordan's long lost sister, although that was huge, but because there were parallels between what Eryx had done for us and what Mariah had done for Jordan. They'd both unhinged their lives for the sake of their younger siblings. It had given Jordan a new perspective, made her see Key's feelings about Eryx in a different light. Nothing was ever black and white, and Jordan learned another shade of gray when Key found Mariah.

"What about Kyros? Do you think he loves Jordan?"

"I don't know. He's so closed off and hard to read, it's impossible to say."

"She'll be here to visit soon. I need to get up and put myself back together before she comes."

"You have plenty of time. I'll ask Mathilda to bring you some dinner."

"Did you eat?"

"No, I waited for you."

She fell quiet, and I continued to pet her silky soft hair and knew when she felt better because her scent grew stronger.

I pulled my hand back when she moved, expecting her to get up, but she came closer and sat up and I knew what she wanted. I reached out and plucked her from the bed and settled her in my lap. She twined her arms around my neck, just as she'd done before, and rested her head on my shoulder.

Olga rubbed against my back and purred.

We sat like that for a long, long time and I felt odd. Almost at peace.

"I don't talk about it," she said against my shirt, her voice soft and muffled. "I've never talked about it. I have no real friends and never have. I remember girls at school. I called them friends, and we got on fine, but they didn't know me at all. They talked about guys and clothes and music and movies, and I had nothing to talk about, nothing to add. I was always the quiet one, but not because I'm a quiet person. It was because I had nothing to say that was appropriate, that wouldn't make them uncomfortable. And I never wanted to be a victim, never wanted to be defined by what was happening to me. Even after he was dead and I lived with Marta, my life was different than theirs. They were poor – everyone was poor – but none of them worked for their living. They lived with family." She lifted her head and looked into my eyes. Inches away. "I like that you know about him. I don't have to pretend. And I wanted you to know that." She pressed a kiss to my cheek and returned her head to my shoulder.

"You should talk about it, Mariah. Maybe you'd feel less afraid if you got it out of your head."

"Maybe." She slid her fingers into my hair. "But not now, Phoenix. I'm tired, and hungry, and Viorica will be here soon."

"I should get up and call Mathilda."

"Yes." She made no move to get off of my lap.

I was glad. I'd never been this close to another human being for this long, not even Jane, and I never wanted it to end, never wanted her to move. It occurred to me that she'd had very little affection in her life since she was six years old and went to live with Nadia and Emilian. Marta had evidently been kind-hearted, but gruff, and I doubted she'd given Mariah much in the way of affection. Maybe she'd tried and Mariah rebuffed her. She didn't like to be touched. Except right now she was glued to me.

I gathered her closer.

There was a knock at the door, and I debated setting her off of my lap, but couldn't bring myself to do it. Whoever was there could think whatever they wanted. "Come in," I called.

Mathilda stepped inside the room and smiled at us. "Is our puir lamb feeling better, Master Phoenix?"

"I think so. She's hungry."

She came close and bent to peer into Mariah's face. "Zee said you aren't feeling well, child. Do ye need some Tynedol?"

"I'm all right," she said without lifting her head from my shoulder. "I went with Zee to follow a Skia and it scared me. That's all."

Mathilda patted her leg and stood straight. "How about a nice beef stew? Would you like that?"

"Yes, please. Thank you."

Her soft brown eyes met mine. "Would ye care for some supper?"

I nodded and she disappeared.

Mariah moved so that her nose was against my neck. "Mm, oranges." She sighed, sending a tiny breath across my skin that woke things up that didn't need to be awake. I quickly thought about the slides I'd looked at under a microscope that morning. Viruses were not sexy.

"Thank you for staying with me," she whispered.

"I wouldn't want to be anywhere else."

"I didn't dream."

"Do you usually?"

"Yes. Nightmares. I hope when I go to sleep later that I don't dream. After today . . ."

She shivered and I tightened my arms. "He's dead, Mariah. He can't hurt you ever again."

"You don't understand," she mumbled.

"I want to. Tell me."

"I dream every second of it, always just as it was. Then I

wake up and it's so real, it's like he's there. It takes me some time to realize he's not, to remember he's dead, and in those moments, it happens all over again."

She hadn't told Key outright that Emilian had raped her. She'd never said so to me. As far as she knew, all we were aware of was that Emilian abused her. Sexual assault was the elephant in the room, but she'd just pointed to it, maybe because she was still upset, or maybe because, at the moment, she felt as close to me in spirit as she was in body. And she was very close.

I debated what to say, whether I should go forward, or wait for her to say something more. It was a huge risk. I might spook her. But she'd handed me an opening, and I had to take it. When she didn't speak again, I asked, "Was it always at night, when you were asleep?"

"Always," she whispered. "It was part of what he liked, scaring me awake. At first, I reacted just as he wanted me to, but after Olga came, I knew when he was there, and I'd have time to wake up and escape."

"To the rug by the fire?"

She nodded. "He tried to kill Olga, but it's almost like she knew to stay away from him. He could never find her, and a few times he chased her after she woke me, but she always escaped."

She probably disappeared, taken into another realm until Emilian forgot about her. "So when you dream, it's always the same?"

"Yes." Her head turned so that her chin rested on my shoulder. "Except that sometimes he has his knife. Sometimes, he doesn't."

It took all I had to stay calm and keep my body relaxed. Someday I'd be in Hell, and when that day came, I'd find Emilian and cut *him*. Until then, I hoped he suffered endlessly at Lucifer's hands. "Do you have scars, Mariah?"

She didn't answer for a while and I feared I'd gone too far, but then she said, "They're where no one can see. No one will ever see."

I convulsively held her tighter and swallowed the lump in my throat. "Show me." If I couldn't heal her mind, I could at least heal her body.

"You're not serious."

"We're friends. We can talk about anything, do anything, and it's only between us."

"Friends don't look at one another naked, Phoenix. Just leave it. I'm only telling you this so you'll understand why I don't want to go to sleep, especially tonight. I know I'll dream, and it'll wake me up, and I'll be more afraid than usual because of seeing that awful man who looked *just* like him."

"I'll stay with you."

"All night? You mean you'll sleep with me and be here when I wake up afraid?" She lifted her head to look at my face. "That can't possibly end well."

"I've lived without sex for almost a hundred and twenty five years."

"This doesn't make me feel less anxious about sleeping with you."

"I will never mark you, Mariah. Never, I swear, even if you wanted me to. You are completely safe with me."

"What if we climb in this bed and I decide I don't like you in it with me?"

"Then I'll sleep on the floor."

"You'd do that?"

"I'll do anything if it helps you get past what he did to you."

She shifted and things aligned provocatively. Her eyes widened. "I can never forget that you're a guy."

"I hope not. I'm rather fond of being a guy, with all the accompanying equipment. It makes yours so much more interesting."

"Again, this isn't making me feel better about sleeping with you."

I shrugged. "Everything still works, and it occasionally does what it was designed to do, even when I don't want it to, especially when I'm asleep, but that doesn't mean anything. It's a bodily function like any other. It'll go away." I moved my lips across her soft cheek and made myself think about deadly viruses under a microscope. "Let's give it a go and see if it helps you."

Her lips curved into a small smile. "Trying to fix me,

Phoenix?"

"I want to more than I've ever wanted anything."

"I told you, fixing me won't change what happened with the other . . . with Jane."

"No, but it will make you whole again. I'm responsible for you."

"So, I'm a duty."

"You're my friend." I'd been slowly coasting my lips across her soft cheek and realized I was now kissing her soft cheek. And the lobe of her ear. And her throat. I should have stopped, but didn't. "I want you to be at peace, and not afraid of what's in your own head." Her scent grew stronger, and I considered it a small victory.

It occurred to me that she was letting me kiss her. In fact, she tilted her head back to expose more of her throat and I ran little kisses all the way to her chin. I was *this* close to her lips, and wanted to keep going. *So* badly, I wanted to kiss her full on the mouth.

She blinked at me. "Maybe the lap thing wasn't such a good idea."

I thought she was talking about this overwhelming need to kiss her, but realized when she shifted again that she was talking about what was happening just below her perfect ass. I cleared my throat. "The lap thing was an excellent idea. I just shouldn't kiss you. Anywhere."

"It's not fair, Phoenix. I've never wanted to kiss a guy, *ever*, and when I finally find one I do want to kiss, I can't."

I pulled her back to me and stroked her beautiful hair. "There'll be someone else. Someday."

"And you'll be okay with that?" she mumbled against my shoulder.

"Yes," I lied.

She sighed and we fell quiet again. I have no idea how many minutes passed before she whispered, "Don't hurt me."

"I would never—"

"I know you wouldn't, but you'll break my heart. I should get up and make you leave and not talk to you ever again."

"Then why don't you?"

Her arms tightened around me. "Because I've never had

this, never felt this way, and I can't help myself."

"Things will change after you've been here for a while. You'll get to know everyone and feel at ease and comfortable and your fear will diminish. I'm just the first person to get this close to you, so you naturally feel more connected to—"

Startling me, she sat up suddenly and held my head in her hands. "Stop talking."

"Why? I was just saying that—"

"You're spouting a lot of nonsense because you want to convince yourself it won't matter if I'm with someone besides you. Stop lying, Phoenix. I may not be all you'd hoped I'd be, but I'm what you've got, and it'll drive you insane to see me with someone else. You can pretend it's about me, and talk big about me finding my perfect soul mate among the Luminas, but in the end, you're entirely too selfish to let me go."

"That's low, Mariah. Yes, I'm selfish, but I'm trying so damned hard to do the right thing for you."

"This isn't a field trial where you get a cookie for good performance. This is my *life*, and you're jacking it up because of your need to absolve yourself of guilt over a woman who's been dead for more than a century."

"How am I jacking up your life? I'm here, aren't I? I want to kiss you so much, it hurts, but I won't because you don't want to be Mephisto."

"Oh, right." She focused on my mouth. "Remind me again why I don't want to be Mephisto."

"You have to kill people."

She was coming closer, her hands still holding my head, and when she was half an inch from my lips, she whispered, "We're doomed to this. You realize it, don't you?"

"I wouldn't say doomed, exactly. For one thing, that's highly negative, but also, we can overcome the . . . ." Her lashes were long and dark above those deep blue eyes. I could feel her soft breath on my mouth. "Overwhelming, uncontrollable, all-consuming . . . ."

"If it's like this for the next hundred years, we're toast. If it's like this until the end of next week, we're goners for sure. If it's like this ten minutes from now, it just *is* going to happen."

Her lips brushed across mine and I came closer to the breaking point. "Letting hormones drive a decision like this is immature and foolish. You're upset right now, understandably so, and because we're friends and I know your past, and you want to feel something besides pain and fear, you think kissing me will—"

"This isn't a new development, Phoenix. I've wanted to kiss you since the first night I was here, when you came to my room and apologized. As for hormones, we'll both still have them tomorrow, and the day after, and next year. Do you think they'll go away? Will there be a time when we don't want to kiss each other? Say yes and I'll get up right now and we won't talk about it anymore."

A mental picture of Jax and Sasha popped into my head. I was forever catching them kissing when they thought they were alone – in the TV room, behind the stairs, in the gym, on one of the hiking trails. They'd been together daily for over a year, slept together, did everything together, and they still couldn't keep their hands off of each other.

Looking into Mariah's beautiful eyes, I pulled on my well of self-control and found the bucket dry as a bone. I would *not* kiss her. I reminded myself of all the reasons I couldn't. "We're only doomed if we choose to be."

"I see. So I'm supposed to join you in your martyrdom."

That made me mad, which paradoxically made me glad because it allowed me to set her off of my lap. "Why do you keep picking at it?" I got up and moved away, but it didn't help. I wanted her so much, I could almost taste her. The fire had died to embers, so I laid a couple more logs in the grate and poked at it until the coals caught fire. "You *will* find someone else. You're Anabo, capable of loving anyone."

She went into the bathroom, and I could see her standing in front of the mirror. "I look horrible." Reaching into a drawer, she pulled out a hairbrush and began running it through her hair. "Wonder what's keeping Mathilda?"

I stalked to the door of the bathroom and glared at her. "Why are you ignoring what I said?"

Turning, she continued brushing her hair while she frowned at me. "Because I'm tired of you assuming so much about me because I'm Anabo. How would you like it if I said I don't believe you can be a nice guy because you're a son of Hell? What if I assumed everything you do is for an ulterior motive, that you're evil at heart?"

"I really hate rhetorical questions. Of course I would hate that. But the fact remains that you *are* Anabo, and you have a choice. Once you become immortal, kissing means you're permanently Mephisto. I'm a strong guy, but I do have my breaking point. I'd eventually be compelled to seduce you, and once we do that, you're marked as *my* Mephisto and stuck with me forever. And I mean literally *forever*." I hoped what I said would jolt her back to reality. I didn't want to frighten her, but she had to understand that there was no going back.

The hairbrush stopped. "Wait. You just said that if I'm immortal, Mephisto is permanent. What if I'm not immortal?"

"You can ask Lucifer to return you to who you are now."

"And after that, I could become immortal and a Lumina?"

"Well, yeah, but it's complicated, and you might like being Mephisto, so you wouldn't want to go back, and I think you should—"

"Does it really matter what you think I should do? It's not that I don't value your opinion, Phoenix, but you're way too involved to be objective at all." She was staring at my mouth. "I think we should go for it, and next week, before I become immortal, I can do whatever it is I need to do to go back to original me."

"No."

"Why?"

"Because it's like Pandora's box. I can't kiss you for a week, then say peace out and there's an end to it."

"At least I could finally kiss somebody." She paused, then said, "And by somebody, I mean you. I don't want to kiss just anybody. Only you. And you could break your fast, at least for a little while. I'm not seeing a downside."

"You have no idea what you're asking me to do." I kind of hated myself for saying it, for the drama of it, but she really didn't understand yet exactly what was inside of me. Along with muscle and bone was something dark and twisted that I couldn't control. My best hope of keeping it contained was not doing anything to wake it up. Like kissing Mariah.

She reached for the knob and halfway closed the door. "I have to go."

"Where?"

She huffed out an impatient breath. "I have to *go*. And when I open this door, we are not talking about kissing. We'll eat dinner, Viorica will come for a visit, then I'll take a shower and go to bed. If you're in it with me, fine, but don't tell me again how much you want to kiss me unless you plan to follow through."

She didn't exactly slam the door, but she wasn't quiet about it.

I turned and went to the fireplace to wait for Mathilda, and think very seriously about whether Mariah's idea had merit, or whether I should go ahead and kill myself and be done with it.

CHAPTER 11

~~ MARIAH ~~

All the comfort Phoenix had given me about Viorica flew right out the window as soon as she walked into my room. Tonight, not only was she wearing her fake smile, her sweater was inside out, and her ponytail was crooked. I suspected she'd just come from Key's room, and while I didn't want to think about why her clothes were on wrong, I noticed she had puffy eyes. She'd been crying. I hoped Key was kind and helpful to her. If I ever learned he wasn't, I'd hurt him. I wished I could be helpful, but she was determined to treat me as an honored guest who was set to leave soon. She had no clue what had happened in my life since Sunday night, but she'd know soon enough, and for now, if it made her feel better to think of me as a guest on holiday, what was the harm? At least I was one less worry for her.

And she was extremely worried. She took a seat on the chair opposite mine and instantly began picking at the tear in her jeans.

Mathilda had walked in right behind her, bearing hot cocoa and oatmeal cookies, clucking as she set the tray on the desk. She stood straight and folded her hands in front of her apron while she said to Viorica, "I won't be easy until you are here with us for good."

"Just over a week to go," she said as the hole became an inch bigger. "Thank you for the hot chocolate." She beamed at me. "Mathilda's cookies are to die for."

"I know." I'd eaten my weight in them yesterday after snowshoeing.

"Enjoy yer visit, girls." Mathilda disappeared.

"I can't stay long," Viorica said, waving away the plate of cookies when I offered it to her. "I have a ton of homework."

"Why does doing homework matter if you're about to leave the real world?"

She shrugged and sat there stiffly, picking at that tear. "I can't help myself. It's a compulsion to do what people expect of me, and my dad thinks I'm going to Yale in the fall. He wouldn't understand if I blew off school. Besides, slacking isn't who I am. What about you, Mariah? Do you intend to go to college?"

I lied like I was born to it. "I'm saving to enroll at university next year. I'd like to be a doctor. A pediatrician."

She lied equally well. "How wonderful! You'll make an exceptional doctor."

I decided I hated this. I wanted to have a real relationship with her, and all the subterfuge was driving me crazy. For a hot minute, I considered fessing up.

But I didn't. I went along with her rambling, surface, pointless conversation for another painful twenty minutes – and ate the rest of the cookies – and when she stood and said she had to go, I hugged her more tightly than usual.

"Is everything okay?"

I clung to her. "I love you, Jordan."

Surprising me, she squeezed me so hard, my breath came out in a whoosh. "I love you, too, Mariah, *so much*, you have no idea."

Then she was gone and I had a premonition of something about to go horribly wrong. I passed it off as nerves over Lucifer's omen and seeing Viktor Petrov's lookalike face.

After I showered, I sat by the fire and read more of the romance novel I'd picked up earlier while I was waiting for Viorica. This one didn't hold my attention as well as the first two, maybe because the heroine was too perfect. I wanted her to have some flaw, some characteristic that made her human. I didn't get what the hero saw in her.

Then, around page forty, it became clear that she'd been programmed to be perfect because part of her brain was robotic. She'd had a head trauma in a car wreck and it was assumed she'd die, but the hero, who was her husband, had taken her to a crazy doctor who fixed her by replacing part of her brain with machinery. She was gracious and charming, entertained beautifully, had crazy hot sex with the hero, and never argued with him, no matter how belligerent he was. He picked fights on purpose, and she went along with whatever he said. The poor guy was crazy with grief, because he had his wife, but he really didn't. I was well and truly hooked by the time Phoenix came to my room, dressed in long cotton boxers and a motorcycle T-shirt. His feet were bare.

"Another one?" He came close and peered at the cover. "Why would a woman like that drive a race car? She's wearing a suit. It's a nice suit. But it's a suit."

"The hero is a race car driver. He thought he was invincible, but he had a wreck and she almost died." I told him the premise, and he was intrigued, so I read it to him until just past chapter ten, when he said, "It's late. Save the rest for tomorrow night." He watched me bookmark the page and set it aside. "Do you think he knew she'd be like that when he took her to the mad doctor?"

"At first, I thought it was because he wanted to keep her alive at any cost, but after what happened at the dinner party she hosted for his sponsors, I wonder if he wanted her to have no opinion of her own. She was against his racing before her accident. Now, she's on board, but it's obviously killing him she's such a robot."

"Be careful what you wish for?"

"Something like that." I eyed the book. "Isn't it a male fantasy to have a woman with no opinion, who goes along and does what she's told?"

"For some men, probably. Some would like a very strong woman who takes care of everything and tells *him* what to do. Still others want an equal partnership. And the rest would be happy with a sheep."

"You mean a woman who follows without question?"

"No, I mean an actual sheep." His black eyes were laughing. "I'm kidding. It's just that some guys are so awkward, they don't know what they want."

"Like Zee."

He nodded. "It's going to be insanely interesting when an Anabo lands in his life."

"He'll tell her he doesn't believe in love." I saw his questioning look and said, "He told me his views while we were waiting outside that club in Moscow." I smiled. "I predict she'll tell him she doesn't believe in it before he can. Then he'll try to prove her wrong."

"Like I said, it's going to be interesting."

"If you could choose, what sort of girl would you go for?"

His eyes were no longer laughing. "You do realize that's a loaded question coming from you?"

"You've already told me I'm out, and I have no expectations anyway, so just be honest."

He stared at the fire and said quietly, "She'd go with me to out-of-the-way places to see unusual, beautiful things, and try different foods, and meet interesting people, and sail and surf and ski and hike Everest and ride bikes across Mexico, and kiss me a lot, and never cut her hair, and tell me stories, and let me make love to her once a day and twice on Sundays."

"Never cut her hair?"

He looked at me. At my hair. "Every guy has a thing. Mine happens to be hair." He cocked a smile. "Of all that, the only thing you comment on is the hair?"

"None of it surprised me. Not even the hair, really. But I had to say something."

"You think you know me, Mariah?"

"I survived until now by being extremely observant."

"What kind of guy would you go for?"

"I wouldn't. I don't like guys."

"Only because you're afraid of them."

"I'm not afraid. I just know what they're all about, and I'm not interested." He looked as though he couldn't decide if he was sad or argumentative. The play of emotions across his handsome face was fascinating. "With one exception, I'd do all of your things, Phoenix."

"Then we'd be friends and not lovers."

"Isn't that what we are now?"

He was thoughtful before he nodded slowly. "Yes, we are."

"But you won't do any of those other things because you

think giving up everything you enjoy is what you have to do to make amends."

"Something like that."

"What about me? Suppose after I become immortal, when Eryx is no longer the threat he is now, that I do all those things? Would it bother you?"

"It wouldn't bother me."

I could see that it would, and he was lying. Remembering the day we skied, his grin, his laugh, his obvious enjoyment of every moment, I knew he was never cut out to be an indoor, bookish sort of person. Just like me, his love of books was solely because he'd figured out a way to live vicariously through fictional people. If he couldn't climb Everest, he'd read about someone who did. He built motorcycles for everyone else on Mephisto Mountain because he wanted one, but wouldn't allow himself. I wondered if he went to all the trouble just for the excuse of test-driving each one he built?

With a vague idea to shake him up a little, I sat up a bit straighter and went off, becoming more enthusiastic as I talked. "You know, if I have to stay here, I might as well take advantage of who and what I'll be. Key says he has piles of money, and with the ability to transport myself, I can go anywhere and do anything, can't I?"

"Yes."

"I always wanted to see the pyramids. I'll go there first, and land right on top of one, then I'll ride a camel, and eat lamb kebobs. After that, I think I'll learn to scuba dive and go to Australia and swim with sharks. I won't care if one bites me because I'd heal right away. Oh, and then I'll rent a Jeep and hire a guide and drive across the Outback. How awesome would that be? But first I have to learn to drive. Will you teach me?"

"I'll teach you." He was completely deadpan.

"There are thousands of museums in the world. I'll see them all, and go on a photo safari in Africa, and take a raft trip through the Grand Canyon, and ski in Switzerland. Maybe I'll jump out of an airplane." Just the thought of it made my heart race and my face flush with excitement. "Can you imagine flying through the air like that?"

"No." He looked depressed.

I kept going. "I won't want to do all of this by myself, so as soon as I become a Lumina, I'll get to know the others and find someone who'd like to go adventuring with me." What began as a way to point out that he should move past Jane and reclaim his life had turned into honest enthusiasm. I really could do all those things. I *would* do them, with or without Phoenix.

Suddenly, without consciously deciding, I was one hundred percent on board with staying with the Mephisto. I'd have to work, of course, but I'd have time off. I imagined all the marvelous things I could do and felt like laughing with joy.

He was staring at me.

"What?"

"You're happy right now."

"Yes. I'm just realizing that staying here will have definite benefits."

He stood and said abruptly, "I'm going to bed. I'm tired."

I got to my feet and met his gaze. "Why are you so aggravated? Would you like it better if I didn't do any of those things and never left this mountain?"

"Yes." He scowled. "*No.* Of course not." He turned and stalked to the bed, turned back the covers and waited for me to get to the other side. The lights went off, but I could still see because of the fire, which he'd stoked with a new log a little earlier. He peeled his shirt off and tossed it to the chair by the bathroom door, then turned and sat on the bed with his back to me. "Are you going to get in, or stand there and stare at me all night?"

He was beautiful. I couldn't stop staring. "You have the same tat that Zee does."

"It's a birthmark. We all have one." He looked over his shoulder at me. "When did you see Zee's arm?"

"He was getting dressed when I went to find you."

Olga jumped on the bed and meowed at him. "She's not understanding why I'm here."

"She'll get used to you in a bit." I petted her, then nudged her out of the way so I could get in bed. Once I was under the covers, he turned and stretched out on top of them, his very big feet just reaching the end of the bed. "Are you comfortable?"

He crossed his arms behind his head. "I'll be fine. Don't fret, okay? Just go to sleep and I'll be right here when you wake up."

I snuggled into the covers because I was cold, and frowned at Olga when she curled up next to Phoenix. "Traitor."

"She likes me." He was quiet for a while before he turned his face toward me. "You don't have to find a Lumina. I'll take you to do those things."

"That would be wonderful, I'm sure, but I wouldn't want you to change who you are on my account. You stay here and build your bikes and read and plan takedowns and be true to yourself. I'll be fine on my own. Or with a Lumina. Maybe Jordan would go with me. She's already been lots of places, though, so maybe not. Maybe Sasha. Or, you know, Zee would go with me. I think Zee and I are going to be very good friends."

"You don't want me to go?"

I heard the hurt in his voice, and while it bothered me to cause him any pain at all, I inwardly celebrated a small victory. He wanted to break free of his guilt so badly, wanted to live his life and find his own joy, but couldn't admit it. He would cloak his eagerness behind his supposed duty to me. I decided to let him. "Of course I want you to go. We're friends, right?" I snuggled in more. "Damn cat. She's my heater, and there she is next to you and you're not even under the blanket."

He moved around to get beneath the covers, upsetting Olga, who meowed then jumped off the bed. Before I knew what he was about, he'd turned me over and pulled me next to him, my entire back half surrounded by his big body. He had one arm around my middle, and his chin rested against the top of my head. "There. Now you won't be cold, and nothing and no one will bother you."

"You're not a heater – you're a furnace. Why are you so hot?"

"It's Hell."

"Oh."

He chuckled. "Not really. It's that we generate so much energy, we run a higher temperature than humans."

Olga jumped back on the bed and curled against my belly. I

fell asleep thinking this was about as close to perfection as it could get. If only I wouldn't dream, it'd be the best night ever.

Hours later, I woke in total darkness. The fire had gone out, and Olga wasn't on the bed. I wondered what had woken me, then I heard Phoenix mumbling. I rolled over and moved close enough to hear him, but he spoke in English. He sounded distressed and I could feel the tension in his body, which was completely out of the covers.

While I laid there wondering if I should wake him up, he whispered my name, then murmured English words, then said my name louder. He began to move against the sheets, rolling his head from side to side, calling my name while his arms twitched and his legs restlessly kicked. He became more physical and louder until he suddenly sat straight up with a sharp gasp. "*Jesus*," he said into the darkness just before he quickly reached for me, his hands roaming across my body. They stilled against my hip and he took a deep breath, as if he was relieved. He laid back at the same time he pulled me next to him and wrapped me in his arms.

I didn't say anything, didn't let on that I was awake. It seemed such a personal episode. He'd dreamed about me, that I was being harmed in some way, and after he woke and reassured himself I was fine, he nearly crushed me in his relief.

I stayed awake until his breathing became deep and even, and eventually, I drifted off again.

Then, I dreamed.

It was always the same. Always. Right down to the sound of the water pump's rhythmic *badump-badump* from the dye factory two blocks away and the smell of stale cigarette smoke that permeated every inch of Emilian's house. It was dark but for the yellow light from the downstairs hallway that filtered up and through the open door to my room. I always focused on his shadow on the wall because it was a featureless, silent monster rending the flesh of the shadow below – a girl who felt no pain, heard nothing, remembered nothing. I envied the shadow.

I fought. In my dream, I always did. I couldn't escape to the rug by the fire because in dreams, there is no escape. The horrors in my mind replayed over and over, every detail crystal clear. He smelled of vodka and vomit and an unwashed body.

He called me horrible things, said disgusting words, and the more he said, the more worked up he became. I fought harder and he went into a rage and grew more excited. Holding me down with the weight of his body, his cold, bony fingers pushed my T-shirt above my breasts and he pulled his knife from his pocket. I flung my fists at him and kicked and struggled to get away, praying that this time would be different. This time I'd escape.

I never did.

I finally stopped fighting and stared at the shadow and prayed to God that he'd cut me deep enough that I'd bleed to death.

He never did.

I flinched when the cold blade slid into my flesh and gagged on my own spit when his horrible hand pushed my legs apart, heard his guttural grunts and his demand that I move, fight, speak, scream, show my fear, give him what he wanted.

I remained still as stone and watched the shadow and prayed he'd die.

"Mariah, wake up."

A deep, warm voice flowed over me and I turned my head to see who had spoken. Phoenix stood next to the door. "You're dreaming. This isn't real. Wake up now."

I looked up from my bed and Emilian was gone. I tugged my shirt up to see my breasts, and they weren't bloody. I focused on Phoenix. "How are you here?"

"I came for you. I came to take you home."

Home. Yes. *Good.*

"You made him disappear." My voice had a note of wonder. I was awed.

"I will always make him disappear. Come on now and wake up."

Crossing the line from unconscious to awake, I realized I'd been talking, and so had he. I blinked my eyes open and he was there, right next to me, stroking my hair. He'd lit the candles in the sconces around the room, bathing everything in soft, warm light. My pajama top was above my breasts and I hurriedly began shoving it down, but he'd already seen. He held his hand against mine and stopped me. "Don't, Mariah. Let me fix you."

Squeezing my eyes shut, I whispered, "Can't you just forget that you saw?"

"I don't want to forget. Let me do this for you. I can't make it so it never happened, but I can erase this constant reminder."

How was he not revolted? I could scarcely stand to look at myself in the mirror, but when I was naked, I never, ever looked. "They're so . . . horrible. So ugly. You must be—"

"Sad. Also raging mad, but not letting it show because what's the point? All that can do is upset you." His hand rested against my ribcage and his thumb rubbed lazy circles against my birthmark. "I won't do this unless you say yes."

"How can you fix me?"

"I can heal any living thing." He came closer and kissed my forehead, my nose, my chin. "Will you let me?"

When I nodded, he raised himself to his elbow and gently closed his hand around my right breast. Many minutes passed while I felt heat pulsing into my body and when he moved his hand, my breast was smooth and pink without the jagged, puckered scars. He repeated with the left breast, and when he was done, he tugged my shirt down, slid his arms around me and pulled me close, pressing my cheek to his chest. We stayed like that for a very long time, me listening to the beat of his heart, Olga purring behind me, Phoenix squeezing me tighter and tighter.

I was half afraid he'd say he was sorry about what Emilian had done to me, or talk about how brave I was. I'd read so many accounts of adult survivors, I knew it was common when people found out about the past to try and lose the awkwardness, to smooth it over and make the person feel better. They didn't understand that nothing would make it feel better. This was something that was a part of me now, and while I accepted that, I also did all I could to not think about it, not dwell on it, and not let it be all of who I was. It was a part, but not the most important part because I wouldn't let it. I wouldn't allow Emilian to ruin the rest of my life. He'd had his time to torture and torment me, and he was no longer in control.

Except in my dreams, and I hoped as time passed, he'd show up less and less.

I should have known Phoenix wouldn't be like most people. He would never take the easy road. It made him difficult, but it made him real. He was the only person I'd ever opened up to, and not once had he reacted as I'd feared.

He didn't now. "Tell me what he did."

Just that simple. And just that complicated. *Tell me what he did.*

I knew he would ask again, and again, and later on, again. He wouldn't leave it alone until I told him. I was warm and relaxed and so close to him, our legs were entwined. Through the layers of our boxers, I felt the hot line of his penis against my pelvis, but it wasn't hard. It wasn't frightening. It just . . . was. "I don't know if I can get through it. I don't know if you can stand to hear it."

"Just tell me as much as you can. If you can say it, I will listen."

I began, hesitant at first, but he asked a million questions, and my answers led to more talking, and all the while, I was there next to him, in a cocoon of warmth and security. I didn't cry. The pain and horror of what Emilian had done to me was way beyond crying. It had forever altered me, and I had long ago grieved the loss of who I was before he raped me that first time.

"You hate him." He stated it as fact.

"With all my soul. Yesterday, when I thought Viktor was him, it all came back, every memory I worked so hard to lose. I was fourteen again with no way to get away from him."

"Why didn't you go to Marta?"

"He told me he'd kill anyone I told, then he'd kill me. I believed him." I pulled away and rolled to my back to stare up at the ceiling. "I wished I would die. I prayed he would die. When he did, I swore I'd never be like that again."

"Abused?"

"Dependent. If I'd had the ability to take care of myself, I could have left. I'd have run away and hidden from him and made my own way, but I knew what waited for me could be worse than him. The world isn't kind to young girls on their own. When he died, I was elated, and Marta was kind to take me in, but I worked for her, for my keep. I was sixteen when I went to work for Gustav and began earning real money. I saved all I could, hoping I'd have enough to live on my own. Then I decided to go to university, to become a doctor. My grades were very good, and I was always smart in sciences and math. Sophia, Gustav's fiancé, told me I'd qualify for scholarships."

He'd raised himself up to his elbow and rested his hand against my belly. "And now you're here, and everything's ruined for you."

I looked up at his face, at his black eyes and the shock of dark hair that fell across his forehead. "I won't lie and say I'm not upset about it, Phoenix, but my life never seems to stay on course. If I'm anything, I'm adaptable."

"Why aren't you angry? I don't understand how you told me all of this without anger. Is it that you hide it so well?"

"The night he died, I shouted at him. I threw things at him. I knew he wasn't going to live because he was helpless, lying there while the flames consumed the bed. It felt like I was burning up as well, and when I was so hoarse from screams and smoke that I couldn't speak anymore, I went to get Olga and the picture book and ran downstairs and out the door. While I watched his house burn down around him, I wasn't angry. I felt reborn, like I was new again. I remember it so clearly."

Turning my head, I looked up at the ceiling. "I let him die, and accepted that I'd go to Hell for it, but I made my peace with it. I'd spent all those years since my parents died being angry and resentful. Nadia and Emilian were just the most horrible, evil people, and I hated them, hated that I had to be there. I snuck out and went to mass every Saturday afternoon, and the priest listened to my confession and told me to pray for deliverance from my hatred. Then he'd say he would go to see them and try to intervene and I said no, because I was certain Emilian would kill him."

"Why wouldn't he have gone anyway? What kind of priest knows a young girl is being brutalized and doesn't do anything to help?"

"He only knew my first name, and they never went to mass, so he had no idea who they were. I was careful never to say their names because if he'd gone to see them, I was convinced

Emilian would kill him." I got up from the bed and walked around the room, pushing my hair behind my ears over and over. Something hit me and I wondered why I hadn't thought of it before. It would explain so much. "Was Emilian a lost soul?"

Phoenix sat up and rested his forearms on his bent knees. "M says no. He chose to be merciless and cruel, probably because he was severely abused by his father when he was young. He took out all that rage on you."

A rush of adrenaline coursed through me. The top of my head tingled, and I was breathless, as if I'd just run a mile. I stopped beside the desk to look across the room at him. "What does that mean? That it wasn't *personal?* He didn't actually hate *me,* he was just *mad at his dad?*" My voice grew progressively louder, until I was almost shouting. I couldn't help it. "I was small and helpless and therefore a convenient *punching bag?*"

"I'm sure he hated you. He hated everyone and everything, and blamed the world for all his difficulties. His father was somebody in the communist party before the Romanian revolution, and they had more money than most, but by the time Emilian died, he'd spent all of what his father left to him."

Breathing hard, my hands clenched, my heart raced, and I was so hot, I began to sweat. I continued pacing, my mind a jumble of scattered boxes, all the lids off, all the memories crowding into my head. "He never talked about his family. He never talked about much of anything. He'd stare at television for hours, and drink and smoke, and sometimes go out to buy more vodka. And eat. Nadia always cooked huge meals and they'd eat and I'd clean up, but only after she'd thrown all the leftovers in the garbage. She told me I was getting too fat and didn't need to eat. This from a woman who was three times Emilian's size. She'd bake – always baking, and it smelled so delicious, and she'd tell me if I would finish my chores in some impossible amount of time, I could have some. I never did, and she'd sit there like a giant cow and stuff all that food in her face and laugh at me. She'd laugh and laugh. And I was so hungry, I'd beg, like a ravening dog." I stopped pacing and sucked in a deep breath. "Sometimes, she'd take what she didn't eat and throw it in the yard, in the dirt, and I'd eat it, Phoenix. I ate dirt because I was *so fucking hungry*."

"How old were you?"

"It started when I was eight." I took off again, pushing my hands through my hair, shaking with rage or relief – I wasn't sure which. "I'd wait until they went to bed, then go to the rubbish bin and pull things out to eat. If I pilfered from the pantry, I was punished. She spent all day cooking, reading gossip magazines, and watching the TV in her bedroom. I loved going to school because it was a respite from them. I'd volunteer every day to stay after and do something for the teacher, and I think they knew, because they always gave me some task that would keep me there a little bit longer. I fainted once from hunger and a doctor came and after that, I had free lunches at school. She was very kind, and wanted to help, but when she came by the house to see Emilian and Nadia, they wouldn't open the door. He was so mad that she came, he locked me in the closet for a week. I used to pray to die. I wanted to die so much, and be with my parents, with God, where there's no pain and no cruelty." I grabbed the back of a chair and looked at him, at his handsome face, his dark eyes, and loved that there was no pity. No anger. Only acceptance. "But I didn't die. I just kept living."

"You're here now, Mariah. Nothing and no one will ever hurt you again."

I felt sick to my stomach. Shaky and anxious. "Talking about this is making me sad."

"And mad."

"And mad. Yes, mad. *Furious.* They had *no* reason, Phoenix. None at all. I was never a bad kid. I tried to make them like me, and it always backfired." I walked around the chair, back to the desk, to the bathroom door, and back again. "They called me Anna's accident because my mother was older when she had me. They said it was my fault my parents died, that they had to drive back and forth to Bucharest to find work to feed me and Viorica, and they were too tired because they were too old to have children, and that's why they had the wreck and died. Nadia said they were stuck with me, and I got what I deserved because I'd killed my parents. Who says that to a little kid? Who's that cruel and vile?" I stopped at the edge of the bed and met his dark gaze.

"You didn't believe them, did you?"

"A part of me did. I missed them so much, and Viorica. I dreamed about her every night, standing there crying while I left her. I made bargains with God. If I could stand what Nadia and Emilian did to me, he had to make sure Viorica was safe. I hated not knowing. I went back to the orphanage at least a hundred times, hoping to see her in the play yard, but I never did. I knew later that she was adopted barely three months after she arrived, taken to the United States, given a new name, a new family. I was certain she forgot me. And our parents. And I wasn't sad because that meant she also forgot Emilian and Nadia."

"Was he cruel to her?"

"If she got in his way, but I tried to keep her away from him. I couldn't always because he'd put me in a closet. I'd hear her scream, then cry for me, and it was more painful than when he hit me. I never regretted taking her to the orphanage."

"Why did he put you in a closet?"

"To punish me, but whatever I'd done wrong never made any sense to me. Now that I'm grown, I realize he got off on it. He got some sick twisted enjoyment out of knowing I was in there, suffering. So many times, he'd lock me up, sometimes for days and days, in the dark, with no food or water, no toilet. And when he'd finally let me out, I'd beg for water, and he'd be so mad because I'd have peed myself, and he'd take off that belt and hit me over and over because I'd soiled the floor. Nadia would make me clean it up, even though I could barely stand because I was dehydrated. If I passed out, she kicked me until I woke up. I was so glad when she died. Then we came home from her funeral and I was alone with him, and because she was gone, I was the one who cooked, who bought the groceries. He stopped locking me in the closet. He stopped shouting at me and hitting me. Instead, he came to my room when he wasn't too drunk and raped me, and the more afraid and angry I was, the better he liked it."

I focused on the painting above the bed, a pastoral scene of the moors in Yorkshire, blooming with heather. "I hate him so much, and you are *so* wrong that I didn't mean to kill him. I did, and I watched his horrible, cold, cruel hands shrivel up in that fire and felt nothing but joy. I laughed like an insane person, because I knew he'd never touch my sister, never hurt me again, and I will *never* be sorry I didn't save him. Never. I hope he's in Hell."

"He is."

"Maybe I'll be there, too, and maybe I'll deserve that, but it will be worth it. I'd dance with Lucifer himself if it meant sending the evil bastard to the lowest pit of Hell."

Phoenix murmured into the quiet of the room, "Rage of angels."

"What?"

"You're not going to Hell, Mariah."

Hearing something in his voice that wasn't simply a reassurance, I looked at him, only then realizing I had tears on my face. Ignoring them, I said, "How do you know?"

"I asked my father." He swung his legs over the side of the bed, got to his feet and came to me. He grasped my arms in his big, warm hands. "Emilian was dead already when the fire started. He had plans that night to kill you, and himself, but he was so drunk, he couldn't find his knife."

"He couldn't find it because I hid it."

"He lit a cigarette and had a stroke a few seconds later, fell on his bed, and it went up in flames. When you saw him, he was already gone, and people don't go to Hell for being glad someone kicked it, or failing to move a dead body out of a fire."

"But I didn't—"

"It doesn't matter what you did or didn't do. If my father says he's not coming for you when your time comes, he's not lying. He knows. Ease up on yourself, Mariah, and leave Emilian to Hell."

I blinked up at him, feeling such tremendous relief, I was exhausted. "Don't stare."

"Why? Are you embarrassed to cry? Don't be. You need to cry for a long, long time."

"I hate . . . crying."

"I know." Bending, he picked me up, then sat on the bed

and settled me on his lap to hold me close while I sobbed like a child.

CHAPTER 12

~~ PHOENIX ~~

She cried herself to sleep. While I held her soft body next to mine, I listened to the hum of Olga's purr and relived every moment of the past hour, since the instant I woke to the sound of her rapid breathing. She'd been straight as an arrow, stiff as a board, every muscle in her body tensed, and I knew what she dreamed, what was happening to her in her mind. I told her to wake up and she asked how I was there. Still asleep, she brought me into her dream. And Emilian disappeared. She lifted her shirt in her sleep to see that he hadn't cut her, and unknowingly showed me what I was certain no one had ever seen. No one but Emilian. Both of her breasts had been severely mutilated, large sections of flesh missing, healed over with angry red scars.

I drew her closer against me and swallowed hard, blinking back tears.

I'd never felt rage like that. Never. I have no idea how I had remained so calm, except that I was determined to focus on her, to help her. But Jesus God, in all the centuries of chasing lost souls and witnessing the horrors they inflicted on others, I'd never felt this kind of helpless fury, this bone deep grief. She was so soft and gentle. How could anyone hurt her like that? I couldn't fathom the pain she'd suffered.

Healing her had been almost impossible to do without losing it. I'd wanted to cry and shout and hit the wall and break things. She wasn't aware, but I had held her as close as possible and nearly squeezed her to death because it was all I could do to keep myself grounded.

Then she told me all the things he did to her and it was infinitely worse than anything I'd imagined.

M's words came back to me. *". . . nothing you've lived through in a thousand years of life could help you understand what she has endured, because you've never been overpowered or helpless. Let her use all that rage to her advantage. Teach her to fight."*

I'd thought altering her gentleness was the wrong thing to do, and I still wasn't completely comfortable with it, but now, knowing what she had to live with in her memories, I wondered if having the ability to kick ass and take names would make it better, make her feel empowered, even if only to fight in her dreams?

It made sense, but for one problem: me. It always came back to the problem of me. Mariah becoming Mephisto meant I was her only choice, and now more than ever, I knew I could never be with her. If I turned my back on my past, on what I owed to Jane, what I'd promised Lucifer, and went after Mariah, there would come a day when she'd know all my secrets. She'd despise me, and I wouldn't blame her, but by then, she'd be stuck with me, with no way out.

I looked down at her beautiful face and wished all over again that I was different, that I could deserve her.

But wishes are worth exactly what you pay for them.

I began to make a plan, and the more I thought about it, the more certain I was that this would work. It would kill me to do it, but my life was totally screwed anyway. I would do this for her, to make her whole again, and whatever it did to me, I'd just have to deal. If I couldn't deal, there was always death. And eternity with Lucifer.

I recognized that it might come to that without my death. What I planned would either go off without a hitch, or infuriate Lucifer so much, he'd take me out without blinking.

But I had to try. For Mariah.

When she stirred in my arms, I stood, turned and laid her on the bed. As I smoothed the covers over her, she opened her eyes and looked up at me solemnly. "You're upset."

"No."

"Liar." She closed her eyes. "I got carried away telling you things, and now I feel awkward."

"You can feel anything you like, but you should never feel awkward with me."

"But you've seen my . . . and I told you everything. I've never told anyone. I didn't even tell Father Michael about Emilian."

I sat next to her and held her small hand in mine, tracing the half-moon cuts with my finger, healing as I went. "You regret telling me because you think it changes how I see you, but it doesn't, Mariah. You're Anabo, intended for me, so it's my instinct to want you, and extremely difficult not to act on that. But it's more than just instinct. I genuinely like you. You're not afraid of me. You call me on my bullshit."

"Only because you said we should be honest with each other."

I reached for her other hand and traced the cuts to heal them. When I was done, I let go and stretched out next to her, propped up on one elbow so I could look into her face. "I don't feel sorry for you, if that's what you think. It's not in my nature to feel sorry for people, even an Anabo. I wish it had been different, and I wish I could fix you and make it all go away so you wouldn't be in so much pain, but as much as anything, I'm enraged, and even that has more to do with me than you. It grieves me that he's dead, only because I will never have the satisfaction of killing him."

"You would do that, even though he wasn't a lost soul? Wouldn't you be in trouble?"

"Lucifer has a strict rule against killing people who aren't lost souls, so yes," I slid my fingers into her so soft hair and rubbed my thumb across her lower lip, "I'd be taken out and sent straight to Hell. But I'd do it anyway, and he'd know who I am and why I'd want him dead."

"I'm glad he's already dead. I'd be sad if you went away."

"Would you?"

She nodded and looked at my mouth. "Are you going to kiss me?"

"Yes. Close your eyes."

She did, and her trust made me feel like crying again. Great God, between Key and I, we would turn the Mephisto into a pansy party. But I didn't cry. I bent my head to hers and took my time. Her scent was intoxicating. Her skin was smooth and tinged with pink in her cheeks, because she was anxious, maybe embarrassed. I touched my lips to hers, just barely, and even that tiny touch made my whole body tighten. I thought about viruses. I thought about algebra. I thought about a thousand things that would steer my mind away from where it wanted to go.

Feeling stronger, I turned my head slightly and kissed her. A sweet, chaste Jimmy Stewart movie kiss.

Redirecting my thoughts made no difference. Absolute awareness of who she was and what she'd been through didn't change anything. The sweetness of the kiss was irrelevant. Desire streaked through me, taking my breath away. I lifted my head, closed my eyes and prayed to a God who couldn't hear me to give me patience; give me what I needed to not screw this up. I'd known it would be like this. I'd known, but did it anyway. For her.

"Phoenix? Are you done?"

That made me smile, which did give me a drop of relief. I opened my eyes and looked into hers, noticing they were a shade lighter than they'd been only moments ago. "Not yet."

"I thought there must be more. Although that was very nice." She closed her eyes. "Do it again."

I did. Several times. Always gentle, no tongues. I was just thinking this was going okay, certain I had complete control over what lay sleeping inside of me, when she curled her arm around my neck and rolled to her side, flush against me. I'd failed to put my shirt back on, which meant the only thing between me and her soft, round perfect breasts was the skimpy top that went with her pajama bottoms. It was half falling off.

I imagined a tiny army in my head, lifting their swords and spears to Heaven, shouting *Freedom!*

They should have been shouting *Get away from her!*

Amazing what we can convince ourselves of when want collides with responsibility; justifications that would never hold up under rational scrutiny. I hadn't touched a female in a sexual way in 125 years. A pure-hearted Lumina would have been sorely tempted. I was a son of Hell, capable of unimaginable things. All I wanted to do was touch her. Just this once. What could it hurt?

I slid my arm around her, drew her still closer, and nudged her lips open with my tongue. The part of me that was standing back and shaking his head wanted her to be shocked and pull away. He was doomed to disappointment. Mariah touched my tongue with hers, hesitant for a nanosecond before she moved her head and took the plunge.

Our teeth bumped and she laughed against my mouth. "Is this the awkward part?" she whispered.

"It's the awesome part," I replied.

She kissed me again, and maybe she'd never done it, maybe I was out of practice, but damn it was hot. At no time had I ever enjoyed a kiss that much. The tiny army was cheering.

And other things were happening even more than before. I was becoming shaky, hot, and sweaty. My body wanted what it hadn't had in over a century; primed, ready, and beginning to be pissed off at me for not cooperating.

I know she could feel me. How could she not? Wasn't she afraid? I tried to move my hips back a little, but she followed. We were tighter than two coats of paint. "Mariah."

"It's okay. You said it does that even when you don't want it to."

So trusting. If she had an inkling what was racing through my mind, she'd shove me off the bed.

But she didn't. With her delicious mouth on mine, I slipped my hand beneath the thin fabric of her top to cup one breast.

The wee army went wild.

I unequivocally decided there was nothing in the world as soft as Mariah's breast; full enough to fill my hand, with a pretty pink nipple that grew tense beneath my fingers. I needed to stop, had to move my palm away from her perfect, lush . . .

She drew back an inch and looked right into my eyes. "You don't have to be nervous. You've already touched them once this morning."

"That was different."

Sliding her fingers through my hair to hold my head, she smiled up at me. "You fixed them. I think that gives you the prerogative to touch them if you want to."

If I wanted to? I'd give up breathing. "It doesn't bother you?"

"They've been hurt for so long, I tried my best to ignore them. I couldn't actually feel anything that touched them. Nerve damage, probably." Her eyes were sleepy and dreamy. "But now, your hand is so strong and warm, and that feels . . . it's just . . . lovely." Blowing my mind completely, she slid the top up and over her head and tossed it away. Her arms went around me, mine went around her, and skin to skin, we kissed again. The scent of heather was all around, making me euphoric.

Then the strangest thing happened.

All the tension drained away and left me with a feeling I'd never had before. I was at peace. I still wanted her beneath me, wanted to be inside of her beautiful body, wanted to make love to her until she knew what it could be, but the insidious demand of that dark and twisted part of me was gone. I was awed. The tiny army disappeared and all that was left was me and Mariah and this incredible, indescribable feeling of contentment. I had the extraordinary thought that I had come home. Finally.

"Phoenix?" she whispered.

"Yeah?"

"Do you feel weird?"

"I feel wonderful."

"It's hot." I started to pull away and she clutched me tighter. "No, I mean on the inside, like I drank tea before it cooled. And it's going all through my body."

Mephisto. She was already turning. Despite my determination not to, I thought of Jane, and remembered how many times we'd kissed, and how she was scarcely closer to Mephisto after three months than she'd been when we began.

But we'd never kissed like this. Jane would never have stripped off any article of clothing, much less her top, and pressed herself against me. If by some miracle, she had, she'd have felt my erection and completely freaked out.

Mariah was lying there smiling at me like I was the greatest thing in the universe, her tantalizing breasts pressed against my chest, her belly nestled against my very ready penis. She wasn't afraid. She trusted me.

After all that time, I suppose my cluelessness meant I was an obtuse ass, but I recognized that Jane had been nervous of me. Not afraid, exactly, but anxious. Wary. And it hadn't been because she was worried about sex.

She hadn't consciously known the truth, but her instincts knew.

My constant companion, Mr. Guilt, plopped himself right down there on the bed, but for once, I chose to ignore him.

I kissed Mariah again.

I have no idea how long we laid in her bed and kissed and whispered, but I know for sure it was the happiest I'd ever been. I didn't think about what would come, or how she'd change, despite the fact that I'd kissed her for just that purpose. I'd think about it later. At that moment, all I could focus on was Mariah and her soft, sweet lips, her slender, beautiful body.

Not until Deacon's deep, solemn voice announced, "Breakfast is served. Allah is good," did I remember reality.

I looked into her eyes, still dark blue, but far brighter than they'd been after Zee brought her home from Moscow. I hoped what I planned would work. She deserved happiness, unconditional love, and peace with her past. If I was successful, she'd have all those things.

I kissed her one more time. One last time. Forcing all emotion out of my head, I got off of the bed and retrieved my T-shirt. While I pulled it on, I lied to her. "I have to spend the day in Washington, working on the takedown we're planning for Jordan's birthday party. I'm sorry. I wish I could hang out with you instead."

"It's okay. I'm going to see Ty's animals this morning, and Denys offered to show me more of the mountain this afternoon."

"I'll probably not get home until very late."

"Will you come to see me?"

The hope in her voice nearly made me falter. I looked at her lying there, so soft and beautiful, and cursed my inheritance of M's faults and my inability to rise above them. "Yes, I'll be here." But by then, she wouldn't care. She wouldn't look at me as she did now. She'd look at me as she did my brothers – a friend. Nothing more.

Before I said goodbye, I bent and stroked her silky hair, catching her scent for the last time.

CHAPTER 13

~~ MARIAH ~~

For the first time in many years, I looked at myself in the mirror before I got in the shower. Running my fingers across the smooth skin of my breasts, I was still in awe of what Phoenix had done. Healing me was the greatest gift I'd ever received. Not only was the physical reminder gone, but giving voice to all the things I'd never even been able to consciously think about had made it not so horrific and frightening. His calm acceptance of what I'd stored in all my mental boxes was as incredible as it was freeing.

I was enormously grateful to him, but more than that, I was practically giddy with infatuation. I'd never felt anything like it, and wrapped it around me with all the wonder of a child. I didn't think about his constant reminder that we would only ever be friends. At that moment, I didn't care. Just being his friend was enough for me, although I admitted I'd be disappointed if he never kissed me again. I could never have conceived that kissing was so marvelous. Emilian had never tried to kiss me, and now I understood why. Kissing was an exchange of trust and affection, something that increased desire. What Emilian did to me was never about desire. It was about violence and control and hate.

Shaking myself, I forced him from my mind and concentrated on the warm, delicious feelings coursing through me. I was so glad my first kiss was with Phoenix. Someone who understood what it meant to me. It didn't hurt that he was most excellent at it.

I blushed and grinned as I turned to get in the shower, and

while I washed my hair, I hummed the Nora Jones tune Zee had played for me. For the first time I could remember, I felt at peace. Happy. Excited about the future.

By the time I made it to the dining room for breakfast, it was all but over. I was hungrier than usual, and must have looked panicked. Deacon said, "We never run short of food, Anabo. Sit and I will serve you." He disappeared.

I took my seat and moments later he reappeared with scrambled eggs and bacon, toast and fried potatoes. I thanked him and made no comment when he scooped an extra serving of eggs onto my plate. It was as if he knew I needed more than usual. I wondered how? Did I look different? I knew I *was* different, but didn't think it was outwardly evident. I could feel my body regenerating itself, the energy was incredible, and everything seemed in sharper focus. I could hear noises from the kitchen I hadn't noticed before. But I was certain I didn't look different, so I had to wonder how Deacon knew. He said as he placed more bacon on my plate, "Protein is most important. Never skip it."

I nodded and picked up my fork.

The only people left at table were Ty, Denys, and Sasha, and none of them appeared any different in their manner than before. They didn't know I was changing, which meant they didn't know Phoenix had kissed me. I was relieved. Whatever happened between Phoenix and I needed to remain between us. I couldn't deal with the rest of them talking about it. I had lived so long within myself, my thoughts known only to me, I would never be okay with others peeking inside my head, or my heart.

Sasha took a drink of coffee before she asked, "So what's on the itinerary today?"

Ty said, "I'm taking Mariah to see the animals."

Sasha beamed. "I love hanging out in the stables. Can I go with you?"

"Of course." Ty looked at Denys. "What are you doing this morning?"

The youngest Mephisto grinned at me. "Headed to Mountain Village to buy Mariah some cross-country skis. Snowshoeing is too slow, and I want to show her the other side of the mountain this afternoon."

Sasha's smile seemed less genuine. "Maybe you should wait until Phoenix can go with you. He'd probably like to show Mariah around over there."

"If showing her around was important to him, he'd have stayed on the mountain today. Mariah's leaving day after tomorrow."

Sasha became interested in the contents of her cup and Ty focused on smoothing marmalade on his toast.

I had the distinct feeling there was more subtext here than the lie that I was leaving, but Sasha and Denys were both smiling, and Ty concentrated on his food.

I continued eating and made no comment.

Half an hour later, after I'd gone upstairs for a coat, gloves and a wool cap, I met Ty and Sasha in the grand hall, and he reached for my hand to transport us.

We spent all the time until lunch in the stable and barns. I was completely captivated by the horses, goats, sheep, chickens, and the dogs and cats. Everything within the stone buildings was clean and neat, well maintained and clearly well loved. I met at least ten Purgatories who spent all of their time looking after the animals. In the corner of the smaller barn was an area used as a veterinary clinic, with various sizes of kennels and crates that held wild animals, including a possum, a baby owl, and what looked like a tiny wolf, but Sasha said was a coyote. They'd all been injured and were staying here until they were healed.

While Ty fed the owl through an eyedropper, I asked, "Why do you not heal them with your hands and let them go?"

"We're forbidden to heal anything unless we caused the injury." He looked up from the small owl in his big hand. "Or if it's an Anabo."

Thinking of Phoenix's hands on my breasts, I wanted to smile, but didn't, hiding my secret behind my usual expression that gave away exactly nothing.

After lunch, I met Denys in the mudroom on the ground floor at the back of the mansion, half expecting Sasha to show up and ask to tag along, especially after she suggested again at the table that Denys wait for Phoenix to take me to the other side of the mountain. No one else seemed to think it mattered, but I had a feeling she'd want to go with us.

She never appeared, however, so it was only Denys and I who struck out across the frozen garden, headed for the forest just beyond. It took a bit for me to get the hang of cross-country skiing, but it was enough like downhill that I caught on quickly.

The sun was bright in a sky more blue than I'd ever seen, and the mountain in snow was more beautiful than my mind could completely grasp.

Denys was his usual gregarious self, teasing me, joking, laughing when I went too close to a tree and a low branch dumped snow on my head. An hour into our adventure, he stopped next to a rushing stream, leaned against a boulder, and pulled a couple of energy bars from his jacket pocket. "Want one?"

Of course I did. I took it and leaned with him, watching the crystal clear water as it tumbled over the stones. "Are we heading back now?"

"Not just yet. There's something I want to show you."

Minutes later, we were on our way again, winding through the forest another half hour until we came upon a tiny log cabin in the center of a small clearing. It was picturesque in the snow, with a stone chimney, two small windows, and a covered porch that ran the length of the front. "What's this?" I asked. "Does a Lumina live here?"

"No, it's not part of Mephisto Mountain, even though it's above the Kyanos mists that keep people from finding us. It was probably built in the late eighteen hundreds as a rancher's summer rest when he came up to check his cattle."

"So it's empty."

He gave me an odd look. "No."

"Why are you being so mysterious?"

"I never knew it was here until a few months ago. I noticed Sasha was acting weird, so I followed her and this is where she came."

I looked away quickly. "Is this somewhere that she and Jax—"

He laughed. "God, no, nothing like that. It's not about Sasha at all. She's just the one who led me here. She doesn't know because I never told her, but I could see it made her nervous that I was bringing you to this side of the mountain."

"If it's not hers, or have anything to do with her, why would she care if we found it?"

He said as he skied away, "Come on, and you'll see."

I could never resist a mystery, and my curiosity was keen. As soon as we'd taken off our skis, we stepped on the porch and removed our boots, then Denys turned the latch and the door swung inward. In just my socks, I walked in ahead of him, unprepared for what was inside. Before I could compose myself and hide my reaction, I gasped, my gloved hand flying to my mouth.

It was exactly like the room in my mind, the safe haven I escaped to when I had nowhere else to go. There was the braided rug before the stone hearth, a small rocker set to one side and a larger one on the other. There was the painting of sheep in a meadow above the nicked, worn mantel. There was the odd dark stone in the midst of all the pale ones. Even the fireplace tools were identical. The only thing missing was Beet.

Denys stood close, his dark gaze watching me. "You look like you've seen a ghost. What's wrong?"

"Why did you bring me here? How did you know? How is it the same?"

"The same as what?"

I remembered myself and carefully concentrated until I had my expression under control. Smiling at him, I said, "It's very much like the family room in the house where I grew up."

"Not surprising. It's hard to make a cottage with a stone fireplace look much different than every other cottage with a stone fireplace."

Maybe so, but this wasn't a different cottage. This was the room in my head. But how? I'd never been here, never seen it. I was grieved that my memory of my home with my parents and Viorica was gone, replaced by this one room cabin in the middle of the Colorado wilderness. All the photos I had that were taken in our house didn't show the room – just Viorica and I, or Mama and Papa, not enough of the setting to know details. The braided rug in those photos was similar to this one, but I knew now that my escape wasn't that. It was this.

Still confused and upset, I looked at the rest of the room, noticing there was a bed with an old quilt in one corner and a hutch that held a microwave in the opposite corner. A very small refrigerator sat next to the hutch, and on the other side was a small sink with an ancient faucet. The remainder of the walls were covered with floor to ceiling shelves that held dozens of boxes in myriad sizes, from very small to dress boxes to hat boxes. Some were ordinary cardboard, some made of wood, and some covered with antique paper.

Denys removed one, lifted the lid and held it out to me. Inside was an assortment of ladies accessories from back in the day; a silk fan, opera glasses, elbow length white gloves, and a small tapestry coin purse. I looked up from the box. "Jane?"

He nodded, replaced the box, and pulled another one. It had a rose satin ball gown inside. The next held a parasol and at least a hundred handkerchiefs. In a hatbox was an enormous royal blue hat with a sprig of crumbling dried heather pinned to the crown. Next was a string of pearls and a cameo brooch.

I handed it back to Denys and wished he hadn't brought me here. I was confused, sad and feeling that much more less-than. So maybe Phoenix hadn't loved her enough to be redeemed – he'd loved her enough to live his life under a blanket of guilt for over one hundred years. He'd loved her enough to bring her things to this secret place and keep them safe and treasured. I glanced at the bed. Did he come here often?

"He disappears sometimes for a week at a time. We always thought he went to Yorkshire, to her grave, but now I think he comes here."

Denys took a seat on the big rocker. Rather than take the other, I pulled out more boxes, looking in each one, my heart falling further. Her entire life was here, stored away as if waiting for her to return. Did Phoenix sit in one of those rockers and stare at the boxes and imagine she was still alive? Did he wish she was still with him, that he'd had long enough to love her as he'd wanted? Did he take her things out and look at them, turn them about in his big, strong hands and remember her?

I opened a box that was filled with writing paper, her elegant script scrawled across the pages. I was wishing I could read English when it hit me that I could. It didn't come easy, but I read that first page on top of the stack and understood well enough. "This is a novel."

"It is," he said softly. "And that isn't the only manuscript. There are three others, and I've read them all. They're incredible. She was born in a time when women weren't encouraged to be anything but a wife, and their opinions were ignored or silenced completely."

I replaced the lid and slid the box back on the shelf. I pulled out another, some inner demon insisting I look in each one, torture myself until I'd examined the contents of every single box. This one held another gown, blue silk – the one she wore in the portrait in the grand hall. The golden, jeweled phoenix was nestled in the folds. I pulled it from the box and slipped it over my head, tucking it beneath the turtleneck of my sweater. The metal was cold against my skin.

Denys didn't notice. He waxed on about her amazing talent. "Her stories are about women of her era overcoming desperate situations. I wonder if she tried to get them published? Her work is so good, I'm certain she'd have found a publisher. It's not really surprising, I guess, because she loved to read, loved anything to do with literature. Did you know I'm a reader?"

I shook my head, only half listening. This box held a stack of photographs, a pictorial history of Jane's life. There were many surprises. Like Jane with a twin, and Jane in a wheelchair. I'd had no idea. Then she stood next to her parents, who were seated. No sign of her twin, and there was no doubt the girl in the photograph was Jane because she wore the phoenix around her neck. There she was, standing next to a Grecian column, holding the leash of a spaniel, the one in her portrait. I wondered if Phoenix had healed her? What happened to her twin?

While I continued obsessively pawing through Jane's pictures, Denys said, "My favorite things have always been books. My brothers assume whenever I leave the mountain that I've gone to a pub or a nightclub, and they're mostly right, but they don't know I spend a lot of time in bookshops and libraries. I see girls there and always wish one of them would be Anabo. Someone I could bring home to show our library, and she'd stay for that and be with me."

I heard something in his voice and glanced over my shoulder at him. His smile was gone, and I saw abject misery in his eyes. "Why did you bring me here?"

He was intensely uncomfortable, I could tell. He'd stopped rocking and sat stiff and still. He swallowed but didn't look away. "There's something about you, Mariah, something I've never known in anyone else. It's like . . . like you *know*."

I considered whether to sit down, but decided he'd have an easier time with this if I remained where I was, methodically pulling out the boxes to look inside. "I do know. I don't understand why no one else does."

"How do you know?"

"I can see it in your eyes. I can feel all that pain rolling off of you, and no matter how many jokes you tell or how hard you laugh, it never goes away. Why, Denys?" This box held a china doll, well loved, her little purple silk dress faded and her painted mouth all but gone, she'd been kissed so many times.

"I was in love with Jane."

Oh, God.

Sliding the doll back onto her shelf, I read the label on the next box: ST. CLAIRE MILLINERS, BOND STREET. Another hat. I almost didn't reach for it, but my compulsion to look in all the boxes had me slipping it from its spot.

"Did you hear me?"

"I heard." The lid came off and I said, "How is that possible, Denys? Zee told me the Mephisto can only be with an Anabo whose scent they know, that it's impossible for any of you to be attracted to one who has no distinct scent." I stared down into the box and wished so hard that Denys hadn't brought me here. A dried posy of tiny roses. Two golden rings tied with white satin ribbon. A small Bible bound in white leather, yellowed with age. A gossamer lace veil. And in the midst of it all, a love letter from a bride to her groom on their wedding day.

Dearest Phoenix ~ It's taken some time, but I realize now how barren my life would be without you.

"The night Phoenix brought her to meet us was the first time we'd seen Jane, and he'd found her over two months earlier. I was late, and drunk, but I remember feeling like I'd been struck by lightning, she was so beautiful. I stumbled and accidentally knocked her to the floor, and while we were there, I kissed her."

You are my dearest friend, and while it will be enormously difficult to leave this life, I'm filled with happiness to spend eternity with you.

"Was Phoenix angry?"

"Furious. What he didn't know, and I never told him, is that Jane kissed me back."

Reverend Moss has agreed to marry us in the bower we love in Hyde Park at nine this evening. It grieves me to become yours outside of a church, and the reverend was very clear that this will not be a legal union, but all of that is unimportant. We will be married before God and that is what matters.

"Did she visit again after that?"

"Yes, but I always made sure I was away from home. I couldn't take seeing her, knowing I could never have her. I hated Phoenix so much, and while I know that's unfair, I couldn't help it."

I love you all the more for agreeing to exchange vows before I am with you.

"You didn't fall in love with her after one very brief meeting, during which you drunkenly stumbled into her, knocked her down, and stole a kiss. You went to see her, didn't you? Behind Phoenix's back, you visited her."

He sounded defensive. "I went to apologize. It was entirely innocent."

"Not entirely. You wanted to kiss her again, didn't you?"

He sighed. "I wanted to steal her away and never come back. But I didn't, Mariah. We sat in her room and talked about books, and the world, and religion, and Eryx. I went back the next day and the day after that."

"And never told Phoenix?"

"No," he said solemnly. "When she died, I wanted to die too, but I could never say so, never show it. He's spent the past one hundred years rolling around in guilt, and I've spent them with a broken heart."

All the obstacles we have faced are gone now, Phoenix. We

will be happy, of one accord, and I will love you all the days of my life.

"What happened that night?"

"I've never known for sure. None of us do. I was in a London pub and, out of the blue, I was hit with acute awareness of something different, something awry. Even halfway to drunk, I was able to concentrate enough to know it was Jane. I knew where she was. Before that night, we didn't know about the Mephisto mark. A few hours later, Eryx abducted her, and we all knew immediately because she was in our heads. Phoenix was nowhere to be found, had even disappeared from a mental search, which is next to impossible. We were afraid he'd been taken out by Lucifer, but couldn't fathom why. It wasn't until we gathered before leaving for Romania to rescue her that he showed up, beat all to hell. He wouldn't say where he'd been or what happened."

You say you don't love me as you should, but I have faith that our friendship will become more as time passes. Passion comes in all colors, and we are both committed to defeating Eryx. We will build on our bond of high regard for one another and passion will follow.

What did that mean? This read like she was trying to convince herself that this was the right thing to do. Passion will follow? Did she mean she felt nothing for Phoenix beyond the love of a friend?

Intuition nagged, and I had to ask Denys, "Did Jane have a particular scent?"

"Sometimes, when I was with her, I'd smell cloves. I wanted to believe it was because she was meant for me and Phoenix got it wrong, but she had a little doll that was stuffed with cloves."

Thinking of oranges, I asked, "When you find your Anabo, I wonder if you'll have a certain scent to her?"

"I don't know. Jane told me once that I smelled like laundry, like freshly washed sheets drying on the line in the sun. We laughed because can you see me doing laundry?"

No, but I could see him with Jane. "When you went to Romania, was she . . . had Eryx already—"

"No. He waited for us. The fucker knew we'd come after

her, and as soon as we appeared, he cut her throat. Phoenix ran for her, caught her before she hit the floor, and tried to bring her back, but she never responded. He took her to her home, to her room, and laid her on her bed for her parents to find. Her father hired Pinkertons to investigate, but of course they found no suspect. The morning of her funeral, without telling us, Key took her body from the casket and replaced it with stones. Her parents buried a weighted coffin in the churchyard, in holy ground, at the same time Key and a group of Luminas buried her in a plot close to our home in Yorkshire."

That choked me up. Key knew how important it was to visit the dead, to have a place to grieve. He did it for Phoenix. Key was a hard guy, quiet and serious, but his love for his brothers and his commitment to his leadership of the Mephisto was obvious in everything he did. I thought all over again that he and Viorica were perfect for one another. And I remembered what Zee had said about God never sending an Anabo who wouldn't be compatible.

Phoenix's list of things he'd like in a girl came back to me: *She'd go with me to out-of-the-way places to see unusual, beautiful things, and try different foods, and meet interesting people, and sail and surf and ski and hike Everest and ride bikes across Mexico.*

Everything I'd seen in Jane's boxes indicated a homebody, a woman who loved to read and write and play the piano and have tea with close friends in the cozy comfort of her morning room. I knew from the handbills and newspaper clippings I'd seen in the boxes that she was passionate about social change in England; helping the poor and saving women who'd been forced into prostitution in order to feed their children. She'd been handicapped, which would have affected her interests, but in all I'd seen, in every box, and I was close to the end of them, there wasn't anything to indicate she had the slightest curiosity of anything like climbing Everest or visiting unusual places. Even after she was healed, she was content to be home. She was not the adventurer Phoenix wanted.

So why would God send a girl like Jane to him?

I was terribly afraid he had not, that Jane was intended for Denys and by some twist of fate, some awful screw-up in the cosmos, a tragic mistake had been made.

"Do you visit her grave, Denys?"

"Sometimes. Mostly when I'm positive Phoenix won't be there. I hate myself for feeling this way, Mariah. You have to believe that. As much as I get pissed off at Phoenix, and think he's carried on the guilt trip for way too long, and resent that Jane was his, he's my brother. I'd never do anything to hurt him, and if he knew how I felt, and still feel, about Jane, it'd kill him."

I began to wonder if Phoenix knew, if he figured out that Jane wasn't for him. If so, was it any wonder he could never escape the guilt? Not only had she died because he wasn't on top of things, he'd taken a girl meant for his brother. And she died.

It was all purely conjecture, of course, but I knew there would come a time when I'd have to ask Phoenix for the truth about Jane. If I could open up and tell him about Emilian, he could tell me about her and the night she died.

For the moment, I reminded myself that Denys didn't know I was aware that I was Anabo, or that I was intended for Phoenix. Maybe that's better, I decided. He'd be more open and honest because he'd assume I had no vested interest in Phoenix or his past. "Why couldn't he bring her back?"

"Eryx claimed he'd replaced Phoenix's mark with his own, and we assumed that was why, that if an Anabo is marked, she can only be brought back by the one who marked her."

Maybe she could only be brought back by the one who was her intended. I imagined how it had been, learning Eryx had raped her, the horror of seeing her murdered right in front of them, Phoenix's desperation to bring her back, and her dying in his arms. Had he known then? Was it too late for him to see which brother was her intended, to see if he could bring her back? Or had he known in that moment that it would never be right if another of his brothers brought back the woman who loved him? And she did love him, I didn't doubt for a second. It was a sweet, deep love, not one of strong desire and passion, but Jane was still young, and totally innocent.

How had she felt about Denys? He said she kissed him back. Had she wanted to kiss him again when he came to visit?

I would never know.

And perhaps in the grand scheme of things, it didn't matter. She was gone, and it was time for Phoenix to let go of her death. I would confront him with all I'd learned, and make him face it, make him talk about it. Not for me, and not for what might come to pass between us, but for him. He needed to let go of this crushing burden he'd carried around for more than a century.

And for Denys. Turning away from the shelves with all the boxes that held another woman's life, I watched him stare up at the sheep picture, his hands clenched around the armrests of the rocker.

Out of nowhere, I remembered the night I met Phoenix, when he came to my room to apologize. He'd stared at me with that strange yearning I didn't understand, but it spoke to something in me and there was a connection. I understood now. Maybe it was instinct, maybe it was a divine promise, or maybe it was simply fate, but a bond was formed between us that night, and nothing in the days following had done anything but build on it. I trusted him, and for me that was huge. I didn't trust anyone, even those closest to me, like Gustav.

Yet, in a very short period of time, I'd grown close to Phoenix, had slept in the same bed with him, had shown him what I kept in the boxes inside my head.

Had this been what happened between Denys and Jane? One moment, one look, one unspoken connection. Not love, because love was so much more – but an indefinable tie that couldn't be broken by time or another person or even death.

My heart broke for him. As difficult as it had been for Phoenix, it was in some ways worse for Denys. He'd been unable to grieve openly, had kept all of it inside. Until now. I went to him and stroked his hair. "Let's get out of here. We'll go somewhere and talk. You can tell me all about Jane, and maybe you'll feel better."

He looked up at me and smiled, but not his fake one that hid his true feelings – this one was real. "I could use a whiskey."

He had a serious issue with alcohol, but now wasn't the time to give him a lecture. "Come on, then, and we'll get one."

Outside, we put our ski boots on, gathered up our skis, and

he popped us back to the mansion. I went to my room and slid into a pair of regular boots, then met him in the grand hall. "Where can we go?" I asked.

"I want to take you to my favorite pub."

"But I'm not supposed to leave the mountain. Can't we just get your whiskey and go somewhere here, somewhere private?"

"Nowhere here is private. It'll be fine, Mariah. Trust me."

He reached for my hand and seconds later, we stood on the sidewalk outside the Rose and Crown. "Is this London?" I looked all around me, at the beautiful buildings and the pedestrians out and about at midnight. A double-decker bus passed. Excited and eager, I asked, "Can we go around and see some things?" It would be awesome to see Big Ben at night. And the Thames. We could stand on the bridge at the Tower of London and watch boats pass beneath.

"Maybe later," he said, tugging my hand. "Let's go inside."

I followed and we took a seat in a booth not far from the bar. The pub was fairly crowded, most of the tables occupied, some guys standing in the corner, laughing. It was lovely, with lots of gleaming wood, brass, and thick, bottle green carpet. I wished Gustav could afford to fix his place up like this. He tried to make improvements, but money was so dear, he'd not been able to do much. His enthusiasm almost made up for it. I had no doubt he'd someday own a nicer pub than what he now had. I would miss him in some ways; not in others. He was my past, and even though he'd always been kind to me, protective even, he was a reminder. Not that I'd ever forget, but after this morning, I realized for the first time that I could eventually put it behind me, could lose the pain of it.

Thanks to Phoenix. I inwardly smiled, wondering what he was doing at that very moment. Was he in the White House? Would he come to see me tonight? I felt a little breathless, thinking about it. I hoped he'd kiss me again.

A pretty blond girl arrived almost immediately, and she knew Denys. Quite well, it appeared. She was smiling at him very happily. "I haven't seen you in a while."

"I've been busy," he said with a grin and a wink. "Brianna, I'd like you to meet my cousin, Mariah, from Romania. This is her first time in London."

She smiled at me. "How d'you do?"

"Fine thanks. It's nice to meet you."

"I know what this one wants," she jerked her head toward Denys, "but what can I bring for you?"

"I'd love some tea."

As soon as Brianna left, Denys lost his smile, gazing at me soberly. "He kissed you, didn't he?"

I didn't answer.

"You just spoke perfect English, Mariah. I'll ask again – did he kiss you?"

I hadn't realized. Speaking English had been automatic. I supposed there was no point dodging the question. I'd outed myself without thinking. "Yes."

"So you know."

I nodded.

"Are you going to stay?"

Again, I nodded.

"As Mephisto? Are you going to take the jump and be one of us? Are you going to be with him?"

I hadn't thought about it since this morning, since Phoenix kissed me and began my metamorphosis into Mephisto. He'd said I might like it, and I began to understand what he meant. I was energized, hyperaware of things I'd never noticed before, and the fear that never left me, whether conscious or subconscious, was at a low simmer instead of close to boiling over. Not feeling so afraid of the world, of life, of what was always in my head, was pretty righteous.

"I'm not sure," I said honestly. "I'd thought to be a Lumina because Mephisto means I have to kill people. I still don't know if I can do that, but things are . . . not quite the same as before."

He was clearly bitter, his dark eyes filled with anger. "He'll never let you not be Mephisto, never let you get away from him, surely you know this. Maybe you think he's not so bad, maybe he's been nice. I'd assume so if you let him kiss you." He leaned forward and grabbed the hand I'd rested against the table, squeezing hard enough to hurt. "He'll never leave you alone. *Never.* If you have any sense of self preservation, get out while you can. Lose Anabo. Go back to your life. Don't stay with him."

"Let go of my hand."

He released me and sat back, his grin instantly returning with the arrival of Brianna and our beverages. He flirted with her. She flirted back. There was a suggestion of later. I wondered how many girls Denys had slept with in his lifetime? And I wondered if they all hoped for something more, or were they content to only be a sexual release for him? Then I wondered why I was so judgmental? It wasn't like me and I was disturbed that I wanted to tell her she should stay away from Denys, that he would never be serious about her and she was wasting her time, her kisses, her body.

I concentrated on my tea, plopping the silk bag in and out of the wee teapot, hurrying up the steeping. And all the while, I chastised myself. I had major issues with sex, which was understandable, but knowing I had a problem and dealing with it were two entirely different things. I hoped I wasn't always so freaked out by it, or critical of girls who liked sex for what it was and didn't attach any significance to it. Maybe Denys was good at it. Maybe Brianna knew it. Maybe she liked sex and didn't have any expectations beyond getting naked with him.

When she was gone again, I looked up and met his gaze. "I don't understand your anger."

"He destroyed Jane. He took her to bed, then abandoned her. Why was she alone that night? If I found an Anabo meant for me, there's no way in hell I'd leave her within an hour of our first time. He didn't love her because he's incapable of it. Please, Mariah, save yourself from an eternity of misery. Lose Anabo and live the rest of your life like ordinary people."

"What about my sister? Have you forgotten her? If I go back to my life, I'll never see her again, and we've only just found each other."

"Key will grant an exception for her to visit you. Even if he doesn't, she'll do it anyway. Jordan will do what she will and Kyros needs to get used to it."

I poured the tea into the cup and took a sip. It was marvelous. "Why do you think Phoenix is incapable of love?"

"Because he had the chance. He had Jane, and she was

perfect. Beautiful, smart, educated, funny, kind and absolutely loyal. He couldn't love that, so what does that say about him?"

"It says she wasn't right for him."

"She was his intended."

"Says who?"

"Says God. He sent Jane for Phoenix and not only did he not love her, he let her be murdered."

I was already tired of the Mephisto, and not because they were sons of Hell, eternal bad-asses charged with saving the world, which gave them a certain aggravating arrogance. No, I was tired of the guy thing, and they were so steeped in testosterone and over a thousand years of striding across the planet with absolute entitlement because of their size, their looks, and their sheer strength, they failed to understand simple human interaction. Dialogue. Conversation. Discussion. Why talk it out when they could simply launch themselves at one another and roll around on the floor and punch and kick and curse and shout?

"You look like you're disgusted."

"I am. With the lot of you. Over a century has passed since she died. You silently grieve, he stalwartly feels guilty, and I don't doubt the others are equally tightlipped about it. No one, in all those years, has ever talked about what happened to Jane. You say you have no idea where he was that night, or why he was beaten when he finally showed up. Did it ever occur to you to ask? Did you never consider just telling him how it was with Jane? Maybe he'd be hurt, or feel betrayed, but it's better than having this huge, festering secret between you. You're so filled with rage toward him, you're trying to get me to leave. Listen to yourself, Denys. Would the others want me to leave? Jordan told me there are no other Anabo, that we're so rare, she thinks maybe M asked God to send more. Would you wish your brother, who you claim to love, to have no one for all eternity? Because I'm it for him. And maybe it's unfair that he's had two Anabo, but how can you be sure he has? How do you know Jane wasn't intended for you, all along? Maybe he didn't know. Maybe you guessed at it. But you'll never know, and you'll never move past it if you don't *talk to him*."

He blinked at me. "And here I thought you were more the

202   STEPHANIE FEAGAN

quiet type."

"Not hardly." I drank more of my tea. "Can we get something to eat? I am starving."

He waved at Brianna, who hurried over. "Bring my cousin some fish and chips, with mushy peas. Bring a slice of steak and kidney pie, as well. And if you have any left, let us have some treacle cake."

As soon as she'd flirted a bit more and left, he settled back and drank his whiskey, watching me drink my tea. "You're kind of a surprise, Mariah. I wonder what goes on in that head of yours?"

If he only knew. I shrugged. "We all have our crosses to bear, don't we?"

"I'm a son of Hell. No crosses for me."

I told him my thoughts about religion and he was surprised, I could tell.

He told me what he thought, and it was my turn to be surprised.

The food came and it was delicious. He ordered more whiskey.

Time passed, he drank more and became tipsy, then drunk. Our conversation swung between serious and funny, and at some point, others gravitated to our table, pulling up chairs, laughing and cheering when Denys ordered round after round for everyone in the pub. He told joke after joke, flirted with everyone there, held them in the palm of his hand, and all the while, through his drunken, raucous laughter, I saw the pain in his eyes.

After my second pot of tea, I had to go to the ladies. I excused myself, and one guy said with a warm smile, "Don't be long." For the first time in my life, I didn't feel an underlying threat. Not that I believed every male who showed an interest in me was threatening – just that he was, by virtue of being male, a threat.

I nodded and struck out for the restrooms, located down a narrow hallway just past the bar. In the ladies, when I was done, while I stood at the sink to wash my hands, I was suddenly aware that someone else was there. And the door hadn't opened.

Alarmed, I reached for it and the lock turned, right before my eyes.

Wheeling around, I saw a guy in a pale pink dress shirt and dark gray trousers casually leaning against the wall, hands in his pockets. He was almost as good looking as Denys, and bore a striking resemblance to Key – to all the brothers. His hair was black as midnight, nicely cut, his jaw was covered with a light stubble, and his black eyes were dead, without a spark of life. Beyond creepy, they were disturbing. Even terrifying. And yet, I didn't feel so very afraid, despite who he was.

"We meet at last." His lips curved into a slight smile, almost wry. "Hello, Mariah."

"Hello, Eryx."

CHAPTER 14

November 6, 1888
Yorkshire

I drop my arms and step back from Jane. I will the candles on her desk to light, and we stare at one another. "What happened tonight?"
"I was hoping you didn't notice."
"Why would you kiss my brother like that? Why is it never that way with me?"
She moves to the chair by the window and sits, her back ramrod straight. Is it distress, or her corset? I decide I hate fucking corsets.
"I felt sorry for him. He was so embarrassed and humiliated, my heart went out to him."
"You feel sorry for lots of people and you don't stick your tongue down their throats."
She scowls at me. "There's no call to be crude."
I stalk closer to her chair, angry and frustrated. "You didn't kiss him because you felt sorry for him. You kissed him because you wanted to, because you felt an instant attraction to him, the second he appeared. Isn't that true?"
She looks up at me, meets my gaze directly. Boldly. I'm a little taken aback. Jane is never bold. "Very well, I won't deny it. Yes, I was instantly attracted to him. What difference does it make? I love you, not him. Are you going to carry on like this every time I'm attracted to another man? Because you should know, I've been attracted to a number of other men."
"Again, I'll point out that you don't kiss men you find attractive. Until tonight." Remembering, my heart squeezes.

"That was hurtful, Jane."

She's instantly on her feet, sliding her arms around my middle. "It was nothing, Phoenix. I'm sorry. He kissed me, and I responded. I'm only human, after all."

I bend my head and kiss her and this time, it's better. It goes on for a while and gets even better. When I lift my head, she blinks up at me. "It's just all new to me. You and yours, walking again, and learning to live with what happened to Georgiana – it's a lot to become accustomed to." She pulls away and turns around. "Will you undo me?"

My lascivious mind takes that way past what she means. While I'm unbuttoning her, sliding the gown down her body to pool at her feet, then unlacing her corset to toss it aside, then reaching for her shift to pull over her head, my mind already has her in the bed, beneath me, crying out, kissing me with uninhibited desire and passion.

She turns to face me, clearly shy about her nakedness. I stare, unable not to. "You're so beautiful. I don't deserve you."

"Do not start that again. It's such a damper." She steps around me and goes to the bed to retrieve the night-rail she'd left there earlier. I catch one last look at her sweet body before the thin fabric hides her from me. She moves to her dressing table, sits and begins to remove the pins from her hair. I watch, mesmerized as golden curls fall one by one to trail down her back. She begins to talk and I can scarcely pay attention, I'm so caught up. When she's done with the pins, she picks up a hairbrush and pulls it through her curls, slowly, carefully, apparently oblivious to me watching. She is still talking, and I realize she's telling me something important.

". . . another month, and spend that time getting to know your family. I also want to learn more about Eryx, and the people who follow him. I can't understand why someone would turn their back on God and pledge themselves to a charlatan."

"They don't know he's a charlatan. He's very charming and people trust him because he fakes sincerity so well. He tells them God has abandoned humanity and they look around at all the suffering and they believe him. He offers them the achievement of all they think they need to be worthy, and it's always based on whatever it is they feel is missing in their life.

Georgiana was convinced she needed the adulation of every aristocrat in England, and your infirmity was holding her back. To most anyone, this is shallow, but to her, how she was seen by others was all important. Eryx has the unique ability to see through a person, to know what they want, and he's cunning in his method of convincing them he can give them what they need to get what they want."

She begins to braid her long hair and I realize I've missed the opportunity to touch it, to comb my fingers through its softness. Next time, I promise myself.

"Let's try again on Friday night," she says, finishing the braid, turning to face me. "We'll forget tonight and start fresh."

I nod my agreement, but I know I won't be able to forget watching her kiss my brother.

~~ PHOENIX ~~

It was rare for me to be afraid of anything, but I almost chickened out and popped back to Mephisto Mountain. All that kept me going was remembering Mariah's soft voice, telling me the horror that was her life; remembering Jane's beautiful face as she died, her eyes filled with her heartbreak.

Grave injustice was mine and I owned it a long time ago, but not until now did I have the chance to make it right.

That it meant meeting Lucifer again was terrifying. The last time, his minions had rearranged my face and pulverized most of my internal organs. And while the dark overlord vented his rage at me for my deception, Eryx was abducting Jane, taking what made her Anabo, stealing all hope of her resurrection. He was able to do that because of me, because I'd held on to her, knowing she wasn't mine to keep.

In the alley of St. Paul's Cathedral, moments after I'd been climbing the steps to go inside and end everything, Lucifer had told me I wouldn't be allowed to die unless and until I admitted the truth to my brother, and made amends to Jane. He went still further and said when and if I found an Anabo meant for me, I could never have her until I'd met his demands. Incapable of any kind of filter, lying in the filth of the alley, my body broken and my spirit destroyed, I'd pointed out that my disappearance was best for everyone. He hauled me to my feet and said, "Only best for *you*. Of all your brothers, you are most like your father." He shook me until my bones rattled. "Compassion is not a means to an end. Sacrifice isn't about *you*. Love isn't a prize to be won." He tossed me back to the puddle of refuse. "Make this right, Phoenix. Live your life with honor. Then come and talk to me about what's best for your brothers."

He disappeared and I laid there and stared up at the stars in the narrow strip of sky between the buildings. I could still feel Jane, knew she waited for me. While I wondered how I could ever make things right, her presence in my head felt different. I sat up and concentrated more carefully, and I knew. She was in Romania. Eryx had taken her.

Her murder made half of my promise to Lucifer invalid, and the other half . . . I hadn't seen the need to tell him. Jane was gone and it was all my fault. He would hate me forever, and while I certainly deserved his hatred, I knew it would cause enormous problems within the Mephisto. It would alter trust and we depended on trust to do what we did. What was the point?

And so I never told him. Someday, I would, but not yet. I wondered if Lucifer would punish me for putting it off. I was awash in fear, despite knowing he was always painstakingly fair. I acknowledged my fear wasn't of what he might do to me, but what he would say. I'd never known shame as I had the night Jane died. No physical pain could compare.

Lucifer was very good at shame. It was one of his reasons for existing.

Humans believed he was a tricky chameleon who'd suck the souls from the unwary, the unfaithful, and the sinners, but that was all bullshit.

Lucifer was the reason for the darkness of humanity. His existence instilled the pull of evil that resided in every human soul other than the Anabo. He was the dark to Heaven's light, the down to God's up, the balance of choice. And yet, nothing in any written or spoken word came close to the actual being who was Lucifer. People forgot he was once an angel, closer to

God than any other. I didn't know why he fell. All I knew for sure was that he didn't exult when people did bad things. His was not an existence of triumph, but of sorrow, grief, and eternal penitence. He wasn't about gathering followers. The groups of people who thought to worship him were laughable, if only because they had no clue who it was they lauded. He was the reason humans had the choice between right and wrong. He was man's conscience. Whatever perversions and horrors they committed against one another was entirely their own choice. And if they remained unrepentant, they would spend eternity with Lucifer, not in a fiery pit, but a dark, cold place where there was no dignity, no love, no solace.

Unless they gave their soul to Eryx, ensuring a future more dark and grim than Hell. If we failed to capture them, their soul would cease to exist when they died, absorbed into his to bolster his quest for domination of all.

I'd spent most of the day revisiting old haunts, standing at Jane's grave, walking through the frozen dead gardens at the Longbourne estate. I tried and failed to figure out a way to make things work with Mariah. I wanted her with all my soul, would have done anything to stay with her, but she deserved so much more than a lying piece of shit like me. And once she knew what really happened with Jane, she'd despise me. Better that I step back and leave her alone.

And so I wound up in the Arabian desert in the middle of night, chanting the ancient words that would open the gates to Hell on Earth. It was all I had, the only possibility of calling Lucifer. He would know the absence of any Skia or lost soul, and pay close enough attention to realize I wanted to talk to him. Would he come? I didn't know, but I had to try. If this didn't work, I'd be forced to call M and solicit his help, which would mean telling him everything – and Lucifer's rage couldn't compare to my father's if he knew the whole truth.

Lucifer had a flair for drama, and he didn't disappoint. The wind began to blow ferociously and lightning crackled across the cloudless night sky. In the midst of stinging sand, I ceased chanting and lowered my arms to wait, but instead of Lucifer appearing, a piece of paper flew at me, plastering to my chest. I peeled it off and saw that it was a handbill from 1968 for a

Beatles concert at the Royal Albert Hall in London. It was an odd place for a meeting, but I wasn't about to question it.

Folding the handbill into my coat pocket, I popped myself to London and landed just in front of the beautiful round hall Queen Victoria had built in memory of her husband. No one was about. It was almost one in the morning, and I stood well away from pedestrian thoroughfares next to the huge statue of Prince Albert at the top of the steps to the south entrance on Prince Consort Road.

A voice came to me from the other side of Prince Albert. "You've more nerve than any of your brothers, Phoenix. I'm not quite sure if this elevates or lowers you in my regard."

He stepped out and I was instantly freezing. It was cold in London and the sky threatened snow, but this was a different kind of cold. This was the coldness of death, absolute and eternal. "Do you know why I'm here?" I asked him.

"Not entirely, and I could guess, or mine your mind, but I believe I'd rather you tell me why you've called me into the light."

He didn't have a memorable presence. He had face and form, but I forgot it even while looking at him. I questioned my fortitude, yet again, and clung to thoughts of Mariah. And my brother.

I didn't preamble, didn't go into any explanation. There was no need. He knew everything. "I want Mariah to be his."

"You're assuming I can do this, even though she was made how she is by God, and sent specifically for you. He will have his, someday, but it won't be Mariah. She is for you and it's not in my ability to change that. You need to ask God."

Was he joking? No, couldn't be. Lucifer was many things, but not a jokester. "He can't hear me."

"I'm aware."

"Then how can I ask?"

"You can love her, find your redemption, and talk to God for hours on end. He'll hear every word."

"But then—"

"You'll love her and have to give her up. Ironic, yes? You took what was your brother's, and now, to repair what you destroyed, you'll have to sacrifice what you want most, what's yours to have, if only you deserved her. You'll love her, but have to watch her with him all the rest of your life, and know that it would have been different had you not given in to your selfishness. I wonder, when it comes down to it, if you'll give her up for him? Or will your basest nature, what makes you Mephisto, rise up again and deny justice?"

I honestly didn't know.

"Your first step, to exemplify sincerity in your quest, is to tell him. You've procrastinated this duty I demanded for well over a century. If you fail in this, I can't help you at all and, even were you to love her and be redeemed before God, he won't take you at your word. Lies and secrets between brothers are as gangrene to a limb, eating away at the lifeblood, killing it. Come clean, Phoenix. Once you do that, you can move forward."

"He'll despise me. He'll never trust me again."

"Man up. Tell him."

I swallowed, imagining his reaction, already hurting for him, for the pain I would cause.

"Not everything is as it appears, you know. Sometimes the truth is colored with prejudice and arrogance."

"What does that mean?"

He moved closer and I shivered from the bone-chilling cold. "You have an insurmountable hurdle just to love her. You feel affection and lust, as you did with Jane. You grieve for Mariah, for what she's suffered. And you hear the whisper of how it might be, the indescribable joy that's within reach. But at this moment, you don't love her in any way that doesn't directly affect you. It always comes back to you, doesn't it? What will it take, I wonder, for you to love her earnestly and selflessly?"

"Doesn't what I'm doing now indicate the sincerity of my feelings for her?"

"It indicates your need to relieve your guilt. You believe transferring the prospect of Mariah fulfilling the Mephisto Covenant to him will make it right. She's merely a pawn. I repeat, the first step is to tell your brother of your deception. That night, you knew because you were warned. My message was crystal clear. Yet you married her before God and lay with her anyway, took what wasn't yours, and committed a grievous wrong against her, your brother, me, your father, God, and all the Mephisto."

"I loved her. Maybe not enough, not yet, but I'd grown attached. We were very close. How could I let her go?"

"I never said it would be easy. I offered my help and that of your father. Until that day, you didn't know. As much as your brother was wronged, so were you. But once you knew, once it was clear that she wasn't yours, you had the opportunity to do the right thing. You failed, monumentally, and she died because of your weakness. That wasn't love, but selfishness and arrogance. You spent all the years afterward running from it, Phoenix, never realizing it wasn't behind you, but ahead. You're running toward it. You are here because it's much closer than ever before."

I was drowning in shame.

"If your tie to Jane was strong enough to tempt you into betraying your brother, what makes you think you can give up Mariah?"

I faced the reality of never kissing her again, never talking to her about anything intimately personal, never again experiencing what had happened this morning, that euphoric feeling of coming home. In a very short time, I'd grown more attached to her than I ever imagined possible. I knew her and understood her far better than I'd ever known Jane.

"It's because of what I feel for her that I want to do this. She needs someone like him. Not me. I could never make her happy. She'd be miserable forever."

He was quiet for so long, I came close to panic. Was he angry? Disgusted? I had no idea. I resisted the overwhelming urge to fidget.

"Tell her," he said at last.

"About Jane?"

"All of it, and tell her of your intention to request divine intervention. If you will do this, if you lay your soul bare to her, I'll make it so that any of your brothers could claim her. What happens after that is a question of personalities, hormones, and fate. If she chooses another, whether the brother you wronged, or any of the others, you will step aside and not interfere. If she chooses you, I expect you to honor her. But nothing happens unless you make it right with him and tell Mariah."

He wasn't going to let this be easy. I could think of nothing more difficult or painful than meeting his demands.

But I'd do it, because Mariah deserved this. She was so gentle, so soft and unassuming, beautiful and patient and wounded. I would do what had to be done so that she would be at peace.

"I wonder whether you will find what eludes you?" He came closer and dropped his voice to a whisper. "What can lift you up beyond your father's legacy and make you into the man you wish to be? I wonder . . ."

He began to fade, and then he was gone, leaving me alone with Prince Albert and my never-ending guilt.

I wandered around for several hours, stopping to stare up at Big Ben, always beautiful at night, then popping over to the bridge at the Tower of London to watch the boats pass beneath. It grew later and I became hungrier. I had missed dinner hour at home, and all the pubs were closed in London. A barge sluiced through the river below and the name painted across the back was *Lily*, which made me think of a favorite spot of ours in West Hollywood.

I decided Lily's would do for dinner, and popped myself to L.A. It was mobbed, as always, but I handed a hundred to the hostess and within ten minutes, I was seated in the middle of the place, ordering from a guy named Bo who acted like he knew me, which was weird because I'd never seen him before. I recognized some of the other wait staff, even had a wave from a girl named Gloria, but Bo wasn't familiar at all.

I ignored his creepy familiarity, as well as the overt looks I got from a couple of good looking young women seated close by. It had been a very long time, but I still remembered how this worked. In spite of their fear, or maybe because of it, girls were easy to attract, especially in places like Lily's, dimly lit with sexy music and lots of liquor. I'd barely need to say anything and one of them, maybe both, would go with me anywhere I liked. When we were done, I'd bring them back, buy them a drink and disappear into the shadows, erasing their memory of me as I went.

In all the years since Jane's death, it had taken enormous willpower to ignore looks from beautiful girls. I rarely went out for that very reason.

Tonight, I had no problem at all ignoring them, but their interest sent my mind tripping down a path I wished I could avoid. I was thinking way too much about naked bodies and sweaty skin and the orgasmic joy of wild and crazy sex. I remembered my dream about Mariah in exquisite detail. I remembered the feel of her soft, beautiful breasts, the taste of her, the desire in her smoky blue eyes.

Shit. I had to get a grip.

Bo brought me a salad, then he brought crab cakes, and after that he brought a steak with some kind of puffy potatoes and tiny asparagus. While I polished off the food and drained two more beers, I gave considerable thought to my next move.

What I wanted to do was go home, go straight to Mariah's room, and kiss her for an hour. I wanted to take her clothes off and hold her next to me for another hour. And I wanted to seduce her during all the hours after that.

Would that I could. If I took that step, and it was a big if anyway because of her past, wouldn't I be making the exact same transgression against my brother?

Telling him the truth and giving up my claim to Mariah was the right thing to do. It would absolve me of guilt. It might go a long way toward mending the horrible rift I was about to make between us.

But it meant losing Mariah, and everything in me fought against it. My tiny mental army stood on a hilltop and shouted *Mine!*

He would love her, eventually, and she'd be much happier and more content than she could ever be with me. He had a gentle nature and would always be considerate and kind. He was a much better mate for her.

It didn't change that I wanted to die at the thought of letting her go.

I was just pulling cash from my pocket to pay the check when Zee walked into the restaurant. I remembered then that it was Friday and Arcadia was playing tonight at Fawkes on Sunset. Of course he'd be there. It was his favorite band. And of course he'd come to Lily's beforehand. It was a favorite of ours.

But it was still freaking me out that he walked in at just that moment. Way too coincidental. Thinking of my too-friendly waiter, my mind flashed a mental picture of the barge named *Lily* at the same time I glanced down at the ticket to see how much I needed to pay. Right below the line for the tip were the words, *Tell him. Now.*

CHAPTER 15

His low voice echoing in the hard, cold, tiled bathroom, Eryx asked, "Surprised to see me?"

"A little. Everyone thinks you're too busy chasing Jordan to pay attention to me."

"Ah, but you're one of the most important things in her life. If I'm to win her, I'll have to win you as well, won't I?"

"How did you find me?"

"Dumb luck, really. I've been occasionally following my brothers, hoping they'd be arrogant and stupid enough to take you into the real world. Makes sense it'd be Denys who'd screw you over. His life can be distilled to the bottom of a bottle. It'd be sad if it wasn't so pathetic."

"What do you want?"

"I'd like to take you to my home, to get to know you, and show you around. After Jordan comes to live with me, I want you to join us. She'll be better situated if she has you there."

He was clearly operating in an alternate reality. "Is she coming to live with you?"

"She doesn't know it yet, but yes, she is."

I turned and unlocked the door. "A gracious offer, but no, thank you."

It locked again and he was right behind me. "Come along with me for a brief visit. I'll bring you right back and the drunken fool will never even know you were gone. At this very moment, he's taking the lovely Brianna to the manager's office for a little slap and tickle on the boss's sofa."

I turned and looked up at him. "Why would I believe you? If

what they say about you is true, you're incapable of honesty."

He was very close now, staring down into my face. I squashed my instinctive need to put space between myself and another human being. I would not show any of my quirks, phobias or fears. I had no choice but to go with him. I couldn't run from him, and even if I screamed, even if Denys heard me, by the time he popped in here, I'd already be gone. I would go with Eryx and he would kill me.

I thought of all the times I'd wished I could die. Now, when I felt more hopeful than I could ever remember, when I had the promise of something wonderful, I was going to get my wish. If it weren't so tragic, it'd be hysterically funny. I wasn't afraid. I was pissed. But I'd never let him know it.

His expression was odd, almost sad. "Will you go with me?"

"Like I have a choice?" What else was new? The only thing it appeared I'd ever get to choose was which underwear to put on after my shower. Everything else hinged on the whims of others. God, I was so tired of it. "Let's go then, and get this over with."

He looked more sad. "Aren't you afraid of me?"

I shrugged. "I'm afraid of very few things. You're not on the list. But I can fake it if you like."

"Are you good at faking things?"

"I could win awards."

He took my arm and everything went dark.

When I could see again, I was in a library. It wasn't as large as the Mephisto library, but impressive all the same. Like the Mephisto house, there were a multitude of candles in sconces all around the room, illuminating the bindings of the books and the polished walnut in a pleasing blend of soft colors. I glanced around as he stepped away from me. "A reader, are you?"

"Yes, always. Eternal life on Earth can get very boring. And for me, very lonely. I survive by reading." He was watching me. "That surprises you, doesn't it? Did you think I sit in a cave and plot the demise of mankind while twirling my moustache and laughing maniacally?"

"Would you be crushed if I told you I haven't given you or your daily routine much thought at all?"

"A little. I like to instill fear, but you appear to be perfectly calm."

"Yes, well, I've now seen the library. Very nice. Can we continue the tour so you can kill me and get it over with? Dragging this out isn't going to be fun for you because no matter what you do or say, I won't be afraid." I wasn't faking this. I really wasn't afraid. Sad, because I'd only just realized how lovely life could be, but not afraid. After Emilian, I wasn't afraid of pain or death.

So Eryx would kill me and Phoenix would grieve and Denys would feel guilty. I'd be in Heaven, with my parents and God. There was no escape, so why give him the pleasure of watching me try? He might also rape me, and the thought made me extremely anxious, but I would deal with that by mentally escaping.

"Have they told you about me?"

"That you raped Jane, then murdered her? That you killed my sister and plan to infiltrate the U.S. government with your followers? That you have a master plan to grow powerful enough to take over Hell? Yes, I know all about you, Eryx."

"For the record, I didn't actually rape her."

"What did you actually do to her?"

"I convinced her of certain truths about the Mephisto. Then I kissed her, and things got very dodgy after that. I didn't want to kill her, but it became necessary."

"Are you always a liar, or just when it suits you?"

"Not always, but I lie quite often. It's part and parcel of what I do. In this case, however, I'm not lying. Oh, I told Phoenix I raped her, but you have to understand brothers, Mariah. We're a nasty bunch in the best of times, and taunting each other, getting in fights, aiming always to be on top is simply a byproduct of male sibling rivalry run amok. I wanted to dish back a bit of it. They've always hated me because I was my mother's favorite. Except Key. He tried to kill me a few times because of his jealousy, but he never hated me."

"None of them hated you until you murdered your mother."

"True, but they resented me. Our father was never around much, and I took on the role of head of the house." He shrugged. "I didn't rape her. It may strike you as strange, or even funny, but I'm much too fastidious. I'm very attractive to females, other than Anabo, so raping women isn't necessary. I find willing partners with ease."

"Rape isn't about sex. It's about power and control."

"Yes, I understand, so think about who I am. I've gathered millions of souls over the course of a thousand years. You don't get much more control than that. I want to control all of humanity. Why would I find any kind of satisfaction in controlling a woman long enough to rape her? I wouldn't. It's disgusting. So you see, while I readily admit I killed Jane, I assure you I didn't rape her."

"I want to believe you. I'm sorry that I don't."

There was that wry smile again. "You're very much like your sister in this respect. I can't get her to believe anything I say."

"You're kidding me, aren't you?"

He sobered. "Not at all. She won't believe my sincere regard for her and my wish to make her happy."

"You're blowing my mind."

"I begin to perceive your astonishment, but be assured, I'm not kidding. As for yourself, I confess I'm equally stunned. Will you tell me how you can be so calm when others would be shaking, crying, trying to run away?"

"No. Just know that I'm prepared for pain and death, and won't react in any way that might gratify you. So do us both a favor and get on with it. No need to show me around on some lame pretense of me considering living here."

"It's the sensible thing to do, to ensure you never become Mephisto and take up the fight against me, or bear Mephisto children who'll grow up to join the war, but as much as it's practical to kill you, I can't. Jordan would be upset."

"I thought your plan was to use me for leverage."

He shook his head. "That won't work with your sister. Although it would wound her terribly to let you die, she would because she's stronger than my will." He had a look of wonder on his handsome face. "She's the most extraordinary person I've ever known, and considering I've been alive for over a thousand years, that's saying a lot."

I peered at him, looking for any hint of sincerity. Incredibly, he seemed seriously enamored of my sister. I was certain he was incapable of love, but what he felt for Viorica went way beyond lust and infatuation. He actually appeared to admire her and want to please her. Very strange. "Why are you allowing yourself to believe she'll willingly come here and be with you? She won't, Eryx. Ever."

He smiled and just like the other brothers, it changed his face. That's when I saw the charm. In spite of his dead eyes, he looked warm and friendly. "We'll see." He walked to the door and waved his hand. "Shall we?"

I walked out the library door, into a wide corridor, and wondered if I might actually make it out of here alive.

Eryx moved close and looked down at me from those dead, black eyes. He was still smiling when he plunged a knife into my heart.

~~ PHOENIX ~~

Zee saw me as I stood. Our eyes met across a sea of tables and people, and something in the way he stared at me gave me chills. In that weird, inexplicable way he had, he knew something. But what? I looked down just long enough to throw some cash on top of the ticket and when I looked again, he was gone.

I hurried out of Lily's and saw him striding off down Santa Monica, his trench coat flying out behind him in the strong Santa Ana winds. I ran after him, and when I caught up, he said, "Go with me to Fawkes."

"Zee, I—"

"Just go with me, Phoenix, and don't say anything."

Fawkes on Sunset was way too far to walk, but I guess he wasn't ready to be there yet, so we continued walking. I debated what I would say to him, but nothing absolved me, nothing made it sound any better than what it was – complete and total betrayal.

Ten minutes later, when anxiety had reduced me to a mass of knotted nerves and dread, he came to a dead stop in front of Fred's Dry Cleaners, grabbed my arm and pulled me around to face him. "How did you know? I was so fucking careful, made

damn sure I never let it show. How did you know she wasn't . .
. that I was . . ."

He *knew*. All along, he'd known she was his. Why had he
never said anything? Confused and stunned, I answered, "A
message from Lucifer the day we were to be married."

"So you knew when you . . . when—"

"Yes, brother, I knew. And I did it anyway. I never had a
clue that you knew she was for you. All this time, I—"

"You've lived with the guilt. You gave up everything as
some sort of twisted atonement. Did you plan to ever tell me?"

I couldn't stop swallowing. Seeing the hurt in his eyes, I
wanted to scream. I wanted to bang my head against the plate
glass window of Fred's Dry Cleaners until it shattered, until I
was bleeding. "That night, after . . . I was eaten up with guilt. I
realized what a horrible mistake I'd made, how badly I'd
betrayed you, and her, and I left. I told her to pack, that I'd be
back to get her, but I wasn't going back. I walked around
London, wishing I had it to do over again, that I could change
it. I tried to gather the courage to find you and tell you, but I
couldn't do it. I figured one of you would go to her, eventually,
and take her home and look after her. I thought you'd realize
I'd gotten it wrong, that she was intended for you all along, and
you'd be with her and she'd finally be happy. She was never
happy with me, Zee. She tried, and I know she loved me, but it
was never right and I didn't know why until that day. I was
headed into a church to off myself, was actually on the steps of
St. Paul's, when a group of guys jumped me, hauled me into an
alley, and beat the shit out of me. They were Lucifer's. I was
told I wouldn't be allowed to die until I made it right with you.
And with her."

"And while you were getting your ass handed to you, she
was with Eryx."

The wind blew my hair in my eyes. I scrubbed my hands
across my face and shoved it back. "How did *you* know she
was yours?"

"I'm reconnaissance, remember? I went to all the houses,
checked out all the lost souls before the takedown at the
Rothschild ball. I saw her and thought she was Georgiana, and
was confused, because she had no shadow. She glowed. I got

closer and she smelled like the ocean. There's no ocean in Yorkshire. And I knew."

He'd known all along, and never said a word. He hadn't known I was aware, and to spare me more pain, he'd kept it to himself. I had to wait a bit to speak. I finally asked, "Why didn't you tell us? Why didn't you claim her?"

He turned and began walking again. "Because I was afraid I'd kill her."

Catching up, I wondered if I'd heard him right. "What? *Kill* her? Why, Zee?"

"I knew what she would look like. I dream about her every damn night of my life and have for centuries. And I always kill her. When I saw the dancing instructor who was Skia, I followed him and he led me to Georgiana. Finally, my dream made sense. She was so beautiful, but she was lost, and I thought, this is my mind's fucked up way of telling me I can't have what I want. I found perfection, and I'd have to kill her. When I went back for reconnaissance, when I found Jane and realized they were twins, realized she *did* exist, just as she was in my head, I knew if I claimed her, if I talked to her, I'd be obsessed. I'd take her home and bind her to me, and then I'd kill her."

His agony and fear was so clear to me now. He'd always and forever been strange, sleepwalking, talking to himself, odd in his manner of speaking, blunt to the point of rudeness, extremely sensitive to moods of others. And his intuition was freakish. Until that moment, I'd not realized it was all a coping mechanism. He lived in a world within his mind, and it was his best friend and his greatest enemy. "In your dream, after you kill her, don't you bring her back?"

"She's already resurrected. She's mine. She's Mephisto. I carry her into a church and lay her on the altar and smother her with my hands. I'm on fire and in so much pain, but I can't die until she's gone."

"You couldn't kill her if she was resurrected. Why would you dream something that can't happen? Why are you afraid of committing a murder that would be impossible?"

He stopped walking again, this time in front of a sushi bar. "For a guy who reads a lot, you're way behind on metaphors. I

don't think I'd kill her in a literal way. I'd kill her because of
what I am. She'd have only me – you've said it yourself. Once
they're immortal and Mephisto, they're stuck with us."

He leaned against the building, next to a metal fish. "I'm not
right in the head, Phoenix. I've known since I was a kid, long
before I made the jump. If you knew . . . there are things in my
head no one could fathom, no one would believe. Some days,
it's all I can do to get out of bed. Some days, the noise is so
loud, so disturbing and horrible, even the music can't drown it
out. I've tried every drug known to man and they do nothing.
Heroin, weed, coke. I've popped a thousand pills. Nothing.
Booze makes it worse. I can never get away from it. The only
thing that makes life tolerable is music."

I was a clueless idiot. How could my own brother be in this
much pain and I never fully understood? *Selfish*. Lucifer had
me pegged exactly.

"It all got worse after Mana died, but it really cranked up
when we left Kyanos. I realized other people don't hear
someone screaming all day and all night. They don't hear
snatches of conversations that aren't real, that are going on in
someone else's head. They don't ever see the whole world in
monochrome. Sometimes, everything is red, or purple, or black
and white. And sometimes, especially late at night when I wake
up and know I've been sleepwalking, I find blood on my
hands. I don't know where it comes from."

No, I'd never known. I couldn't go back, couldn't be a
better brother to him, but I promised myself, standing there in
the dry wind on the sidewalk of Santa Monica Boulevard, I'd
be more aware in the future. I'd spend more time with him and
less time brooding, or escaping into my books, or building yet
another motorcycle. How much he had suffered, and I was so
caught up in my own little world of guilt and misery, I missed
all the opportunities to be with him and make his world less
frightening.

His expression was resigned. "I'm fucking crazy. What
woman could live with this and not die a little more every day?
Think about Jane. She was fine and kind and capable of deep,
profound love. Now imagine she loved me. She wakes up in
the middle of the night and what am I doing? I walk through

some days without complete awareness. So she talks to me, kisses me, makes love to me, and I'm not even there. Her soul would shrivel and die."

He pushed away from the wall and continued down the street. "I will never have a mate. I've known it my whole life. When I found Jane, I thought about ways I could make sure she wasn't at the ball, to keep her from any of you, but as much as it would have been best for her, and for my brothers, I couldn't let her go. If I couldn't have her for my own, I could at least have her in my life. I could see her every day. I could love her as my family. It seemed like such a good idea. And in the end, I'm as responsible for her death as you are. The irony isn't lost on me."

We walked in silence for a long time, and after an ambulance screamed past, I said, "She smelled like heather. How did she have a scent if she wasn't for me?"

"The night of the ball, before we all left for London, I took a bunch of heather and mixed it in with the fresh flowers that were scattered around the matrons' room. I knew she'd be in there, because she couldn't walk, because her family tried to hide her away and shuffle her off where they wouldn't have to see her. I felt so bad for her. And I knew you would be the one to take all the old ladies outside before we set the fire. I knew you'd find her, and smell the heather. She loved it as much as you do, and she pinned sprigs of it to her hat. You never questioned that she was yours. Until tonight, when I walked into Lily's, I didn't know you were ever aware that she wasn't."

"And you knew tonight because—"

"You planned to tell me. I don't know how or why I know some things and not others. It just pops into my head and I know. I walked into Lily's and saw you and I knew."

"I don't know how I can ever express how sorry I am, Zee."

"You've spent over one hundred twenty five years being sorry. For fuck's sake, don't spend any more time wallowing around in this, Phoenix. What good does it do? She'll always be dead and I'll always be crazy. What happened is as much my fault as yours. If I'd stepped up and said, here she is and I can't claim her, if I'd been honest, maybe things would have been different."

"But I knew and I still—"

"You're a selfish bastard, I won't argue that, but it's not like any of us were born to be choirboys. If any of the others had been sucked in as you were, if I'd tricked any of them like I did you, I have no doubt they'd have done the same thing. I know for sure Denys would have. He was crazy for her, did you know?"

Still reeling from what appeared to be forgiveness, astonished that he didn't despise me, it was difficult to be more shocked, but I was. "I had no idea." I remembered when he kissed Jane, and she kissed him back. I tried to remember what Zee had done, the expression on his face, but couldn't. I'd been too angry at Denys and disturbed about Jane to notice anyone else in the room.

"I think because I never claimed her, she was sort of a free agent. That's the only way I can explain how he was attracted to her in the first place. He became obsessed. He went to see her behind your back. Did you know?"

"No." I'd felt resentment from Denys for so long, I'd forgotten there was a time when we were friends, when he liked me. Or maybe I'd just been so wrapped up in my own misery, I failed to notice it had started after Jane's death.

As we walked, I had to face that I'd checked out of everything but planning takedowns and the most basic interaction with my brothers. Jax and I had always been close, but we mostly talked about Eryx, or basketball, or takedown plans. When he found Sasha, I'd been there for him, but it was always about him and Sasha. I'd closed myself off completely, and they'd spent the last century tiptoeing around me. Denys had resented me having Jane, and when she was murdered, his resentment had grown to rage. I'd abandoned her, allowing Eryx the opportunity to take her. I remembered him shouting at me right after Key brought Mariah to Mephisto Mountain. Now I understood where all that fury came from.

"You're having an epiphany, aren't you?"

"Yeah, you could say that. And I always thought I was so smart. Turns out, I'm the village idiot."

Zee looked at me and smiled. *Smiled.* Unbelievable.

"Welcome back," he said, grasping my shoulder, squeezing hard.

I stopped him and hugged him and didn't give a damn who saw us. And I cried. Just a little, but enough to be embarrassing.

He stepped back and said solemnly, "I love you, Phoenix, just like I love all my brothers. It's not in the cards for me to be with someone, but you can. You have Mariah. Don't screw this up. She has problems, but so do you. And you're both fixers who want to pick up what's broken and make it work again, make something ugly into something beautiful. You're perfect together because you have all the years ahead to fix each other."

I'd been handed the opportunity, and before I could rethink it, before I could renege, I told him, "I'm releasing my claim to Mariah."

He stared at me with no expression on his face. "For a brilliant mind, you can be so fucking stupid. What, you think she's like a dog or a cat you can hand over to someone else? Mariah's a fully functioning intelligent human being with her own ideas about who she'll be with."

"I understand it looks impossible, but time changes things, Zee. If she could be claimed by you or Ty or Denys, who's to say it wouldn't work out?"

"Do you think giving her up absolves you of what you did with Jane? Because it doesn't."

"What will?"

"You're gonna have to figure that out for yourself. Don't you think there'll come a time when you regret disclaiming her?"

"It's not like I want to." I looked away from him and watched the cars zip past. "I'm convinced she'll be happier with somebody else."

"You're convinced you don't have what it takes to step up. You judge Denys because he can't let go of the booze, but you're no different. Instead of alcohol, you're addicted to strangling yourself, living like a damned monk. You think if you let go of that, you'll hate yourself even more than you do now."

I'd never been a fan of talking about my own emotional garbage. I wasn't going to start now. "You don't know me, Zee. Nobody does." Except Lucifer, because there was no hiding from him.

I suddenly remembered what Mariah had said to me when I told her she was wrong about a hidden side to me. *"Oh, there's a side, and it's wild and scary and if you let it loose, you don't really know if you can control it."* How did she know? Why wasn't she afraid of it? Because she should be. I was.

"You may be more screwed up in the head than I am." He took off walking again.

I watched him until he was a block ahead, then transported to catch up and walked beside him in silence.

"No arguing?"

"No."

"How do you propose for this to work? None of us are attracted to her. We can't be. You claimed her the night you shouted at her and called her a whore."

"Yeah, that was romantic. I'm a real catch, aren't I?"

"The thought of her with anybody else made you lose your shit. Why do you imagine for even a second that you can step aside and let her be with one of us instead of you?"

"It's not about me. It's her, and what she needs. I'm not it. I know I can never make her happy." I told him what Lucifer would do as soon as I told Mariah about Jane, and all the time I was speaking, he was shaking his head.

"That's maybe the worst idea I've ever heard. It's also completely pointless. Do you *seriously* think she'd fall for me, or Ty, or Denys when she's already falling for you?"

"She's not falling for me. I'm just the one closest to her right now, somebody she feels comfortable talking to."

He cut the air with his hand. "All right, then. You tell her all about Jane, and me, and what you did. Tell her you've asked Lucifer to take away your claim so we can all have a shot. When it blows up in your face, I'll be a total asswipe and say I told you so."

"It'll be hard. It'll be damn near impossible, but for her sake—"

"*What* is *wrong* with you?" He stopped dead and I had to

back up. "If you're so convinced you can't be the guy she needs, then fucking *change*. *Be* that guy, Phoenix. If you throw away the miracle that is Mariah without even trying, than yeah, you're right – you *are* a worthless piece of shit."

I couldn't think of even one thing to say to that.

"You have no idea who you are, do you?"

"No, Dr. Phil, but I'm sure you'll tell me soon enough."

He scowled at me. "Fuck you, man. I'm going to Fawkes. Like now. If you want to go with me and be stupid some more, I'll be at the back entrance." He disappeared.

I stood there on Santa Monica, alone, and cursed Mephistopheles. If the son of a bitch had just kept his dick in his pants, none of us would be here.

Zee didn't expect me to follow, but I did.

Seconds later, I stood at the alley entrance of Fawkes. A guy was banging some chick against the back of the building, and I thought it must be painful for her. Bricks and a naked ass didn't go well together. With Mariah in my head, I moved close enough to figure out if she was a willing partner and decided from the look on her face and her breathless moans that she didn't mind the bricks.

They were unaware of us, partly because they were so involved and busy, but also because it was mostly dark in the alley, the only light coming from a vapor fixture attached to the building behind Fawkes. I, of course, could see them very well. Too well. So maybe it'd been 125 years since I'd had sex, it wasn't as if I forgot what it was like.

It was a bummer to see that at this particular time in my life, when thoughts of sex, specifically sex with Mariah, were eating away my brain.

Zee knocked, the door opened, and a blond guy almost as big as us smiled at my brother. "Zeenose, my man, glad you could make it. We got a surprise for you."

"Hey, Kel." Zee returned the fist bump the guy gave him. "I hate surprises."

While Kel laughed, we stepped inside and the door closed behind us.

"This is my brother, Phoenix."

Humans were typically afraid of us and I was a bit bemused

that Kel didn't seem the slightest bit anxious. I shook the guy's hand, then he pretty much forgot me as he led Zee through the trunks, cases and miles of cord crowding the narrow space backstage. "John got himself a new bird," Kel said. "She's British, and so hot, but man, wait 'til you hear her voice, and she's righteous on keyboard. Funny story. She's a concert pianist and has been since she was like ten. Kind of a prodigy. Anyway, she bugged out from a performance in New York and went to see Arcadia at Blackbriar. John asked her to play for him, and the audience went nuts, so he talked her into joining the band."

"She abandoned her career to play in a band?"

Kel shot Zee a look. "She's kind of different, if you know what I mean."

We were now stopped at a door, which I assumed led to the dressing rooms and practice studio. Zee said, "No, I don't know what you mean. Different like mentally challenged?"

Kel glanced at me, almost as if he wished I wasn't there, then lowered his voice and said to Zee, "Like skating close to batshit."

"Most musicians are batshit."

"True, but she's just . . . different. You'll see. Come on and see John and meet her." He opened the door and walked into a narrow hallway.

We followed and I whispered to Zee, "Should I go out front?"

"No, stay with me."

Kel stopped at a door, knocked twice, then opened it and waved us inside. This was the practice studio, which also served as a green room, a place to hang out before the club's evening line-up began. Arcadia was headlining, but another band would play a few sets first, and that meant a lot of people in the room. All guys, some with long hair, some with short hair, some with no hair, all with tats and piercings and grunge clothes. Some held a beer, some were tossing back shots, a couple were sharing a joint, and a few were drinking Gatorade.

The exception sat at an upright piano and played Mozart, her back to us, her unbound hair long and golden blond with a slight curl. It reminded me of Jane. I glanced at Zee and realized he hadn't seen her yet. He was talking to John, lead guitarist of Arcadia, about geek computer stuff. John had been a doctoral candidate at MIT who had a garage band that went viral, and now here he was, touring the country and Europe instead of becoming a professor. But once a computer geek, always a geek, and Zee was as much an over-the-top tech nerd as the best of them.

"I want you to meet Euri," John said, nodding toward the blonde. "She's amazing, and dude, she writes code like a poet."

Zee glanced her way. "Her name is Yuri? That's like a Russian guy name."

"Her parents had the bad judgment to name her Euripides, and she goes by Euri."

The piece she played ended on a somber note, and she stayed where she was until it faded. A few of the guys clapped, and one of them said, "Holy shit, that was gorgeous."

Turning on the piano bench, she stood and walked toward us.

I was instantly dizzy, blinking rapidly, my heart rate accelerating so fast, I began to sweat.

Dressed in a shimmery pale pink über short dress with no sleeves and a pair of black heels taller than the Empire State Building, she was graceful, refined and elegant. Her legs went right up to her neck. Her eyes were cornflower blue in a perfect, beautiful face. She looked like she'd stepped out of the pages of *Town & Country*, like she rode polo ponies and sipped champagne cocktails at the country club.

Except she had a tattoo of a question mark on her right forearm, a tiny diamond stud in her nose, and streaks of pink in the long, blond hair framing her face.

She had the glow of the Anabo.

And she looked exactly like Jane.

It wasn't a resemblance. It was as if Jane had come back to life, slipped into modern clothes, and walked into our lives again.

I have no idea how I didn't pass out. I shot a look at Zee and I knew . . . I *knew* she was for him, just as Jane had been. Outwardly, he looked cool and collected, unlike my sweaty hot mess of gobsmacked disbelief.

I kept repeating *What the fuck?* in my head, over and over.

She reached us and John made introductions, but she never spared even a glance for me, or John. She was completely focused on Zee. "Have we met?" she asked in a soft, cultured voice. British. Christ, she even sounded like Jane.

"No."

"You're very familiar. Why are you wearing a diamond in one ear? Did you lose the other one? Or is this from your girlfriend, like in The Breakfast Club, and she's wearing the other one right now and thinking of you?"

"I don't have a girlfriend."

"That's unfortunate for every other girl in the world, but extremely marvelous for me." She stepped closer to him and despite her height, even in the shoes, she still had to look up at him. "You smell like hot cross buns, delicious and yeasty. How peculiar."

Zee's nostrils flared and I knew he caught her scent. I wondered if she smelled like the ocean? He didn't say anything, however. Just stared at her with absolutely no expression on his face. He was almost as good at that as Mariah. The only indication of his inner thoughts was a tiny twitch at the corner of his eye.

"Why is your name a letter?"

If I searched the world to find a female version of Zee, I'd wind up at Euri. She had that same odd way of peppering a person with questions that were just a shade too bold not to be rude. Blunt, without artifice of any kind.

"It's short for Xenos."

"Which is Greek for crazy and mixed up. Are you crazy?"

"Chances are excellent. Most crazies don't realize their shortcomings."

"I've been told I'm one note short of a symphony. I have dreams, sometimes when I'm not sleeping. Music fixes it." She smiled. "Do you play?"

"Yes."

"What do you play?"

"Everything."

"No one can play everything. I think you'll need to demonstrate."

He stepped back and said, "I think I need to leave." Without a goodbye, he turned and walked out.

Well, hell.

I said to John, "I'm sorry. He's . . ."

John nodded. "I know. It's okay."

I looked once more at Euri, who was staring at the open door. I freaked out all over again at how much she looked like Jane. "He's not usually rude," I lied. "It's just that he—"

"No need to apologize for him. I understand. He's shy, and awkward, and I frightened him. But he'll be back. He can't not come back."

I met John's gaze and he lifted one brow in an age-old gesture that meant, *I have no clue what she's talking about.*

I knew. In those few brief moments, that indefinable connection was made between Anabo and Mephisto, and no matter how far he ran, or where she wound up in the world, they'd find their way back to each other. How Euri knew that was anybody's guess. Maybe she knew things the way Zee knew things.

My head exploded with possibilities. I couldn't let him run away from her.

I mumbled goodbye, and followed Zee out the door. I found him outside, in the alley, watching the lovers have a post-coital make out session. "Unfuckingbelievable," he said as soon as I came outside to stand next to him.

"I assume you're talking about Euri and not that girl's ass, which has gotta be rubbed raw from those bricks."

"We need to call a war room meeting with our father. We need to find out what he's up to. In nine hundred years, we found only one Anabo. Now, in less than two years, we've found four. And how coincidental is it that tonight, of all nights, we meet Euri? He's jacking with us, Phoenix. And I have to wonder if Lucifer is aware, because if he isn't, if M is interfering, this could end badly."

"How could M have anything to do with it? Anabo come from God. Last time I checked, M and God aren't golf buddies."

"I don't know. That's the point. I think we should ask him and make him tell us what's going on."

"Or, we could not look a gift horse in the mouth."

"What are the odds she'd walk into my life tonight? What are the chances she'd be crazy like me?" He looked at me. "What the fuck?"

"I don't know, brother. Let's go inside, I'll have a whiskey, we'll see her with the band, and we'll talk about it."

"What's to talk about? I'm just as wack as I was when I found Jane. Nothing's changed."

"It appears she may be as wack as you are. Maybe she's what you need, Zee. If anyone could understand you, maybe it's her. You'll never know if you don't try. Come on, have some faith. Let's go see her sing, and you can think about your next move."

Once again, he blew my mind. Looking me right in the eye, he said solemnly, "The last thing I need is a head case like me. Not interested. The more I think about it, the more I think maybe Mariah and I would be good together. Coming from her background, she may be the only Anabo I'll ever find who could survive me. So you do what you have to do to release your claim, and count me in. I'll win. She already likes me." He glanced at the couple, who were about to go at it again, and said in a loud voice, "For fuck's sake, man, get a damned hotel room."

Then he disappeared, and I was left staring at the guy, who of course thought I was the one who told him to get a room.

He let go of the girl, who scrambled to pull her panties back on, and headed for me while he zipped his jeans, fury in his eyes.

I should have left.

I didn't.

And that guy did get a room, but not in a hotel. I didn't leave until I heard the ambulance the girl had called.

CHAPTER 16

~~ MARIAH ~~

I was in the little cabin, sitting on the big rocker. Beet was curled up just in front of a cheery fire in the hearth, and across from me, in the smaller rocker, a petite dark haired woman with olive skin and the bluest eyes I'd ever seen was crying. She was a female version of Zee. This had to be the Mephisto's mother, Elektra.

This could not get any more weird.

I knew I was dead. I just couldn't figure out why I was in this cabin with Elektra, a woman who lived a thousand years ago, but was dressed in holey jeans and a Woodstock T-shirt. Woodstock? Okay, it could get weirder. Was this Heaven? If so, I was disappointed. I'd expected something more beautiful. Certainly more spacious. Spending eternity in this tiny room wasn't my idea of Heaven.

"I'm sorry," she whispered, ineffectually waving her hand in front of her face, as if that would dry her tears. "I'm the angel, Mary Michael. I've been visiting you in your sleep since you were very young. Because it's difficult for Anabo to live in a dark world, God sent me to be a help to you."

Mary Michael? Why? Her name was Elektra, which I thought rocked. Why did she have to change her name to be an angel? But I didn't ask because I was more curious about the little cabin. "Do we come here for our visits?"

"Yes."

No wonder this was where I mentally escaped. "I appreciate the thought, but if I never remembered you, how were you a help? You know I was abused, tortured, and raped, right?"

She cried harder and nodded.

"And no matter that I supposedly don't have Original Sin, I hated him so much I made no move to save him from death. Maybe the church has it wrong, but they teach that it's a sin to hate, no matter the provocation. So while it's real nice that you brought me here for cozy chats in my sleep, it didn't change that I hated him, and it sure didn't make my life suck any less hard. I don't mean to be critical, but maybe it would have been more help if you'd gotten me out of there."

Softly, she said, "I did."

I was surprised. "Are you saying you took him down?"

"He was going to kill you."

"What about free will? Does that not apply to angels? Can you kill people because they're bad?"

"I didn't kill him. He had a stroke. He may have been helped along when I visited him, because he was very disturbed to see an angel in his room, but his death was not by my hand. He was in bad health, and nature will have her due. I wish it could have been sooner, but it wasn't. I did my best for you, Mariah, and now . . ." She swiped at her tears and sat up straighter. "I'm going to do the right thing for you."

"You're their mother, aren't you?"

She nodded.

"Do you visit them in their sleep?"

"No, I'm not allowed to see them. Just the Anabo."

"Are you the one who'll take me to Heaven?"

"If you wish to go, yes, I'll take you there, but I'm hoping you'll go back. Eryx is trying to bring you back."

I was even more surprised. "Can he do that? There seems to be a lot of confusion as to who can bring an Anabo back to life."

"Because of their immortality and the blood of Mephistopheles, any of them can bring an Anabo back, even if she's already begun her change to Mephisto, even if she's marked."

"Then why did Phoenix fail with Jane?"

Fresh tears spilled over and rolled down her smooth cheeks. "She lost Anabo."

"How? Why?"

"Eryx convinced her the Mephisto were lying to her. He reminded her that Phoenix killed her twin, and even though Georgiana had given her soul to Eryx, it didn't mean she had to die."

Now I knew what happened to the twin in the photographs.

"Jane was extremely attached to her sister, as most twins are, and part of her was always afraid of Phoenix, because she felt her sister's fear."

"Did Jane pledge her soul?"

"No, but she wavered in her faith. She was confused and in so much pain. She wanted to believe she could still save her twin, and Eryx made her believe he cared, that he isn't the monster his brothers made him out to be. He told her if she was no longer Anabo, she could ask Lucifer's help in getting her sister back from Hell on Earth, give her a chance to reclaim God and be sent to Heaven instead."

"So she chose her sister over Phoenix." That made me sadder for Phoenix. Had she instinctively known he wasn't meant for her? I wanted to know more. I wanted to know why Phoenix left her alone that night.

"Jane was a perfect storm, Mariah. So many things happened when she was found, and not all of them good. I'll say no more. Just know that she's in Heaven now and happy. More, I think, than if she'd stayed."

"Maybe I'll be happier in Heaven than if I stay. Life so far hasn't been anywhere close to easy, and going back to Eryx will be extremely dodgy. He'll never let me return to the Mephisto. I'll be with him forever."

She shook her head. "I'm certain he'll take you back to that pub. He won't do anything to anger Jordan, and he really believes you'll join her when she is with him, and he's convinced she will be."

"Why would he believe that? It's stupid, and from all I've learned about him, he's nowhere close to stupid."

"He's obsessed with Jordan, and a lot of what he's doing now is in direct opposition to what he's done for over a thousand years. No one saw this coming, Mariah, least of all me. It makes me wonder if he's not as lost as we thought."

"Not calling you a liar, but let's be honest. You would

naturally think so and give him the benefit of doubt because you're his mother." I got up from the chair and wandered to the shelves, but couldn't move the box I wanted to look inside. It was one of three I hadn't inspected when I was here earlier.

"You have no form, Mariah. You're a spirit, unable to move things."

It was dark outside, but the moon was full, shining on the blanket of snow in the clearing outside the little cabin. I looked out at it and wondered why some people's lives went according to plan while others, like mine, were constantly changing course. "If I go back, I'll be immortal, which means I'll be Mephisto forever, won't I?"

"Yes, but it's not a bad thing, is it? I think by joining them, doing what they do, you'll finally come into your own."

"I don't want to kill people, no matter that they're lost souls. What does that mean, anyway? It seems extremely harsh that a person can't recover from a mistake, even one that takes them away from God. I haven't felt all that close to God in a long time. I only pray when I'm afraid." I turned away from the window and frowned. "I really wish you'd stop crying. It's making me feel bad. I get that you're upset that my life sucked, and now I'm dead, but if you're supposed to help, I don't think crying about it will make any difference."

She stood and dried her eyes and said, "You're right, and I'm sorry. Come take my hand. We're going to see some things."

I hesitated. What kind of things? I was at least ninety percent leaning toward telling her to take me to Heaven. The ten percent was only because of Phoenix, and even for him, I didn't know if going back was worth it. He had become my friend, had been nothing but wonderful, and I was infatuated with him, but how well did I really know him? I remembered how he'd acted the night I arrived on the mountain, the side I'd seen of him that wasn't friendly or nice. He was a wild child waiting to get out, and did I really want to be there when he did? Not just there, but *with* him. Stuck for all eternity.

I really wished Eryx hadn't stabbed me and I wasn't dead. I needed more time.

"We don't have much time, Mariah." Mary Michael seemed

far less weepy now, and much more commanding. Like a mother.

I went to her and took her hand.

I expected her to take me to see a few lost souls, or a Skia, to illustrate how awful they were for mankind, to convince me of the need to take them out.

The level of my mistaken thoughts was staggering.

She took me to a place devoid of humanity, a dark, horrific freak show.

She took me to Hell on Earth.

"You see your life as a long succession of tragedies, of terrible luck and helplessness, but what doesn't kill you makes you strong. You're a compassionate, intuitive soul who was forced to see the underbelly of man because of the sacrifice you made for your sister. I asked to show you this and was allowed because ironically, of all the Anabo, you are the one who will be most affected, and the only one who can withstand what you see. Eryx and the Mephisto believe Jordan is strong. She is, but not like you, Mariah. No one has ever been here and returned to the living. None of my sons, no other Anabo, none other than Lucifer has ever seen this place."

"And you," I whispered, gripping her hand with all my might.

"And me. Look around you and know this is nothing like where Mephistopheles carries souls entrusted to Lucifer. Hell is for penance, and all who wind up there are regretful. They yearn for a return to God, to light and kindness. Those who give their souls to Eryx and are captured by the Mephisto are here, and they are not repentant. They're angry. Lost to God. Lost to humanity. These are the souls you believe you can't kill. These are the souls you think you can save."

We stood high on a ledge in a huge cave, dimly lit by small spots of orange and red scattered across the walls, which seemed to breathe, in and out, in and out.

"This is deep within the Earth, where some rock is liquid. Lucifer formed these caves not long after Eryx began collecting souls, and it's his will that keeps the walls from collapse, his spirit that holds the souls within. If you had form, you'd be too hot to live. Those who believe in Hell think this is what it is. This is the fire and brimstone so beloved by those who seek to frighten humans into submissive faithfulness. There are other abscesses in the Earth linked to this one. They are all the same, filled with desperation and rage."

A teeming mass of people shuffled along the floor of the cave, wandering endlessly. "Why are there no bodies? Don't the lost souls die when they are sent here?"

"They are sustenance to the Skia."

If I wasn't only a spirit, I know I would have thrown up.

"They fight over the lost souls' bodies, and kill each other again and again, but always revive. For the Skia, there is no death." She looked at me. "If the Mephisto are successful, this is what Eryx gives to those who believe him and renounce their faith in God. None but Eryx's followers wind up here. You can't see all the spirits of the dead in this room, but they are here, and they are legion. If Eryx is vanquished, they'll have one last chance at redemption and Heaven. Those who don't make it here before they die are eternally lost, their souls absorbed by Eryx to increase his strength."

"And the Skia?"

"They give him their souls when they become immortal. They're robots who do his bidding with no will of their own. This is a horrible place, and the Skia exist in abject misery, but the lost souls are better off here than dying within humanity. At least this place gives them some hope, however small, and however much they don't deserve it. Yes, it's harsh, but they always pledge with their eyes wide open, well aware of what they're doing."

"Why do they do it? I don't understand why someone would do it."

"They turn their back on God for many reasons, but the heart of their motivation is always the eternal search for worth. People want to be worthy, they want to feel important and special. They'll go to extreme lengths to get it, even handing their soul to Eryx. They don't recognize the irony until it's done, that worthiness comes from within, and no amount of props from others will ever fill the void. They could find peace and ease if they stopped trying so hard, because God gives every man dignity. Eryx gives them lies."

I couldn't stop staring at the Skia below. They were old and young, every race, male and female, tall and short. They were all naked and skeletally thin. Hungry. I knew what it was to be hungry. They looked up when the earth rumbled and I saw hope in their blistered, sweaty faces. When nothing happened, when no lost soul came hurtling into the cave, they resumed shuffling. Fights broke out occasionally, vicious and bloody, but worst of all, in an area closest to the wall with the least light, females screamed in agony and I didn't have to look to know what was happening to them.

I couldn't stop crying.

I couldn't stop my heart breaking.

"Life is all about choices. We can't always control what happens to us, but we have a choice in how we live through it and who we are. You're here right now because God chose you to be Anabo, because you sacrificed yourself for Jordan, because you are one of those rare people who have compassion even for those who choose evil."

"That's not true. I never felt sorry for Emilian."

"Feeling sorry for people means you have sympathy, which isn't the same as compassion. What you feel for all others is hope. Regardless of who they are or what they do, you hope they'll change, that they'll be at peace. You never lose hope, never give up. You had many opportunities to kill him in self-defense, Mariah. Why didn't you? Why did you keep trying, even in the face of his rage and hatred?"

I turned my head to stare at the stone behind us, unwilling and unable to look at the room below me any longer. "I wanted him to stop. I wanted him to be different. I hated him so much."

The screams were killing me. They were me. They were my screams. The ones in my head, the ones into my legs while I sat on the roof, the ones I swallowed to keep him from hurting me worse. "Please take me away from here."

Instantly, I was back in the little cabin, standing on the rug, Mary Michael's arms around me. "We're out of time, Mariah. You have to decide now if you will go back, or if I'll take you to Heaven."

I stepped away from her. "I could forget it all in Heaven. I'd never remember him, or what happened to me."

She nodded slowly. "You'll forget Phoenix and the Mephisto. All that will remain is your memory of your parents and Viorica. You'll be sublimely happy, always safe, without sorrow, surrounded by love. Heaven is a marvelous state of being, and it's well within your right to go there. Staying means you never lose the memory of Emilian. It means living with the insanely messed up boy who is my son. And it means taking the lost to Hell on Earth." She began to fade. "Staying will be difficult, but potentially full of joy. Now, child. Decide now . . ."

I looked at Beet, whose tail was wagging. He barked. Bending to stroke his soft fur, I thought of Olga. Zee and Sasha and Kyros and Denys and Mathilda and all the rest. I thought of Viorica – Jordan. I'd barely had a chance to know her. Then I thought of Phoenix. Healing me, kissing me. *Tell me what he did.* An insanely messed up boy, and he was meant for me, an insanely messed up girl.

Beet barked once more before he disappeared.

In the end, the decision was a no-brainer. This was my destiny, what God intended for me. If I'd made it this far and survived, how hard could the rest of eternity be?

I said to the now empty room, "I'll stay," and darkness fell.

"Welcome back," I heard Eryx say. I felt his hands on my torso, felt heat pulsating through me.

Blinking my eyes open, I looked up at his face, at his dead eyes. "Of course I won't kill you," I mimicked his low, deep voice.

Withdrawing his hands, he smiled and stood from where he'd kneeled next to me on the library sofa. "I couldn't risk you dying and not being brought back. My brothers can screw up a train wreck."

"How do you do it? How do they do it?"

"It's a simple matter of sharing our life force with one who is dead."

"Can you bring anyone back?"

"Not just anyone, no. My immortals belong to me before they die, so I can bring them back, kill them again, do whatever I like with them. My brothers aren't allowed to resurrect anyone who's not Anabo. They have rules. I don't."

"What about the Luminas?"

"They're brought back by God."

At a console below mullioned windows, he poured liquor into a cut crystal tumbler and brought it to me. "Have this. It'll steady you." He offered his hand and pulled me to a sit, then held out the glass.

I took it and sipped, appreciative of the heat as it travelled down my gullet and into my stomach. "What happened to my sweater?" I was wearing a black sweater that was much tighter than mine, and a pair of black stretch pants. "And my jeans?"

"You bled all over them. I've had my housekeeper dispose of them."

"Whose clothes are these?"

"Does it matter?"

"No." But I was curious. Had he bought clothes for Jordan? Was he that confident? Or did he have another girl who lived here with him? I tried not to think about him undressing and redressing me while I was dead. That took creepy into the stratosphere. "How could you be so sure I'd come back?"

"I wasn't sure, but I weighed the odds and decided you'd be unwilling to leave your sister. My certainty grew after you died and I found this beneath your sweater." He held up the golden phoenix I'd swiped from one of the boxes. "So you're intended for Phoenix. I'm curious. What does he smell like?"

I wondered how he knew about the scent of Anabo and Mephisto? It seemed like something he shouldn't know, like the Mephisto Covenant. The less he knew, the less he could use it against the Mephisto. "What a peculiar question. He smells like a guy. Sometimes like aftershave, sometimes cologne, sometimes sweat." Always marvelous.

"If an Anabo is intended for a Mephisto, they have a certain scent, don't they?"

I shrugged. "I wouldn't know. I haven't been with them that long. As for the necklace, I stole it, in case I went back to Bucharest. I could get a lot of money for it."

"Why would you need money?"

"Why does anyone need money? To spend it."

"No particular reason? Did you imagine you'd find a better

place to live? Were you thinking of buying a car? Maybe you want to travel."

He was good at digging, but I was equally good at never poking my head out of the hole. "I just thought it'd be some money. Now it doesn't matter because I can't go back to Bucharest, thanks to you."

He handed me the phoenix, then poured himself a whiskey and took a seat beside me to drink it. "You were gone a while. Care to tell me where you went?"

"Hell on Earth. I said hey to all your converts."

"You have a macabre sense of humor."

I drained the whiskey and stared down at the candlelight reflected in the crystal. "Okay, so I didn't say hey. I just watched their misery and thought that as horrible as their existence is, yours is worse."

"Oh?"

I turned my head to look at him. He appeared fascinated by me, staring into my eyes, clearly waiting for me to explain myself. "You want what your brothers have."

"I have no light, no sentimentality, no love, no shred of honor. What makes you think I want brotherhood?"

"I don't."

"What, then?"

"You want hope. You think my sister will bring you hope."

He surged from the sofa and went to set his glass down on the console. "We need to get back. Denys will sober up enough to miss you soon. I'll have to give you the tour of my home some other time."

I slipped the phoenix around my neck and let it drop beneath the sweater before I stood and walked toward him. He stiffened, which surprised me. I set my glass next to his and took his hand.

Seconds later, we stood in front of the bar in the empty, dark pub, scarcely lit by the streetlamps through the windows. He looked down at me as he released my hand. "You're wrong, by the way."

"Maybe, but I don't think so."

"We'll talk about it later, when you're living with me."

"Even if by some bizarre twist of fate my sister did agree to stay with you, I wouldn't follow."

"Don't tell me you've fallen for one of my brothers."

"I've been to Hell on Earth."

"And you can't wait to find more of my followers to send there?"

"I can't wait to hand you your Waterloo."

His black gaze swept me from head to toe and back again. "You're almost as small as Jordan. A tiny warrior, are you, Mariah?"

Remembering the sweaty faces of the Skia, their skeletal bodies, their utter hopelessness, I said, "You have no idea."

He bent low and looked closely at my face, at my eyes. "So much rage," he whispered. "All for me?"

"No, it's all for The Man."

That made him laugh. He was still laughing when he disappeared.

I walked toward the hallway to the restrooms, but cut left this time and opened the door that said MANAGER on the nameplate. Denys was stretched out on a leather couch, sound asleep, naked as the day he was born. He held equally naked Brianna next to him.

Welcome to Awkwardtown, population, me.

I stood there and thought about my room in the Mephisto mansion. My bed. Olga. I wanted to be there now. It was nine in Colorado, almost time for Jordan's visit. And later, Phoenix would come. I wondered if he'd stay the night with me again. I wondered how he'd take the news that I'd become immortal.

I was still in shock, I think, and the enormity of it hadn't yet hit me. For now, I wanted familiarity. I wanted my room and my cat and Mathilda to bring cocoa and her sweet British lilt. I didn't want to wake up naked Denys and Brianna.

I could almost imagine I was there, in my room.

Gasping, I nearly fell down when darkness enveloped me, I felt the rush of transporting, and I *was* in my room.

I staggered a bit before regaining my balance and looked around, stunned. From the end of my bed, Olga meowed.

I grinned at her. "Righteous!"

Unimpressed, her eyes went to half-mast and she purred.

My delight in transporting dimmed a little when I realized

Denys would wake up and completely freak out when he couldn't find me. What a pain. He really needed to lay off the liquor.

I petted Olga, then concentrated on the spot where I'd stood before I left the pub manager's office, gratified when seconds later, I was there once more.

Denys was still snoozing, but Brianna had moved. Her eyes were open and she saw me appear out of thin air. I opted to pretend it didn't happen. "I've really got to get going. Will you wake him up and tell him I'll be outside the pub, waiting?"

She blinked in confusion, but nodded, and I walked out of the office.

Ten minutes later, after I heard a heavy door close and assumed it was Brianna leaving via the back hall, along with Denys, who would have to pretend to leave as well, he popped into the pub as if this was all completely normal, his usual grin firmly in place. "Sorry about that, Mariah. I must have dozed off."

"You were passed out."

"Aw, come on, don't be mad. Let me buy you some dinner and then I'll take you home."

"Denys, it's the wee hours of the morning here and nine in Colorado. Let's just go home now."

"You're mad."

"No. Tired. It's been a really long day." I was also ravenously hungry and decided I'd go to the kitchen and ask Hans to give me some leftovers or something. "How are you this sober? Because earlier, you were clobbered."

"It's immortality. No drug lasts long in our system." He grinned. "Takes a whole lotta booze to even get a buzz."

"Does it help, Denys?"

His smile lost some of its brilliance. "Nothing helps, really, but it's something to do." His eyes narrowed and he came close to stare at me curiously. "You look different. Are you okay? What did you do while I was, uh, napping?"

"I helped Freddie clean the bar. Sort of like old times, you know?"

"Seriously?"

"Seriously."

He wanted to believe me, so he did. People are funny like that. Give them an out when they act badly, and they'll take it, every time. I should have told Denys what really happened, but I was feeling weird about it, and wanted to tell Phoenix first. I also wasn't up for Denys's inevitable guilt trip when he discovered I'd been taken by Eryx. I was back, no worse for wear. Well, other than being murdered and resurrected. And my new clothes were ruined.

But, really, otherwise, I was fine. No need for him to feel guilty, and besides, it wasn't as if he forced me to go with him. Now, I just wanted to go home.

He took my hand and as we landed in the front hall, Deacon turned from dusting Jane's portrait. "You've been missed."

"That's nice," I said.

"You misunderstand, Anabo. No one knew your whereabouts and there is a search taking place. It was assumed you were with Denys, but Kyros was unable to locate you at the establishment where he was imbibing too much liquor and disrespecting a female." He went to the intercom box and his solemn voice echoed through the house, announcing my arrival, calling off the search.

"Oh, hell," Denys mumbled. "I'm in for it, now."

I moved a little closer and said under my voice, "I'll tell them I wanted to be alone for a while and you took me to a church in London, where I was perfectly safe because it's holy ground."

He jerked his head around to look at me, astonishment in his eyes. "You'd lie for me? About *church?*"

"I'd rather not have to answer a lot of awkward questions. Just go along with what I say."

"You can try, but for the record, you're not safe inside a church. Eryx can't go in, but Skia and lost souls can because, even though they no longer belong to God, they're not born of Hell. That's how Sasha became immortal. A Skia followed her inside a church in St. Petersburg and killed her."

"Who brought her back?"

"Jax."

"How? If he went inside—"

"He died trying to save her." Denys gave me a solemn look.

"He made the ultimate sacrifice because he loved her, and God gave him back his life."

"The Mephisto Covenant." Would Phoenix ever die to save me? I didn't think so. Oh, he liked me, lusted after me, and I had no doubt we'd be friends for all eternity – but he was way too selfish to off himself on my behalf. Still, wouldn't it be amazing for someone to love me that much? I couldn't imagine it at all.

Kyros appeared first, quickly followed by Jax, Sasha, and Ty. Phoenix and Zee were no-shows, which made me glad. It said a lot about my character, but I didn't mind telling a fib to this group – lying to Phoenix would have bothered me.

His face creased with worry, Kyros came to me and grasped my upper arms, inspecting me. "Are you all right? Where were you? We did a mental search for Denys and found him at the Rose & Crown, but you weren't there." He shot an angry look at Denys. "Where the hell was she while you were drunk, doing the barmaid?"

"How do you know what—"

"I saw you! You were so drunk, I couldn't wake you up. I looked all over the pub, fanned out across London hunting for her. We finally decided she'd stayed here, and was maybe somewhere in the house, or lost in the—"

"I asked Denys to take me to church, so he did and left me there and came back for me a couple of hours later. Don't be mad at him. He was just doing what I asked."

His hands tightened on my arms. "Mariah, you have to understand the danger. If Eryx finds you, if he were to take you, he could—"

"Look, this was just something I had to do, and now it's done, and I'd prefer to skip the lecture." I pulled away and stepped back. "I apologize for worrying everybody, but it's very hard to be here, not knowing when I can ever leave."

Instantly, his expression softened and I felt awful for playing on his sympathy. It added insult to the injury of my lie.

"So, you know."

I jerked a nod. "I know."

"Are you going to stay?"

"Yes. Right now, I'm going to get something to eat, then get ready for Jordan's visit."

They all looked at each other before Key said, "She's not going to make it tonight, Mariah. She went to visit Matthew today, and while she was there, he made a miraculous recovery. She went home with him and stayed late, and now she says she's way too tired and emotionally wrung out to visit. She'll come tomorrow night, after the winter ball they're having at her school."

"A miraculous recovery? How? Did Jordan heal him? Isn't that forbidden?"

"She says she didn't, and I believe her, because if she had, Lucifer would have taken her out immediately. We don't know how it happened, but she's elated, as you can imagine."

"Yes, I can." I wondered how he'd been healed? It was odd, unexpected, and too coincidental, but I'd most likely never know, and since I was beginning to feel sick at my stomach with hunger pangs, I opted not to be overly concerned about Matthew. I was disappointed not to see Jordan, but on the other hand, I'd feel the need to tell her what happened with Eryx, and I wasn't ready to do that. Not yet.

Kyros walked with me to the dining room and continued through to the kitchen. When we were there, before I could ask Hans for something to eat, he said, "In the future, don't lie for him. He has a serious problem, and covering it up only enables him."

"Why do you think I lied?"

"Because you're Jordan's sister. The only time she won't look me in the eye is when she's not being completely truthful, and you just did the same thing. The similarity is amazing. So where were you, really?"

"Can I tell you later, Key? I really feel sick, I'm so hungry."

For a moment, he looked like he'd press the issue, but he didn't. Instead, he waved his hand at Hans. "Let's get something for Mariah to eat. Lots of protein." Hans asked if I'd like steak and eggs. I nodded, feeling uncomfortable. I suspected Kyros knew what happened to me, especially when he said, "Have your supper, then get some rest. Sleep is crucial right now." As soon as Hans's back was turned, he leaned in and whispered, "I know he kissed you. I can tell a difference.

You're becoming Mephisto."

He appeared to be extremely happy about this, so I went along, glad he didn't suspect I was now immortal. "I didn't really want to tell anyone. It's personal."

"I can see why you'd be an extremely private person, Mariah, but you'll have to get used to everyone knowing everything. All of us in one house would make it difficult to keep secrets, but we're also all connected, so it's next to impossible to hide what happens." He pulled one of the stools out from under the counter and waved me toward it. "Have a seat. If you need anything, I'll be in my office."

I sat and he squeezed my shoulder at the same time he bent and kissed me on the cheek. "I'm so glad you're staying," he murmured.

Then he was gone, and it was just Hans and I, speaking German, talking about omelets.

⨯⨯⨯

Phoenix never showed up. After my shower, I finished the book about the perfect woman with the robot brain, hoping he'd turn up at my door. At midnight, I accepted he wasn't coming and went to bed. Lying in the dark with Olga, I wondered where he was. I was hurt, which pissed me off. I did not want anyone to have any kind of hold over me, emotional or otherwise. I would necessarily have to be dependent on Kyros for money and my living, but it wasn't exactly a handout. I'd be expected to work for my keep, which wasn't so different than working for Marta, or, if I had become a doctor, I'd work for money to pay for living. It seemed a fair trade: I'd take out the lost souls and Skia, Key would feed and house me and give me money to play.

As soon as I was able, I would go to Egypt. I'd go by myself and see the pyramids. I would like it and not care I was by myself.

Screw Phoenix. If he did show up sometime before morning, I'd tell him he couldn't stay, that I wanted distance.

Because I couldn't live like this. I wanted him, badly, and that meant ceding a measure of control over my emotions. I'd just have to back off for a while and get my bearings, and then we could be friends.

Feeling slightly better, I eventually drifted into sleep. I dreamed about Hell on Earth, and in the sea of faces, Emilian stared up at me and begged me to help him. I laughed, dangling an apple, taunting him. He began to cry, which made me feel bad, so I threw him the apple. The others covered him immediately, and I heard his screams as they ripped him to shreds.

I woke with a gasp, shaky and perspiring. When I sat up, blinking, reorienting myself, Olga meowed and rubbed her head beneath my chin. I petted her absently, sucking in great gulps of air. I didn't want to go back to sleep. I couldn't have that dream again. The other one, the one I had over and over, was preferable.

Out of bed, I went to the windows, opened the drapes and pushed up one side of the square panes, welcoming the frigid air on my hot body. After a while, I went to the chair by the fire and sat to stare at the banked coals, but they reminded me of the walls of Hell on Earth. I switched focus to the painting above the bed, soothed by the moors and the heather. Someday I'd go to England. I'd find out when the heather bloomed and go then.

I dozed off, and when I next awoke, I was in bed, cocooned in warmth, my arms and legs entwined with Phoenix's. "You're here," I murmured.

He kissed me, tasting mostly of toothpaste, but underneath the mint was the flavor of whiskey. I reminded myself of my decision to tell him to leave. I gave myself a lecture about how I was only getting in deeper and it would make it that much harder and more hurtful when he did what it was his nature to do. He'd leave. I'd be alone again. He'd come back for this, for conversation and company, and when he'd had his fill, he'd leave. It would be eternity of this, and I'd be hurt over and over again. I wanted so much more. I deserved more.

I kissed him back. I listened to him whisper that I was beautiful, that I became more beautiful to him every day. I ran my fingertips across his bare back, loving the smooth heat of him, his thick muscles, the odd comfort I found in his huge body. By rights, I should have been scared to death of him.

I wasn't.

I pulled back and lifted my pajama top over my head. Then he was kissing me again.

Nothing felt real. I was hazy and sleepy and deliriously happy, captivated by the feel of his warm, strong hand on my breasts, surrounded by the sweet tangy scent of oranges.

Something was different and my muddled mind sought to capture it, to define it. He was more intense, more focused, more determined.

I knew how this was going to end and I was evenly split down the middle – inwardly shaking in terror and jubilantly shouting, *Yes, thank God, finally.*

Maybe if I hadn't been so foggy and caught up in the moment, I'd have done something different. Like pushed him away and demanded he get out. Maybe I'd have gotten off the bed to pace around my room and methodically go over every step and tell him how I felt about it, so he'd know, so he'd not scare me. In all my boxes of terrible memories, there was logic and order. Self-protection. But it seemed so inconsequential, maybe even irrelevant, held up to this overwhelming need. I was so lonely, so alone. I craved intimacy and affection like a crack junkie's desperation for his next hit. I'd chosen immortality primarily because of the Mephisto and my sister. Family. A place to belong. People who wanted me, who needed me, who *liked* me.

"Mariah?" he whispered.

"It's okay."

"Oh, God, don't hate me."

"I could never hate you."

"Don't let me do this to you."

"I want you to do this *with* me."

"Semantics, *puica.*"

I loved that he called me a Romanian term of endearment. It was what sent me the last little bit into absolute certainty that I wanted this to happen.

He was up on his elbow, hovering over me, kissing me, his hand drifting from my breasts, across my belly, beneath the waist of my pajama bottoms, and there, to a place I never allowed myself to think about, a part of me that was pain and disgust. "You can't want to touch me, Phoenix," I mumbled against his mouth.

"I can, and I do. I want to touch you . . . I want to be a part of you more than I've ever wanted anything in a thousand years of living."

"But I'm dirty and . . . used, and—"

"What you are is the sum total of everything in your life since you were born, and you're all I want, what I need. Soft, gentle, beautiful. Jaded and naïve at the same time. You're smart and wise and passionate." He kissed me yet again, slower this time, gently sweeping his tongue across mine, while his fingers dipped into my most private place and I . . . instinctively, I wanted to close my legs, to clench myself into a tight wall of resistance. Desire, something I'd never known until today, insisted I open up and find out for myself if the earl's wife and Danielle and the robot heroine were all figments of their creators' imaginations, or fiction imitating real life.

Despite this insistent need I felt throughout my body, even though I reasonably thought there had to be something amazing about sex, I couldn't distinguish between now and then. His hands on my body felt right and wrong, all at the same time. I wanted so badly not to freak out, but I could feel myself beginning to lose my breath, lose myself. My mind was trying to take me to the braided rug by the fire and I didn't want to go there. I wanted to be here, with Phoenix.

He raised up at the same time all the candles in the room were lit. He knew it would be better in the light. "Stay with me, Mariah." His fingers were doing interesting things down there and I moved my legs restlessly. "This is what feels good. This is what makes you wet and ready. This is . . . no, don't look away. Stay right here with me. You see, it's just me, and I'd never hurt you, ever, and the instant you tell me to stop, I will. Do you have any idea how beautiful you are?"

"I'm not beautiful, Phoenix. You're infatuated with me because I'm Anabo. Because I'm your Anabo."

He gave me a wry smile. "Infatuated. Is that what this is?" Lowering his head, he kissed me again, and his fingers never stopped. "Your lips, your mouth . . . I could kiss you for hours and hours and still want more. Until the end of time, I'll want to kiss this perfect mouth. So full and soft and . . ." He slid his lips across mine, smiling. Shifting slightly, he was closer, his chest against my breast, his erection pressing against my thigh. And still, those fingers.

"I don't know what to do."

"Just keep looking at me, and don't think about anything but how this feels."

"This is so strange, Phoenix, and I'm embarrassed and awkward. Maybe you should just go ahead and—"

"Not until you're ready." He dropped his head so that his mouth was just next to my ear. He whispered, "When we were reading about Danielle and Rupert, what were you thinking? How did it make you feel?"

I laid there and blushed like I was twelve years old. "I think you know."

"Good. Then imagine we're them. You're Danielle, an innocent, and you're wild about me, Rupert, and you were never hurt, never taught that sex is horrible. You're a blank canvas and everything is new and intriguing."

I closed my eyes and tried to pretend I was Danielle, that I was innocent and this was my first time. I moved my arm and my hand brushed against his penis. I jerked it away, then hesitantly moved it back. He had on long boxers and I thought Danielle would be curious enough to slip her fingers beneath the elastic band and . . . it was incredibly hot. Hard, but the skin was so soft. I still had my eyes closed, but I kind of wanted to look.

"I'm not nearly as pretty as you," he whispered, his face still next to mine, "but maybe you should see what I look like. Danielle would look."

"She was a painter. Of course she would."

"All right, so you have to paint me, nude – shouldn't you study the subject?"

"Will you take your boxers off?"

He chuckled as he rolled away and complied.

When he was back, he said, "You're blushing so hard, you may wind up with a tan. It's okay, Mariah. It's just me. Open your eyes and look."

I turned my head at the same time I opened my eyes and he

was smiling at me. So good looking, it was a sin. No guy should be this spectacular. He kissed my nose. "Are you going to look? I'm starting to feel shy."

"Liar. You probably walk around naked all the time."

"True, but I'm alone."

I touched him first, then moved my head to look down at my thigh, at the length of him stretched across my skin. I spent some time inspecting him, touching him, and other than a couple of deep breaths, he didn't do anything. When I looked back at his face, his eyes were heavy and his expression was intense. "You said you wouldn't do this. Why did you change your mind?"

"Can we talk about it later? I'll explain everything, I swear. For now, I want you so much I'm close to begging. I want you to like this, want you to understand it's not painful, or ugly. I want you to know what it's like to completely let go. There's nothing like it, no way I can describe it so you'd understand. Please, Mariah, just stay with me and talk to me. Tell me if you're unhappy with anything."

"Did you bring . . . do you have a condom?"

"It wouldn't do any good. They lose effectiveness because there's some kind of chemical reaction that . . ." he cleared his throat, "they disintegrate when we . . . well, after we . . ." He took a breath. "It doesn't matter. I can't carry any kind of disease, and even if I could, it's been a hundred and twenty five years. And I can't get you pregnant unless you're immortal and you want to get pregnant."

"All I have to do to prevent pregnancy is just not want it?"

"That's all."

With my hand wrapped around him, he shifted again and was half on, half off of me when he kissed me, his fingers never stopping. My legs moved, then my hips, and I focused on how he tasted, and the scent of oranges, and the feel of his big body beneath my palm. I have no idea how long we kissed, how long he touched me, but when he moved to slide my pajama bottoms off, along with my panties, I wasn't alarmed, wasn't afraid. I wasn't on the braided rug. I was in bed with Phoenix, and while I was enormously anxious, I honestly didn't know if it was fear, or desire. I knew I was ready and told him so.

Still kissing me, he lifted me up, moved my body and slid into me sort of sideways. He wasn't on top of me. He knew it would be too much like my memories, and in that moment, I knew I was doomed to fall in love with him. For all that he was difficult, he was the best thing that had ever happened to me.

"Oh, hell," he murmured, looking down into my face. "You're crying. God, have I—"

"No, it's . . . I'm just a little . . . that you did this like, that you knew . . . not on top, Phoenix." I slid my arms around him, clung to him, and when he began to move, I moved with him. It was extraordinary and nothing at all like I'd imagined, or feared.

He kissed me again and again. He was all over me, enveloping me, and yet I didn't panic, wasn't afraid. If I'd told him to get away from me, if I said stop, I was unequivocally certain he would. He'd be frustrated, disappointed, and terribly unhappy, but he'd do it. That knowledge gave me comfort, made me at ease, allowed me to be in the moment.

The meeting of our bodies, his inside of mine, the look in his black eyes, which I'd call love if I hadn't known better, the scent of his skin, his soft words of encouragement, the realization that I was irrevocably putting my past behind me forever – every moment was glorious.

"This is *not* infatuation," he murmured against my mouth. "Do you understand?"

I mumbled something incoherent, losing my ability to think of much beyond what my body was doing. Every nerve ending was on high alert, my senses overwhelmed, and my muscles took on a will of their own.

He lifted his head and stared down into my eyes, his expression fierce and determined, his rhythm increasing, his body slamming against mine. "Do . . . you . . . *understand?*"

"Yes . . . no." I grasped his upper arms and held on, rising to meet very thrust, losing my breath, losing my mind.

That side of himself he hid so well came fully awake and shoved his calm, controlled façade off of a cliff, and then it was only me and the real Phoenix in my bed. Honest. Wild. Uninhibited.

This was who he was, who I would love. I knew I would. And it would never be easy to love him or be with him, but I'd been born for difficulty. And it wasn't as if I was exactly easy.

He nipped at my throat and his voice was hoarse and raw. "Give over, Mariah. Give me what I want. Do it *now*."

I had never had a climax. I'd never touched myself in any way that was sexual. I had no clue what it would feel like, or how to make it happen. "Kiss me."

He did, and his hand slid across my body, down to where we were joined.

One touch and I jerked my mouth away from his to suck in a deep breath, my back arched from the bed, and I closed my eyes. I shook uncontrollably as pure pleasure radiated from the center of me, from a place I'd long considered taboo, a place I refused to even think about. That such an exquisite feeling could come from the same place that had brought so much agony completely blew my mind. When the feeling subsided, I was breathing hard, as if I'd been running, and I watched his face when that feeling came over him. He opened his eyes in the midst of his climax and looked at me with so much joy, I almost cried again.

Then everything got dicey. I began to burn, deep inside, and struggled to get away from him. "Phoenix, it hurts, it *burns*. Oh, my God! Ah, damn!"

He held me close, stayed inside of me, wouldn't let me go, never looked away from my eyes. When I was still, when the pain was gone, he said, "It's not fair to you at all, and I should be sorry for marking you, but I won't lie and say I'm sorry, because I'm not." He came closer. "Tomorrow, everything will be settled, but for now, you're mine. You're everything. You're my whole world. And no matter who you're with, that will never change for me."

"Why do you think I'll ever be with someone who isn't you?"

In a blink, he was back to calm, controlled Phoenix. He gave me a lazy smile and didn't answer.

Instead, he kissed me, and I was so exhausted, physically and emotionally, I let him get away with avoiding the question.

CHAPTER 17

~~ PHOENIX ~~

I'd only intended to sleep with her, to kiss her, and when we woke, I'd tell her everything. It would end what we had, and I'd want to die, but I'd have this night to remember what it was like when she was mine.

Instead, I'd had sex with her. No doubt Lucifer would shake his head in disgust. I was just the worst kind of person. *Of all your brothers, you are most like your father.* Selfish always, except when it was convenient not to be. M could be generous, even jolly, but when it came to his own pride and comfort, it was always all about M. Even his love for our mother hadn't been enough for him to do the right thing. I thought Eryx's life must break her, over and over, even in Heaven. All because M didn't love her enough.

Lying in the dark, holding Mariah, surrounded by her scent, I was awed by her ability to conquer her worst fear. That she'd opened herself up to me, gone along and stayed with me until that one golden moment when her expression went from anxious to rapturous joy – I'd never forget it as long as I lived. The air around her shimmered, and her eyes became a shade of blue I couldn't name. Like nothing I'd ever seen.

Listening to her soft breath and Olga's purr, I was enveloped in a euphoric post-sex moment of peace so calm and tranquil, my soul had no room for guilt.

I fell asleep happier than I'd ever been in my long life.

And woke up with the worst guilt trip I could imagine. She was still next to me, so soft and trusting, her breath against my chest, her sweet beautiful face relaxed and a little smile on her lips. What did she dream? Something wonderful. And when she woke up, I'd kill that smile, murder the bond between us.

It had to be late in the morning because the light shining through the break in the drapes was intense, and a thousand birds were chirping. I could hear voices from downstairs, Hans banging pots and pans, Deacon intoning instructions for the Purgatories. No words, but voices. I heard Key, who sounded close to singing, he was so happy.

That's when I remembered they would all know about the mark. No hiding what I'd done to Mariah last night.

I closed my eyes and wished for the four hundred billionth time that I could make this work, that I could do as Zee said and change to be the guy she needed.

How did a person change? Where would I even start?

I had no idea. All I knew was that she deserved someone who wasn't me, one of my brothers who could make her happy. He'd replace my mark with his and I'd want to kill him, but I'd have to stand aside and let it happen and carry on. The past 125 years had sucked, but the rest of eternity promised to be Hell of my own making because I couldn't let go of who I was.

You don't really know who you are, do you? Zee's words came back to me and I realized the truth to them. I'd remained a celibate, guilt-ridden control freak for so long, I couldn't remember what it was like before Jane. I didn't know what was important to me, what it meant to wake up and look forward to the day, how it would feel to accomplish a goal. My whole existence was takedown plans and guilt. I wasn't a guy, a friend, a brother – I was a robot.

"Hey," she whispered sleepily, sliding her leg between mine, tightening her arm around my middle, gently stroking my back.

That was all it took. I was hard and ready all over again.

I made love to her again, and this time, she wasn't afraid at all. She smiled up at me and my heart raced and I forgot all about my plan to disclaim her.

In the afterglow, she mumbled against my shoulder, "I'm starving. I mean, I could eat ten eggs and a pound of bacon and a million waffles and—"

"I think we slept through breakfast. I hear Hans prepping for lunch."

"Then I'll eat cheeseburgers."

"Hans will be insulted if we ask for cheeseburgers."

"Doesn't he ever cook boring food? I love cheeseburgers, and it's not like I ever got to eat many."

"I'll get you some cheeseburgers."

"And fries and a chocolate shake?"

I grinned. "Whatever you want."

She buried her face in my neck and whispered, "All I really want is you."

Now was the time to tell her. Now. Right now. This minute. *Get out of bed, put your boxers on, and tell her. Before you take another breath.*

I kissed her and whispered, "Stay here and I'll be back in twenty minutes."

I popped to my room, pulled on some jeans, a T-shirt I grabbed from a chair, and some stupid looking house slipper things with sheep shearling that Mercy had brought Thursday. Grabbing my coat, I fished out some money and shoved it into my pocket, then popped to Shake Shack in New York, the one at midtown, and ordered six cheeseburgers, three orders of fries, and two large chocolate shakes. It was Saturday, the restaurant packed with what seemed like a thousand kids, and my order took forever. While I stood around and waited, Eryx walked through the door. He smiled at me.

I didn't smile back.

"Nice shoes."

"I was in a hurry."

"Was there a fire?" He was clearly offended by my footwear. He, of course, was dressed in GQ style, as always.

I hated him, loathed him, but had to admit, he had excellent taste in clothes. I wished I cared enough to be a sharp dressed man. "What do you want?"

"Checking on Mariah. Have you seen her today?"

Alarms began to sound in my head and the tiny army was shouting, *Danger!* "Of course I've seen her. Why?"

He peered at me curiously for a while. "You don't know, do you?"

The army was ready to shoot arrows, chuck spears, swing broadswords. "Know what?"

He grinned. "She's wily, Phoenix. Has a poker face to beat the best of them. You should pay more attention, and never underestimate her. I'm not surprised, really. She's Jordan's sister, after all."

"And you would know what she's like, how?"

"I got to know her ever so slightly last night, when she came for a visit."

Aware of a tableful of children right behind me, I lowered my voice. "What the *fuck* are you talking about?"

He lost his smile and came closer. "Enjoy her company while you can. She'll be with me as soon as Jordan is mine."

"You're a fool." No way was he going to get a rise out of me. Not now. Not today. I'd go home and ask her what she'd done yesterday, if one of my brothers had taken her off the mountain. I was already angry about that – I couldn't waste energy on Eryx.

"I suppose we're all fools at one time or another. For instance, you never comprehended how important Jane's sister was to her, not until it was too late. I wonder if you'll make the same mistake with Mariah?"

"She'll be Mephisto, but not mine."

"Unlike her, you're so bloody transparent, I know exactly what's going through your mind right now. You're wondering how I could have taken her and no one was ever aware. No alarm was sounded, no rescue party came after her. Poor Mariah, it's as if she's doomed to be invisible, always on the fringe, the forgotten one. She's not flashy, is she? Quiet and calm, beautiful in an understated way, but underneath it all is brilliance and rage I'd respect if I were you. She's unafraid of anything."

My mind was reeling. How had he taken her? From where? Who was she with?

"As usual, you'll focus on things that don't matter at all. You'll want to exact revenge on whomever wasn't careful with your little chippy, instead of learning more about her. I made her immortal, Phoenix."

I was speechless. *Why?* What did he think to gain by

making her immortal? Because Eryx never did anything that wouldn't somehow be of benefit to himself. How had he done it? Did she suffer? My hands clenched and I had to hold myself back from attacking him. He'd frightened her. He *killed* her.

But she came back. For him. My confusion ramped up to severe anxiety. Everything was getting away from me.

"I see that shocks you, but will you ask her what happened? Will she tell you she visited Hell on Earth? No, not unless you ask, but you won't. You'll spend time trying to figure out how this could have happened, who's to blame, and all the while, she'll be there, waiting for someone to notice her, to pay her the attention she deserves. She'll get tired of waiting and come to me, to Jordan. There's nothing in the universe more precious to her than her blood, her sister."

For Jordan. He'd made her immortal so she could stay with Jordan. His obsession had taken him so far off of his usual path, he was unrecognizable, like a monster in the forest who steps into sunlight and is revealed to be nothing but a humble woodsman. For the first time since he'd jumped, I felt almost sorry for Eryx. He'd bought into the delusion that he could have Jordan, and he wanted her enough to abandon his quest. It was surely temporary. Once he realized he would never have her, he'd return to his old self with a vengeance.

"She gave up a lot for Jordan, didn't she?"

"How would you know?"

"I have people in Bucharest, investigating. She's had a terrible life, but she's resilient and strong. And she'd do it all again for her sister. A little like Jane and Georgiana."

"You lied to Jane."

"And because she loved Georgiana with such a pure heart, she risked believing me. I intended to take her home, Phoenix, where she'd marry a like-minded do-gooder aristocrat and live to be an old lady."

"You can rewrite history all you like, but it doesn't change reality."

He came still closer. "She loved you. I don't know why, but she did. When she realized what she'd done, she was hysterical because it meant she could never be with you. I killed her because she wouldn't have married the aristocrat and moved on. She'd lost Georgiana, Anabo, and you. She went a little mad, Phoenix. As much as I enjoyed your misery, that wasn't my primary reason for taking her life. It was mercy."

"If I didn't want to punch you in the face, I'd laugh. The last time you felt mercy was the night you killed our mother."

"You're probably right." He shrugged. "Doesn't matter now. She's dead and you've moved on, haven't you? It's a bit of a repeat, except the stakes are a lot higher. You didn't love Jane, but you're deep in it with Mariah, aren't you? I can smell her on you, brother."

He turned to walk back to the door, and said over his shoulder, just before he pushed outside, "She's not like Jane at all." He looked back at me. "But you know that better than anyone, don't you?"

Then he was gone.

Waiting became torture. I almost left without my order, so anxious to get home and ask Mariah what happened. I remembered how exhausted she was last night. Newly made immortals usually slept an enormous lot just after they were brought back. They were ravenously hungry until their metabolism evened out, typically a week or two. I'd taken her at her word about being tired, and passed off her enormous hunger to Mephisto. Once an Anabo began the change, she was far hungrier than usual.

But not like an immortal.

How had it happened? Was she afraid? I wanted to be with her when she crossed, and not only was I not, neither was anyone else. Just Eryx. Of all people. Had he been cruel to her? Why hadn't she told me? After I had picked her up from the chair and carried her to bed and laid down beside her, she woke up and kissed me. She let me make love to her and never said a word about what happened to her.

Somewhere between a kid running into me as he barreled toward a table and an elderly man asking where to find the ketchup, the obvious truth hit me like a sledgehammer. Her immortality meant my mark was permanent.

I should have been upset. I should have railed at fate and my own stupidity and selfishness. I should have been buried in an avalanche of guilt, not only for her, but for Zee. Had he been serious last night, or was his decision to go for her a result of freaking out because he'd just found Euri? It no longer mattered, did it? Mariah was mine. *All mine*. Forever. At a minimum, I should have worried about her, and her future happiness.

Instead, I wanted to stand on a table and announce to everybody at Shake Shack that I was the luckiest son of a bitch on the planet. I wanted to throw my arms up in the air and shout, *"Fuckin' A!"*

Finally, the burgers were ready. I claimed the bags, walked outside to the crowded sidewalk and disappeared, popping back to her room. She sat in the middle of the bed, cross-legged, still naked, pointing a remote at the TV that now hung on the wall beside the fireplace, flipping channels. "Zee must have brought it yesterday, while I was gone. Do you know how awesome this is? I can understand everything they say. Look, this lady is talking about Jordan's dad." She frowned. "But she's being a real nasty hag about him." The channel changed. "Oh, cartoons!" Finally, she looked at me, her gaze moving to my feet. "Nice shoes."

"I was kind of in a hurry." I couldn't believe it, but a lump formed in my throat. She knew. Last night, she knew what it meant to have sex with me and she did it anyway. In her own quiet unassuming way, she accepted me as I was. Overcome, I set the bags on the small desk.

She moved over and patted the bed next to her. "Let's be heathens and eat right here."

I pulled off my T-shirt and spread it on the bed like a picnic blanket, then emptied the bags in the middle. Ditching the shoes, I took a seat beside her and we watched Bugs Bunny while we ate.

"These are delicious," she said, halfway through her second burger. "Where'd you go?"

"Shake Shack in New York."

"Let's go to New York. I want to see the Statue of Liberty, and the Empire State Building, and all the museums. I know we can transport there, but could we maybe fly? I've never been on an airplane before. Oh, and can we go to the opera? I've always wanted to see an opera."

"We'll go wherever you like. Guess who I ran into at Shake Shack?"

"Eryx?"

I jerked my head around. "How did you know?"

She shrugged and reached for her third burger. "You look weird, like you're afraid and excited and maybe you'd like to cry. When you left, you were very chill, and since I seriously doubt anything at a burger box place would make you want to cry, I assume the person you ran into was Eryx, who's been stalking all of you lately, and he told you what he did to me."

"When were you going to tell me?"

"As soon as I finished these cheeseburgers." She waved her hand toward the TV. "Let's see the end of Bugs Bunny and I'll tell you all about it."

There was such an element of surreal comedy to it, what could I do but go along with her? I ate my food and watched cartoons and continued reveling in absolute unequivocal glee.

When Bugs was done and I'd taken all the trash to the bathroom and tossed it, I went back to her bed, stripped off my jeans and laid down, pulling her with me. I kissed her and her mouth was cold and chocolaty. She reached between us, wrapped her hand around me, and mumbled against my lips, "Insatiable."

Our third time, and it was nothing like the first two. I was bemused. To me, sex was always sex. Different face, different girl, different language – but the mechanics were always the same and my objective never wavered.

With Mariah, it was like it had been in the very beginning, when we first joined humanity in the real world, when we figured out how to attract females into dark places. Every touch, every caress, every look, every kiss felt new and different. It took all my self-control not to be too aggressive, too over-the-top. She was small and delicate, still hesitant and unsure of herself, of me.

In the middle of things, I slipped. My self-control took a walk.

"Phoenix, what are you doing?"

Carrying her to the chair by the fire, I said, "Remember when I told you to imagine you're Danielle and I'm Rupert?"

"I remember, but—"

"This is me *not* being Rupert. He was a nice guy. Mr. Gentleman. I'm not nice, Mariah." I sat and turned her so she had to straddle my thighs. Watching her eyes widen in surprise as I maneuvered her body to slide down onto me, I was gratified.

"Oh," she whispered. "*Oh.*"

Her scent was heady, as if I stood in a field of heather. Her eyes were closer to midnight blue. I slipped my hands into her hair and cradled her head while I pulled her close for a deep, hot kiss. "Move for me," I whispered. I was insane with need for her. "Make it happen for you, Mariah."

She began slowly, shyly, but it wasn't long before she forgot to be self-conscious. She loved the control, reveled in her ability to set the rhythm. I have no idea how I lasted as long as I did. Watching her was tantalizing and so erotic, the sway of her perfect breasts, the rise and fall of her breath as it increased, the tightening of her muscles around me – I was scarcely a nanosecond behind her climax. Her head went back and she cried out, her body quivering. As I completed, I snatched her close to hold her tight against me. I never wanted to let her go. I would never let her go. She was mine, and I was overcome with protectiveness and aching affection for her.

We stayed like that for a while before I gathered her up and carried her back to the bed. She snuggled beneath the covers, her eyes drifting closed.

I laid down next to her. "Now would be a good time to tell me."

She burrowed deeper under the covers. "Mm, yeah, but let's take a nap first."

If I let her go back to sleep, it'd be hours before she'd wake up. I moved on the bed to lean against the headboard, and pulled her along with me, propping her against the pillows, pulling the covers up to her waist. "I promise you can sleep all you want, just as soon as you tell me."

She pulled the covers up farther, covering her breasts, but not before I noticed her birthmark. She was almost entirely changed to that unique blend of Anabo and Mephisto that would allow her to take out the lost souls, and still have the capacity to love me.

Probably a very bad idea to think about that at the moment. We were friends, and now we were friends with benefits. Could I love her? I didn't know, mostly because I wasn't entirely sure what it meant to love someone. I loved my brothers, and I loved Sasha. I didn't doubt I'd someday love Jordan. I loved Mathilda and Deacon and Hans – all the Purgatories meant something to me. And the Luminas.

But to love a woman selflessly and completely? How did that happen? And how could she ever love me if I didn't love her? Eryx was right. Jane had loved me, but I realized now it was more like the love I felt for Sasha. Close and warm, but not intimate. When we became intimate, it was a disaster. She'd cried and sobbed and wanted her sister. I'd felt like an ass, and there'd been so much blood, I was totally freaked out. In retrospect, it hadn't been that much, but I'd expected a little spot. Instead . . . what I didn't know about females was pretty much everything. I said I was sorry at least fifty times, until she told me to stop, to just leave her alone for a while so she could pull herself together. That's when I left, and I knew I wasn't going back.

The contrast to how it was with Mariah was night and day. She had taken all I had to give and returned it to me tenfold. Even now, she was sitting in bed completely naked, trusting and comfortable with me. Jane had never been easy in her own skin, and I had no idea whether that was a product of the times and her upbringing as an aristocrat, or because she knew on some level that I wasn't her intended.

It didn't matter now. It was done and she was gone and I'd made peace with my brother. I may have screwed it all to hell again by sleeping with Mariah, but I'd deal with it. I'd make it right however I could.

Mariah began her story. "Just after lunch, Denys took me to see the other side of the mountain." She leaned away and looked into my eyes. "I'm not going to tell you unless you swear not to go all commando on Denys. Swear?"

"I swear." But I was already wondering if he'd done something out of resentment or spite because he was so angry at me.

"You're lying, Phoenix. I'm serious. Don't get mad at him and get in a fight, or say something cruel to him. Promise me."

I wasn't liking this at all, but my need to know outweighed possible retribution, so I nodded and said, "I promise."

She meandered through the day, describing everything, including the little cabin where I'd stored all of Jane's things, which I'd gathered piece by piece over a couple of years after her death. Her parents never noticed. They'd closed up her room and moved on with their lives. When one of the maids boxed up what was left of Jane's belongings to take to a charity house, I took them all before they ever reached their destination. I put them in the little cabin I'd found in the wilderness, and as time passed, I was drawn back to it, again and again, some kind of penance, I suppose.

I found it odd that the cabin was where Mariah mentally escaped to when things were too much for her mind to handle. She'd never seen it until yesterday. I wondered why, and she said, "I'll get to that in a while."

She talked on and I was hanging on every word, feeling bad all over again for Denys, who'd been as hurt by Zee's cover-up as Zee and I. It was terribly sad and I wished so much it could have been different.

When she got to the part about Eryx taking her, I could no longer sit still. I got up, put on my boxers, then went to build a fire, taking my time, finding comfort in a task I'd done a million times in ten centuries.

By the end of her story, I was reeling. So much to absorb: her nocturnal visits from an angel who turned out to be my *mitera,* her unprecedented visit to Hell on Earth, Eryx joking with her, Eryx telling her he didn't rape Jane – and Mariah believed him, Denys completely clueless of what went on while he was banging the barmaid then passing out cold. She'd had the most extraordinary day, yet she sat there and told me all without the slightest hint of upset.

I stood behind the chair in front of the fire and watched the flames lick the split logs. "Why didn't you tell me last night, Mariah? Why did you let me make love to you? It's permanent now, and you can never go back."

"I don't want to go back."

I looked across the room at her, sitting in bed, her long dark hair flowing across her shoulders, her hands resting on the covers, her eyes ten shades lighter than they'd been yesterday morning. Her Anabo glow was beginning to show. Was she happy? She was looking at me with that poker face, giving me no hint of what she was thinking or feeling. "You're stuck with me."

"I was stuck with you the night I arrived. Why put off the inevitable?"

"You make it sound as if you're simply resigned to your fate."

"Oh, come on, Phoenix. Do you want me to tell you I love you madly, deeply, and will as long as I live, which will now be until the end of time? I've known you a week. A lot's happened in that week, but still – it's a week. Maybe I'll love you, maybe you'll love me. Does it matter? We're friends, and now we're friends who have sex. Let's just let it be and carry on." She slid further back against the pillows. "It's your turn to tell me why you changed your mind about the sex thing."

"You won't like it. You're going to regret letting me mark you."

"Regret is something I refuse to have, ever. I did what I did and I won't be sorry, even if you tell me I'm right and Jane was intended for Denys, and you knew it and had sex with her anyway."

"You're a scary girl, you know that?"

Her eyes widened. "Me? Scary?"

"It's like you know things, and then you throw them out there and point to them and kill any chance of secrets. Don't you know, people hide things because they're ashamed of them?"

"Are you joking? Until you, I hid every single thing in my life because I was so ashamed. Get over yourself and tell me the truth about Jane. All of it, even the parts that make you feel like a douche."

"I don't *feel* like a douche. I *am* a douche. And a jackass, and a liar, and a very bad guy."

"Says who?"

"Lucifer. He said it the night Jane died. He said of all my

brothers, I am the most like my father."

"So you've actually seen Lucifer. That's heavy. I want details. But first I'll say, maybe he meant you look like him, or that you have the same personality. Why assume he meant that you have the same character flaws?"

I began to pace. "I'll tell you the story, and you'll know exactly what he meant."

She nodded and folded her hands across her belly. "Okay, go."

For a guy who isn't big on talking, I was a guy who couldn't stop talking. I went on and on. She asked questions and I answered, but mostly she watched me pace and listened.

I fully expected, when I got to the end, that she would tell me to get out and never come back.

But, then, Mariah never did what I expected.

She sat up in bed and said, "That's all well and good, but you still haven't told me why you changed your mind about sex. Two nights ago, you said you'd never mark me, even if I wanted you to. The very next night, we were naked and I was marked. I'd love it if you said it was because you were overcome, that you couldn't help yourself, that I'm irresistible to you, but the truth is—"

"That's exactly why."

"Bullshit!" She scrambled out of bed and stalked toward me in all her naked, beautiful glory, her blue eyes snapping with indignation. "You and your brothers are like wolves, claiming their territory. I'm surprised you don't pee on things so the others know, *Hey, this is mine. Back off.* You told Zee you'd step aside for my sake, for his sake, but you didn't do that. You never *intended* to do that. The instant Kyros brought me here, the second you laid eyes on me, there wasn't a force of nature strong enough to make you let me go. You can kid yourself that you tried to do what you think is the right thing, but why lie? You knew when you climbed into bed with me that I'd wake up with your mark. Maybe you should go out there in the hall and howl so they'll all know you've claimed me."

"I don't need to do that. They're aware." But I really did have an insane urge to throw my head back and shout at the top of my lungs. Maybe I'd beat on my chest for good measure.

The thought was a little funny.

"You're smiling! This is serious, and you're *grinning*."

I advanced on her and she didn't back up.

"You've got to be kidding. I'm not done yelling at you."

"Bookmark your place," I said, a little hoarse, whether from yacking so long or because I was ridiculously emotional, I don't know. I lifted her off of her feet and turned her in a circle.

"Put me down. I'm not going back to bed with you."

I stopped turning and looked into her face. "Really?"

She went still in my arms. "No, not really, but honestly, Phoenix, you're impossible. Why did you think, even for a second, you could give me up? And why did you imagine I'd give you up? I'm not an object you can hand off to someone else. Zee is right. For a brilliant mind, you can be a real putz."

Hours later, I woke and knew she was having her dream. She was stiff, her breathing way too rapid. I moved closer and stroked her hair. "Wake up, Mariah. You're dreaming. This isn't real."

She mumbled in Romanian, "How are you here?" Once again, she'd drawn me into her dream world.

"I came to take you home."

Even in sleep, her expression was one of wonder and awe. "You made . . . disappear."

"I'll always make him disappear. Come on and wake up now." I wondered how much longer she'd be haunted by this nightmare? I hoped someday she'd fight him in her dreams and win, and maybe then she'd stop seeing him. Except I knew dreams didn't work like that. When the day came that she was past it, when she felt strong enough to fight him off, she'd not have the dream. I was overwhelmed by sadness for her, that the bloody bastard still tormented her, even in death.

She blinked open her eyes and I instantly gathered her close. She clung to me, shaky and unnerved. "I wanted so badly not to have it any more."

"I know." I hugged her tighter. "I know."

"How could you ever think I'd not want you," she whispered. "You're the best thing that ever happened to me.

The very . . . best."

"It's only that I'm the one you opened up to, Mariah. If you were as open with—"

"I wouldn't open up to anyone else. It's you. There's something about *you*. Maybe you are selfish, maybe you're wild. But not to me, Phoenix." She nuzzled into my neck. "Not to me."

We laid like that for a long time, me petting her hair while I held her close, and her mumbling grossly exaggerated praise into my neck. I could almost transport to an alternate reality and imagine that she loved me. Really loved me.

Even more outlandish, I could imagine that I loved her. I'd do anything for her, slay all the monsters, stay with her every night for all time and be there when she woke up, happy, sad, or scared. I didn't know about love, not really, but I did know there was no one in my life, in the world, that I'd rather be with.

Someone knocked. Expecting Mathilda, I called for her to come in, and had a shock when Zee opened the door.

He walked to the bed and stared down at the two of us, still tighter than a sailor's knot beneath the covers, Mariah's face half buried in my neck. "I assume this means your plan is null and void."

I nodded.

"You do realize I'd never have gone through with it, right? I only said as much because I knew it'd make you crazy, make you do exactly what you did. You're the most hardheaded, stubborn asshole on God's earth. It takes something extreme and harsh to get you to pay attention." His gaze moved to Mariah. "It's our duty to ensure the comfort and happiness of all Anabo, Mariah, and I was chosen to do the honors. Are you well? Is everything okay? You have only to say the word, and he'll be dealt with accordingly."

She turned her head and said, "I'm horribly embarrassed, but that's not his fault."

"Why are you embarrassed?"

"Because I'm in bed, naked, with your naked brother, and you're here looking at us, and everyone in the house knows what happened last night."

"Of course we know," he said in his usual blunt, reasonable, Zee way. "He marked you. This is how it works. Perhaps it'll make you feel better that no one will know about any subsequent sex. Unless you yell a lot. Some girls like to yell, which seems a little overdramatic to me, but whatever. Are you happy?"

She'd turned her face into my neck again, no doubt ten shades of red. "Very," she said, her voice muffled.

"Good. Don't forget to practice your scales. Every day. Lesson on Wednesday at nine. Be sharp." He paused. "B sharp. Get it?"

"I get it. I'll be sharp. Thank you for the TV."

"Welcome. I also bought you a laptop, which you need to let me teach you how to use. Phoenix will do it wrong."

Offended, I said, "I beg your pardon. I'm not some Luddite who doesn't know—"

"You're an amateur. She needs me to teach her."

"Fine."

"Fine." He turned away. "Try and make it downstairs for dinner. Key is leaving just after to go with Jordan to her school's winter ball. He's asked Sasha fifty times to adjust his bowtie, and Mathilda is about to bean him with a skillet because he keeps freaking out that his tux trousers are wrinkled. He's put his hair in a ponytail ten times, taken it down ten times, and now he's wondering if he should pull it back again. It'd be pathetic if it wasn't so funny."

This, I had to see. When Zee was gone, I asked her, "Are you up for this yet?"

"I may as well get it over with." She raised her head and looked at me. "And I am kind of hungry."

"Kind of?"

She grinned. "Okay, I'm starving." She tickled me. "Luddite."

Bouncing around on her bed, scaring the shit out of Olga, I couldn't stop laughing. Life could never get better than this.

CHAPTER 18

~~ MARIAH ~~

Isak Dinesen wrote in *Out of Africa* that the Earth was made round so we can't see too far down the road. That night, the first time I remembered those words was when Key came back from Washington and called a war room meeting.

I was in the basement with Phoenix, in his lab looking over all of his potential plans for the takedown that would happen during Jordan's birthday party. I was impressed by the detail, the absolute attention to every facet. Faking deaths was tedious business, and Phoenix rarely got it wrong – at least, according to Hetta, a Lumina who was a biomedical engineer before she came to be with the Mephisto. She worked with Phoenix when the plan involved death by anything internal, whether poison, or virus, or a health issue like a stroke or heart attack.

She was explaining her work with a particularly nasty foodborne virus they were considering, one they would hand off to M to use for the doppelgangers at the party, when Key's voice came through the intercom, announcing a war room meeting.

Phoenix walked toward the door of the lab, then turned and looked at me expectantly.

"What?" I asked.

"You need to come with me, Mariah. You're one of us now."

Feeling extremely weird about that, I followed him out into the narrow hallway and walked beside him to the room from which everything flowed, like command central, or a brain, or the queen bee. The Mephisto basement was like a medieval castle, with flagstone floors, stone walls and many candles. There were computer banks in various niches and rooms, all giving out additional light, and the lab had been brightly lit with electricity, but for the most part, everything was lit by candlelight. The war room was a mix of ancient and modern. There was a large, oval hickory table with a repaired crack down the middle, and nine chairs, the newest one for me, a world map and a white board with colored markers across one wall, and a huge flat panel screen on the opposite wall. An iron fixture with at least fifty candles hung from the center of the high ceiling.

They were all there when we arrived, sitting around the table, Ty with his mastiff, Gretchen, next to him, Key still dressed in his tux, although he'd undone his tie. His hair was down, as it had been when he left, mostly because he'd run out of time to pull it back again.

As soon as Phoenix and I sat down, he said, "There was an incident at the dance tonight. Jordan somehow got it into her head that I might consider defecting to join Eryx. He was talking to me, and she went ballistic. Shoved him, then punched him, and if I hadn't stopped her, she'd have jumped him and continued hitting him. I carried her out of there and she cried so hard, was so hysterical . . ." He sighed and ran his hands through his hair. "It's too much for her. Being there, being Mephisto, trying to act normal – it's killing her. I want to vote on my plan to tell her when she comes later tonight that she's not going back." He looked at Phoenix. "Hoping, actually assuming, you'd all agree, I went ahead and asked M for a doppelganger, a brain aneurysm."

I said, "If she can't go back, she won't have the time that's left with her dad."

"Maybe it's better this way," Sasha said. "I've been thinking about how hard it was going to be for her at her birthday party, knowing she was about to leave him."

"She could have weathered that," Key said, "but lasting another week in the real world? I don't think so. Eryx is the problem. He's relentless. He told me tonight that he's giving up, but I don't believe it. He's up to something, and I'm convinced we need to bring Jordan home to make sure she's safe from whatever he plans."

Everyone nodded and Key said, "Hands for aye." We all raised our hands. He stood and said, "I'm going to my room to wait. I'll explain when she gets here, and tell her the vote was unanimous."

I almost offered to help, but didn't. Jordan and I weren't close at all. She'd lean on Key, which I supposed was how it should be.

When we stood to disburse, Phoenix said, "She'll be glad you're here, once the shock wears off."

"You think so?"

"I know so." He took my hand and led me from the war room.

"Are we going back to the lab?"

"Not right now. I'm going to have to dream up a whole other plan."

"Because now there won't be a birthday party where a lot of lost souls will be gathered."

He glanced at me. "Now, there'll be a memorial service."

I felt chilled. No matter that her death would be fake, the idea of a memorial service for my baby sister made me shaky.

Wrapping an arm around my shoulders, he walked me down the hall toward the stairs. "Let's do something to take your mind off of it."

"If you're thinking of—"

"A movie. Let's go to the TV room and watch a movie." He shot me a meaningful look. "Unless you were thinking of something else?"

I smiled, which was what he intended. "Later. For now, a movie sounds good."

Everyone else had the same idea, so there was a crowd sprawled across the sofas and chairs to watch *The Bourne Identity*, evidently a family favorite. I was sucked in fairly quickly, taking my thoughts away from the sadness my sister was about to endure, but not entirely. It was there in my subconscious, humming along, waiting.

When the movie was over, everyone took a bathroom break and we reconvened to watch the next Bourne movie. Mathilda brought popcorn and sodas, and all the while, I wondered what was taking so long. Shouldn't Jordan be here by now? Maybe she'd arrived and Kyros was telling her.

The second movie was done and we were halfway through the third when there was a loud crash right above us. Zee immediately paused the movie and we all exchanged looks. Another crash, followed by glass breaking, then an anguished scream that went on and on, making the hair at the nape of my neck stand on end, bringing instant tears to my eyes.

It wasn't female. It wasn't Jordan. It was Kyros.

One heartbeat later, we all popped upstairs to the hall outside his room and everyone looked at Phoenix, as if by silent consent, he would be the one to go inside.

We crowded around the door when he opened it and collectively gasped. Key had broken everything inside and thrown most of the furniture out the windows, smashing them completely. He was leaning out, into the heavy snowfall, screaming in agony. Phoenix went into the melee and retrieved Key's cell phone from the littered floor. Bending his head, he read the small screen, then looked at us from over his shoulder, horror on his face.

Turning back to his brother, all he said was, "Kyros."

He wheeled around and saw Phoenix standing in the midst of the wreckage, Key's phone in his hand.

Phoenix said solemnly, "Now you know."

Falling to his knees, Key buried his face in his hands and sobbed.

We waited in the hall an eternity before Phoenix finally came out. He looked around at all of us before he focused on Jax. "She wrote an email but didn't send it. M did. Eryx visited her and convinced her she could help him, that if she kissed him, there was a chance he could change, that she could share some of her light and the war for Hell would be over. She said he looked different, and she had to take a chance for Key, because he loved Eryx so much, but it backfired and she lost Anabo and Mephisto."

Jax swallowed so hard, I heard it. "She's immortal, so if she's not Anabo or Mephisto, she's . . . ."

Phoenix took a deep breath and let it out slowly, leaning

against the wall to stare up at the ceiling. "She's like Eryx."

I wrapped my arms around myself and moved back, away from the group, shaking so hard, I don't know how my teeth weren't chattering. Lucifer's omen repeated in my head. *"The Mephisto will suffer a great loss by straying from the path."* I never dreamed it would be my sister. All I'd done hadn't been enough. Not in the end. She would suffer a million times worse with Eryx than she would have with Emilian. She was lost. To her, there was now no God, no Lucifer, nothing but Eryx. What would happen to her? Was her soul still her own, or did it now belong to Eryx?

"She knew what was happening to her when she wrote the email," Phoenix said, "and I suppose by the time she was done, she'd already changed enough that she lost the motivation to send it, which is why M added his own note and sent it. Key says he's going after her, that he'll take her back to God and hope it works."

They deflated and stared at the floor. Zee said, "To do that, he'll have to die."

Dead silence.

"We'll all go after her," Ty said, and the others spoke at once, agreeing they would all go, then throwing out ideas about how to do it.

I moved next to Sasha and said, "I want to go, too." They stopped talking and turned to face me.

"We get why you'd want to, Mariah," Sasha said, looking as though her heart would break, "but you're not immortal. You're not yet able to do what we do."

I looked to Phoenix, thinking he'd tell them, but he was still staring at the ceiling.

"Even if you were immortal," Jax said, "you haven't had any training. You'd be a liability, and going to Erinýes is way different than anywhere else. He has the castle and grounds on lockdown, so we can transport in, but not out. We have to leave his property, which is acres and acres in the Carpathian mountains."

"But she's my sister. I want . . . I have to see her before she's taken. Before she's . . . gone." I willed Phoenix to look at me, to acknowledge me, to stand up for me.

He never said a word, his focus on the ceiling, his thoughts all for a master plan, his mind working in overdrive. And no doubt he was devastated to lose Kyros. I would lose my sister; he would lose his brother. All because of Eryx.

I said to the rest of them, "I understand." Turning, I walked away, toward the stairs, up to the third floor, then further, up to the attic floor. I heard them agree to reconvene in the war room, then there was only silence.

And me.

I went outside to the tiny terrace to stand in the snowfall. Nothing in my life had ever hurt this badly. I couldn't get her sweet little face out of my head, standing there on the steps of the orphanage, her lip trembling while she held her rabbit and watched me leave.

I couldn't stand this. I cried until I had the hiccups, and when I went back inside, there were all those shelves, so organized and tidy with all those boxes of God knew what – clutter from the past, things that no longer mattered.

Standing behind the last shelf, the one closest to the door onto the terrace, I reached out and pushed a box so that it slid through to the other side and fell to the floor. I pushed another and another, until I'd shoved all the boxes on that shelf to the floor. Things broke, papers scattered, boxes ripped, and the more I destroyed, the more I wanted to destroy. Fury took hold and I became vicious, shoving them harder and faster, repeating her name every time one hit the floor. *"Viorica . . . Viorica . . . Viorica . . ."*

It was almost morning and I was nowhere close to sleepy. I paced the attic, scowling at the remaining shelves. In a rush, I ran at them and pushed with all my might, gratified when they dominoed and fell in a spectacular crash.

I was raging and frustrated, grief ripping my heart to shreds. Had my whole damned life been a waste? Had all those years of misery been for nothing? I'd saved her from abuse and sexual assault, but she'd lost her soul, lost God, lost love.

She was all I had. She was everything to me. Without her, I didn't know who I was. Nothing mattered. Nothing made sense. She'd been my anchor all of my life, what kept me sane, what gave me a purpose.

I stood in the middle of the massive mess I'd made, breathing hard, and didn't know what to do. I couldn't go with them, couldn't be any help to Kyros, wouldn't be there when he took her away. I'd never see her again and I'd never get past it. Never.

My mind tried to nudge me toward thoughts of Phoenix, of his complete and total lack of compassion, of notice, of anything. It was as if I didn't exist. The rational, logical side of me understood. He was thinking of Key, trying to dream up something that could save Jordan without his brother having to die. But the lonely, hopeful dreamer side of me was bleeding.

I forced it from my mind. I wouldn't think about it. I wasn't surprised. I'd always known he'd hurt me, and I was an idiot because I'd let it happen.

It didn't matter. All that made any difference was Viorica. I had to see her.

I closed my eyes, imagined I was in my room, and seconds later, I was. Olga meowed.

I'd take myself to Eryx's castle. I'd been there, and I was certain all I had to do to be there again was imagine it. I wouldn't have the ability to leave by transporting, but I'd worry about that after I'd seen Viorica. I would see her one last time.

With a plan and a purpose, I showered and dressed in jeans, a pale pink sweater, Ugg boots and my ski jacket. I twisted a scarf around my neck, pulled my hair into a ponytail, petted Olga goodbye, then headed downstairs. Through the windows of the dining room, I saw that dawn was breaking. It was almost seven in Colorado, close to three in Romania. In the kitchen, I asked Hans, "Do you have some energy bars? I'm going for a hike."

He smiled and went into the walk-in pantry at the other end of the kitchen, reappearing moments later with a box of the bars. I stuffed four of them in my pockets, said thanks, goodbye, and left.

In the mudroom, I closed my eyes and imagined I was in Eryx's library.

When I opened my eyes, I was in Eryx's library, but things were very different than they'd been last night. Loud hip-hop music came from somewhere just outside the room and I heard laughter. I moved toward the doorway and saw people in the hallway, all with shaded eyes. Skia. Of course everyone in Eryx's castle would be Skia. I was surprised to see so many. Were these people always here, or had they come just for the occasion of my sister joining their ranks? Eryx must be elated. He'd said Jordan would be with him, and now she was. The smell of alcohol was strong, along with the sickly sweet scent of weed.

I darted in and out of doorways, hiding, making my way through the first floor until I came to a bedroom wing. I was just reaching for the door of the first room when the door at the end of the hall opened and Eryx was there, still dressed in his tuxedo from last night's dance. He smiled at me. "I've been waiting for you."

"How did you know I was here?"

"You've been marked."

"How stupid of me to forget." I wondered if Phoenix would mentally search for me and know I was here? I doubted it, but it didn't matter. I was here to see my sister. I had to focus.

He waved me toward him. "Come and join us. We're having a bite to eat and some champagne."

I walked to the end of that long hall, growing more anxious with every step I took. When I was there, he stepped back and waved me inside what appeared to be his bedroom. It was huge, twice the size of the Mephisto's suites, and those were ginormous. I swept my gaze around the room, searching for Viorica.

She sat at a small table in front of a fireplace so big, a horse could have fit inside. She smiled at me. "Eryx said you'd be here. Come sit down and eat some of this paté. It's fabulous."

Her beautiful bluebell eyes were now as black as Eryx's, and just as dead. She wore a skimpy black dress that hugged her curves and showed most of her cleavage, her hair was up, and she wore a pair of dangling diamond earrings. She was sexy, elegant, beautiful – and lost.

I sat and made certain I had no expression on my face.

"Are you staying?" she asked.

"For a while."

"Nonsense," Eryx said, almost jovial as he took his seat. "You need to stay indefinitely. Jordan will like that, won't you?"

She shrugged. "Sure, if she wants." She smiled at him. "But she's been marked, so your brothers are sure to come after her."

He gave me a level look. "Somehow I don't think so. What do you think, Mariah? Will they plan a rescue mission for you?"

"No."

He almost looked like he pitied me, and I was wondering why, and how he knew the Mephisto would have forgotten about me when Viorica said, "It's really nice that you're here, Mariah. Eryx has a marvelous library, and I know how much you enjoy reading. His nearest neighbor is Castle Dracula. How awesome is that? He says he'll take me to visit. You can go, too."

"Sure," I agreed, although I knew it would never happen. Sometime soon, the Mephisto would arrive to rescue her, and this charade would be over.

We ate paté and drank champagne and pretended it was all very normal. Eryx had an impressive stereo system, not as elaborate as Zee's, but exceptional, and he put on classical music.

"I have a room prepared for you," he said, smiling at me. "One of my assistants purchased all you'll need, but if anything's missing, you have only to ask. I want you to be comfortable here, Mariah."

I thought of Olga. I didn't really need anything except Olga. But I wasn't staying, and neither was Viorica, so my need for my cat was irrelevant.

He talked about Erinýes, told us the history and some of his plans for improvements and modernization. He talked and we listened. Or, at least, I listened. Viorica was busy eating, staring off into space, twiddling with one of her earrings. Eryx appeared not to notice her lack of attention. He mostly spoke to me, but he'd give her an indulgent smile every so often. She was like a pet, a toy, an object of his desire, and there was no doubt he desired her. The sexual tension was enormous. Once he'd gotten what he wanted from her, how long would he remain interested? The strength he'd found so attractive was nowhere to be seen. My sister had lost her spark, her energy, her glow. She was self-absorbed. I thought Eryx was still riding the high of his conquest and hadn't yet noticed that she'd changed. He'd killed what it was about her that he'd wanted so desperately. Would he appreciate the irony once he figured it out?

When I couldn't stand seeing the travesty of her sweet short life ending for one more second, I stood abruptly and said, "I'm very tired. Will you excuse me and show me to my room now?"

"Of course." He stood and waited for me to say goodbye to my sister. I bent low and kissed her cheek, then began to back away from her.

She looked at me and her lip trembled. "Where are you going? Don't leave yet. Don't leave me here."

"It's just for a little while. I'll see you later."

"Promise?"

"I promise." I lied, just as I had all those years ago. It was next to impossible to remain expressionless, but I managed somehow, and turned away before I lost it.

Eryx led me down the hall to one of the bedrooms and opened the door. It was large, decorated very prettily in yellow and blue, with a lovely painting of daffodils above the fireplace and a small, feminine desk beneath the window. He went to the closet. "My assistant got your sizes from the clothes you wore last night, but some may not fit. Just let me know and we'll make sure you have what you need. If you require something to eat or drink, or need help of some kind, the bell pull is right there by the bed. My housekeeper will answer your ring." He moved to the door. "We will see you for dinner." He smiled. "I'm very glad you're here, Mariah."

I nodded and gave him a fake smile.

He was closing the door when he stopped and looked at me soberly. "By the way, in the event the Mephisto do show up to take you back, it's up to you to decide whether you go or stay, but they can't have Jordan. She's lost to them now, and if you love her, you'll keep them from taking her. Otherwise, they'll send her to Hell on Earth."

The door closed softly and I stood staring at it, my mind racing for logic, for truth. Key planned to take her back to God. Could he? I thought of her dead black eyes and honestly didn't know. I didn't know what to do. If I told Eryx they were coming, he'd be ready. He'd protect Viorica. No matter what she was or how lost, I couldn't bear for her to be in Hell on Earth. I'd go there myself before I'd allow her to be there.

I sat on the chair next to the fireplace and listened to the steady thump of bass from the party, the sound of laughter and revelry. I made myself focus, made my mind avoid everything but the facts, without emotion.

All those people out there had shadows across their eyes. They'd given their souls to Eryx. They were like robots. Viorica had no shadow. She must still have her soul, and even though it was marred by Eryx's influence, she didn't belong to him in the same way as the lost souls and Skia.

He was deviously clever, and any kindness he exhibited was solely to suit his purposes, never actual consideration. He was being effusively nice to me. Why? He wanted me to stand between Jordan and the Mephisto. He was playing on my love and devotion to her. If I told him the Mephisto were coming for her, I'd be giving him exactly what he wanted.

If I did nothing and Kyros took her to holy ground, she would lose immortality and die. Would she be in Heaven? Whether she was or she wasn't, at least that course of action offered hope, and staying here forever meant no hope, no life of her own, no happiness.

I continued to plan what I would do next. The party became louder and more boisterous. I debated leaving and went to the window to investigate how difficult it would be to go out that way. The forest was many meters away, and I risked being seen if I chose that direction. Trees stood closer to the castle further to the east, so I'd have to find an exit in that direction. That meant I'd have to go back through the Skia party, and I might not be so lucky this time. Instinct told me they'd know what I was – hadn't Zee said the Skia knew the Mephisto? Chances were good that Eryx had briefed all of them on what might happen today. If I saw me, what would they do to me?

I seriously doubted they'd offer me a cocktail, or wave me on my way to the other end of this castle so I could leave.

There was a knock and I steeled myself for who might answer when I called, "Come in."

I was surprised it was my sister.

She shot a furtive glance over her shoulder before she slipped into the room and closed the door behind her. "We don't have much time," she whispered in a stage voice. "You've got to help me, Mariah. Please. I know you're upset by what's happened, and believe me, I never dreamed I'd wind up here, like this, but what's done is done. The thing is, I'm afraid he's going to kill me. He's going to make me have sex with him, and then he's going to kill me."

Her fear was palpable. "He can't kill you."

"He can do lots of things the Mephisto can't. He has so much power, so much more than they do, because of all the souls he carries within. He's almost as powerful as Lucifer. Yes, he can take me out, and I know how he thinks. He'll give me the ultimatum of giving him my soul to become Skia, or he'll kill me. I can't lose my soul, Mariah, and I don't want to die. If I die, where will I go?" Huge tears formed in her black eyes. "I'm so afraid! I need time. I need to think and make a plan. I need to get away from him. Please, will you help me?"

"I'd do anything for you, Viorica. You know that. But I can't see how I can help." I couldn't tell her about the Mephisto plans. She'd tell Eryx, I was sure of it.

"I'm certain Kyros will come after me, but he doesn't know that Eryx is aware. He's waiting, and all those Skia are here because he plans to capture Key and hold him hostage."

She had to be lying. The Skia were drunk and stoned, laughing and dancing, partying with abandon. They weren't anticipating a Mephisto arrival. "I don't know what they plan to do. They may do nothing. You're lost to them, so why would they risk coming here to get you?" Key would risk it because he loved her, but I didn't say that.

She came closer. "You live with them now. You're immortal and marked. You're fully Mephisto. Why don't you know their plans?"

"It's complicated. They don't know I'm here. I came to see you because I had to, one last time."

"So you never intended to stay?"

"How can I stay and be who I am?" I stood and went to the window. "I love you, will always love you, no matter what, but I have to go."

"Take me with you!"

"I can't."

She rushed toward me and threw her arms around me, crying into my shoulder. "I'm so sorry. So . . . sorry."

Returning her embrace, I wished there was some way I could let her know she wasn't doomed to be here for all time, but it wasn't a chance I could take. I couldn't trust her any more than I could trust Eryx. As much as anything, that broke my heart.

"The only place he can't go," she mumbled into my shoulder, "is Hell on Earth. If I could go there, just for a little while, I'd have time to think, time to make a plan."

"It's a horrible place and you'd be miserable."

"But I'd be safe from him, and I'd do *anything* to get away. He's scary, Mariah. I wish so much that I hadn't believed him. He's so sincere, such a master at faking people out." She cried harder and clung to me and I was overcome with grief. "He keeps talking about sex, and what he's going to do to me. It's . . . unnatural. I don't want it, I don't want to do it. I'm so afraid."

I remembered his speech about rape, that he thought it was disgusting. "He won't make you do anything you don't want to do. I'm sure of it."

"Are you joking?" She pulled away and stared at me with wide eyes. "This is Eryx we're talking about. He's evil worse than Lucifer. He has no conscience, no light, no clue what it is to be afraid. He loves to instill fear in others, but he doesn't know what it's like." Her face crumpled. "What am I going to do, Mariah?"

"Just be patient and tell him you want to wait, and you can think of something."

"I could ask Lucifer for help. Do you think he would help me? God can't hear me anymore, but Lucifer can. He knows."

She brightened. "That's the answer, I'm sure of it. I'll ask Lucifer."

I didn't think Lucifer could hear her any more than God, but I didn't say so. "He may take you to Hell, Viorica."

"Wouldn't that be better than this?"

"I don't know. I have no concept of Hell or what it might be like."

"I know from what Key told me that it's not like Hell on Earth, and it's not like it is with Eryx. Lucifer is balance, and he's not about inflicting evil. He would help me, I know he would. Please, Mariah, take me to Hell on Earth. That'll get his attention. He'll come there and talk to me."

"Even if I wanted to, I couldn't take you. I can't leave Erinýes unless I walk out."

"You never know until you try. Maybe Hell on Earth is different."

"Viorica, you've got to understand, there's nothing I can do to help you. It's not as if I talk to Lucifer. Why do you think he'll hear you there any more than he will here?"

The door opened and Eryx stood there, scowling at Viorica. "You said you'd be right back. What goes on here?" He came in and closed the door, advancing toward us with a thunderous look of rage on his handsome face. "You're not trying to leave, are you?"

I wasn't sure if he was talking to me, or my sister, but all my protective instincts came screaming forward and I stepped in front of her. "What is wrong with you? Can't you see she's afraid?"

"Of course I see. I'm not blind. Now step aside."

"No."

He grasped my arms and shoved me, than grabbed Viorica and kissed her. She fought to get away, but he held her fast and pulled the neckline of her dress below her breasts, squeezing them so hard, she cried out against his mouth.

Furious, I launched myself at him and pushed with all my strength, gratified when he stumbled backward, clearly shocked. I didn't wait around to see what he'd do. Taking my sister's arm, hoping it worked, I closed my eyes and imagined I was on that narrow ledge within Hell on Earth. I knew the instant heat consumed me that we were there.

I opened my eyes and saw Viorica smiling at me as she tugged her dress up to cover her breasts. "You did it! You really did it! I didn't think you would. I said you weren't this gullible, but he knew. He's so smart, knows exactly how to get people to do what he wants. You really fell for it and brought me here." Her face was perspiring.

So they had tricked me. They'd used my love for her and my horror of rape to make me do what they wanted. "Why?"

"To get rid of you, of course."

"If he wanted to be rid of me, why did he bring me back to immortality? Why didn't he just let me stay dead?"

"For me. He wanted you to be there for me. He didn't realize that I couldn't care less, but once he understood, he knew he'd need to dispose of you, so you can't be any help to the Mephisto. Eryx can visit here, but he can't bring anyone with him, and he can't take anyone out. He was delighted when you said you were brought here while you were dead. Even as a newly made immortal Mephisto, you can transport to places you've been. But Hell on Earth is like Erinýes, on permanent lockdown. You can come here, but you can't leave."

"And you can?"

"It's part of what Eryx gave me when he kissed me. I'll be with him always, and grow in strength as he does, and someday, we'll own the world."

"Why would you want to?"

"Because it's power. Everything in the universe belongs to those with power. I realize now, all pleasure comes from power. Your whole life, you've been a powerless nonentity, so I don't expect you to understand."

I couldn't breathe because of the heat and the lack of oxygen, and yet I didn't die. Agony and no death. Hell on Earth. The shuffling crowd had stopped moving and were shouting and screaming at us. "I love you, Viorica."

Her expression went from ecstatic to disgusted in a nanosecond. "My name is *Jordan*. I haven't been Viorica since I was a baby, but you just can't let go, can you? You should have gotten a life. Instead, all you've ever done is sit and wait for life to happen to you. You love people and hope they'll love you back, but nobody loves an invisible girl. You hated Emilian, but it turns out, he's the only one who ever cared anything at all about you. At least he noticed you exist." She stepped back. "Goodbye, Mariah. Enjoy eternity here."

"You're a clever one," I said with a smile. "I always knew you were the smartest of us, the brightest and prettiest. I wish you well, Viorica, and hope you find your way back to God, someday."

That made her angry. Turning to look down at the sea of raging faces, she shouted, "Silence!" When they quieted, she said, "Meet Mariah, the newest Mephisto!"

The rage became hysteria, all of them surging forward to shake their fists and scream at me, call me filthy names and hurl threats.

I leaned close and kissed Viorica's sweaty cheek just before she disappeared and I was alone. Again. I tried to transport and wasn't at all surprised that I couldn't.

I didn't hate her for this. She was like him now, without a conscience, without compassion.

I began to pray, even though I felt certain God couldn't hear me. This was Lucifer's domain, a place to keep Eryx's followers from recruiting others. God didn't live here in any way.

I began to pray to Lucifer. I prayed to Mephistopheles. I prayed to Mary Michael.

Time passed and nothing happened.

The Skia were insane with fury, trying to climb the stone wall to the ledge where I stood. They'd find a way, eventually, and take me down and tear me to bits. They'd rape and torture me and I'd owe it all to my baby sister, who loved me until Eryx poisoned her soul.

I'd taken off my jacket, had lost my scarf, and now I pulled off my sweater, then my jeans, until all I wore was a bra and panties. I sat on my jacket and labored to breathe while I watched my skin turn red and blister. I wondered what Phoenix was doing, if he'd discovered I was missing yet? Would he be able to mentally search for me and find me here?

I closed my eyes and thought of him, trying to do my own mental search, but I came up with nothing and didn't know if it was because I didn't know how, or if a mental search wouldn't work in Hell on Earth.

What difference did it make anyway? He couldn't come here to get me for the same reason I couldn't leave. I was stuck here and no amount of wishing and praying and hoping would make a damn bit of difference.

I had no concept of time, but eventually I grew hungry. I pulled one of the energy bars from my jacket pocket and turned to face the wall while I ate it. There were three more, hardly enough to last forever. I was destined to be hungry, skeletal and desperate. Would I look forward to a lost soul landing in this cave because it would mean food?

Unable to help it, I threw up the energy bar all over my sweater.

That's when I noticed the Skia were louder, closer, more enraged. They knew I had food. I saw a hand on the ledge just before one of them, a man, slid up beside me, then another, and another. They were climbing on top of one another to reach me. I tried to kick them away, but the weight on the ledge was too much and it gave way, sending me hurtling into the middle of the mob.

CHAPTER 19

For maximum energy, in a long-standing pre-takedown ritual, we ate as much as possible, and today, as fast as possible, then convened around the onyx *M* in the front hall. Each of us held a box of plastic explosives, and Jax held the detonators. He grimly looked around the circle. "Is everyone completely clear on what you're to do?"

We all nodded, except Zee, who said, "I still think it's dicey to blow up Erinýes. There's no reason to do it other than revenge, and it's going to take time, which means more opportunities to be discovered by Eryx's Skia. If he realizes we're there before we're ready for him to know, he'll take Jordan somewhere else and we'll have to start all over." He looked at Key. "Time is all important, and what you plan to do won't make any difference if she's already crossed the line. No way she's getting into Heaven if she's helped him take a soul."

"She's been with him ten hours, at the most," Sasha said, "and they haven't left Erinýes, I know, because I've been holding on to my mental search ever since I found out what happened. It's not like he's going to go hunt down a convert when he just got her there."

Zee said, "There's also the possibility he'll try to mark her, which may or may not be possible, but once she's taken that step, getting her back to God might be a lost cause."

Hands gripping his box, Key looked close to losing it again. "This will work, Zee, and it's not just about revenge. You saw the text he sent me. He's so pleased with himself for having the ability to trick an Anabo, comparing it to Lucifer's temptation of Eve, he's certain he's close to being powerful enough to confront Lucifer. He has to know that he's not. We have to show him he's nowhere close, because if he openly declares war, it'll be chaos and anarchy of Biblical magnitude. Humanity will suffer because he's still tied to the world, and the only way he can draw Lucifer out is by trying to destroy it."

"And you think blowing up his castle is the way to show him he's not ready to take on Lucifer?"

"It's that we *can*, Zee. You went there and saw for yourself that he's allowing everyone in the castle to slack off. He's so cocky right now, he thinks we can't touch him. He thinks we're *afraid* of him. We have to make it real clear that he's not as powerful as he believes, and he won't win if he calls Lucifer out. Stealing Jordan and blowing up Erinýes will do that."

Zee shifted the box he held and said, "I wish to God what she tried to do had worked."

"We all do," Ty said, his voice hard. "But it didn't, and we owe it to her to get her out of there, to save her from what she's become."

Jax began a count.

On three, we transported to Romania, to Erinýes. I materialized in the main bedroom corridor, the one with modern bathrooms, the one with Eryx's at the end. I went in the first room and quickly set the plastic, affixed the charge, then moved across the hall to the next bedroom and set another one. Most of the Skia were in the great hall, dancing to hip-hop tunes and getting crazy drunk, but one occasionally came my way and I remained inside a bedroom as they passed. I stealthily worked my way down the hall, avoiding rooms with Skia, and set the last charge in the room closest to Eryx's, this one with the most plastic to ensure his room was destroyed.

Back in the hall, I saw a couple leaving a bedroom I'd skipped, so I went back to set a charge in there. When I opened the door, I caught the faint scent of heather. I worked the plastic, thinking of Mariah, of how difficult it would be for her to get past losing Jordan. She hadn't come downstairs to the war room, I assumed because it was too much for her. How could she plan her own sister's death?

I'd essentially planned my brother's, but for me, it wasn't

quite the same. Mariah had given up so much for Jordan. To see it all end like this had to be worse than devastating.

I couldn't think about that. Not now. Not yet. We did this for Jordan, and for Kyros, because he loved her. So much, he would die for her.

I noticed a scarf on the chair and thought it looked familiar, but there was no time to look and see if it was Mariah's, if she'd maybe left it here when Eryx brought her.

I could hear gunfire. We had started.

I slipped a mask across my face, reached into my pocket to retrieve a switchblade, then swung the assault rifle around from where it'd been riding my back.

In the hall, I moved through quickly; any Skia who wasn't already passed out from inhaling the canister gas Zee and Sasha were dropping across the castle I shot. If one came at me before I could get off a shot, I stabbed them. Some of them rallied enough to get pistols and rifles, but I made it to the other side of the castle without wounds.

My objective was the wing of rooms where Eryx's resident Skia worked, where they had computer banks and records similar to ours. Zee would have already taken hard drives and flash drives, but we wanted to make sure when Eryx came back, there was nothing left of his operation. He would have to start from scratch.

I found the hall, set the charges without incident because the Skia were all unconscious, then ran back to the front of the castle, leaping over the bodies littering the floor, running through the open doors and down the steps to the grocery truck Ty had commandeered from the village ten miles away. I was last, and as soon as I leapt for the truck, Ty sped away.

Fifty yards from the castle, he stopped and we all jumped to the ground. Jordan was unconscious. Key laid her across a stack of boxes inside the truck, then joined the rest of us.

Jax handed each of us a detonator. "On three."

We punched the remotes and felt the ground shake while we watched Eryx's castle explode, blasting everyone inside to bits. They were immortal, so they'd be back, but it would be a while. It took several weeks to come back from being blown to pieces. And it would take months, even years, for Eryx to rebuild and replace what he'd lost. When he came back, he'd know the Mephisto had won this round. He'd know he wasn't ready to take on Lucifer.

We climbed into the back of the truck, and Key sat on a cabbage crate, settling Jordan in his lap, holding her against his chest. I watched him and wished with all my heart and soul this could be different. I'd alternately hated and loved him, all of my life, but no matter what, he was always there, always solid and strong. I would miss him like I'd miss my arm or my leg. I'd survive, but I'd always feel handicapped, a part of me gone forever.

Another five minutes and the truck passed through the gates that marked the edge of Eryx's land, freeing us to transport again. As we slowed, Key looked across at me and I solemnly looked back at him. I didn't say anything. He believed if I'd had the choice with Jane that he now had with Jordan, I'd have done it. But would I? It was a question I didn't think I'd ever have an answer for. All I'd felt for Jane had been bastardized over a century, until it was so wrapped up in guilt and shame, it bore no resemblance to reality.

Key looked at Sasha, who was crying, then at Denys, who said, "I'm glad you're my brother." His gaze moved to Zee, who lunged across the space between them to hold Key's face in his hands and kiss his forehead. "I love you," he whispered before he disappeared.

He looked to where Ty was standing behind the truck. Our tallest brother swallowed hard and said, simply, "Good-bye, Kyros."

Finally, he looked at Jax. "You'll make sure Mariah is safe?"

I wasn't angry that he said it. I understood. Nothing I'd done about Mariah had been right – none of it had been in her best interests. Key was asking Jax to make sure I didn't screw it up worse than I had already. Even now, he was looking out for the Mephisto.

Jax nodded, and Key said, "You'll be oldest now. You'll be the one who leads. Keep these filthy animals in line, understand?"

Jax gave up trying not to cry. "I'll miss you all the rest of my life."

Key looked down at Jordan's beautiful face, clutched her a little tighter to his chest, and disappeared from Romania. From our lives.

We stayed in the truck while Ty drove it back to the village, and didn't transport away until he'd parked and killed the engine. We materialized back in Colorado and everyone split up to grieve in their own way. All the Luminas had gathered in the living room and I could hear their murmurs, no doubt praying for Key. There was no one on Mephisto Mountain whose life wouldn't be affected by Key's absence. He was respected and loved.

I popped upstairs to Mariah's room, hoping she'd be there, disappointed when she wasn't. I almost made a mental search, then didn't because that was a bad habit to fall into. Everyone deserved their privacy, and unless it was called for because of a very good reason, we had an unwritten rule not to search for each other.

I wandered back down her hall, and saw a marble on the third to last step of the stairway leading up to the attic. I bent to pick it up and saw other odd items on the stairs, like a game piece from an old Monopoly set and a pipe Zee used to smoke over a hundred years ago. I continued climbing, continued finding random items until I reached the fourth floor and went into the attic. I was stunned. What had once been total organization was now mass chaos, a giant heap of broken boards, torn boxes, and things long forgotten that Mathilda packed and stored because she was so sure someone would want it again.

I didn't have to think hard to know Mariah had done this. I felt so bad for her, and understood her need to deal with her anger and grief. I was in a state of confusion and shock that my brother was gone. Jordan had been everything to Mariah for so long, how much greater must her pain be? I wanted Mariah. I needed to be with her, to offer comfort, and maybe in return, I wouldn't have this horrible urge to cry like a little girl. I couldn't stop thinking of Key, all through the years, always with his long hair, his stern face, his absolute dedication to the rest of us. Most boys aspire to be like their father. I always aspired to be like Key.

My hatred of Eryx ramped up yet again. Someday I'd have the joy of killing him. I didn't know how it would happen, but it would, and I'd show no mercy, just as he'd never shown us an inch of compassion.

He would know when he returned to the living that Key's soul had disappeared from Earth, but despite how close they'd once been, Eryx wouldn't grieve in any way. He'd be glad.

I turned to make my way back downstairs, a little surprised by how long I'd lingered to stare at the mess in the attic, and was halfway to the third floor when I heard Sasha shouting, "They're here! Oh my God, Key and Jordan! *They're back!* They're in her room!"

Like a thundering herd, the Luminas and Purgatories and Mephisto flowed up the stairs to the third floor and burst into Jordan's room. They wouldn't all fit, and those in the hall were crying, hugging one another, slapping high fives.

I waited my turn and went inside the room and saw Key practically breaking Jax's back, he hugged him so hard. I saw his eyes and, just like Jax's, they were no longer black. Almost, but not quite. They were dark gray. He was smiling so wide, his face had a shine to it, a little like the Anabo glow. Divinity. He still had the lingering traces of divinity. Had he gone to the gates of Heaven as Jax had, and pleaded for God to take Jordan? Had they told him his love and ultimate sacrifice meant he'd fulfilled the Mephisto Covenant, and he was now redeemed before God?

I hoped so. I'd not seen anyone look this happy since the day Jax walked out of that church in St. Petersburg, holding Sasha's hand.

When it was my turn, I hugged Key and slapped his back and told him I was more glad than he'd ever know that he was with us again.

He said, "I love you," and I said, "I love you, too," and then we parted and someone else was hugging him. I was on my way to Jordan when she looked around and asked, "Where's Mariah?"

"You just hugged her, goof," Key said. "I saw you." He glanced around and frowned. "No, I suppose that was Mercy."

He looked at me. "Do you know where she is?"

I shook my head, my memory flying back to Erinýes and the scarf in that bedroom, where I caught the faintest scent of heather. Then I remembered she could transport. But she didn't know how. Did she? A terrible thought began to take hold. Had she been at Erinýes when we blew it?

Jordan looked at Kyros and said, "I was certain Mary Michael would rescue her, but she should be back by now."

Sasha said from where she stood at the window, "I'm mentally searching and she isn't anywhere. It's as if she disappeared."

My heart hammering, I did my own search, and just as Sasha said, there was nothing. No sense of her, anywhere.

I looked at Jordan. "What do you mean, Mary Michael would have rescued her? Where is she?"

She instantly began to cry, became hysterical, close to hyperventilating, and kept repeating, *"Oh my God,"* over and over until I wanted to shout at her to stop, to tell me.

Key grasped her arms and held her still. "Jordan, calm down. You have to tell us where she is."

Turning her horrified tear-streaked face to me, she whispered, "Hell on Earth. I left her in Hell on Earth."

I almost couldn't draw breath, fear for her overriding everything. I wanted to know how. *Why?* But that would have to come later. I jerked my head around to look at Jax. "I'm going."

"You can't. Nobody can go there except Lucifer."

I exploded. "You think I give a shit about *rules* right now? I'm going to be with her. You just make sure Lucifer comes to get us."

"Phoenix, please, I know this is horrible. The worst. The very worst. But rushing off is foolish. Let's call M, right now, and he will help." He was already drawing his phone from his pocket.

We waited for him to arrive, which took the longest thirty seconds of my life. Jordan was hysterical. I ignored her.

When M arrived, he was smiling, but he quickly stopped when he saw Jordan losing it. "What's happened? What's wrong? This should be a happy—"

"Mariah is in Hell on Earth."

He wheeled around to face me, his expression one of complete shock. "How? No one but Lucifer goes to Hell on Earth. No one!"

Jordan tried to speak up, but she was crying too hard to make any sense.

"Mariah is not no one, and she *is* there, and I *am* going to find her."

He looked more freaked out than I'd ever seen him. "If you go, you can't leave."

"Lucifer will come for us. All you have to do is tell him, and he'll be there."

"He's going to be angry. Furious. This could mean far more than punishment. It could mean he'll take both of you out."

"There's no choice, M. I'm not leaving her there by herself. If Lucifer's angry, I don't care. Just make sure he knows."

I looked at Jax, who nodded.

Steeling myself, I closed my eyes and transported to the one place on the planet I would never want to be, and the only place on Earth I could possibly be.

I had no concept of what it would be like, no grasp of where to materialize. I instantly felt intense heat and when I opened my eyes, I had a nanosecond to get my bearings before a mob of naked, skeletal Skia attacked me. Even in their reduced state, they were stronger than humans, and it was all I could do to fight them off. I had my switchblade, but it would eventually be a losing battle, their sheer numbers giving them tremendous strength.

I had to find Mariah. Desperately fighting to keep them from dragging me to the ground, I mentally searched, thankful that it worked when I found her. She was close, but not here. I imagined I was next to her, hoping I'd transport.

Nothing happened.

The noise was deafening, the angry shouts of the Skia echoing around the cave. I kept my mental search for Mariah front and center while I hacked and punched and shoved my way through the mob. Their numbers and their rage would be my undoing, but I had to get to Mariah before they tore me to pieces. They'd already torn off my coat, and my shirt was in tatters.

I made my way into a narrow tunnel, crouching down to move through, the switchblade becoming harder to grip because of blood and sweat. I was soaking wet. My hands were blistered. I couldn't breathe. I kept moving.

In the next room, much bigger than the last, all the Skia were massed together at the other end, bodies writhing as they tried to push their way through to the front. I heard her screams. Her agony.

With raging Skia on my heels, I ran and gathered myself for a jump, then leaped into the air and sailed over the heads of the mob, landing on top of the one who was next in line. I yanked two of them off of her and reached down to scoop her into my arms. Bloody and bruised, her beautiful face unrecognizable, she fought me and continued to scream, her neck stretched taut, her eyes wild with terror. She saw me and didn't know me. To her, I was another face, another male, another rape.

My heart broke into a million pieces. I knew, no matter what happened, or how soon we got out of here, she'd never recover. She would never come back.

They were all over us, but I wouldn't let go of her. They took me down, they kicked and punched and ripped my flesh from my bones, and I would not let go of her. I would live through this. I was immortal. And my rational mind understood their fury. I was the enemy. I sent them to this Godforsaken place. They were Eryx's drones, incapable of compassion. The best I could hope for was a reprieve from their hatred when there was nothing left of me to destroy.

Some of the meatier ones tried to pull Mariah away, but my arms were a vice grip around her. They broke her arms, trying to get her away from me. They ripped out her beautiful hair, scratched her face with their claw-like fingernails.

One of them tried to rape her, even while I was holding her, and I kicked him in the nuts.

Mariah never stopped screaming.

A snarling woman stuffed a piece of my shirt into her mouth and yelled for her to shut up.

I called for Lucifer, shouting his name until my throat was raw. I had no concept of time. I faded in and out of consciousness, but I never let go of Mariah.

CHAPTER 20

I was in the room with the braided rug, and the fire, and Beet, but instead of my mother, Mary Michael sat on the old rocker and worked a basket in her nimble hands. I watched, intrigued by her skill, talking to her even though she never replied. Beet licked my face and it felt cool on my hot skin. Such a love. I'd always wanted to get another dog, but it hadn't been possible. They were expensive to keep, and Marta didn't like dogs.

It didn't matter so much now. Here was Beet, wagging his tail, licking my face, wiggling his little body with pleasure when I rubbed his belly.

I would never leave here. Ever. I would be happy here. Content. At peace. And nothing would ever hurt me again. Sighing, I laid back on the rug and looked up at the crossbeams of the cabin, at the hewn logs placed there so long ago by a hard working rancher. I wondered if he came here alone, or did he bring his family? Did he have a family?

I heard a booming voice calling my name, and I turned my head to look. There was the rancher, and he held a posy of flowers in his hand. He gave them to Mary Michael and she smiled and kissed him. He took off his coat and sat on the big rocker and told us all about his day, about the cattle and the meadow and crossing the stream on his horse. Mary Michael continued making her basket. I thought the rancher looked like the Mephisto. He was dark and handsome, and had a gleam in his eye that spoke of a joker, a man who liked to tease. He flirted with Mary Michael and she told him to hush, pointing at me as a reminder that children were present and he should behave.

My body moved. I knew I bled, but I felt no pain. I saw nothing except Mary Michael's startling blue eyes and the rancher's boots and Beet's tail wagging.

I wanted the fire to go out because it was so hot.

I didn't wish for death. I knew that was beyond me now, and all that was left was this small room. I'd worried that this was the extent of Heaven, but now, I was ecstatic to be here, would be here for all eternity and that would be lovely.

I began to hum. I might have sung, except something was blocking my voice, clogging my throat, not letting any sound come out. Oh, well. I'd hum, and wasn't that wonderful?

CHAPTER 21

~~ PHOENIX ~~

It had been three weeks since Lucifer came for me and Mariah. I didn't know until we were back on Mephisto Mountain that we'd been in Hell on Earth for over thirty-six hours. My photographic memory wouldn't let me forget even one second of the time we were there, but I was shocked to learn it was almost two days. Jax said M went immediately to Lucifer, to ask him to rescue us, and as he'd predicted, Lucifer was furious. He left us there to teach us a lesson. No one was to go to Hell on Earth, but it hadn't ever been an issue because who would want to? Entry was open because it had to be for the lost souls and Skia, but there was no exit, except for Lucifer. According to M, that Jordan had left caused an enormous amount of anxiety for Lucifer because it meant Eryx had gained enough power to override his will. While she was with Eryx, Jordan was an extension of him, able to draw on his power to do what he did.

As it turned out, our mother hadn't been given permission. She'd taken Mariah there all on her own, and while Lucifer had no say or control over her actions, I didn't doubt she was in hot water with God.

Maybe Lucifer was unaware of what more time in Hell on Earth would do to Mariah. Maybe he knew already that she was forever lost in her own head, and taking her out of Hell on Earth the minute he knew she was there wouldn't have made a difference. Maybe the lesson he wanted to teach was to me.

I knew it wasn't Jordan's fault, and she was massively depressed, but I still didn't want to see her. She came to

Mariah's room numerous times each day after we came back, and I wouldn't let her in. I wouldn't let anyone in, even Mathilda. I popped down to the kitchen for meals and took them up to Mariah and watched her eat with no expression on her face, no light in her eyes, no recognition of me or her surroundings. She was there, but she wasn't.

Every morning, I took her pajamas off and got in the shower with her and washed her hair and sang to her. I dried her hair and combed it out, then led her back to bed. I read to her, played movies, and talked. Endlessly.

The fourth day, Key came to visit and wouldn't let me turn him away. He sat by her bed and talked to her and something sparked. It didn't last, but there was something there. He asked me to let Jordan see her. When I said no, he said, "She can't eat, can't sleep, can't stop crying. This is cruel, Phoenix. Please, if you won't do it for Jordan, do it for me." He'd looked at Mariah. "Do it for her. Maybe Jordan can bring her back."

"Maybe Jordan would scare her farther away. Let's not forget, she's the one who took her there."

"Would Mariah hold it against her?"

I had to admit, "No."

Key cried and my resolve crumbled. I was at wit's end, had no idea what to do for her, what was best. Key said, "You've got to let people see her. Talk to her. You can't stay here all day and all night for all time."

I relented and allowed Jordan to visit. She and I talked for hours, and I peppered her with questions about Eryx, storing it all away for later. My hatred of him had elevated to another level. I was determined to destroy him.

A steady stream of visitors came after that, and if someone didn't leave when I told them to, I physically picked them up and took them out to the hallway. That side she'd once told me about came screaming to the fore. I lost it a lot, and broke things and cursed and shouted – but always away from her room. When I was there, I never raised my voice, never allowed myself to become angry.

Mathilda was in Mariah's room daily, sitting by the bed, knitting, talking constantly, telling Mariah stories of her childhood growing up in Surrey. She brought treats which

Mariah ate with the same enthusiasm she ate everything – none. Food appeared and she ate it, but it might as well have been gruel.

I brought all of my work into her room and planned Jordan's memorial service takedown on the little desk. It went off without a problem, and when it was over, I told Key not to count on me for making any plans until Mariah was back.

I knew he didn't believe she'd come back. No one did.

But I couldn't let go of hope. Couldn't let go of her.

After three weeks, however, hope began to wane. It had been a particularly difficult day. During our daily shower, for some reason she actually saw me – not me as Phoenix, but me as a male, and she began to cry. She jerked away from me and cowered in the corner. It took half an hour to coax her back to me, and afterward, when I had her back in bed, she looked farther away than ever.

I sat there for hours, praying to God, even though he couldn't hear me. Sometime around two in the morning, I changed into my boxers, laid on the bed, and gathered her close, just as I did every night. And like always, she was limp and unresponsive.

"What is her happiness worth to you?"

I opened my eyes and there was Lucifer, standing at the end of the bed. "Everything."

"She sleeps to heal her mind, but some wounds never quite go away. Let her go, Phoenix. Let her go to God."

I clutched her tighter to me, but I nodded.

"If she could wake up right now with no memory of what happened, if she could be here, be Mephisto, find love amongst your brothers or the Luminas, what would you do to make that happen?"

"Anything."

"Get up."

I kissed her cheeks and her nose and moved away from her to get off of the bed. I stood and faced Lucifer, prepared to go with him.

"You'll never see her again. You'll be with me forever where there is no warmth, no love, no kindness. You'll work, hard, and I'll never let up. Ever. For all time, even when the end of the world has come and gone."

"I'm ready."

"Do you love her?"

"Does it matter?"

He disappeared.

He would be back. Until then, I'd spend the time with Mariah and say goodbye.

I sat on the chair next to her bed and watched her beautiful face in sleep. Where was she? Did she live on the rug by the fire? Was her mother there? Was she happy?

I began to cry and couldn't stop. Falling to my knees, I grasped her hand and held it within my own and rested my head on the bed. "Please, *please*, wake up now. You can do all those things you wanted, and be here with your family, with Jordan and my brothers. Please, *puica*, let me see you smile just one more time before I go. I love you so much, Mariah."

A hand came to rest on my head and I jerked up, thinking it was her, but she was still asleep and unmoving.

Turning, I blinked away my tears.

Like a beacon in darkness, lit by divinity, an angel smiled down at me.

~~ MARIAH ~~

The rancher had gone, and sometime later, another man arrived. He wasn't nearly so good-humored as the rancher. I wasn't sure if he was handsome, or ugly, or somewhere in between. I kept trying to see his face, but I couldn't remember what he looked like, even when I was looking directly at him. He talked about me as if I wasn't there. He said things like, "Heal her mind," and "Let her go, let her be with God."

I sat up and said, "I'd love to be with God. Mary Michael, can I go be with God? It's not that I don't like it here, but you're going to leave me, I know you are, and then I'll be all alone." I began to cry. "I'm so tired of being alone. Please, if I could just be with God, I'll never be alone again. God loves me, I know he does."

She never looked at me. Slowly, she faded and was gone. I grabbed Beet and held onto him, but he also disappeared, leaving my arms empty. The light began to fade and then there was only me and the man, in a circle of light in the middle of darkness. He reached out and I laid my head in his hand and sighed. Now I knew who he was. This was Lucifer. "Why are you here?"

"I came to take you home. Do you want to go home?"

"I want to belong. I just want to be normal, and belong, and matter. Why do I never matter?"

He stood and pulled me up and drew me close and hugged me tight. "You matter to those who love you, like me, and God, and Mary Michael. You matter to Viorica."

"She brought me here. She's lost."

"Kyros brought her back to God, and they're waiting for you at home."

"I'm glad. So glad."

"You also matter to the brothers, especially Phoenix."

"He forgot I existed."

"He never forgot you. It was his way of protecting you."

"It sucked."

"I didn't say it was a good way, just that it's his way. He'll always be one who compartmentalizes, which you can surely relate to. Everything in your mind is in its place, where you can find it or ignore it, depending. Sometimes you'll be in a place in his mind that's safe, where he can find you after he's taken care of what's in the other spaces of his mind. It never means those things are more important. Just that they have to take priority in his thoughts. He can't help it, Mariah. It's how God made him. It's why he's so good at his plans. He loves you."

"No."

"He came to get you."

I leaned back and looked up into his face, but couldn't remember his features, even while I looked. "You mean in my dream? He comes to get me from my dream."

"When he discovered you were in Hell on Earth, he went there immediately, and stayed with you until I arrived."

Horrific memories slammed into me and I couldn't breathe. So much pain and blood, terror and evil. And Phoenix, fighting, shouting, holding them back while I screamed. Holding me, trying to keep them from taking me. I'd scarcely begun to remember when the memories were gone.

"I've taken them, Mariah. It's as if it never happened and you were never there, and you'll never remember. It's my gift to you, so when you open that empty box in your mind, think of me and know that despite who I am and what I stand for, there is a slice of warmth still in my soul, and I am capable of affection for those I admire."

Affection from the devil. I was oddly humbled.

"Phoenix waits for you, Mariah."

"Where is he?"

"In your room, hoping you'll wake up. But if you want to go to Heaven, I'll make that happen and you'll never wake up."

I peered up at him, trying to hold on to his features, but it was impossible. "Why you? Why not Mary Michael? Wouldn't she be the likely candidate to take me to Heaven?"

"She is his mother, so all her persuasions would come with an ulterior motive. Same goes for his father, although he'd never admit to it. Mephistopheles likes the illusion that he's impartial, and for the most part, I let him." He smiled and I knew I'd remember that. "I'm the one here now because it's my will, because I want you to fully understand what it is to be with Phoenix. He's not the worst of his brothers, but perhaps the most complicated, like his father. He's an odd blend of good and bad, exacting precision and a complete mess. I always favored him because he's never been one to hide from his mistakes, and he's had a lot of mistakes."

"He can be very kind and considerate when he wants to be."

"And selfish and nasty when he wants to be." He stroked my hair. "He's been acting badly the past few weeks, breaking things, yelling at his brothers and the Purgatories and Luminas. When they launched the takedown at Jordan's memorial service, however, he was his usual careful, methodical self and it all went off without a hitch. As soon as they were back, he began issuing orders and guarding your bedside and telling the rest of them to back off and let you rest."

"Where have I been for all that time?"

"Asleep in your mind. You get up, you eat, you take a bath, but you're not there. You never speak, never focus. You're a functioning body without life. I put you to sleep to let your mind heal, and now I've erased the remaining memories that would cause you to relapse."

"Even Emilian?"

"No, that's part of who you are, Mariah. It's what life handed to you and I have no call and no right to make it go away. The other . . . I do have some authority, and I believe you can be perfectly well-rounded without remembering." He stroked my hair again. "I see why he's so fascinated with your hair. Always did love a woman's hair." His hand stilled against my head. "He does love you to distraction, child. So much, I lost him, just last night. He broke down and cried and begged God to send you back and promised he'd love you forever and never, ever not be grateful. You know, groveling sometimes works."

I smiled at that.

"He was sincere and God recognizes sincerity. It doesn't mean Phoenix won't ever be overbearing or ill-tempered again. You need to keep this in mind before you decide."

"So he loves me. Does that mean he's redeemed? I thought I had to love him back."

"You do. We all know it. You know it. God knows it. Yes, Phoenix can look forward to Heaven when the end finally comes, or when Eryx is defeated, but redemption isn't a free pass. He must live a life of honor. When he screws up, and he will because he's Phoenix, he'll need to be repentant. Not guilty. Guilt is a joke if repentance isn't real." He stepped back from me, out of the light so that I couldn't see him any longer. "What say you, Mariah Ardelean? Shall I deliver you to God, or return you to Phoenix?"

"Suppose I left the decision to you? Where would you take me?"

"To Phoenix, of course. I need Mephisto to fight Eryx."

I didn't think that was the only reason, but I appreciated his honesty. I nodded and the next moment, I heard Phoenix's voice. He was reading.

". . . *do not have patience for your base, loathsome advances. I really must insist you leave, my lord, before I set the gardener on you.*" He cleared his throat. "That's harsh. The gardener is a giant. He'll mash the poor man like a bug.

Honestly, Lady Mavis should blow off Lord Whatshisname and go for the gardener. Being a really big guy, he'd have a spectacular . . . well, he'd be well endowed, wouldn't he? There's something about him, anyway. How many gardeners would know so much about the law? He's undercover, mark my words. He's gunning for Lord Whatshisname, who's clearly about to swindle Lady Mavis. The guy has an unpronounceable name. Never trust a guy whose name you can't pronounce. Moving on."

I heard pages turned.

"Okay, skipping all the boring stuff. There's a ball, and Sir Gouty Guy steps on her toe . . . blah, blah, and there's a tiresome garden party . . . oh, ho! The gardener is lurking in the bushes. I knew it! He's eyeing Lord Whatshisname. Lady Mavis says, *'Max, what are you doing here? This is most unseemly.'*"

He read that in a falsetto, and I'd never had such a hard time remaining expressionless.

"Max is a big ox and a bit slow, but is he really? Now he's carrying Lady Mavis off to the old abbey ruins on Lord Whatshisname's estate. He's kissing her. She's kissing him back. Aw, that's nice." It was quiet for a while, then he said softly, "I wish you'd wake up and kiss me, Mariah. God, I miss you so much. I'd give anything just to see you smile, just to have you look at me and know me." The bed moved. "And love me."

I felt his hands on me, stroking my hair, touching my shoulder, smoothing the covers. Then I felt his lips against mine, kissing me gently, and I kissed him back. He jerked away in surprise. "Mariah?"

I opened my eyes and looked up at his beloved face. "I am so glad you don't write romance novels."

Huge tears welled in his eyes and spilled over and rolled down his cheeks. He bent low and slid his arms around me and nearly crushed me, he held me so tight. "You came back," he whispered against my ear. "Oh, God, you came back to me. Mariah, I love you so much it makes me crazy, makes me sad and happy and just . . . crazy."

I had to ask, "Are you sure it's not just guilt? You forgot

about me."

"I never forgot. You have to believe I didn't forget." He raised up and blinked down at me, his face an inch away. "I could never forget you. Ever, in a million years. I just get caught up, and that night, Key was so bad off, needed me like he'd never needed me before. I knew how bad it was for you, but I thought you wouldn't want to hear what we planned, because it was Jordan, your Viorica." Tears began anew. "I know it will get old, probably already is, but I'm always going to be a clueless wonder, Mariah. A big ox, just like Max, so you're going to have to tell me when I'm doing it wrong. I'll try, always, and I swear I'd never hurt you on purpose."

"I know. I knew it then. I just had to see her, one last time."

"And you did, and she tricked you."

"I took her to Hell on Earth to get her away from Eryx, but it was all a ruse, and then she left me there." I thought of Lucifer's gift. "I don't remember what happened after that. The box is empty."

"It needs to stay that way. Will you see Jordan? She's been very depressed, blaming herself."

"Why? It's all on Eryx."

"She knows, but still, she's the one who took you. You've been here, but not here, for over three weeks. She comes every day, sometimes three times a day, to check on you. She reads to you, and talks to you until I make her leave."

"Why?"

"Because I'm a selfish bastard and I want you to myself." He smiled at me. "Okay, not entirely. It's just that there are so many who wanted to be here and hang out and talk to you and cry about you, and I didn't know how much you might be aware of. I didn't want them making you tired, or sad."

He kissed me again, soft and gentle.

"Do you really love me?"

"I really love you. Last night, I talked to God and he listened, and I'm certain you love me back, because I was visited by an angel who told me I was redeemed."

"Was it your mother?"

He shook his head and said soberly, "It was Jane."

Now it was my turn to cry. I hugged and kissed him and we

had an epic cryfest.

"Let's never tell anyone how pathetic we are," he said, rubbing his eyes with the heels of his hands.

"Deal."

Deacon's solemn voice came through the intercom. "Dinner is served. Allah is good."

The familiarity of the announcement was unimaginably comforting. "I want to get dressed and go down there and see everyone."

"Are you sure?"

"Absolutely sure."

"Come on, then, and let's get you in the shower." He offered his hand and pulled me out of bed and began undressing me. When I was naked, he pulled off his T-shirt and unzipped his jeans.

"What are you doing?"

"Giving you your shower. We do this every day."

"But, Phoenix, I'm awake now. I can bathe myself."

He nodded. "I'm aware. Humor me."

"Are we going to—"

"No, not yet. This is just a shower. I swore when you woke up, I'd get in there with you and run soap all over your body and not feel like a perv."

"Did you feel like one while I wasn't here?"

"You have no idea." He held my hand and took me in the bathroom, where we took a shower together, and didn't have sex because he said it was too soon, that he wanted me to be home for a while, wanted to make sure I was fully healed. I had a feeling he was talking about whatever happened to me during my time in Hell on Earth, but I didn't ask. Lucifer said I wouldn't remember, and I was glad.

I wore the black dress and a pair of beautiful heels to dinner. Phoenix walked me downstairs holding my hand and when we entered the dining room, everyone stood and clapped. Mathilda and Hans and Deacon and Dani and Mercy were all there, along with Mirabelle, who I recognized from her portrait in the library, and a big man I didn't recognize who was introduced as Gunther, the newest Lumina.

Jordan – I was determined to think of her as Jordan from

now on – rushed toward me and stopped just short of running into me, her eyes wide with worry. They were the color of bluebells again and I glanced at Kyros, who appeared as worried as Jordan. I hugged her and she cried and I heard Phoenix mumble, "Key should buy stock in Kleenex. We're turning into crybabies."

"Shut up, Phoenix," Jordan said from my shoulder.

"As you wish, sister. Now, stop getting snot all over Mariah's dress and let her sit down so she can eat. She's been eating gruel for three weeks."

She pulled away and said, "I love you, Mariah. I'm so sor—"

"No, none of that. It was a bad time. You weren't yourself. Let's look ahead and put it behind us, okay?"

"Okay." She swiped at the tears on her cheeks and gave me a watery smile. "We're going to see Euri play in New York later. Do you want to go?"

Euri? I shot a look at Zee, who said, "Don't read anything into it. She won't know . . . we're just going to see Arcadia. Nothing else. You should go. They're most excellent."

I glanced at Phoenix, who sighed. "Just for a couple of hours, and no alcohol."

"Thanks, Dad."

"You're still my patient until I decide you're well." He did look concerned. "Now sit down and eat. Hans made your favorite. Short ribs."

"How do you know it's my favorite?"

He led me to a chair and pulled it out for me. "Because I'm the master of observation. Also, Hans told me."

I looked around at their faces, so glad to be back. "Did I really eat gruel for three weeks?"

Deacon said from behind my chair, "No, Anabo, you ate quite well. Phoenix was making a joke." There was a pause, then, "Heh."

It was the Deacon equivalent of laughter, and I caught a look from Phoenix that indicated he had no idea why the big man thought it was so funny.

Dinner was delicious, as usual, and afterward, everyone transported to New York, to a club called Blackbriar in Hell's

Kitchen. Phoenix held my hand while we listened to Arcadia, and Zee was right – they were amazing. Euri was incredible. I noticed the lead guitarist staring at her and wondered if he was in love with her. I also noticed Zee couldn't look away from her.

I whispered to Phoenix, "Is it weird to you how much she looks like Jane?"

"A little, but not the way you're thinking." He looked down into my eyes and smiled. "It's all tied off, Mariah. Over and done. Euri is Euri, not Jane, and it will take a lot of time and probably a lot of work to get her with Zee, with us, but at no time will I think of her as Jane."

"Maybe because you saw her as an angel?"

He sobered. "Because I've let it go. I love you, Mariah."

I kissed him and didn't care who saw.

When the band took a break between sets, I swept my gaze around the club, and stopped at a guy who casually leaned against the east wall while he stared at our group.

"Phoenix, Eryx is here."

"I know."

"He's staring."

"He turns up everywhere we go, but I don't know why. Don't care. He had a major setback after we retrieved Jordan." He finished his whiskey and looked down at me. "We blew up Erinýes. He's homeless and all of his work is gone. He's bitter, I'm sure, and will no doubt try to take his revenge. We'll deal. Let's ignore him and enjoy tonight, okay?"

"Okay." I did ignore him, and I did enjoy myself.

At exactly two hours into the evening, Phoenix said, "Time to go."

I didn't argue. I was tired, and we said goodnight to everyone and left, walking down the street a block before we disappeared and returned to Colorado.

When I was ready for bed, Phoenix was there, getting in with me, Olga curled up at the end. "Did you sleep with me while I was away?"

"Every night." He drew me close and sighed into my hair. "And every night I'd wish and hope that you'd wake up in the morning and be yourself. I'm so happy, Mariah, but a little scared. I can't help worrying something will go wrong."

"Of course it will, Phoenix. Life is things going wrong. It won't matter. We'll fix it and move on."

"I love you more than any guy has ever loved any girl in the history of the universe."

"Hyperbole."

"No way," he mumbled sleepily. "It's true. I win at love."

I snuggled against him and went to sleep, strangely unconcerned about what I might dream.

Good call, because as it turned out, I dreamed that Deacon opened a comedy club.

AUTHOR NOTE

15% of sexual assault and rape victims are under age 12.
29% are age 12-17.
44% are under age 18.
80% are under age 30.
12-34 are the highest risk years.
Girls ages 16-19 are 4 times more likely than the general population to be victims of rape, attempted rape, or sexual assault.
7% of girls in grades 5-8 and 12% of girls in grades 9-12 said they had been sexually abused.
3% of boys grades 5-8 and 5% of boys in grades 9-12 said they had been sexually abused.
Nearly 30% of child victims were between the age of 4 and 7.
93% of juvenile sexual assault victims know their attacker.
34.2% of attackers were family members.
58.7% were acquaintances.
Only 7% of the perpetrators were strangers to the victim.
Victims of sexual assault are:
3 times more likely to suffer from depression.
6 times more likely to suffer from post-traumatic stress disorder.
13 times more likely to abuse alcohol.
26 times more likely to abuse drugs.
4 times more likely to contemplate suicide.

If you or someone you know is being victimized, go to http://www.rainn.org/ Rape, Abuse & Incest National Network and find help. There are many people who care what happens to you, including me. I'm donating a portion of the profit from this book to RAINN. ~ Stephanie

"The only thing necessary for the triumph of evil is for good men to do nothing."
– Edmund Burke

ACKNOWLEDGEMENTS

Many thanks to Kristen Droesch for stellar editing, and for the email out of the blue that made my day. Thank you Kim Killion for the marvelous cover design. Thanks to Kelly Simmon. Special thanks to first readers Damaris Cardinali, Kate Sowa, Sarah Evans, Aujah Irvin-Jenkins, Ashley Carroll, Kenzie Ellis, Katie Gillary, Jen Showalter, and Stacy Vandever Wells. Your thoughts and editorial suggestions were a tremendous help, and I appreciate your time. Sometimes, it really does take a village! Huge thanks to the awesome bloggers who helped spread the word about this book. You're all treasures, fellow bibliophiles who inhabit the Mother Ship with me, and I love you for it. This book exists because of readers who said they wanted more Mephisto. My sincere gratitude to all the Facebook Peeps who are always lovely and were so supportive of my efforts to get this book published. You're why I stay up late!

AUTHOR BIO

Stephanie Feagan is a multi-published RITA winning author who loves travel, books, and smart guys. A practicing CPA, she lives in the outback of west Texas with her husband and a mean cat. For bonus content and more about the Mephisto, visit her website at www.stephaniefeagan.com.

BOOKS IN THE MEPHISTO COVENANT SERIES

Please Note: These were written and published as Young Adult novels under the pseudonym Trinity Faegen.

Book One - *The Mephisto Covenant: The Redemption of Ajax*
Egmont USA
Available in hardcover, paperback, and eBook. See website for   information   and   buy   links:
http://www.stephaniefeagan.com/books/trinityfaegenbooks/the-mephisto-covenant-the-redemption-of-ajax/

Book Two - *The Mephisto Kiss: The Redemption of Kyros*
Egmont USA
Available   in   hardcover   and   eBook.   See   website   for information   and   buy   links:
http://www.stephaniefeagan.com/books/trinityfaegenbooks/the-mephisto-kiss-the-redemption-of-kyros/

COMING IN MARCH 2014!
THE NEXT BOOK IN THE MEPHISTO COVENANT SERIES…

CRAZY FOR YOU

We are Anonymous. We are Legion. We do not forgive. We do not forget. Expect us.

A year ago, Euri was a freshman at Cambridge, a concert pianist whose boyfriend was a fellow computer geek she'd known since childhood. Occasionally they hacked into ultra-secure databases just to prove they could, and participated in a few Anonymous ops. Then Euri left England on a concert tour and when she returned, Miles had become a violent, angry stranger, talking incessantly about a guy he met online known only as Anonymous66X. Miles was never a druggie, but after he overdosed and died, Euri became obsessed with finding Anonymous66X, to stop him from preying on others. She walked away from school, her career and her aristocratic family to join an indie band whose lead guitarist, John, is rumored to be 4Jane, one of the best hackers in the world. She tours with the band and, with John's help, works into the wee hours every night, searching for Anonymous66X. His follower numbers continue to grow, but he's elusive and she comes no closer to discovering who he is. Then Euri meets Zee, and everything she thought she knew about Anonymous66X, her music and herself becomes so much garbage code, a jumble of disjointed meaningless script.

Zee is mentally wack and knows it. A son of Hell, he's no choirboy, but he can't convince himself to claim Euri, can't doom her to eternity with him and his crazy mind. When he learns she's searching for Anonymous66X, he knows if she finds him, he'll kill her. Anonymous66X is Eryx, his oldest brother, sworn enemy and mankind's greatest threat. Zee is certain he can convince her to back off, and once she gives up and goes back to her life, he'll disappear and grieve the loss of her for all time. But Euri won't give up, and worse, she's getting closer to finding Anonymous66X. In a manic haze of fear and lust, Zee abducts Euri, and nothing will ever be the same for either of them.

The next installment in The Mephisto Covenant Series begins a new chapter in Eryx's war for Hell. He's back, stronger, smarter, and more determined, unleashing all the fury of his dark, hopeless soul. Unless the Mephisto can find a way to outwit him, they'll lose more ground and Eryx will be ever closer to taking the reins of Hell, eradicating free will, ensuring the doom of all mankind.

www.ingramcontent.com/pod-product-compliance
Lightning Source LLC
Chambersburg PA
CBHW032143190626
46814CB00005BA/1817